NIGHT RUNE

PROF CROFT 8

BRAD MAGNARELLA

THE PROF CROFT SERIES

1

Arnaud Thorne was sitting on the metal bench at the back of his cell, legs folded, slender fingers interlaced around his knee. The drab robe he wore over his prison scrubs was police issue, but he managed to make it appear regal. It was his bearing, erect yet relaxed. As his yellow eyes found mine through the window, his lips turned up at the corners.

"Mr. Croft," he said with false cheer. "To what do I owe this pleasure?"

The magic that warded his confinement warped the air between us, bending his grin into odd shapes. The effect was nauseating, but no more so than the reason I'd come to him. And knowing he'd been expecting me.

"Where are they?" I asked.

He leaned forward, fine eyebrows rising up his waxy brow. "And to whom are you referring?"

"My teammates," I said. "The ones I entered the time catch with."

"You're going to have to be more specific."

Struggling to keep a neutral expression, I exhaled slowly through my nose. His powers couldn't penetrate the cell's defenses, but he was a master manipulator, something he could manage through words alone. It was why I had given the guards strict instructions to keep the speaker off at all times. In fact, I'd ordered the guards out before turning it on. Arnaud and I had the holding area to ourselves.

"There were four," I said. "A young minister, a druid, a half-fae, and a mermaid."

"Indeed?"

"Yes."

More than ten hours had passed since my return, and the Upholders were still no-shows. For a time, I held to the hope they'd delayed their return from 1776 New York to allow everyone to heal. Malachi, along with several of the half-fae, had suffered injuries from cannon fire, and some of the recovered druids, including Jordan's wife, had been weakened by possession. But hours here would have been days there.

By first light this morning, I had to accept something had gone awry.

"Ah, yes." Arnaud sat back and tucked a strand of fine white hair behind an ear. "You were quite a motley outfit. Fascinating to observe. And surprisingly capable." He tsked. "A pity."

"What's a pity?"

"Well, that you journeyed all that way to rescue their friends, and you returned empty handed."

He opened out his own hands, his smile revealing his sharp teeth. He was baiting me to fire back with something to the effect that we'd destroyed a pair of Strangers, or that I'd managed to capture him. He wanted to stoke my emotions into a smoky blaze that would cloud my reasoning. But past experience with Arnaud had prepared me.

"Where are they?" I repeated.

He stood and straightened his robe so that it fell into neat pleats around his baggy pants. Clasping his fingers behind his back, he began a slow stroll around his cell in a pair of canvas shoes.

As I awaited his response, I examined him for symptoms of being cut off from the infernal realm. He did appear thinner. And under the harsh fluorescent lights, his skin seemed to be yellowing. But if he felt any depleting effects, he hid them well. He pursed his narrow lips in a thoughtful expression, as if he had all the time in the world.

At last, he spun on a heel. "What are you prepared to offer?"

I grunted a laugh. "You're not getting out."

"Then why should I assist you?"

"Because this cell is the only thing protecting you from your master."

"What are you suggesting, Mr. Croft?"

"I switch off certain sigils, and Malphas will see you've been taken prisoner. He'll send up infernal power in an attempt to overwhelm the forces holding you, but when that fails, he'll reclaim you before you can spill more than you already have. Yeah, you've said nothing, but he won't know that." I made a diving motion with my finger. "Back to the Below. And with no way to return to our world, you'll be useless. Not only that, you'll have failed him. I don't think I need to spell out the rest."

Arnaud chuckled.

"Laugh all you want," I said, fighting to keep my throat relaxed. "You know it's true."

"Oh, rest assured, Mr. Croft, I find no humor in the scenario. I imagine that's exactly how events would unfold."

"Then what's so funny?"

"For all your bold talk, you won't carry out your threat."

"No?" I challenged.

"No. And it's because of your lady friend and the little *miracle* she's carrying."

My cheeks prickled with cold heat. "They have nothing to do

with this." I said it too quickly, but I couldn't help it. I didn't want Vega or our unborn child on the demon-vampire's tongue, much less his mind.

"Did I strike a nerve?"

Arnaud was suddenly inches from me, his demonic eyes peering hard into mine through the window. The cell's currents made his narrow pupils appear as if they fell into deep, twisting voids. I shuffled back a half step.

"Ooh, I believe I did," he said, delighting in my reaction. "Let me elaborate, Mr. Croft. If you released me to my master, yes, I would likely be destroyed. But what if I weren't?" He grinned up at me. "After all, I've defied death before. And what if I found my way back to this world? This city? To your child's ... crib?"

While he spoke, I recited a silent centering mantra to keep his words from taking lurid form in my thoughts. I wasn't entirely successful. Flashes of the bloody mess he'd left at the vampire hunters' apartment kept intruding. But I held his gaze, refusing to shrink from his insinuations this time.

"So you see," he said, "even though the odds favor you mightily, sending me to Malphas isn't foolproof, which makes it a non-option. I doubt you even told your lady friend you were considering it."

"She's not here," I said. "Is she."

Instead of responding, Arnaud's eyes gleamed devilishly.

"Good, so let me rehash," I said. "Refuse to help me, and you'll meet your master. Give me something useful—"

"And you'll simply incinerate me?"

"That's right."

He drummed his first two talons against his chin as though pondering the question, but it was an act. I could practically hear the cogs whirring in his scheming mind. Even faced with death, he was working out something.

"Why come to me and not the fae?" he asked after a moment.

The question caught me off guard. My morning's first stop had been the fae townhouse on the Upper East Side. I wanted the butler Osgood to tell me why he hadn't delivered the rest of the Upholders from the time catch—and if needed, to send me back there. But no one answered the door.

"The fae?" I repeated.

"Surely you trust them more than you do me."

Something in the angle of his voice bothered me. "What do they have to do with anything?"

"Oh, come, Professor. A man of your academic standing shouldn't have to be led to the obvious."

Was he saying the *fae* were the reason the others never returned? I shook my head. No, this was just more of the demon-vampire's deceit.

"I can understand your reluctance to consider the question," he continued. "After all, you had *history* with your contact inside the fae."

He was referring to my relationship with Caroline, some-thing he would have known from possessing me the year before. But he was wrong. She wouldn't have double-crossed me. Could someone have overruled her, though?

Dammit, Arnaud was getting inside my head again, rattling me.

"Perhaps you should have followed your own advice and been more skeptical toward them," he pressed.

My fists clenched below his view. "I'll repeat my offer—"

Arnaud waved a tired hand. "Yes, yes, I'm well aware of my fate. Cast down to the master or sent up in smoke. But here's the real kicker." He turned toward me with a triumphant air. "You can't do either."

I laughed, but it came out all wrong. Did he suspect I needed him for something more?

Before entering the time catch, I'd had a sequence of vivid dreams. In the first, I was with Vega and Tony in my apartment, holding our baby girl. In the next, I was at the blood-soaked scene of the vampire hunters' massacre. A half-dead Blade rasped that Arnaud had acquired a bond-negating scepter—which turned out to be true. Blade then transformed into one of the senior members of my Order, Arianna, who said she and the others were trapped in the Harkless Rift. She told me to find Arnaud.

Done, but now what?

Arianna hadn't returned, either in material or ethereal form, and I damned sure couldn't ask Arnaud what she'd meant. He would use the knowledge that I needed him to maximum advantage. I had no choice but to wait on Arianna's next communique, which meant keeping Arnaud alive until that happened.

"And why not?" I challenged.

"Because I'm the only one who can place you in the time catch."

I relaxed slightly—he didn't know about my other need. "Yeah, sure you are."

"And yes, that's where your friends are."

I eyed him for any hint of trickery. "Why didn't they return?"

"You'll have to ask the fae."

"They're not talking to me."

"Hm. That alone should tell you something."

"What do you know?"

Arnaud returned to the bench at the back of his cell. "You asked me where your friends were, Mr. Croft, and I've answered the question. So go ahead, fire up your magic. Incinerate me as agreed."

He refolded his legs, clasping the topmost knee.

The powerful wards I'd constructed brimmed with lethal energies. At a Word, I could release them into him, reducing the demon-vampire to smoke. A part of me burned to do just that—to rid the world of his evil, avenge the lives he'd savaged and destroyed, and protect my family. I caught myself shaping the Word in my mind. But even as the sigils began to glow, Arnaud held my gaze steadily.

"Well?" he goaded.

Swearing silently, I dispersed the gathering energy. The sigils faded.

Arnaud smiled and clapped his hands. "A stay of execution! Splendid!"

"Yeah, don't get too comfortable. I need to check out your claim before I do anything."

"About your friends being in the time catch? Oh, you know that's exactly where they are, but do what you must. In fact, I'd prefer it. Once you discover I'm your one hope of re-entering that place, and you will, our talks will go more swiftly. Especially when I explain the *urgency* factor."

I had started to leave, but I stopped. Reacting to his teaser was stupid—I knew that—but right now he was my sole source of intel.

"And what's that?" I asked.

"After the hostile way in which you've conducted this interview, Mr. Croft, I'm inclined to withhold that information. But very well. I was managing some especially powerful energies in that space. You experienced them firsthand, I believe. Well, what do you think is happening without anyone at the controls?"

As the corners of his mouth forked up, I pictured violent currents of ley energy snaking in directions they weren't intended, bending essential struts, rendering an unstable environment even more so. My final image was of a massive implosion, swallowing everyone and everything inside the time catch.

"Exactly," he hissed.

My heart thumped sickly in my chest as I strode from Arnaud's view.

"I'll be waiting," he called before I could kill the speaker.

2

I arrived upstairs in Homicide to find Vega stooped beside her office file cabinets, midnight hair shifting across the back of her jacket. It wasn't until she turned slightly that I saw the broom and long-handled dustpan. She had a habit of cleaning when her mind was preoccupied, and this was clearly one of those moments.

As she emptied the dustpan into the trash, my gaze fell to her stomach. She wouldn't start showing for at least another six weeks, but I thought about what Arnaud had said. Was I endangering my family by keeping the demon-vampire alive?

"How'd it go?"

I looked up to find her facing me, eyes dark and expectant. I closed the door, kissed her warm forehead, and relieved her of the broom and dustpan. "Interestingly," I said, leaning the cleaning implements against a filing cabinet. "He claims the Upholders are still in the time catch."

"Dammit. Is he telling the truth?"

"I think so." Though Arnaud had made light of my offer of clemency from his master in exchange for info, he'd accepted it, sliding in the response to my question subtly, without fanfare. "Didn't give me much more, though."

"Did he tell you why the Upholders were still there?"

"He made some insinuations about the fae, but I don't know. Felt more like a mind game."

I sat on the corner of her desk. Vega came over and leaned beside me, arms crossed, eyes narrowing toward the opposite wall where several framed certificates hung. "What about the senior members of your Order? Any insights into how he could possibly free them?"

"Not yet. You sound skeptical."

I thought we were going to get into another back and forth over whether Arianna's visit had been just a dream. We'd had that discussion a couple times now. But instead, she said, "I just don't like that he's still alive."

"Well, me neither."

"So what's the plan?"

"As far as learning how he might be key to the Order's release?" I blew out my breath. "We wait for Arianna to contact me again."

"And if she doesn't?"

"Then he'll eventually die."

"How long is eventually?" she asked, continuing to study the far wall.

"Days. He's completely cut off from the infernal realm. He's already looking thinner, weaker."

"You're not planning to extend his time here, are you?" When she looked over at me, a cloud gathered across her face. Arnaud was right. I hadn't told her my plan to use the threat of Arnaud's master reclaiming him as leverage.

"No."

"Are you sure about that?"

The challenge in her voice took me back to our conversation

the night before, when she'd told me about Tony's father, Ramon. After an incident where Ramon imperiled her son, Vega had him arrested and prosecuted for child endangerment. For an instant, I could see the same protective instincts firing hot behind her eyes. But then she grasped my arm and leaned her head against my shoulder.

"I just want this to be over."

"Me too." I placed my hand over hers.

"What's the next step?"

"Recovering my teammates from the time catch."

"I was afraid you'd say that."

I thought about Malachi, Seay, Gorgantha, and Jordan. "I made a promise."

"How are you getting there?"

"I'm going to check with Claudius first," I said, "see if he's had any luck reaching the senior members of the Order. Then I'll try the fae again."

I considered Arnaud's claim about him being my sole key to the time catch, but I decided not to share. Vega was dealing with a lot right now, including morning sickness. Even if he could access the time catch, I had other options.

"Think there's anything to Arnaud's insinuations about the fae?" she asked.

"No," I replied, but without the conviction I needed to feel. I consulted my magic again. It remained in the same neutral state it had been in all morning, no hard confirmations or rebuttals. "I can't see the fae making a deal with a demon."

"Still, it's strange they're ghosting you."

"Well, they're strange, period. I'll get answers." I gave Vega's hand a final squeeze. "I should get going."

"Keep me posted."

"I will." She joined me as I stood from the desk, and we kissed.

My hand was on the door when Vega spoke again. "Is it safe for you to go back into the time catch?"

When I turned, she was holding the broom to her chest. The honest answer was that it depended on whether the time catch was as unstable as Arnaud suggested. Or was he just seeding more doubt?

"I'll be better prepared this time."

She brought her fingers to her lips and waved. I was barely through the doorway when I heard her cleaning again.

OUTSIDE 1 POLICE PLAZA I DUCKED INTO A PARKING LOT TO CALL Claudius. As the line rang, I paced the asphalt, aware that every minute here was twenty or thirty in 1776 New York. Meaning the Upholders had been there for the equivalent of weeks. Throw in Arnaud's suggestion about the time catch's instability—

Stop it, I cut in. *He wants you to rush this. He wants you to screw up.*

I took a steadying breath, but as I exhaled, a prickling wave burned through me. My magic was talking. I spun and searched the parking lot, then the buildings across the street. The fight-or-flight response faded, but the message was all too familiar: someone had been watching me.

"Ah, yes, hello?"

I reoriented myself to the phone but continued to monitor my surroundings. "Claudius, it's Everson," I said. "Any luck reaching the Order?"

"The Order..." His voice trailed off. "Wh-who is this again?"

"Everson Croft," I said sternly. "I talked to you yesterday. I was about to enter a time catch, remember? And you were supposed to be working on reaching the senior members of the Order, the ones trapped in the Harkless Rift?"

I imagined him blinking in puzzlement. "Oh, right, yes, yes," he said at last. "How can I help you?"

God, his confusion was getting worse every day.

"Did you or did you not reach the Order?" I asked as patiently as I could.

"I'm afraid I hit a snag."

"A snag?"

"Yes, well, I... Let's see..." I could hear another phone ringing in the background. "Oh, what now?" he muttered, seeming to lose his train of thought.

"Claudius," I snapped.

"Can we talk in person? I'm having a hard time hearing you."

"Sure," I said, exhaling. "Did you have somewhere in mind?"

I was already cycling through nearby coffee shops and diners he could transport to when the connection disintegrated into static, and a portal the size of a doorway opened between me and a police SUV. At the other end of a tunnel, I could just make out Claudius. He was waving for me to come through.

"It's safe," he said from far away.

"Yeah, and so was the Hindenburg," I muttered, clapping my phone closed.

I drew my cane into sword and staff, not believing I was about to trust a portal opened by someone who could barely manage a telephone, but it was that damned ticking clock. I needed help for the Upholders.

With a final glance around for whomever might have been watching me, I uttered a Word. The surrounding air hardened into a form-fitting shield. Mouthing a quick prayer, I stepped inside. A damp darkness pressed in from all sides, and the ground squelched underfoot. Where in the hell was I?

Better not to ask, I decided, upping my pace.

I was halfway to Claudius when something large flapped

past my face. With a cry, I swung my sword around, but the creature had already disappeared into the darkness.

"Quickly!" Claudius's voice echoed down the portal.

Another set of wet, leathery wings batted past. This time, a cord whipped around my throat.

"Respingere!" I cried.

The shield encasing me sent out a bright pulse. What looked like an albino bat with a long rat's tail tumbled through the air with a shriek and disappeared. I glanced around in the shield's dimming light, now wishing I hadn't. More of the bat-like creatures circled a high ceiling of glistening stalactites. And did one of the stalactites just move?

The pulse from my shield had barely echoed away when a low rumble shook the cavern.

"Run!" Claudius yelled.

The cavern shook again, and I staggered for balance. Something crashed down behind me. I peered over a shoulder. One of the stalactites had fallen. Another landed in front of me and then righted itself. A dozen glowing eyes opened up and down its rocky face.

Well, isn't that nice.

As I veered around the monstrosity, thin tendrils began whipping from its body. I nailed the thing with a force blast, knocking it over.

"Don't look back!" Claudius shouted, waving both hands now.

I immediately craned my neck around. A wormlike creature large enough to fill the tunnel was contracting toward me. Its open mouth showed a humped gullet ringed with rows of nasty hook-like teeth.

A Chagrath? I thought in disbelief. *He sent me through a portal belonging to a frigging Chagrath?* Months before, I had consulted for my friend Jason, also known as the Blue Wolf, when he and his teammates faced a Chagrath in Mexico. One of the last creatures you wanted bearing down on you.

I aimed my sword back and shouted, *"Fuoco!"*

I rarely cast through the blade's second rune, the one the efreet had activated, because it was too hard to control. But right now I was too pissed off to care. The rune spawned a flame of elemental fire. Determined to bring the force under my will, I repeated an incantation of control—which the fire ignored.

In a blinding flash, it roared the length of my sword and geysered into the approaching creature. The Chagrath screamed as bright orange flames broke around its mouth and down its throat. The creature's body shrank back, sending a seismic wave through the cavern.

I stumbled, arms pinwheeling for balance, sword continuing to spew flames. The bat-like creatures shrieked and scattered as arcs of fire sent several up in torches. Even the stalactites were backing away. But the expulsive force was also shoving me from my destination. I shouted one charged Word after another, struggling to recall the elemental power, but it was as if it had a mind of its own.

Without warning, something seized my sword arm and yanked.

3

I landed on a stone floor, the sword clanging down beside me. The rune was dim again. Smoke floated from the cooling blade. When I turned my head the other way, I was eye level with a pair of feet clad in black socks and sandals: Claudius's. He was standing over me in a satin robe cinched at his waist. In a panic, I looked past him, but the portal was closed. The worm hadn't come through.

"A Chagrath's lair?" I shouted. "What in holy hell, man?"

Claudius adjusted his round tinted glasses. "Sorry about that. It was the most direct route, and I thought we'd, ah, catch it sleeping."

"Thought or hoped?"

"Hoped," he admitted.

Grumbling, I pushed myself to my feet. I'd never seen Claudius's workspace, and it looked like a cross between a poorly lit office and a medieval dungeon.

To my left, a massive desk was heaped with telephones, several of them ringing. Piles of notes sat in drifts around a desktop calendar that was five years old. The rest of the stone walls were lined with bookcases, their shelves holding dust-covered tomes and artifacts that buzzed with peculiar energies. Potted plants and small cages hung from a low ceiling. I turned to find one of the plants straining toward me, a mouth set in the center of its bright ring of petals leaking a foul-smelling drool.

"Oh, don't mind him," Claudius said. "Nipped me the other day, and now he has a taste for wizard's blood."

I leaned away from the plant's straining lips. No wonder Claudius always sounded so damned out of sorts. This place was the picture of madness. The aging magic-user tilted his head now, curtains of dyed-black hair shifting around the sags of his questioning face.

"It's Everson," I said, preempting him. "Everson Croft."

"Ah, yes, yes. Everson." He mouthed my name a couple more times, as if to make it stick. "And how can I help you?"

My heart was still racing from the Chagrath encounter, and being underground wasn't helping. Neither was the incessant ringing of the telephones or the mewling cries of the plant jonesing for my blood.

"Is there somewhere saner we can talk?" I asked.

"Saner?" Claudius glanced around before an idea appeared to strike him. "Yes, follow me." As he turned to lead the way, I noticed the back of his head was bald, the hair completely sheared off.

"What happened to your hair?" I asked.

He brought a hand to the crown of his head. "What about it?"

"In back."

His fingers jumped as they encountered the bald skin. He felt around it for another moment, then gave it several pats.

"Oh, yes. That. I was testing possible routes to the Harkless Rift. One realm was made of a living jelly. It gave every indication it would let me pass, but then turned testy when I started wading through it. I'm lucky that's all it ate off." He led the way up a spiral staircase that ended at a landing. "After you," he said, holding a door open.

I hesitated before stepping through a rack of winter coats. Half expecting to emerge into another nightmare realm, I was surprised to find a suburban-looking living room, sunlight glowing through a picture window. Claudius shuffled past me.

"I'll put on some tea," he said. "Have a seat." He waved toward a couch with floral upholstery.

"Where are we?" I called.

"Home sweet home."

"Right, but where?"

"Oh, ah, outside Annapolis, Maryland," he said as he disappeared into a kitchen. "Or is it Peoria, Illinois?"

I could hear him considering the question in a mutter beneath the opening and closing of cupboards. The living room, with its matching furniture set, cream carpeting, and generic landscape prints, looked shockingly pedestrian. Compared to the basement, we could have been in an alternate universe.

The doorbell rang. "Claudi-poo!" a woman's voice called.

From the kitchen, a metal teapot clanged to the floor. "Don't answer that!" Claudius called.

I craned my neck around. Through the diaphanous curtain, I made out the profile of a squat woman with a coif of frosted pink hair. She was holding a tinfoil-covered plate to her chest. The doorbell rang again.

"I have your favorite treat!" she sang.

The kitchen went very quiet. I caught myself hunkering from her view.

After another round of bell-ringing, the woman said, "Well, fudge!" and clopped off.

Moments later, Claudius peered from the kitchen on hands and knees. "Is she gone?"

"Yeah, I think so."

He retreated, then emerged upright carrying a platter with a teapot, cups, and cream and sugar. He arranged everything on the coffee table, then shuffled to the door, opened it furtively, and retrieved the plate the woman had left on the stoop. Returning, he removed the tinfoil from a heap of golden cookies.

"She's in my book group," Claudius explained, setting the plate beside the tea platter. "Recently widowed. Had me over for dinner last month, and I'm afraid I let things go a *little* too far. Makes a tasty gingersnap, though." He popped one into his mouth and poured the steaming tea. "Now," he said as he settled into a soft chair with his cup and saucer. "What did you want to talk about?"

"So, no luck reaching the Order?"

"I'm afraid not. The senior members accessed the rift through their collective powers. I'm not near that level, and my few attempts at shortcuts didn't go so well." He patted the back of his head, producing a slapping sound.

"Any idea how they got trapped?"

Claudius slurped his tea and made a thoughtful face. "I guess I haven't really considered it. Or if I have, I've forgotten."

"Could a demon have done it?"

"A demon? It's possible, I suppose."

Assuming Claudius had also forgotten the story about Arianna visiting my dream and telling me to find Arnaud, I recounted it for him. I also told him about my adventure in the time catch. "So I have Arnaud," I finished. "And somehow that's supposed to free Arianna and the other members of the Order. But there's been no follow-up from her. I'm guessing because she can't reach me."

"No, probably not," Claudius muttered. He was squinting at a note his *amour* had tucked among the cookies. I caught a couple R-rated words. Claudius flinched before disappearing the note into a jacket pocket.

"What if Arnaud's master trapped them?" I asked.

"His master?" Claudius frowned as he polished off another cookie.

"Malphas," I continued. "He's ambitious, powerful. He was manipulating energy in the time catch, we think to create a portal he could enter by. What if he knew that the biggest threat to his plan was a response from the Order?" I was presenting the questions more to myself than Claudius, who appeared more interested in the refreshments. "What if he was the one who trapped them in the Harkless Rift?"

"I don't like where this is going."

I looked up from my tea, surprised to find him regarding me sternly. "Where what's going?"

"You're wondering if the solution is to offer Malphas's servant to him in exchange for the Order's release."

I stared at him for another moment. That was exactly what I'd been thinking, because why else would Arianna have directed me to find Arnaud? "It would be bargaining with a demon master, sure..." I began.

"Never a good idea."

"Well, I happen to agree, but if it leads to the Order's release..."

"I still don't like it."

Neither would Vega, I thought, remembering our talk in her office and the way her protective instincts had flared up. She would never forgive me for releasing Arnaud, no matter what we received in exchange. But I couldn't stop thinking about how, once freed, the senior members of our Order would be able to enter the time catch and recover the Upholders, not to mention boost our firepower against the demons.

After another moment, I exhaled. "All right," I said in concession. "I'll wait for Arianna's guidance. But in the meantime I have to recover the others from the time catch. That's non-negotiable."

"You mean 1776 New York?"

Maybe it was the high volume of ginger he was consuming, but Claudius's mind seemed to have sharpened in the last few minutes.

"Right," I said. "Is there any way you can—"

"Get you there?" Claudius finished for me.

After the Chagrath's lair, I couldn't believe I was even considering the question, but I gave a slight nod.

"Well, I've never attempted a portal to a time catch. I'd need time, no pun intended, and even then there's a good chance you'd lose a lot more than the hair off the back of your head. Have you tried the fae?"

"They're ignoring me."

"Hm. Then maybe you should consult your teacher."

"Gretchen?" I snorted. "She's worse than they are."

"She *was* rather brusque when she called this morning."

I straightened so suddenly, I spilled half my remaining tea. "Gretchen called you this morning? Why didn't you say anything?"

"Well, I don't know." He paused to dip a crescent of cookie into his cup. "I suppose because you didn't ask."

"She's back from Faerie?"

"She suggested as much."

I dug out my phone and accessed the number I'd managed to wheedle from Gretchen, but no one answered. Swearing, I stood and looked around. Where did Claudius say we were? Maryland? Illinois?

"How do I get back to New York? And don't tell me through the Chagrath's lair."

"No, no, don't worry." Claudius finished his cookie before setting his tea down and dusting the crumbs from his lap. "I have a direct portal to Gretchen's place. But here, take some gingersnaps. I'll eat them all otherwise."

"Yeah, there's not really time."

But he'd already set a pile of cookies in the center of the tinfoil and was folding it into a clumpy package. He handed it to me.

"Thanks," I said, quickly pocketing the cookies in my coat. "Do we need to go back downstairs?"

"No, no, right here is fine."

Claudius signed in the air and turned me around. A portal stood inches from my nose. Before I could weigh the wisdom of chancing another of Claudius's portals, the fleshy-looking void sucked me inside.

"Good luck!" he called in a fading voice.

4

I had no idea what kind of portal I'd entered, but it felt like being squeezed through something's digestive tract. Before I knew it, I was being shoved out the other end with explosive force, landing hard on my hands and knees.

"Holy hell," I grunted.

I checked to make sure my cane had made the journey, along with everything I'd stowed in my pockets. Globs of steaming yellow giblets spilled from my coat as I pushed myself to my feet. As the steam dissipated, a basement took shape around me, one I recognized from when the wizard Pierce owned the townhouse.

Another of Arnaud's victims, I thought.

And another reminder of how dangerous the demon-vampire was.

Himitsu paintings, the medium Pierce had used for his divinations, stood in stacks throughout the large space, but Gretchen's hoard was taking over. In fact, the light source for the basement, a golden luminescence, was coming from an especially large pile of her crap.

When something scuffed behind the pile, I readied my cane,

but it was just an antique lantern. It peeked out at me before shrinking away in a contraction of light. One of Gretchen's acquisitions from Faerie, no doubt.

My annoyed thoughts turned to Claudius. *Really, dude? You couldn't have dropped me at the front door?*

Gretchen had a bad habit of not remembering me between her visits to the fae realm. If she thought I was an intruder—which was very likely—I'd be staring down the barrel of some nasty magic.

Grumbling, I activated a tube of neutralizing potion and drank it. The potion would insulate me from her first attack, anyway. Maybe give me enough time to convince her who I was. As the potion spread through me in a tingling wave, I readied my sword and staff and started up the stairs. I was almost to the door when I picked out a pair of shouting voices coming from deeper in the house.

"Who is she?" Gretchen asked.

"Why does it have to be another woman?" Bree-yark barked back. "Maybe I'm just fed up."

"Fed up? With what?"

"With everything!"

It sounded like the goblin was finally having his breakup talk with Gretchen. I'd been cheerleading the move, but did it have to be now? Trying to solicit Gretchen's help on a good day would have been challenging enough.

"Well, where is this coming from?" she demanded.

"I had a talk with someone," Bree-yark said. "Came about ten years too late, but it was the medicine I needed."

"Who?" she demanded.

Oh, c'mon, man. Please don't tell her—

"Your student," he said. "Everson."

My shoulders slumped. *Great.*

"Everson?" Gretchen repeated.

"Might be young, but the kid's got his head screwed on straight. It took jawing with him to get to the truth. This isn't a relationship. This is you stringing along an ugly, lovesick goblin. Been that way ever since we met at that resort in the Mirthers."

"Everson *Croft?*" Gretchen repeated, this time in a roar.

And here I'd been worried she wouldn't remember me.

I was debating whether to step in when something scuffed behind me. I turned to find the lantern a couple of steps below me on the staircase. All of its glass faces had been darkened by smoke save one. Cringing like a frightened child, the lantern rotated its clear face from the door to me.

"It's all right," I said. "They're just having a disagreement."

Gretchen paused long enough in her shouting to grunt. Something shattered against the floor. Great, now she was breaking shit.

"Hey, hey, hey," Bree-yark said in a backing-away voice.

I burst from the staircase and hustled down the main corridor, a shield glimmering into being around me. Though Gretchen was often moody, I'd never seen her in an all-out wrath. I didn't know what she was capable of.

I reached the kitchen to find her two-handing a casserole dish overhead. Unable to tell whether her target was the floor or Bree-yark, I thrust my cane forward and shouted, *"Vigore!"* The pulse shattered the dish in Gretchen's hands, and a pile of what looked like brown cottage cheese and fish guts splatted over her head.

Son of a bitch.

She turned toward me, lips drawn into a bone-white line, eyes huge. Liquid from the mound atop her head began trickling through her wild hair, down her forehead, and off her hooked nose. Bree-yark, who had backed into a corner, grasped a small spatula from the counter and held it in front of his face as if it might hide him. When I waved him over, he wasted no time scuttling to my side.

"Gretchen, listen," I said. "I didn't know there was anything in the—" I made a feeble gesture toward the shards of casserole dish. "I thought you were going to hurt—" I cocked my head at Bree-yark.

Gretchen didn't respond. She just continued to stare, arms above her head as if she were still holding the dish. A dollop of gunk fell from her fingers. When my right calf warmed, I looked down to find that the lantern had followed me into the kitchen and was peering out at Gretchen from behind my leg.

"Hey, maybe we should split," Bree-yark whispered.

That would have been the smart move, but I still needed Gretchen's help. I drew a steadying breath.

"Before you do anything, I want you to hear me out," I said. "The senior members of the Order are trapped in the Harkless Rift. Claudius tried, but he can't reach them. There's a good chance a demon is involved. The same demon has been using a time catch to manipulate energies so he can breach our world." Gretchen squinted slightly, but I wasn't sure whether that was something to be encouraged by. "I'm convinced that the answer to how to defeat the demon and free the Order is in the time catch."

I'd made up the last part. With Gretchen lacking a senti-mental bone in her body, I didn't dare tell her that my true moti-vation was to recover my teammates. But my magic stirred long enough to give a pair of hard nods.

Holy crap, I thought, *I'm onto something.*

Gretchen might have felt it too, because she slowly lowered her arms.

"The fae helped me into the time catch the last time," I said, "but I can't reach them now. I need your help."

"You want me to help you?"

Her voice was so calm, it was creepy.

"Yes, to get back into the time catch."

Gretchen propped her chin on a fist now as though considering the question. The gesture sent a slab of food sliding from her head and splattering to the floor. Why she didn't remove the pile, I had no idea—it would have been as simple for her as snapping her fingers. But why did Gretchen do half of what she did?

"Let's see, he breaks up my relationship..."

"I lent an ear more than anything," I interjected.

"That's true," Bree-yark offered from beside me.

"He breaks into my house..."

"I didn't break in, Claudius sent me."

"He breaks a *casseruola di ricotta* over my head..."

"That you were about to break over Bree-yark's," I pointed out, growing testy. I didn't have time for this crap.

"And now he wants me to help him."

"Yes, and just so you know, I covered your bill for Vander Meer's while you were away." I was referring to her shopping spree at the Dutch furniture store. "That set me back almost three grand. I'm willing to call it even if you—"

"He wants me to *help* him," she repeated.

"Yes," I said, standing firm. "Look, I'm sorry about showing up like this and for the situation with your ... *casseruola*, but this is bigger than any of that. Much bigger. If we don't stop the demon master, Faerie will be threatened too."

"Faerie?" She made a scoffing sound.

"It may already be happening," I said, sheathing my sword back in the cane.

I was riffing off what Arnaud had suggested, which was never a good idea, but if Gretchen had one soft spot, it was her infatuation with the place. Faerie for her was like Disney World for a princess-obsessed preteen. But Gretchen maintained a look of deep skepticism, fists set against her ample hips.

I exhaled hard through my nose. The Order was trapped in the Harkless Rift, the Upholders were stuck in the time catch, a major demon was plotting an attack that could lead to a full-scale demon apocalypse, and the one person who could help was looking at me like I was something she'd curb-scraped off her shoe.

With a hand sign, I opened a small portal to my cubbyhole.

"Here," I said, reaching inside and withdrawing a thick book of maps. I flipped to the page I'd marked with a receipt from Mr. Han's and held it open toward her. "The time catch is here. This is where I need to go."

"Is that right?" she said flatly.

"Can you help me? Yes or no."

Gretchen looked from me to Bree-yark, her lips drawing into a scowl, then down at the lantern. The light source scooted further behind my leg. When Gretchen's eyes returned to mine, her irises were changing colors.

Crap, she's gathering magic.

I tossed the book back into the cubby hole. As the portal shrank around it, I drew my cane into sword and staff again. Gretchen's eyes were twin kaleidoscopes now, the ever-shifting sequence of colors and patterns creating an effect almost as mesmerizing as it was scary.

"C'mon, Everson," Bree-yark whispered, tugging at the back of my coat.

But I couldn't pull my gaze away, even under the protection of my neutralizing potion. Gretchen's magic stalked slowly around me now: probing, sniffing, prodding.

"You want my help?" she asked.

"Everson." Bree-yark tugged harder this time.

Even the lantern was butting my leg, trying to herd me from

the room. But I remained rooted to the spot, unable to do anything but stare into my teacher's eyes. Because beyond their dizzying power, I sensed a promise. A dangerous promise, maybe, but a promise.

"Yes," I heard myself answer.

Her kaleidoscopic irises contracted to points. In the next moment they pounced.

Powerful colors exploded through me, and the kitchen disappeared beneath a mind-reeling series of images. Some of them I recognized as flashes from my past; others were entirely foreign. I tried to decipher them, but they were cycling through too hard and fast. My mind stretched at the joints, threatening to pull apart. Was this Gretchen's idea of punishment?

Stop, I pled.

You want my help? she repeated, this time in my thoughts.

Stop!

And just like that, the cascade of images ceased. I was flat on my back, but not in the kitchen.

I was in an abyss. Four others lay around me, and we were rotating as if on a giant millstone. Energy swirled and piled into giant storm clouds on all sides. I'd dreamt of this damned place. It had followed the dream with Arianna. I struggled to lift my head, to see who the others were—that felt important. But a force held me fast.

"*Liberare!*" I shouted.

Though energy poured through my prism, I remained pinned. Harsh lights crackled and burned the air. Thunder rumbled into low laughter. The sound came from above, where taloned hands were curling through a growing seam. A pair of eyes—enormous, demonic eyes—peered out. Flashes of harsh, ozone-like energy highlighted the contours of a craggy face. The eyes narrowed hungrily.

It was Arnaud's master, Malphas.

I struggled with everything I had against the force restraining me.

"This was inevitable, Croft," Malphas rumbled. "*You* were inevitable."

He reached an arm through the void and punctured my forehead with a talon. A black pain split my head, threatening to drive me insane, but no blood ran. The tip of his talon was on my casting prism. I focused through the agony, focused all my energy on forcing him back out. But Malphas had stolen my power.

"The great *savior*," he mocked.

His talon flicked.

5

Something cold and flat struck me across the face.

I opened my eyes with a gasp to find Bree-yark straddling my chest, his knees pinning my arms to the ground. My lower body was bucking as if possessed by Saint Vitus, but the goblin, with his low center of gravity and compact mass, held fast. In his right fist he clutched the spatula from Gretchen's kitchen.

I sagged to a rest. "It's all right," I panted. "I'm back."

Bree-yark hesitated, the spatula back in striking position.

"I'm good," I said.

With a grunt, he tossed the kitchen implement away and pushed himself off me. Even at a stocky four feet, he must have weighed close to two-hundred.

Drawing a full breath, I sat up. We were on a grassy lawn planted with saplings. A palatial building rose before us. For a moment, I thought we were in Faerie, but when I saw scaffolding around the building's stone wing, I recognized it as the Metropolitan Museum of Art in east Central Park.

"What happened?" I asked.

Bree-yark looked at me askance. "What didn't? One minute

we were in Gretchen's kitchen, and the next we ended up here. Only you were thrashing and screaming like a banshee. I thought for sure she'd snapped your mind as payback for your faceoff back there. Man, you and me must've wrestled for a good five minutes before I pinned you. Knew we should've taken off when we had the chance."

I could only imagine what our tussle had looked like, but I was thinking of the vision.

You were inevitable, Malphas's taunting voice echoed in my thoughts. *The great savior.*

Had Gretchen been responsible for the vision? If so, why? As I considered the questions and the demon master's words, I rubbed the spot on my cheek where Bree-yark had spatulaed me. For the first time I really felt the sting.

"Yeah, sorry about the smack. Even pinned, you were outta control."

When I noticed the closest saplings leaning away from us, leaves blown from their thin branches, I remembered my effort to summon a release spell in the dream, or vision, or whatever the hell it had been.

"Did I cast?" I asked.

"As if the screaming and thrashing weren't enough," he confirmed.

Gaining my feet, I checked to make sure the starter potions in my coat pockets hadn't burst. "Any idea why Gretchen sent us here?"

Bree-yark snorted. "Are you really asking me why that woman did something?"

He had a point, but I couldn't forget the promise I'd felt behind her question: *You want my help?*

"Well, maybe we should take a look around," I said.

"This is the Met, right?" Bree-yark glanced at it doubtfully. "Hell of a search area."

I looked over the scaffolding and piles of building material. The rear of the museum had suffered burn damage during the mayor's napalm assault on the park during the purge campaign. Beyond our island of green, Central Park's charred landscape stretched for blocks, much of it bulldozed into massive debris piles. Replanting was supposed to commence in the spring. Back at the museum, I considered the two million pieces that had been returned to the Met's permanent collection.

"Oh, fuck this," I muttered, anger rippling hot inside me.

I pulled out my phone and dialed Gretchen. No answer, and no way to leave a message. Cramming the phone back into a pocket, I oriented myself toward the road that would take me out of the park.

"Hey, where ya going?" Bree-yark barked.

"Back to Gretchen's."

The goblin hustled after me. "Not a good idea."

"Have you got a better one?"

"Wait, I didn't tell you everything."

I slowed to face him. "What do you mean?"

"She said something before she zapped us out of there."

I stopped. "What?"

Bree-yark was wearing a bomber jacket over a turtleneck that matched his gray wool hat. He fidgeted with the jacket's zipper before answering. "She said neither of us are welcome back there. Only she put it a lot more colorfully and with some serious threats thrown in." By his downcast eyes, I could see he'd taken her words personally.

"Well, that's tough." I resumed my march. "If she dropped me here to find something, she needs to tell me what the hell it is."

Bree-yark jogged beside me. "Look, just give her some time to cool down."

"There *isn't* time," I growled. "That's the point."

"Isn't there something else you could be doing?"

"No."

But as I scrambled down a cindery embankment leading to East Seventy-ninth, I wondered if I was only going to succeed in wasting more time. Gretchen was unlikely to answer her door, for starters. And even if she did, she would only stonewall me. I knew from past experience that any help she proffered was on her terms—and in this case, that help could have already begun. Whether it was the vision with Malphas or transporting me here or something else entirely. I tuned into my magic. Was that a nod?

"Everson?" Bree-yark pressed.

"Fine, I won't go back to Gretchen's."

"Thank the gods," he exhaled as we reached the transverse road.

"There's a fae townhouse not far from here," I said. "They're the ones who delivered me into the time catch. I stopped by this morning, but no one answered. I want to try them again."

"The fae?" Bree-yark made a wary face.

"It's either that or..." I thought of Arnaud's claim that he was my sole ticket to the time catch. "It's either that or I'm out of options."

"Mind if I tag along?"

I looked over, surprised. "To the townhouse? I should be fine."

"It's not just about getting your back—which I've got any time, day or night, I hope you know that. No, it's that I told Mae I'd stop by this morning, but I need some time to pull myself together. I'm still wound up from my talk with Gretchen. Mae would see something's wrong and make a fuss, and I don't like worrying her more than I already have. I mean, she's letting me keep my stuff over there."

"She is?"

"Good thing I had the sense to move it out of Gretchen's, or I'd have never seen it again. I even parked my ride up there. It's just until I can find my own place," he added, as if defending Mae's honor. "We're not, you know, involved in that way."

"I get it."

"Well, not yet."

I was hurriedly saying that he was welcome to accompany me, when the scorched brush at our backs rustled. I spun, energy charging down my cane. But it was just Gretchen's lantern peering at us from behind a bush. Realizing it had been spotted, the lantern dimmed. With a sigh, I recalled my magic.

"What's that thing doing here?" I muttered.

Bree-yark barked a small laugh. "It's all right, Dropsy. Everson's a friend."

"Dropsy? It has a name?"

"She must've gotten caught in Gretchen's translocation spell back there."

"She?"

Dropsy emerged from the brush, her light growing out again. The lantern took a tentative hop toward us, then another. I peeked around to make sure no one was looking, but we had the road to ourselves.

Bree-yark stooped and lifted the lantern by a brass ring. "Gotcha, you little stinker."

Dropsy jiggled anxiously until Bree-yark switched her to his far hand, away from me. "Don't take it personally, Everson," he said. "Took her a few weeks to warm up to me, and that was only 'cause I let her watch cartoons on the big screen TV. She couldn't get enough of 'em."

"Well, can you send her home?"

"Home?" he barked. "That's forty blocks from here, and she doesn't know the city."

I eyed the enchanted item. She looked harmless enough, but

not trusting anything from Gretchen's hoard, I took a closer look through my wizard's senses. The fae magic that powered her was a thin golden shimmer and not particularly strong. Probably a market knickknack of some kind.

"I just don't want any surprises," I said.

"Nah, Dropsy's a sweetheart. Aren't you?" He swung her from his hand. "She won't be any trouble."

"Good, because that inbox is already full."

BREE-YARK SNIFFED THE TUBE I'D HANDED HIM.

"Isn't this what we drank at Epic Con?" he asked.

I nodded and pointed out the emerald-green door off Seventieth Street. "We're at the address of a powerful royal family. The neutralizing potion will protect us from incidental contact with its defenses, but that's about it. Cheers."

I clinked my tube against his and downed the bitter potion.

Bree-yark followed suit, grimacing as he glugged away. Upon finishing, he burped, drew a forearm across his lips, and spiked the tube against the sidewalk, shattering the Pyrex in all directions.

"Hey, I reuse those!" I cried.

But he was blinking up at the townhouse. "Holy thunder, there it is." I could all but see the glamour thinning through his squash-colored eyes. "Man, and I'm usually pretty good at spotting enchantments."

"A few ground rules before we head up. One, let me do the talking. Two, don't touch anything—that's for your own protection. And three, no matter what anyone says or does, please, keep your cool. We're dealing with fae nobility." And if Arnaud's insinuations were to be believed, nobility who had been compromised.

"You've got nothing to worry about," Bree-yark said. "Dropsy and I will stay out of the way." He gave the lantern a little shake.

"I'm not worried about Dropsy."

"Hey, I've been listening to a podcast on anger management. I have a process now."

"Just yesterday you threw a rock at that kid who came for Gretchen's furniture. If I hadn't shielded him, he'd still be leaking brain fluid."

Bree-yark scratched the back of his neck. "He caught me at a bad time was all."

"Well, that can't happen here."

As I peered up the short flight of steps, my stomach churned with the double anxiety that no one would answer the door and that someone might answer. If the fae had abandoned my team-mates, how were they going to react to my visit?

Bree-yark clapped my back. "You've got this."

That got me moving. I took the steps quickly and rapped on the door. Bree-yark stood off to one side. When the lantern twisted and bucked in his grip, he gave me an apologetic look and moved her to his far side.

I was distracted enough by the commotion that I hadn't seen the door open. From the shadow beyond the entrance, a pair of gray eyes glimmered.

"Good morning, Mr. Croft," Osgood said.

6

S truck by the butler's sudden manifestation, I stammered, "Wh-what happened to you?"

The slight, silver-haired fae watched me with cool, unblinking eyes. "And to what might you be referring?"

How in the hell could he not know what I was talking about? I hesitated. *Was* this Osgood? His voice and butler attire were the same, but his bearing had always conveyed a hint of good humor, however subtle. Now he stood as rigid as a statue, his face a porcelain mask. I picked up an undercurrent that was inhospitable, verging on hostile. But it was him. I could sense his prodigious power.

"The time catch," I said. "You delivered us there yesterday evening. You were supposed to bring everyone back."

"Yes," he said simply.

"Then why didn't you?"

"I gave your companions specific instructions. Had they followed them, I would have returned them as agreed."

"*What?*"

"Think back, Mr. Croft."

Subtle magic stirred around me, and it was suddenly evening. I was standing in Fort Jay's central quadrangle with Malachi, Gorgantha, Seay, and Jordan, crumbling buildings rising around us. But everyone and everything appeared spectral. The only solid entity was Osgood. "The best way to return will be from this location," he told us, tapping his foot twice. "Note it when you arrive."

I don't fucking believe this, I thought as the illusion thinned away. *He meant that exact spot.*

Two intersecting walkways marked the present location, but in the time catch, it had been a random place inside an earthworks manned by British soldiers. Short of planting a stake, the Upholders wouldn't have found it.

"So you left them over a *technicality?*" I said.

I was also cursing myself. I should have known to mark the damned spot on our arrival, the fae being the fae. But things weren't adding up. The cheap trick felt beneath Osgood, one. And two, he'd been under orders from Caroline. I couldn't fathom her letting him abandon my teammates.

"I'm sorry, Mr. Croft," Osgood said. "Was there anything else?"

"Yes, there is. You're going to bring them back. Now."

"I'm afraid that's impossible. Not without—"

"Not without them standing in your little spot?" I interrupted. "All right, so here's what you're going to do. You send *me* back there. I'll see to it personally that we're all where we need to be, and then you'll be obligated to return us."

"I can't send you."

"Why not?"

"Because that agreement was fulfilled."

"Then we'll make a new one."

"I lack the authority."

"But not the power."

From the shadow of the entranceway, Osgood returned my stare.

I leaned toward him and lowered my voice. "Do you want to tell me what the hell's going on here?"

Osgood glanced over at Bree-yark, who was still swinging the animated lantern. The goblin stopped and returned a stern nod.

"I believe you have all the essential information," Osgood said.

"So you're not going to return me to the time catch?"

"No, Mr. Croft." For the first time, a tiny wrinkle of what might have been regret showed beneath Osgood's lower lip.

"Then I'm going to ask you to do something else," I said, bringing my voice back under control. I reached into a coat pocket and withdrew a letter. "I need you to deliver this to Caroline." I'd written it hastily that morning, but it explained the situation and the urgency of recovering my teammates.

Osgood shook his head. "I'm afraid I cannot, Mr. Croft."

"Under whose order?" I demanded.

"No one's."

"Bullshit."

"I can't deliver your letter," he said, "because Mrs. Caroline is missing."

My arm thrusting the letter toward him fell to my side. "Missing?"

"Now if that's all."

With my mind juggling everything thrown at me in the last minute, and now this revelation about Caroline, I was too slow to react to the door closing between us. My brain synapses kicked back to life. "Wait!" I cried, thrusting my cane toward the narrowing space. But a thick arm wrapped my body.

"What the—?"

"Whoa, there," Bree-yark grunted, leaning back with his weight until my feet left the ground.

The door closed over my best chance of recovering my teammates. As powerful fae magic sealed the frame, I sagged in Bree-yark's grip. He'd been right to restrain me. The protections over the door were one thing, but those over the threshold would have annihilated my neutralizing magic and protection and then some.

"Didn't want you breaking your own rules," Bree-yark said.

"No, you did good." I patted the goblin's leathery hand. "Thanks."

When he set me back on my feet, I rapped the door several times with my cane, sending up more tendrils of fae magic. Predictably, no one answered this time.

"Dammit," I muttered.

Bree-yark switched the lantern to his other hand. "So what do you think's really going on?"

It sounded like something had gotten to the fae, maybe the same entity responsible for Caroline's disappearance. But I wasn't ready to go there. Arnaud was already right about my teammates being trapped in the time catch. If he were right about the fae being compromised, then I was going to have to consider his next claim—that he was the only one capable of getting me into the time catch.

I blew out my breath. "I don't know, man."

I paced the landing, not ready to give up. I'd gone through Claudius, Gretchen, and now Osgood. Who did that leave? I checked to make sure Osgood hadn't taken the letter like he had the last one, but I was still clutching the envelope to Caroline. I'd addressed it to her P.O. box in the event no one answered. After giving the door a final pair of bangs, I jerked my head for Bree-yark to follow.

"Let's drop this in the mail."

"The letter?" he asked. "But didn't shiny pants say she was AWOL?"

"Coming from the fae that could mean anything."

"True enough," he grunted.

We backtracked two blocks to a mailbox. I licked the envelope and dropped it in, hoping somehow, someway, it would find Caroline. She was my last shot. The alternative was having to tell Ricki I was contemplating a second conversation with Arnaud, this one a negotiation to enter the time catch.

The letter had barely landed when hot pins erupted through my body—the same warning my magic had sent up outside 1 Police Plaza. I spoke quickly, hardening the surrounding air into a protective shield.

"What's up?" Bree-yark asked, sensing the change.

"Someone or something's watching us," I whispered, taking furtive stock of the street and sidewalks.

The goblin's eyes cut around too. Even Dropsy rotated from side to side, checking out the scene for herself. In the next moment, Bree-yark hollered and threw up an arm as something zipped past our heads. Recoiling, I drew my cane into sword and staff. But I quickly recognized our company.

"They're allies," I told Bree-yark, slotting my sword again. "Pixies."

As I tracked the peach and meadow-green contrails, fresh hope stirred inside me. Pip and Twerk had given us a major assist in the time catch, handling the British warships. Were they here to help again? They continued past a line of storefronts and at a corner townhouse undergoing major renovations, veered through a gap in a boarded-over window. What were they doing?

"This way, Mr. Croft," their small voices trailed after them.

I broke into a run, weaving through the pedestrian traffic.

"Wait," Bree-yark called, hustling after me. "You don't think it's a trap?"

"If the fae wanted to hurt us, they would have already," I

called back. Plus, I'd picked up an urgency in the twins' voices. They had something to tell me. I pulled up at a construction fence surrounding the townhouse. A padlock secured the gate, but there didn't appear to be any workers around.

"Quickly, Mr. Croft," Pip cried from inside.

"Mind standing guard here?" I asked Bree-yark as he scuffed to a stop beside me.

"Sure," he said. "Pixies get on my nerves anyway." Dropsy rocked forward and back as if in agreement.

I wasted no time snapping the padlock with an invocation. Removing lock and chain, I passed through the gate and jogged up the steps. At the front door, I smashed the bolt with another spoken Word. Once inside, I held out my sword and called light to my cane. The glow from the opal showed a wooden floor that had been half pried up. I stepped around tools and piles of construction material.

"Pip?" I called. "Twerk?"

"In here," one of them replied in a dismal voice.

They'd flown into a windowless room in the back of the townhouse. I arrived to find the small cherubic beings holding one another in a hover, faces puffy from crying. Bits of their colorful light spilled beneath them like tears.

"What in the hell's going on?" I demanded.

They clung to one another more tightly and began sobbing. The butterfly-like wings keeping the twin pixies aloft stirred their enchanting autumn hair and gossamer garments, but their faces looked miserable. I felt bad now for snapping at them, but my tolerance for strangeness was just about spent.

Remembering the decorum for dealing with pixies, I cleared my throat. "What I meant to say is, what troubles you, fair ones? Why hast thou summoned me here?"

"Something's happened," Pip gasped.

"Something horrible, Mr. Croft," Twerk put in between sobs.

Then just spit it out, I thought in aggravation.

"Is this to do with Caroline?" I pressed gently.

Pip sniffled and wiped her eyes with her little arm. "It's to do with *everything.*"

"Everything, Mr. Croft," Twerk echoed.

At least they were pulling themselves together, but Jesus. "Perhaps you might start your tale at the beginning?" I suggested.

The pixies looked at one another. *Please don't break into song,* I thought.

"*Once all was bright in our kingdom home,*" they harmonized in sad voices. "*But evil stirred in the coming gloam.*"

I sighed. They'd broken into song.

"*He slipped among us, wicked and dark. Casting fear and woe unto noble hearts.*"

It sounded like a demon had gotten into the upper echelon, dammit. "Who has he claimed?" I pressed.

"*Aye, they've fallen under shadow deep,*" the pair continued. "*The—*"

With small popping sounds, the pixies disappeared in bursts of peach and meadow-green dust. I looked all around.

"Pip!" I cried. "Twerk!"

I listened for them, but all I could hear was the sound of traffic outside. I called their names repeatedly as I searched the rest of the house. I even cast a reveal spell. But the two had simply vanished.

"What was that all about?" Bree-yark asked when I rejoined him outside the fence.

"Sounds like a demon infiltrated the fae kingdom connected to the townhouse. Which would explain Osgood's sudden reversal as well as Caroline's disappearance. The pixies were about to tell me more, but they disappeared." I peered back at the townhouse as if I might catch their colorful contrails or hear their voices. I could only hope they'd been translocated and not popped from existence.

"Probably Osgood's doing," Bree-yark grumbled.

"Actually, I think he's the one who let them out."

As Bree-yark raised his brows in surprise, I remembered the regretful look the fae butler had slipped me.

"I don't know Osgood's history," I said. "He's at least as powerful as the nobility he serves, but he's dutybound to obey them for some reason. Caroline ordered him to help us the last time. Malphas must have intervened, possessed someone high up in the kingdom. Now Osgood can't help us, and Caroline's missing." I suspected that the only reason I'd managed to return from the time catch was thanks to my backchannel to 1 Police Plaza. "So yeah, I think Osgood released the pixies to tip me off to what was happening. Until someone in the kingdom shut them up."

Bree-yark nodded grimly. "So now what?"

"Other than having to worry about a demon-possessed fae?" I muttered.

I was dragging a hand across my jaw stubble when the savage prickling from earlier returned. The watcher was back, and with the warning came a whiff of something deathlike. He or she was closer this time.

"You all right?" Bree-yark asked.

I staggered as the surrounding buildings began to warp and bend. And now the whole block was tilting. Or so it seemed. The pedestrians weren't reacting. And except for the troubled look on Bree-yark's face, neither was he.

"We need to get out of here," I said, worried now I was going to lose my breakfast.

Bree-yark wheeled toward the street and released a sharp whistle. When a cab stopped, the goblin opened the door and helped me in. He then joined me on the other side, cradling Dropsy on his lap.

"Just drive," I told the cabby in a shaky voice.

By the time we reached Fifth Avenue and had gotten some distance from whatever I'd felt on the street, the prickling sensation faded and the world around me began to steady. But I still felt strung out and queasy.

Bree-yark shifted in his seat. "Hey, uh, I'm thinking I should see Mae before she starts getting worried."

I nodded. Her place wasn't far, and I could use some space to catch my breath. While Bree-yark gave the driver the address, I peered out the window. Had I just met the possessed fae?

I didn't know, but this entity was powerful.

And deadly.

7

"Everson!" Mae exclaimed. "What a pleasant surprise!"

The elderly woman threw her thick arms around my neck and rocked me back and forth. I'd had second thoughts about coming here—there was so much to process, to figure out —but her embrace had a grounding effect that I hadn't known I'd needed. And her permed white hair, smelling like a grandmother's love, drove out the last vestiges of the death stench from earlier.

"How are you, Mae?" I asked as we separated.

"Oh, not bad for a broad on the rocky side of seventy." She took me by the shoulders and squinted at me from behind her thick glasses. "But goodness, you look as pale as a ghost. Come in and let me get something warm in you."

Mae had decluttered the place considerably since my first visit here. Though a few boxes remained in the main hallway, I was able to step past her instead of having to edge through sideways. Behind me, I heard Mae and Bree-yark exchange tender greetings and kisses on the cheeks. Her drive to organize probably had a little to do with being courted after spending so many years alone.

"Go on and have a seat," Mae called to me.

I followed a lingering aroma of baked bread into her kitchen. Still recovering from my proximity to whatever had been stalking me, I sat heavily at the table. I'd been thinking demon or fae, especially after what the pixies had told me, but now I considered the whiff of death I'd caught before climbing into the cab. The scent hadn't been purely olfactory, had it? No, it had been tinged with magic.

Necromancy?

I nearly shouted when something climbed my dangling coattail and landed on my lap. A lobster-like creature stared at me above a mouth of writhing tendrils, thick claws held aloft. Mae's pet.

"Hey, Buster," I said, wiggling a finger at him.

Buster responded by snapping a claw at my face.

"What's the matter with you?" Mae said, thumping Buster's tail as she tottered past. "Everson's a friend."

Buster dropped his claws in a sulk and bowed his head. As I went to scratch him, he spotted Bree-yark. With a chirp, he leapt to the floor, leaving me hanging, and circled the goblin's steel-toed boots like an eager puppy. Dropsy the lantern craned her glass face this way and that to get a better look at him.

"So Bree-yark tells me you're in the middle of another case," Mae said from the coffee maker.

"Yeah, and it's a doozy."

I gave her a rundown of events since we'd last worked together to rescue the efreet from the demons. As incredible as it seemed, that had only been a few days ago. So much had happened since, and I had to condense the account considerably. Even so, by the time I finished, the coffee had percolated and Mae was setting three steaming mugs around the table. She took a seat opposite me, beside Bree-yark. He'd placed Dropsy on the floor, where she and Buster were making cautious stabs at play.

"And now you need to get back to this time catch to help your friends," Mae said.

I nodded and took a draw of hot coffee. Though not my preferred roast, it felt comforting going down. "Just the small matter of getting back there."

Mae tsked. "Lord, I wish I could help, but that's not my wheelhouse. And you've exhausted all your contacts?"

"Just about."

"Maybe Caroline will get your letter," Bree-yark offered.

"Maybe," I echoed, but doubted it.

"Who does that leave?" Mae asked.

I hesitated a beat before answering. "That demon I told you about? Arnaud? He claims he can get me in. He's going to want to deal, though, and I can't do that." It felt wrong telling them what I'd withheld from Vega, but at the same time it was a big relief. "And not only because he's a demon."

"That would seem reason enough," Mae remarked.

"Agreed, but Vega would flip out if she even knew I was considering it. He's a sadistic killer. He abducted her son a couple years ago, and when I met with Arnaud this morning, he made insinuations against our little girl."

Mae's head tilted. "Little girl?"

"Oh, yeah. We're expecting."

Her eyebrows folded down. "And you didn't mention it till now?"

When she glanced over at Bree-yark, he said, "Hey, don't look at me like that. I'm hearing it for the first time too."

"We haven't announced it yet," I said. "We just got the confirmation a couple days ago."

Mae stood and opened her arms. "Well, come here then." I went over and accepted her second enthusiastic hug of the morning. "Congratulations, Everson Croft. You're going to be a wonderful father to that child."

"Agreed," Bree-yark said.

"Thanks, you two. I hope so."

As Mae released me, she showed her stern face. "But talk to that woman about this demon of yours. She may not want to hear it, but she's got a good head on her shoulders and she's the mother of your child. You'll need to figure it out together."

I nodded even though I wasn't quite ready to take the Arnaud step.

"And Everson?" she said. "I know this is the old-fashioned in me talking, but I hope you intend on making an honest woman of her." She wriggled the band on her fourth finger with her thumb.

"That's the plan."

"Good."

"Of course she has to say *yes* first."

Mae swatted my shoulder. "As if she wouldn't. Well, go on and have a seat. Your coffee's getting cold."

"Actually, I should probably get a move on."

Bree-yark jumped up. "Yeah, we just stopped by so Everson could, you know, help me carry my things down to the car." When I turned, the goblin shot me a look that told me to go along with him.

"That's right," I said.

"So you've found a place?" Mae asked Bree-yark.

"Um, yeah. And I want to get over there today. Set things up and what not." Bree-yark slid me another look as he took Mae's hand and kissed the back of it. "I appreciate you letting me keep my stuff here."

Mae giggled. "Oh, it was no trouble."

"And once I'm settled, I'd like to take you out to dinner again," he said. "You know, to say thanks."

"That would be wonderful."

Despite everything going on, I couldn't help but feel a blush of pride that I'd helped get the two of them together—even if it had meant invoking Gretchen's wrath. They were good for each other.

"Thanks for the coffee," I said.

"Well, here, let me put them in something to carry with you."

"Oh, no, no, that won't be necessary," I said, but Mae was already tottering across the kitchen and reaching for a cupboard. By the time Bree-yark and I gathered his set of duffle bags from the spare room, Mae had already filled two thermoses and was inserting them into the crook of my left arm.

"Dropsy," Bree-yark called. "We're going!"

The lantern reluctantly left her new friend and leapt onto one of Bree-yark's bags. Buster scuttled after her, rising onto his hind legs and snapping playfully before Mae told him to stop. He backed away with a despondent chirp.

"Remember what I told you," Mae said to me as she opened the door for us.

"Talk with Vega before I even think about dealing with the demon Arnaud."

She pinched my cheek. "You're going to make a fine husband. If you need an old woman for anything, you know who to call."

"Will do, Mae. And thanks again. This visit did me good."

"Me too," she said, glowing. She waved past me at Bree-yark. When the door closed, Bree-yark said, "I sure do like her."

"She's great. But why did you lie back there?"

"Oh, just trying to avoid some awkwardness." He used his elbow to press the button for the elevator. "At some point she would've asked if I'd found a place. I tell her no, and suddenly she's offering the spare bedroom."

"What's wrong with that?"

"She's old-fashioned, like she said, and I didn't want to put her in that position. I respect her too much."

"That's noble of you." I meant it, but I hoped he wasn't leaving himself wiggle room to get back together with Gretchen.

As the elevator door opened and we stepped inside, I could feel just how much the visit had helped. My head was clearer and my body stronger, even carrying twenty pounds of the goblin's stuff.

Bree-yark had parked his Hummer a block from the apartment, and he swore when he discovered graffiti on the rear door. Given the neighborhood, it could've been worse. After loading his duffle bags, we climbed into the front seats.

"So where *are* you going to stay?" I asked.

"I'll find somewhere." Bree-yark started the engine. Because of his short legs, he'd had the Hummer modified with hand-powered gas and brake controls. He worked them now, easing us into traffic. "I saw some hotels just up the way that are pay-by-the-week. Could crash at one of those."

"Yeah, I wouldn't."

"It's not forever. Can I drop you somewhere?"

"My place, but only if you let me host you."

"Aw, you don't have to do that, Everson."

I could tell by his tone he wasn't being polite. He really didn't want to put me out.

"One, I've got the space. Two, I'm not old-fashioned like Mae." That drew a barking chuckle from Bree-yark. "Three, you get along with Tabitha, which is extraordinary. And four, I'm going to ask something in return."

"Like halves on the rent? No problem. I'd prefer that, in fact."

"I'm not talking about money," I said. "I need a favor."

Bree-yark looked at me sidelong. "What sort of favor?"

"I need you to get me into the Fae Wilds."

8

"The Fae Wilds?" Bree-yark exclaimed.

"There's supposedly an exiled fae in there, one who has the power to access time catches." Seay the fae had brought him up when we'd met as a team and were brainstorming ways to access the time catch. In fact, it was the option the Upholders were preparing to pursue until Osgood arrived to help us. Now that it was clear we couldn't count on Osgood, I'd been revisiting that horrible option.

Bree-yark shook his head.

"I know it's crazy," I said, "but it's this guy or Arnaud."

"Have you ever been to the Fae Wilds?"

"No, but I've dealt with their creatures up here."

We were speeding down Central Park West, and I stiffened as Bree-yark overtook a line of cars, swerving at the last second to avoid a horse-drawn carriage. The fae lantern hopped up and down on the console.

"Everson, it's not the same," he said. "They're more powerful in the Wilds, and there are more of them."

"Well, you claim to have crossed and re-crossed the Wilds a dozen times," I shot back. "How did you manage it?"

"Being embedded in a thousand-unit army helps."

"Well ... all right, but I have spells and potions."

"Do you even know who this fae is?"

"His name's Crusspatch."

"Gods almighty," Bree-yark muttered.

"You know him?"

"By reputation, and it's not good. He's a crackpot."

That's what I'd been afraid of, dammit. In fact, I'd made these very arguments to the Upholders when Seay and Jordan were pumping the idea. It was weird—and yeah, troubling—being on the other side of the debate, going against my own best judgment. But when your only other option was Arnaud...

"And you think he's just going to help you like that?" Bree-yark snapped his thick fingers, producing a sound like sandpaper. "Even if he agrees, he's gonna want something in return."

I'd made that point to the Upholders too.

"He apparently misses delicacies from his former kingdom," I offered. "That might be all it takes?"

Bree-yark squinted over at me. "C'mon. You really think it'll be that easy?"

"No. But considering what's at stake, I'm prepared to make some sacrifices."

"Even if it means entering into a bargain with a cracked fae?"

"Depends on the bargain. But for my friends?" I hesitated. "Yeah."

He exhaled. "Then you're gonna need someone who knows the terrain."

I shook my head. "I can't ask you to come."

"You're not asking. I'm telling you."

WE ARRIVED AT MY APARTMENT BUILDING AND HAULED BREE-yark's duffle bags to the fourth floor. Inside my unit, we piled them beside the coat rack. Dropsy, who had ridden atop one of the bags jumped down and began peering around the new space.

Already, I was making a mental list of the things I would need to assemble and prepare for our journey. Bree-yark claimed to know of a passage to the Fae Wilds through the old goblin tunnels in Central Park, and he'd remained stubbornly insistent about going with me, for which I was secretly grateful.

"Where's your cat?" he asked.

"Huh?" I looked toward Tabitha's divan, but except for the depression and scattering of orange hair, there was no sign of her. "Good question."

"Hey, Tabby!" Bree-yark called. "Your favorite goblin's here!"

When she didn't answer, I said, "She's probably on the ledge."

"That bad, huh?"

I snorted as I began emptying my coat pockets onto the dining room table. "No, she patrols outside now and again. Makes sure no one's casing the apartment. Magic attracts unwanted attention."

"Gotcha." Bree-yark looked around and made percussive sounds with his lips. "Say, you wouldn't happen to have something to nosh on? Gretchen was in the middle of making breakfast when I decided to have our talk, so I haven't eaten yet." His stomach let out a low rumble. "Probably bad timing on my part."

"I haven't been to the store in forever. Is cereal all right?"

"That'd be great. A few bowls should hold me over."

"Check the pantry. You'll find at least two boxes of raisin bran, and there's some milk in the fridge. Just pour from the plastic jug and not the bottles. That's Tabitha's elite stash."

"No prob—" Bree-yark started to say, then broke off. "Hey,

Everson? I think you should get over here." He'd been rounding the kitchen counter, and now he was staring at something on the floor.

I hustled over. "What's up?"

He pointed a thick finger at where Tabitha lay in a sprawl, eyes halfcocked, tongue lolling. One of her paws was slung across her belly, while the other stretched overhead. My pulse quickened when I noticed she wasn't breathing.

"Tabitha?" I called.

All around her were shards of a whiskey bottle, as if she'd batted it from the opened liquor cabinet above the stove. But there should have been spilled alcohol everywhere. My eyes cut back to her swollen belly. She choked on a breath, then resumed breathing in a wet snore. I exhaled. Not dead. Drunk.

"She do this a lot?" Bree-yark asked, coming to the same understanding.

"Never, and I have no idea what possessed her to do it now." I nudged her with a shoe. "Hey."

She moaned, then resumed snoring. Dropsy, who had somehow gotten onto the kitchen counter, stared down at Tabitha as if trying to decide what to make of her. She edged a little closer and leaned forward.

"Maybe we should turn her onto her side," Bree-yark said. "You know, in case she can't handle her sauce."

"I have a better idea." I scooped Tabitha up and cradled her against my stomach. Her body was heavy and warm. As I carried her toward the ladder to my lab, I could hear the whiskey sloshing in her belly.

Her eyelids fluttered. "Evershun?" she slurred. "Is that you, darling?"

"Yeah, just hang tight. I'm going to have you feeling better in a minute."

"Better? But I feel wonnnderful..."

"I'll bet," I muttered as she dragged a sheathed paw down the side of my head.

Her lids slid up from a set of bleary eyes. As she watched me, her mouth leaned into a smile. "Have I ever told you how much I like your lips? Oh, they're beautiful, darling ... Just scrumptious ... I could snack on them right now." She strained toward my face, but the small effort exhausted her, and she collapsed back into my arms.

"Up we go," I said, scaling the ladder.

Her head lolled so that she was facing behind me. "Yoo-hoo," she called down to Bree-yark.

"Tabitha," he grunted.

"Who *is* that fetching man?" she whispered.

"Bree-yark, and you've met him before. He's a goblin."

"Goblin, hmm." She said it as if she were contemplating a new delicacy. "Aren't you coming?" she called.

"I, um, think I'll wait down here," he said.

"The handsome ones aaalways play hard to get," she sighed.

I set Tabitha on my lab table and dug through my plastic bins of pre-mades until I found what I was looking for: a small vial containing a clear liquid. It was a purification potion designed to eliminate toxins. More than one text claimed it also worked on alcohol, inducing rapid sobriety.

"You know what we need?" Tabitha asked, aiming a wavering paw at my face. "More whiskey."

"Yeah, I don't think so." I spoke an incantation, causing the potion to bubble. "Try this," I said, bringing the dropper cap toward her mouth.

"Ooh, what is—*aack!*"

Tabitha gagged and hacked, but enough went down that it was just a matter now of waiting. By the time she finished spitting, I could see her eyes returning to focus. She winced and brought her paws to the sides of her head.

"I feel fucking horrible," she moaned.

"Better horrible than dead. Care to explain why you lapped up half a bottle of eighty proof?"

"Oh, not now, darling."

"Yes, now," I said sternly.

She sighed. "I told you I haven't been feeling myself the last couple days. Ravenous hunger one minute, complete loss of appetite the next. I thought it was getting better, but after you left this morning, I woke up with the most ungodly sense something was about to happen. Something horrible. I ate, I paced, I went outside, I tried to go back to sleep, but nothing made it better. The dread just grew worse and worse."

"So you dulled it with alcohol?"

"Yes, and it worked. Or at least it *did*." She squinted at me accusingly before wrapping her head back in her arms.

With her succubus nature, Tabitha was sensitive to activity in the Below. And this latest report from my canary in the demonic coalmine troubled me. By defeating the Strangers in the time catch and capturing Arnaud, I believed we'd disrupted Malphas's plans. But Tabitha's reaction coupled with songs about possessed fae suggested Malphas might not be done, that a demon apocalypse could still be on the horizon.

"Any idea where this dread came from?" I asked.

"No, darling," she moaned. "But I wish it would stop."

I retrieved a new vial from a bin. "I have another potion. It'll dull your hangover and help take the edge off, but let me give it to you downstairs."

She waved a weary paw in concession, and I carried her back down the ladder.

"How is she?" Bree-yark asked. He emerged from the kitchen holding a large mixing bowl of raisin bran staked with a serving spoon. Dropsy hopped along beside him.

"I'll survive," Tabitha answered dramatically.

"Hey, Everson and I are going to Faerie," Bree-yark said. "You should come with."

I made a quick cutting motion across my throat, but the goblin was too busy shoveling cereal into his mouth to notice.

"Faerie?" Tabitha moved the back of her paw from her eyes and blinked up at me. "You never mentioned going to Faerie."

A couple years before, she'd given me crap about refusing Caroline's offer to hide us in her and Angelus's kingdom during the mayor's purge campaign. Tabitha's interest hadn't been for our safety but in the food—specifically rumors of a goat milk so rich it separated into layers of thick cream.

"We're not going to a kingdom," I said, setting her inside her vast depression on the divan. "We're going to the Fae Wilds, where the food is suspect at best. We'll be packing what we eat, and it's stuff you don't like."

"Actually, there's a border town I wouldn't mind stopping at," Bree-yark said around another mouthful of cereal. "They have a great market."

Tabitha, who had begun to lose interest, perked up again. "You don't say?"

"Oh, yeah. Roasted fish stuffed with goat cheese and herbs. Dripping lamb shanks on spits. I'm getting hungry just thinking about it."

"That *does* sound delectable," Tabitha agreed.

I glared at Bree-yark, who took a moment to get the message.

"Well, only if that stuff's in season," he amended. "Otherwise, all they have is, you know ... hay bread."

"Hay bread?" Tabitha echoed.

"Yeah, bread made from hay."

Tabitha wrinkled her face. "I can't think of anything more dreadful."

"Oh, it's worse than dreadful. And that's if they have fresh hay. If not, they have to sift it out of the ox manure."

"Hey, would you mind heating up some goat's milk for Tabitha," I said before Bree-yark could make his undersell any more ridiculous. He nodded and disappeared into the kitchen with his bowl of cereal.

"I am *not* eating ox manure," Tabitha pouted, sagging down again.

"Well, lucky you, you don't have to. In fact, I'd prefer it if you stayed here and kept an eye on the place."

Though I could have used Tabitha on demon sentry, especially if the fae were compromised, navigating the Fae Wilds was going to be challenging enough without having to drag forty pounds of attitude on a harness.

"Oh, that reminds me," she muttered. "You had a visitor earlier."

"Yeah? Who?"

"They didn't announce themselves." When she saw I was waiting for more, she sighed. "I'd just helped myself to your scant liquor offerings and was settling in for a nap when a knock sounded at the door. Though really it was more of a scraping. A wretched sound, darling. Thankfully, my senses were already numbing nicely—it was such a relief to be able to relax at last—and I fell asleep. And then you showed up."

"So you don't know who it was?"

"No, darling. I already told you."

A sense of foreboding overcame me. "Did you smell anything?"

"Yes, your whiskey. Too peaty for my taste, if I'm being honest."

"No, besides that."

She started to answer, then reared back onto her haunches. "What *is* that thing?"

Dropsy had come around the back of the divan and was

peering up at her, her glass face glowing with what seemed curiosity.

"It's just a fae lantern," I said. "She's harmless."

"Well, get it away from me!" Tabitha cried, batting a paw at her.

The lantern shrank back and hopped past the hearth toward my bedroom.

Tabitha ground her paws against her eyes. "As if I need a light in my face right now."

"You were about to say something about the smell?"

She muttered as she finished rubbing her eyes and settled back down. "Right before I drifted off, I caught the foulest stink of death."

I leaned an arm against the stone mantel above the hearth and stared at the empty grate.

"Why?" Tabitha asked. "Does that mean something?"

"I picked up the same scent earlier. Something's looking for me."

"Going on the smell alone, I'd say better you than me."

"Thanks."

"Well, why not set a trap?"

I'd been considering the very idea, but I didn't have the time or resources to spare right now. It was going to take everything I had to reach Crusspatch, and if that went well, to navigate the time catch.

Possibly a failing time catch.

Bree-yark reappeared from the kitchen with a steaming saucer. "One serving of goat's milk."

I added the potion absently, and set the saucer where Tabitha could lap it up without having to leave her perch.

"How soon can you be ready?" I asked Bree-yark as I stood again. I was thinking of all the time I'd already spent running around that morning while days and weeks were flipping by in the time catch.

"Just need to change and pack a small bag," he said. "Twenty minutes?"

"Let's make it fifteen."

9

"It's the only way?" Vega asked.

"It's not ideal, I know," I said into the phone. "But yeah, it's what I'm left with."

Bree-yark cocked an eye at me from behind the steering wheel as we motored up Eighth Avenue. I would have preferred to have had this conversation in private—I'd known Vega wasn't going to like my plan—but with time being a factor, calling her on the way to the goblin tunnels was the best solution.

She sighed.

"Look, I started with my most trustworthy contact and moved down the list," I said. "Claudius couldn't get me there, and neither could Gretchen. The fae, well, I told you what happened. This is where we are."

"Crusspatch," she said skeptically.

"Yeah, I don't like the name either. It sounds like a skin condition. But I'm not going alone," I reminded her. She'd worked with Bree-yark just a few days earlier, the two fighting side-by-side in the West Nyack rock quarry to repel a host of demons.

"And Bree-yark knows the Fae Wilds?" she asked. "He knows how to get where you're going?"

The goblin's ears perked up at mention of his name, and he gave me a thumbs-up.

"Yes," I said. "And I have everything I need for the journey. Journeys plural, if Crusspatch can get me into the time catch." I looked past my lumpy coat pockets to the rucksack between my feet. The only thing we were light on was food. With little time to prep, I'd packed the gingersnaps and Mae's coffee—refreshments, basically, until we could find something more substantial.

"When can I expect you back?"

"With the time differentials, it shouldn't be any later than tonight."

"How about an actual time, so I can know when to start worrying?"

I consulted my watch—it was still before noon—and then did a little math. "How about seven o'clock this evening? If for some reason I don't show up by then, call Claudius and Gretchen."

"The two people who couldn't help you?"

"Couldn't help me into the *time catch*," I stressed. "If we run into trouble in the Fae Wilds, one or both can reach me there." I was putting out a lot more confidence than I was feeling. I had no idea if Gretchen was helping me at the moment, and Claudius didn't even know what city he was in, much less the year.

"But it shouldn't come to that," I added.

"All right," Vega said, her voice softening as though to suggest she was through being the concerned girlfriend. "I hate to bring this up, but have you considered what you'll do if Crusspatch can't help you?"

I heard Mae's voice: *Talk to that woman about this demon of yours. You need to work it out together.* But having already passed Penn Station blocks ago, that conversation wasn't going to fit into the few minutes between here and Central Park. Of course, the goal was never needing to have that conversation in the first place.

"We'll cross that bridge when we come to it," I said. "Any updates on Arnaud?"

"I'm looking at him right now." I pictured her staring at the monitor for his holding cell, the grainy light reflecting from her troubled eyes. "He's just sitting there, legs crossed like he's expecting a visitor."

Yeah, me, I thought sickly.

"And he's got this stupid smile on his face. Are you sure he's getting weaker?"

"He is. He just hides it well."

"He does look thinner," she allowed.

"Have the Sup Squad keep an eye on him."

"Oh, that's not changing until he's dead and gone."

"You have your coin pendant on, right?" I asked, partly to change the subject.

"Yeah. Why?"

"Well, when I left your office earlier today, I had the feeling I was being watched. It happened again on the Upper East Side, and Tabitha said someone came to my door earlier."

"Any idea who?"

"No, but there could be magic involved." I left out the part about the death smell—I still didn't know what it meant—but I pictured Mae Johnson frowning her disapproval. "Is Tony at the apartment?"

"Yeah, with Camilla."

"Good, have them stay there. It could be nothing, but the wards will keep them safe. I just want to be extra careful until I know what's going on."

"I appreciate that."

At Columbus Circle, Bree-yark turned right and pressed the hand accelerator.

"We're almost there," I told Vega. "I'll see you tonight, if not sooner."

"Try to make it sooner."

"Are you going to be all right?"

"Do I have a choice?" She sighed. "I'll be better when I know you're safe."

"I have three very good reasons to stay that way," I said, referring to her, Tony, and our pea-sized girl.

I shouted as Bree-yark swerved off road to avoid a line of cement traffic barriers. The Hummer caught air and landed in a series of violent jounces before joining up with a drive that led into the park. A set of wooden barricades greeted us. The Hummer's steel bumper smashed through them, sending planks clattering over the rooftop.

"What's that racket?" Vega asked.

"Um, nothing the city can't replace."

"All right," she said thinly. "I love you."

"Love you too. Give your tummy a pat for me."

She snorted a laugh. "Will do."

I nearly put the phone back in my coat, but the device couldn't make the journey to Faerie. As I placed it in the glove compartment along with my watch, the idea of not having an immediate line to Vega punched my heart. Something told me these types of trips away were going to get harder, not easier.

Bree-yark looked over at me. "That seemed to go pretty well. I never would've been able to have that kind of talk with Gretchen. No, siree." He said it as though still trying to convince himself that leaving her had been the right move.

"Good thing to remember if you're ever tempted to backslide."

"So what do you think Gretchen's doing right now?" he mused, as if my words had gone in one notched ear and out the other.

"No telling," I muttered.

Bree-yark rounded a horseshoe-shaped pond and pulled up beside the old skating rink, now a burnt ruins. As he killed the engine, I eyed a familiar pile of boulders. A couple months earlier, I'd picked my way through them and dropped into the goblin tunnels to stop Damien from reconstituting his five-member cult of devotees. Damien had turned out to be Arnaud, doing Malphas's bidding.

Could we stop Malphas again?

"This is it," Bree-yark said, breaking up the question.

"I thought the mayor said he'd filled in the tunnels."

He grunted a laugh. "Might've believed he did, but goblins are like termites. We dig everywhere."

Dropsy, who had been hopping from one side of the back-seat to the other, jumped onto the console and looked between me and Bree-yark. With no time to leave her at Gretchen's—and her staying with Tabitha out of the question —we'd taken her along. I trusted she'd be all right in the Hummer.

"C'mon, Dropsy," Bree-yark said.

"Wait, she's coming with us?"

"What did you think we were gonna do? Leave her in the car?"

Dropsy faced me with an inquisitive look. Only an hour with the lantern, and I could already read her combos of posture and lighting.

"Well, yeah," I said in a lowered voice.

"By herself and for who knows how long?"

"Can't we just, I don't know, turn her off?"

"She doesn't have a switch, Everson. She's enchanted."

"Look, I've got nothing against enchanted lanterns," I said. "I'm just worried about her slowing us down."

"Naw, I'll carry her."

"Or giving us away. The plan is to travel incognito."

"She can do her own glamours," he said. "Plus, she listens to me. Right, Dropsy?"

Her light swelled before dimming suddenly. And then she was simply gone, wrapped in an enchantment that blended her into her surroundings. She reappeared a moment later and looked back at me expectantly.

"All right," I sighed, hoping I wasn't making a big mistake.

Dropsy bounced as Bree-yark grasped her by the brass ring. I checked all my coat pockets, then slung my pack over a shoulder.

Bree-yark had changed into a fur and leather outfit more befitting of Faerie, complete with a pouch that hung from a strap across his torso. He'd dispensed with shoes, baring his splayed goblin feet. For weapons he was carrying a sheathed blade along with a bow and quiver. Though he owned modern firearms, they were barred from Faerie, thanks to a powerful enchantment that surrounded the realm.

"I still think you should've ditched the trench coat," he said as he closed up the Hummer.

"It's part of my system." I patted a loaded pocket. "Anyway, I don't plan on being visible in Faerie."

He gave me a final dubious up and down before we set out toward the boulders, Dropsy swinging from his free hand.

When we arrived, Bree-yark nosed around, still convinced the goblins had dug more tunnels than the city could fill. I went in search of the hole I'd entered by the last time only to find it plugged with cement. When I backtracked, Bree-yark was standing triumphantly over a slab of stone.

"Find something?" I asked.

He stamped the slab with his foot. "An escape hatch. When we build tunnel complexes, we always have a plan for in case the complex is overrun. A hidden passage that shoots straight to the surface."

"So, what, we lift the slab?"

"Can't. It's anchored from the inside."

I was readying my cane for a force invocation, but Bree-yark shook his head.

"Behold goblin engineering," he announced.

He stepped from the slab and onto a round stone embedded in the ground. It must have been the top of a column, because the stone sunk until I heard something clunk. An instant later, the slab cannoned open to reveal a deep hole.

The sight made the skin over my chest tighten.

Bree-yark frowned. "You all right, Everson?"

"Yeah, I just have this longstanding phobia of being underground. It'll pass."

"Dropsy and I can lead. That way if you faint or something, you'll land on me."

"That's reassuring."

Bree-yark helped the lantern nestle into the top of his pouch until she was secure. He then started down handholds chiseled into stone. I waited until he'd descended about ten feet, Dropsy's golden light swelling around him, before following. The movement would help, I told myself.

"You clear?" Bree-yark's barking voice echoed toward me.

I checked to make sure my head was below ground before answering, "Yeah."

There was some kind of catch where he was, because the slab slammed closed, sending my heart into my throat. Dirt and grit showered over me, some ending up in my mouth. I spat and gathered myself before continuing down, Dropsy's light guiding my holds. In the cooling air, I picked up a faint odor of rot.

"I should warn you," I panted. "The last time I was down here, I encountered some goblin bodies." According to Bree-yark, the goblins who'd occupied Central Park had belonged to a warmongering tribe. If he'd been related to them, it was distantly, but I still wanted to spare him the shock.

"They knew the risks," he grunted.

A few minutes later, I heard him land with a thud. I was soon standing beside him in a short corridor that appeared to dead-end. Bree-yark pawed along the wall until he encountered a small hole. He inserted a hand and struggled with something, the thick cords of his forearm bulging while breath steamed from his gritted teeth. At last, some mechanism yielded and the dead end slid away.

"Goblin engineering," he repeated. "Tighten your laces, 'cause we've got a hike ahead."

"Anything I need to worry about down here?" I asked, drawing my sword from the cane.

"Naw. Only goblins know about the secret tunnel and hatch. And after the city's attack, there's not much of an appetite these days for getting napalmed."

I nodded but kept my weapons drawn as Bree-yark led the way into a small chamber. Dried cement flowed in from a corridor to our left, but the way ahead was clear.

We continued down a network of corridors, Bree-yark remarking proudly on this or that feature of the tunnel complex, but I was too fixated on our destination to follow his narrative. Several times I was tempted to ask if he knew where he was going—he'd never been down here to my knowledge—but goblins had powerful homing instincts. If there was a portal to Faerie, he would find it.

We eventually entered a chamber with a sizeable stone well at its center. Beside it sat a coiled rope and a wooden bucket large enough to bathe in. Bree-yark approached the well and peered inside.

"This is it," he said. "Faerie's on the other side of the water."

I came up beside him. Dropsy hopped from his pouch and stood on the well's stone wall. When I looked down, I expected to be face-to-face with a shimmering surface, but the well was dry for as far as I could see.

"What water?" I asked.

Bree-yark dug into his pouch and came up with a coin of some otherworldly mint. He dropped it over the mouth of the well, and we waited. Eventually, from far below, came the faintest *kerplunk*.

"That water," he said. "You ready?"

"Wait, you're not planning on *jumping?*"

"Relax." He chuckled. "We're heading down in the bucket."

"Of course," I said dryly. "The bucket. Why didn't I think of that?"

I reached for one of my neutralizing potions, an incantation on my tongue, before stopping myself. If I downed the potion, I risked canceling the very magic we would be counting on to get us into Faerie.

Dropsy hopped aside as Bree-yark used his considerable strength to heave the bucket onto the wall ringing the well. A rope trailed from the bucket handle, and Bree-yark began fussing with the rest of the coiled stack. It was only when he pushed it to one side that I saw the pulley system bolted into the ground.

"Goblin engineering?" I asked.

"Damn right," Bree-yark grunted. "All right, go ahead and climb in. I'll push you out."

"In the bucket, you mean?" I looked at the proposed conveyance.

This is frigging crazy, I thought. *But if it's the only way...* I checked that my pockets were sealed before climbing onto the stone wall. Very gingerly, I set one leg inside the bucket and then the other.

"You too, Dropsy," Bree-yark said, taking the lantern and placing her beside me.

Moving my pack around to my front, I squatted low, knees jutting up to my shoulders. It was a tight fit.

"Everyone in?" Bree-yark called, and shoved us into space. The bucket plunged several feet—*holy hell!*—before stopping suddenly. We swayed side to side, knocking against the walls. At one point we nearly tipped over. When we steadied again, I blew out my pent-up breath while Dropsy glowed excitedly.

Above us, Bree-yark was standing on the stone wall, holding the rope that suspended us. It looked as if we'd have to take two trips. But no sooner than I'd formed the thought, the goblin dropped the rope's slack into the emptiness below and began walking down the side of the well like a mountaineer.

"Hey, I'm not sure there's room in here," I said.

Bree-yark turned and planted his taloned feet on the bucket's rim opposite me. Our conveyance rocked dangerously before settling again. When I looked up, his sharp, smiling teeth were glinting in Dropsy's light.

"Next stop, the Fae Wilds," he announced like a proud host. But all I could feel was a nervous foreboding.

The pulley system creaked and the bucket swayed as he began lowering us down.

10

Bree-yark's echoing grunts provided an offbeat to my pounding heart as we descended. The opening of the well had long since disappeared, isolating us in Dropsy's orb of enchanted light. After several more minutes, I had to know how close we were to the water. But as I reached toward Dropsy, she shrank back.

"It's all right," I whispered. "I'm not gonna hurt you."

When she relaxed, I grasped her brass handle. Then I lifted her slowly, craning around until we could both see over the side of the bucket. Some distance below, Dropsy's glow caught a wrinkle of water. Before long, the dancing wrinkle became a round, glittering sheet. Dropsy seemed to transfix on it too.

Oh, this is fae water, all right, I thought.

When it was close enough to touch, I anticipated the splash, wondering what would follow. But no splash came. The water was falling away. I turned toward Bree-yark. "Why are we going back?"

"We're not," he grunted, despite that he was drawing us up hand over hand. "We're through."

"Through?" I peered back down. The glittering circle of

water looked the same as when we'd been descending. But the sides of the wall were made of smooth stone now, not the jagged granite from earlier. And when I looked up, I could make out the opening. It wasn't distant at all, only fifteen or twenty feet away.

Well, holy crap.

When we reached the top, Bree-yark stepped from the bucket. Bracing the thick rope between his teeth, he pulled our conveyance onto the well's rim. Still holding Dropsy, I climbed out and stepped into a cavern whose ground was strewn with pretty autumnal leaves. Natural light entered from an opening a short distance away.

I didn't have to ask if we were in Faerie. The air was unnaturally fresh and clean, everything in my vision several degrees sharper. And beneath it all flowed the magic of the realm: subtle and seductive.

I clapped Bree-yark's thick shoulder. "Well done, sir."

He bowed his head modestly. "Well, I promised to get you to Crusspatch's, and we're not there yet."

"How far a journey are we talking?"

"About a day's march, if memory serves."

"Then let's go ahead and potion up."

I set Dropsy down and retrieved two potions from my coat to cancel fae magic and then two more for stealth. I'd packed ample quantities of both, my coat practically dragging with their weight.

Outside, a bird began to sing. The lilting song brightened my mood, and I caught myself smiling. My coat felt lighter too. Hell, if I flapped my arms, I might even take flight. I snorted a laugh at the thought. Bree-yark, who had been organizing his pouch, looked from me to the approaching song.

"Oh, crap," he said, "that's a satyr's panpipe. Quick, Everson —cover your ears!"

It now dawned on me that for the last several seconds I'd

been smiling stupidly at the potions in my hand when I should have been activating them. But it didn't matter. Nothing mattered except merriment and mirth.

"A satyr's what?" I asked, giggles spilling around the words.

"Panpipe. It's an enchanted instrument, and you're falling under its charm."

The word *panpipe*, especially in Bree-yark's gruff voice, was suddenly the most hilarious thing I'd ever heard. Laughter seized me, and I doubled over. When I struggled to inhale, the ridiculous word floated through my head again, plunging me into another fit of hysterics.

This is serious, I thought distantly. *I'm losing all control.*

"Say it again," I managed, my voice a high whine. "Say p-p-pan..."

But the word was buried beneath another eruption of laughing. Could you die from mirth? I didn't know, but white spots were beginning to float around my tear-blurred vision, while a goring pain took hold in my lungs. I clamped my knees, vaguely aware I was no longer holding the potions.

When I tried to bring my hands to my ears, my arms felt like a pair of soggy noodles. They wouldn't obey. I concentrated toward my casting prism—I needed to invoke shields over my ears. But the image of myself in little magical earmuffs was too much, and I lost it even more. No air was coming in now.

Oh, God. This could actually kill me.

In the next moment, Bree-yark jammed his thick fingers into my ears. Through my tears, he looked like a shapeless blob. The image was comical, but not in the sidesplitting way it would have been just a moment before. With the song blocked, my laughter idled back down to gasps and gurgles, and I could breathe again.

"Thank God you clipped your talons," I managed.

I wiped my eyes and searched around for my fallen potions. I spotted them off to the right. Concentrating into the closest neutralizing potion, I uttered, *"Attivare."*

Tiny gems flashed inside, transforming the liquid into an active potion, one that would cancel the effects of the cursed song. Bree-yark, being a creature of Faerie, must have had some inbuilt immunity. He was singing a song of his own, I realized, drowning out any enchanted music that might be slipping past his fingers.

"Row, row, row your boat," he barked. *"Gently down the stream..."*

That got me chortling, but I nodded for him to continue as I reached for the potion. I had the warm tube in my grasp when, in a savage battering of dark wings, something collided against Bree-yark.

He fell away, his song breaking off mid *"merrily."* His fingers uncorked from my ears. The music of the panpipe rushed in, more charming than ever. I popped the cap from the potion and brought it toward my lips, but my body was convulsing with giggles again. The potion went everywhere except inside my mouth.

Out in front of me, Bree-yark was rolling across the cavern with whatever had attacked him. It wasn't until they came to a stop, Bree-yark on top, that I could make out the part-man, part-crow. A *tengu.*

Bree-yark pummeled its face with his fists, sending the creature's thick beak canting one way and then the other.

"Knock him out," I gasped between laughing fits.

"You screwed with the wrong goblin," Bree-yark grunted.

He seized the creature by its throat and drew his blade, but more tengu were gliding down from recesses in the cavern above. They landed in a flapping of winged arms and surrounded Bree-yark. I felt a faraway urge to help him, to blast them off, but I was shrieking laughter now. The spectacle of a gang of birdmen in ragged loincloths raining blows on my team-mate was the funniest thing I'd ever seen.

Wait, we might have a new contender...

I choked back my laughter long enough to take in the new creature entering the cavern.

He was a small man with a ginger beard and an impressive set of ram's horns that curled around his pointed ears. An instrument of eight or so slender wooden flutes moved beneath his pursed lips. And he was skipping, his furry brown goat legs kicking a little jig in time to his song. I didn't know if it was the dancing or his bright red vest and leather loincloth, or the whole package, but I was suddenly back to dying. I struggled upright and tried to mimic him, but I could only stagger deliriously.

The satyr winked at me above his panpipe. His bright blue eyes cut from my spilled potions to the tengu standing over Bree-yark. My teammate was out cold, and they were picking through his pouch. I looked around for Dropsy—I wanted to get her in on the dancing—but the lantern must have slipped off somewhere.

When one of the tengu stalked toward me, the satyr shook his head as though to say *not yet*. He hadn't stopped kicking his feet, and I hadn't stopped kicking mine, or trying to.

"Hey," I managed between spurts of laughter. "Where can I get a good pair of goat legs?"

The satyr lowered the panpipe from his lips and regarded me with a smile and friendly tilt of his head. "Welcome to Faerie, boyo," he said in a thick brogue, his music continuing to reverberate from the cavern's stone walls.

I was gathering my breath to thank him, when he lowered his head and charged. His ram horns plowed into my gut. My air went out in a dull grunt, and something cracked in my right ribcage. But the thought that I'd just been rammed by a satyr beat everything. Even before I landed, I was dry-heaving more laughter.

"Hope ye enjoy your stay." The satyr was standing over me now, his grin curling into a malicious sneer.

I mouthed more than said, "Think you could teach me how to play that—"

His cleft hoof descended toward my head.

"*EVERSON,*" BREE-YARK CALLED IN A HUSKY VOICE.

My right eye wouldn't open—it was crusty and swollen—but my left one filled me in. I was suspended, wrists and ankles bound to a pole overhead. A pair of tengu carried one end of the pole at a trotting run, and I imagined another pair behind me. We were outside, the stalks of a sun-drenched field whacking my back and sides.

At the sound of the satyr's voice, pain speared through my ribs where he'd rammed me. He was somewhere ahead, swearing at the tengu to pick up their pace. The scrubby creatures had stripped me to my boxers. My cane, pack, and coat with all my potions and spell implements were gone too.

I wasn't laughing anymore.

"*Everson,*" Bree-yark barked again.

When I turned my head, I could make out the bottom half of his trussed-up body. I tried to answer, but a paste filled my mouth. I couldn't move my tongue, much less force out the gummy mass. Which meant I couldn't invoke magic. I remembered the way the satyr had looked at my potions. Must have figured me for a wizard.

Seeing I was awake, Bree-yark said, "They cleaned us out, but they weren't happy with the haul. They're taking us to an ogre who lives nearby. Gonna see what kind of price they can get for our flesh."

Even better.

"So if you can cast," he said, "now might be a good time."

I shook my head to tell him it wasn't possible. I could gather the realm's abundant energy around my mental prism, but without the ability to form words, I couldn't channel or shape that energy. Voiceless casting remained years away for me—assuming I got there. I tested my wrists and ankles. The ropes securing them had been cinched tightly enough to turn my fingers and toes numb.

"Gnarl twine," Bree-yark said. "Not even sure my blade could hack through it. If I still had it," he added in a mutter.

I sagged back into my restraints.

"Some guide I turned out to be, huh?" he said.

I shook my head, this time to tell him it wasn't his fault. I should have downed the potions when we were ascending the well instead of having a mental orgasm over the fact we'd arrived in Faerie.

"If the ogre doesn't butcher us right away, I might be able to negotiate our release," Bree-yark said. "I've still got contacts in the goblin army."

I nodded my head. That was promising.

"Then again, his full name is Humbert the Hungry."

"No speaking unless spoken to!" the satyr shouted. He dropped from his lead position and fell in beside Bree-yark. I couldn't see him, but I could hear his cleft hooves trotting to keep pace. The sound sent a spot throbbing above my right eye, no doubt where he'd stomped me. "Got it, ye putrid *goblin?*"

"At least my dad didn't bang a goat," Bree-yark muttered.

I winced at the sound of my friend being struck.

"Keep it up," the satyr said. "Plenty more where that came from."

"Oh, did you do something?" Bree-yark asked. "I must not've been paying attention."

I wanted to tell the stubborn SOB to shut it as two more blows landed.

"I'd hate to waste valuable *greamaigh* on the likes of ye," the satyr said, referring to the crap in my mouth. "But keep flappin' yer lips, and I'll fill ye to yer eyeballs." He landed a final blow, this one causing Bree-yark to grunt.

The satyr must have seen me straining because he came around to my side. The first thing I noticed was his damp mustache, then the scatter of crumbs down his beard. When he leaned nearer, I smelled coffee and ginger.

The little shit ate our refreshments.

"Have something to add, laddie?" he asked, cocking a hairy fist.

I glared at him another moment before shaking my head. He grinned beneath his hard blue eyes.

"Then relax and enjoy the journey." He lowered his arm. "We'll have ye to Humbert shortly."

Deep down, my magic shifted suddenly, as though trying to tell me something. I stopped wishing for the satyr to choke on one of his own horns so I could focus.

Soon, my magic seemed to be saying. *Soon.*

As the satyr moved away from me, he glanced toward the rear of the pack. Then he did a doubletake, his mouth forming a hole in his crumb-littered beard. Resetting his jaw, he galloped to the front.

"Move your asses!" he screamed. "Faster!"

By now the tengu were peering back too, several squawking in alarm. I tried to crane my neck around, but I couldn't see anything beyond the rush of grass and tengu feet. The creatures behind me dropped their end of the pole, and my head thudded to the ground. The ones ahead dragged me for several more yards before ditching their end and fleeing after the others.

I came to a painful rest on my side.

"What are ye doing?" the satyr screamed. "Pick them up!"

But his voice was fading too. I lifted my head to the sight of scattering bird men. The flapping creatures couldn't lift off—they were gliders—but the wings spanning the undersides of their arms gave them an extra speed. I turned my head the other way just as shadows passed over us and enormous birds swooped low. Tengu caws and shrieks sounded followed by the wet snapping of bones.

Bree-yark, who had landed somewhere off to my left, grunted, "Rocs."

I scooted around until I could see him. His face was lumpy from the beating the tengu had dealt him, and dried blood trailed from one nostril. Charmed or not, I felt horrible for having laughed at him earlier.

"Ruthless birds of prey," he said. "Our best bet is to play dead, wait for them to move on."

He slumped in the tall grass, wrists and ankles still bound to the pole. I did the same, while trying to force the *greamaigh* from my mouth.

I'd read plenty about rocs. With their keen senses, not to mention appetite for living flesh, I didn't share Bree-yark's confidence that they'd move on. Even if they did, we'd still be bound, and it wouldn't take long for another creature of the Fae Wilds to sniff out a helpless goblin and mage.

As the dying squalls of the tengu thinned, I gave up on the paste in my mouth. It wasn't going anywhere. Through the grass, I watched the rocs take flight again with heavy thumps of their wings. At least we weren't going to be bird food. But then three rocs broke from the group and circled back toward us.

Shit.

The immense birds landed nearby, air pummeling the grass around us. The lead roc was the size of a school bus, its wing-span easily fifty feet across. From a dusty blue head, fierce eyes stared down at Bree-yark and me. A thatch of bloody tengu feathers clung to the edge of its sharp beak.

The creature stalked forward on clawed feet. When my bowels jiggled, I considered opening the hatch on the chance it would make me less appetizing. But dignity overruled the notion, and I clenched instead.

C'mon, magic. Talk to me.

Soon, it continued to repeat. *Soon.*

Soon what?!

Feet from us, the roc came to a stop. The other two did the same, holding flanking positions. I didn't realize there had been riders atop the massive creatures until a figure dismounted from the lead roc's back. He was tall and muscular with cobalt blue skin and a mane of bronze hair. A chest plate, silvery and supple, glinted in the sun as he strode toward us. He stopped and stared down at me. Even without his human glamour, he was annoyingly handsome.

"Everson Croft," he said.

I nodded and attempted to moan the name *Angelus*.

It was Caroline's husband.

Without his glamour, the fae prince's eyes were a regal green that complemented his skin and hair. I took a stab at reading them. Curiosity? Contempt? I couldn't tell. They were even more sphinxlike here than in our world.

"We felt your passage into the Fae Lands," he said, which explained the exceptional timing of their arrival. "Why have you come?"

As he posed the question, the paste in my mouth shrank to a wad the size of chewing gum, and my tongue tingled back to life. I spat out the wad and worked my jaw around. Except for a fading bitterness, it was as if the *greamaigh* had never been there. I noticed Angelus hadn't removed our bonds, though.

"Well?" he pressed.

Suspicion raked through me as I remembered the pixies' warning. Was Angelus the one who had "fallen under shadow?" His kingdom controlled the northern portal, which coincided with the fae townhouse. He could have been the one to order Osgood to abandon the Upholders and then stonewall me. If so, and if he knew I'd come here in search of a passage back, the game would be up. For that reason, I didn't dare mention Cruss-patch's name. But I couldn't lie either. He would know.

"My friends are missing," I said.

"Friends from your realm?"

"Yes."

"And you've come to Faerie in search of them?"

"I was told I might find them."

His head angled slightly as though weighing my answers. They were all technically true. The Upholders were missing, and earlier Seay had said Crusspatch might be able to help us access the time catch, where I hoped to find them.

I held the prince's gaze, aware that two more fae, a man and a woman, had climbed down from the other birds. Though they were smaller and their skin lighter in tone, their features suggested kinship with Angelus. I was more distracted by the lead roc, though. It continued to stare at me, its head drawn back as if ready to pluck the flesh from my bones the second Angelus gave the command.

At last, Angelus turned his head and looked off into the distance. "Then your errand will be fruitless. Yours is the only arrival in more than a fortnight."

"Do we have your leave to search anyway?" I asked.

"Neither our kingdom nor any other claims dominion over the Wilds," he said. "You may do here as you wish. But mind the borders." He nodded at Bree-yark. "Your companion will know them."

As my suspicions let out slightly, Angelus motioned with his hand. The twine that bound me to the pole broke apart. I flexed my fingers and rubbed some feeling back into my wrists before pushing myself upright.

Even at six feet, I was much shorter than the fae being before me. His royal attire, which included a fine doublet jacket and glistening boots, had me conscious of the fact I was only wearing boxers. Thank God I hadn't crapped them. Bree-yark hobbled up to my side in a pair of black bikini briefs that made me wince.

"You'll find your belongings among the remains of your captors," Angelus said.

"Yeah, about that." I scratched an elbow. "Thanks for, you know, taking them out."

"And freeing us," Bree-yark put in.

"There are far deadlier creatures in the Fae Wilds than tengu, and help will not always be forthcoming."

"We understand," I said with a nod, but Angelus was peering toward the airborne rocs. They were circling over an area where the field fell to forest. I wondered if they were searching for his wife.

"I was told Caroline is missing," I said suddenly.

I did so in part to gauge his reaction, but I was also worried for my former friend and colleague. Following my encounters with Osgood and then the pixies, I didn't like what her absence suggested. Were there any leads? When his eyes returned to mine, they seemed to hold the same question.

"Have you seen her?" he asked.

I shook my head. "Do you think she's somewhere in Faerie?"

"We're not sure."

I was tempted to bring up the subject of demonic influence and my growing sense that the solution was in the time catch. If Angelus didn't wield the power to get us there, he likely had connections who could. But without being absolutely certain of his allegiance, it would be a gamble.

He stepped forward. "Did you have something to tell me?"

Deciding the gamble too big, I said, "We'll keep our eyes out for her. Is there a way we can contact you?"

Angelus watched me for another moment, then reached into a pocket and withdrew a translucent stone that he set in the center of my palm. As he closed my fingers around its smooth surface, power radiated from his cobalt skin.

"Your word is *Nim-nahn*," he said. "Say it now and open your hand."

"*Nim-nahn,*" I repeated.

A lavender light glimmered to life inside the stone and began pulsing.

"If you see her, hold the calling stone and speak the word. It will summon me."

I nodded and went to place the stone in a pocket before remembering I had none.

"But I warn you, Everson," he added. "Do not engage her."

A husband's threat to his wife's former lover, or something more?

"Why?" I ventured.

"She is not herself."

As Angelus and the others climbed onto their rocs, I considered his words. The lead roc craned its neck from us, its massive body following. In several running steps and prodigious thrusts of its wings, the roc lifted off. The other two followed.

"What was that last bit about?" Bree-yark asked, a hand shielding his eyes from the gusts of debris.

Had Angelus just suggested that *Caroline* was the one possessed?

"I'm not sure yet," I said.

———

WE FOUND OUR CLOTHES STREWN AMONG A RIOT OF BLACK TENGU feathers, and our belongings in sacks and pouches. True to Angelus's word, the rocs had been selective in their carnage and everything was there. When I spotted my cane off to one side, I seized it, never more relieved to feel the smooth ironwood in my grasp.

With the adrenaline of the rescue leaving my system, my head and ribs resumed throbbing where the satyr had struck me. I applied healing magic to the spots as well as to Bree-yark's lumpy head. Before long, I could see through my right eye again, and both of us were moving with less stiffness.

My next act—before dressing, even—was to activate a pair of neutralizing potions for the two of us. I wasn't going to commit another stupid rookie mistake like I had in the cave. Bree-yark and I took down a pair of stealth potions next. Only when we'd begun fading from view did we don our clothes.

I was restocking my coat pockets when Bree-yark suddenly raised his head. "Say, have you seen Dropsy?"

"Not since the cavern."

He began pacing the area, whispering her name.

"She probably went in search of her maker," I said. "Some enchanted objects are known to do that."

Bree-yark relinquished his search with a despondent grunt. He'd apparently grown attached to the lantern.

"I'm sure she's fine," I said.

"Yeah, but it looks like the satyr got away." He pointed out a set of cloven tracks that climbed toward a range of rocks.

"Leave it."

"After what he did to us?"

"Look, no one wants to put a foot up that goat's ass more than me, but we've got a much bigger mission right now." I placed the final potions in a pocket, shouldered my pack, and grasped my cane. "Which way?"

Bree-yark pried his vengeful eyes from the tracks and screwed them toward the forest the rocs had been circling over. The riders had since steered them on, the great birds now dots above the far horizon.

"Well, there's two ways we can go," Bree-yark said. "Around the Kinloch Forest or through it. As an army, we always went around. Of course, we weren't sporting this kind of magic." He looked at one of his spectral arms. That I could see or hear him at all was only because the same magic cloaked me.

"What's the time difference?" I asked.

"Should save us a half day, if not more."

"Dangers?"

"You name it, but it's not like the long way's much safer. Major thoroughfare for giants, not to mention the occasional hobgoblin army." He grunted a laugh. "Did I ever tell you about the time we were on a night march and—"

"Do you know a route through the forest?"

I felt bad cutting him off, but the goblin was an incurable storyteller.

"I know *of* a route," he said.

As the rocs disappeared from view, I regretted we hadn't been able to hitch a ride with them. But when your gut counseled caution, you listened. I would have preferred it had been my magic, but it was still on some sort of meditative retreat.

Bree-yark followed my gaze. "You didn't happen to pack any flying potions?"

"Those require huge energy investments, and their use would burn through our protective potions, so no. That goes for magic-use in general, so I'm really going to need to keep things on the down-low."

"So which'll it be?" Bree-yark asked.

I peered from the valley to the trees. "Let's take the forest route."

We descended the gradual slope of land to where it flattened into a broad vale. Determined not to be ambushed again, I kept a close watch on our surroundings, even as the stealth potions took deeper effect. The sky above remained Windex-blue, while the sun shone exuberantly. I still couldn't get over how vivid everything was, down to the individual stalks of grass bobbing in the breeze.

"Pretty, huh?" Bree-yark said.

I nodded, even though *pretty* didn't begin to describe it. The realm wasn't meant for mortal minds. An hour or two, fine. You'd leave feeling dizzy and overcome, but your brain synapses would still be firing. Beyond that and the realm's ambient enchantments would pluck your sanity away one thread at a time until the whole thing fell open and you were a gibbering wreck. Though my neutralizing potion and magical bloodline blunted the effects, I could feel the potential for madness all around me.

Before long, the forest rose just ahead, its trees tall, dark, and twisting. "The way's marked by a cairn," Bree-yark said. "Supposed to be around here somewhere."

I scanned the tree line to both sides. "I'm not seeing anything."

"There." He pointed off to our right and strode toward the trees.

I still didn't see anything until, deeper in the forest, I picked out a jumble of stones.

"That's the cairn?"

"Yeah, looks like the forest overtook it."

"It looks more like the forest used it for a rock fight."

"Must've gotten tired of things tromping through here."

"Wait." I gripped his arm. "Are you saying this forest is sentient?"

"Most are in the Fae Wilds. Some are just moodier than others. The Kinloch Forest, for example."

"Wonderful."

"We can still take the other route."

I was seriously considering it, when the ground vibrated

underfoot. Bree-yark knelt and flattened a hand against the earth. The vibrations strengthened until the leaves in the trees began to rattle.

"Scratch that," he said, straightening. "We've got a rowdy bunch of stone giants coming our way."

Moments later, a thundercrack sounded and pieces of stone began showering around us. I swore as a fragment the size of a desk buried itself only a few yards away. In the distance, a chorus of whoops rose.

"Sounds like they're clubbing boulders," Bree-yark said. "C'mon!"

We ran into the forest and past the scattered cairn. Ahead, a path wound through the trees. At our backs, more shards rained down through the canopy, one smashing a tree to splinters. We didn't slow until the rumbles and whoops faded far behind us. I peered around, my cane and cold iron amulet drawn. The forest crowded the path now, and strange bird calls sounded from the thick branches overhead.

"This will take us all the way through?" I whispered.

"Straight to the other side," Bree-yark confirmed. "Though it does twist some."

Through my wizard's senses, I picked up traces of the old fae magic that sustained the path.

"Then let's go carefully," I said, "but fast."

I tried to keep watch on all sides as we advanced at the equivalent of a speed walk. More than once, I felt like Bilbo journeying through Mirkwood, and I half expected to see giant spiders or devious wood elves.

Every time I felt my mind starting to adapt to our surroundings of dense, twisting trees, I redoubled my vigilance. Though I'd never been to the Fae Wilds, I knew one of its prevailing enchantments was getting visitors to relax their guards. By the time they realized they were in trouble, it was too late. I suspected that was why I'd been so slow to activate my potions upon our arrival.

For Bree-yark's part, he stomped along, eyes fixed ahead, ears perked to the sides. At length he muttered, "Place is kinda grim."

"You think?" I said.

———

WE'D BEEN WALKING FOR A COUPLE HOURS WHEN A DEEP SHADOW fell over the forest and bird calls became insect chirrups. Through chinks in the tree canopy, I could see brilliant points of starlight. Bree-yark pulled up so suddenly, I almost ran into his back. Even inches away, he was consumed by darkness.

"What's going on?" I asked. "The sun was straight overhead when we entered."

"Kinloch Forest has decided it's nighttime," he grumbled. "And I can't see a frigging thing, even with my goblin vision."

The path ahead had disappeared, absorbed by the same enchanted darkness that now hid the trees and the path behind. I swore under my breath. I'd read of fae forests playing with time, but did it have to pull this stunt now?

"How much longer until it decides it's day again?" I asked.

"When it gets tired of it being night, I guess. I packed some candles, but the trees here are touchy about heat."

"Better we don't use them, then."

"Can you cast one of your light balls?" he asked.

"Not without burning through our potions."

We'd come this far undetected, and something told me the second the forest sensed company, we'd be getting all kinds of visitors. As if to confirm the thought, a blood-curdling scream sounded nearby.

"Damn," Bree-yark whispered, backing into me. I grasped his

shoulders, but my heel snagged on a root and we both tumbled to the ground. Thankfully, our spheres of stealth contained the commotion.

"What are you doing?" I hissed.

"Do you know what that is?" he whispered near my ear.

The scream sounded again, closer this time. "Banshee?"

"Banshee," he confirmed.

I stopped trying to disentangle our legs and froze. Banshees were the cursed spirits of fae, and hella deadly. Their screams alone were capable of killing. It was only by the grace of our neutralizing potions that Bree-yark and I were thus far unharmed. But banshees were also highly attuned to the living, the more powerful spirits able to perceive beyond veilings. And that included stealth potions.

The banshee's next scream was closer still. A terror I'd never quite felt wrapped my heart in icy talons. Bree-yark's compact body began to quiver. His next whisper was barely more than a tremulous breath.

"Twelve winters ago, a single banshee wiped out half a goblin battalion. I don't wanna die like that, Everson."

"Then we need to keep still and stay very, very quiet."

I peeked up at the canopy, hoping for signs of morning—banshees were strictly night creatures—but the stars sparkled as brilliantly as ever. *Thanks, Kinloch Forest,* I thought fiercely. *You big prick.*

Worse still, the stealth spell enveloping us was going to need replenishing soon. But the magic to activate the potions would be like sending up signal flares. Bree-yark squeezed my hand hard enough for my bones to creak.

"Hey!" I complained.

"See that?" he asked.

A female specter in tattered robes drifted beyond the trees. The halo of light surrounding her was pale and sickly. From inside a tangle of hair, vicious eyes roved back and forth, searching, searching. Breath clamped, I hunkered lower with Bree-yark, but our position on the path was too exposed.

The banshee's gaze swept past us, stopped, and then back-tracked slowly.

I adjusted my grip on my amulet at the same time Bree-yark slid his goblin blade from its sheath.

A scream split the air as the banshee flew at us.

12

The banshee's scream felt like an axe cleaving my skull and wedging deep into the brain matter. My thoughts fragmented. My vision went blurry. An unnatural terror shook my core. But throughout the banshee's vocal attack, I maintained a death grip on my cane and cold iron amulet and repeated a single mantra:

If I lose my nerve, we're done.

As the scream faded, I pulled myself together. The banshee sharpened into focus. She was rushing us headfirst, empty eyes wreathed in white flames, lips stretched from a mouth of ghastly teeth.

The time for stealth was over. I'd deal with the consequences later.

With an uttered Word, warm energy filled me, burning through the remaining effects of the potions and haloing my amulet in blue light. The banshee passed through the final tree separating us. I stepped over Bree-yark, who was still trembling on the ground, and thrust the amulet at the banshee's yawning mouth.

"Disfare!" I shouted.

A blue blast discharged from the iron in a silent roar. But instead of scattering the being as I'd hoped, the force sent her tumbling off into the trees. I stooped and helped Bree-yark to his feet.

"The heck happened?" he moaned, clamping his brow.

"You succumbed to the banshee's scream. No shame in that, but we've gotta make tracks."

"Is she destroyed?"

"Displaced," I said. "She'll be back."

"Everson ... your hand."

I followed Bree-yark's wincing gaze to my amulet hand. The skin over the knuckles was blackening, thick puss oozing from a network of soggy cracks. I moved the glowing amulet to my cane hand and splayed my fingers. The veins were darkening, turning the color of ink. A piece of flesh fell from my fifth knuckle, exposing a white knob of bone. But I didn't feel a damned thing.

"Did she touch you?" Bree-yark asked.

"I must've made contact when I blasted her."

I angled my cane down and uttered words of healing. The cane's opal glowed softly, enveloping my hand in a cottony light. But though the black ink stopped spreading, the tissue wasn't repairing. I pushed more power through the spell, but the necrotizing effect of the banshee's touch dug in.

This would require powerful fae magic to cure.

And I could already see the damned banshee circling back.

"Stay close," I said to Bree-yark, who had pivoted toward her spectral form.

At my word, light pulsed from my cane and hardened into a shield around us. I fed it additional protection through the iron amulet—and just in time. Though muted, the banshee's scream punched through my mind like a hot spike and shook our protection. Bree-yark's hands went to his ears.

The scream trailed off, but not the banshee. Her approach

was more cautious this time, eyes fixed on my still-glowing amulet. Even so, I wasn't sure I could repel another direct attack. The invocations and spells I'd just cast in a rapid sequence had cost me energy. Maybe too much energy.

"If she was flesh, I'd give her a taste of goblin steel," Bree-yark growled. "Then she'd have something to scream about."

"She was once," I said, cycling through everything I'd read about the beings.

According to legend, banshees had been fae of extraordinary beauty and conceit. In death, however, their whole-soul obsession with themselves made them susceptible to an ancient curse said to reside in the darker forests of Faerie. The curse twisted those fae inside out—their ghastly, shrieking insides becoming their immortal forms, doomed to wander an eternal darkness. I could only imagine the kind of individual we were talking about, given how self-absorbed most fae already were.

The banshee dove in.

"Respingere!" I cried, sending light and force from our shield.

The banshee withdrew and hovered a safe distance away, watching.

"Holy thunder, she's ugly," Bree-yark muttered.

I resumed parsing through my knowledge of all things banshee until one feature of their condition suggested a weakness. And it related to what Bree-yark had just said. "Do you have water on you?" I asked.

"Yeah, a whole skin."

"Grab it."

While he did, the banshee swayed back and forth, as though searching for an opening.

Bree-yark held up the swollen skin. "Got it."

"Pour it out."

"Onto the ground?"

"The shield, technically, but yeah."

He upended his skin until water began glugging out. Our shell of hardened air buckled slightly as the water landed. At one time I hadn't been able to cast or hold invocations in the presence of liquid, the medium too disruptive to the conduction of ley energy. But with time and practice, I'd prevailed.

And a good thing.

I repelled the banshee's next slashing attack with another pulse. But she veered back around, the eyes that peered at us radiating the most unnatural hatred. She wasn't leaving here without a kill.

"Water's all out," Bree-yark said.

I glanced down at the puddle around our feet.

"Good, now jump straight up on my word. Now!"

As our feet left the water, I shouted, *"Protezione!"*

A second orb of hardened air manifested inside our original protection, and we landed on dry shield. I grew it out until the water flattened between the two layers. I pushed harder, forcing the water into a paper-thin sheet that separated us from the banshee. The inrushing specter stopped suddenly and hovered inches away.

Take a good look, sweetheart, I thought.

Beyond the water, her head tilted one way and the other. She raised a taloned finger in front of the shield, then lowered it suddenly. Her mouth fell as her expression shifted from belligerence to naked horror. In a cyclone of hair and ragged robes, the banshee fled into the trees, a forlorn wail trailing after her.

I waited until I could no longer hear her before dispelling the shield. The sheet of water splashed to the ground.

Bree-yark chuckled in disbelief. "What the heck just happened?"

"Banshees still think they're the femme fatales they were in life," I answered wearily. "Her reflection revealed what she really was. When that sank in, well..." I gestured toward her path of flight. "She flipped."

"Freaking brilliant, Everson."

Though I nodded in response to his shoulder punch, it was too early to celebrate. I had a hand that was half rotted, and I'd just broadcast our presence to the rest of Kinloch Forest in giant stadium lights.

I activated another cocktail of protective potions, and we drank them quickly. I then recalled the power from my cane and amulet, snuffing their light. Darkness collapsed around us. "We need to get moving," I said. "Even if it means feeling our way along the path on hands and knees."

"Um, the forest might have other ideas."

Snaps sounded, and a faint luminescence grew over Bree-yark's face. I spun to find tangles of roots ripping up from the ground and taking large humanoid shape, a green swamp-like gas enveloping them.

13

"Oh, c'mon," I complained. "Now what?"

"Tanglers," Bree-yark said with a grin. "And good news. *These* guys can be cut."

He lunged past me. Roots and earth flew as he ripped his jagged blade through one of the tangler's midsections, effectively chopping it in half. With a grunt, he wheeled and took off another creature's reaching arm.

With my damaged hand, it took time to pocket my amulet, separate my cane into sword and staff, and then move the sword to my good hand.

Though tempted to activate the fire rune and torch the tanglers—and Kinloch Forest while I was at it—I didn't want to compromise the fresh dose of potions already taking tingling effect in my system. Instead, I swung at the nearest tangler's neck. The blade disappeared beyond a superficial layer of roots before being seized, twisted, and thrust out again.

"You've gotta put your body into it," Bree-yark said.

He hacked through one of the tangler's legs, dropping the creature to his own height, then demonstrated his point with a ferocious blow to the neck. I leaned back as the tangler's head shot past.

"Like that," he said.

I skipped around to confront another approaching tangler. But the goblin kicked the one he'd just dispatched, and in three running steps used its fallen form as a launch, thrusting with his thick legs. He caught impressive air and landed feet-first against the new tangler's chest. As the creature toppled backward, it wrapped Bree-yark's feet in roots. Anchored now, Bree-yark swung his blade like a lumberjack, one savage blow after another. By the time they reached the ground, the tangler was in pieces.

Bree-yark and I were fully cloaked now, leaving the final two tanglers groping in search of us. But rather than sneak away, Bree-yark saw it as an opportunity to go full bore. When he finished, he waded from their demolished bodies and peered around, his face glistening with goblin sweat in the fading glow of swamp light.

"Any more?" he panted.

"That was all of them."

"And here I was just getting warmed up." He returned to the path. "We make a good team, Everson."

I was about to point out I hadn't really done anything when a groan sounded, low and shuddering. And was it my imagination, or were the trees a lot closer than they'd been a couple minutes ago?

"You're not gonna like this, Everson," Bree-yark said, "but I think we're standing on a Grumus."

I stared at him to be sure I'd heard him right. When he nodded, we took off down the path. Within a few paces we were beyond the dying glow of the dismembered tanglers and buried in thick night. I heard the collision of a body against a tree trunk followed by Bree-yark staggering and swearing.

"It's no damned good," he complained. "Still can't see a blasted thing."

Another groan sounded. This time the trees shook around us. Grumuses were living entities found in the deepest forests of Faerie. They blended in by supporting the forests' natural growth, but layers of roots and soil hid a vast digestive tract that was always hungry. And a Grumus's mouth could open anywhere and very suddenly. The only reason it hadn't yet was because we were cloaked.

"We've got to get off this thing," I said.

"No kidding. But without a light, we'll have to wait till morning."

"You mean until whenever the forest decides it *wants* it to be morning?"

"More or less. And I wouldn't be surprised if the forest and Grumus are in cahoots."

I swore as I peered around the blackness. Beyond the trees, a banshee-like glow caught my eye. And it was coming our way.

Oh, for fuck's sake.

Bree-yark saw it too. "Her again?"

"Either that or another glowy denizen of Kinloch."

Suddenly, hobgoblin armies and stone giants playing boulder baseball felt like a day in the park compared to this never-ending nightmare. All we could do was remain still and hope that neither the Grumus nor our newest company drew a bead on us. With any luck, the forest would tire of night and switch to day again.

Bree-yark choked on a laugh. "I don't believe it."

"What?"

"It's Dropsy."

I squinted at the glow, not so sure. Before I could stop him, Bree-yark took off running down the path. I watched helplessly as my teammate closed the distance, my mind cycling through all the horrible things the light could be besides an enchanted lantern—banshee, wraith, will-o'-wisp...

As Bree-yark neared it, the light released a bright pulse, sending my heart into my mouth. It wasn't until Bree-yark lifted it up, and I could see his grinning teeth, that I relaxed.

"Would you look at her?" he said as he rejoined me. "Came all this way to find us."

He held the lantern in the crook of an arm like he was cradling an infant, her light still pulsing excitedly.

"It's amazing, and I'm grateful," I said. "But can we coo over her later? We're still on top of a frigging Grumus."

Bree-yark straightened. "Yeah, yeah, sure. Follow me."

He led the way at a run, the path seeming to unfurl in Dropsy's enchanted light. I matched Bree-yark's speed, one of my strides equaling roughly two of his, until we settled into a good pace. Behind us, the Grumus continued to moan. At one point I heard it rip open, as if mouthing blindly for us. But we eventually transitioned from creature back to forest, because the moaning and ripping stopped.

About two hours later, we passed a jumble of fallen stones. Bree-yark reared back suddenly, a forearm thrown to his face. I arrived beside him and swore as sunlight nailed my eyes too. Forming a visor with my hand, I blinked around. Behind us, the forest remained buried in enchanted darkness. But ahead, mountains and meadows were soaked in a stunning alpenglow of late-afternoon sunlight.

We'd made it to the other side.

"See those trees over there?" Bree-yark asked.

I followed his pointed finger down to where a distant lake glittered, a thick crescent of green wrapping its far shore.

"That's where Crusspatch lives."

14

———

By the time we reached the lake, the setting sun was transforming the sky into a stupendous canvas of pinks and purples that the lake's placid surface caught and enhanced. To safeguard my mind, I focused on the narrow path that wound around the shore. As we approached the trees, I dropped my gaze to the backs of Bree-yark's heels.

"Lots of stories about this guy," he barked.

"Crusspatch? Any of them reliable?"

"About as much as a story that gets passed around dozens of times can be, I guess. According to one, a group of orcs set up camp on the edge of these very woods. Next thing they knew, Crusspatch had joined them at the campfire. Just humming a tune, like the orcs weren't even there. And he had a big chunk of something on a skewer that he was rotating back and forth over the flames." Bree-yark peered at me over a shoulder. "Turned out it was their captain's severed foot."

"Really," I said dryly.

"The rest of the orcs attacked, but fire balls leapt from the blaze and bored holes through their chests. Dropped them all 'cept one, a young orc who'd stayed back. He said Crusspatch never even turned his head. In fact, he was still staring at the sizzling foot when he said, 'You're welcome to the heel, but the toes are mine, mine, mine.'"

"Well, it's like you said, time and the number of tellings tend to inflate these stories out of all proportion."

"Yeah, but there's always a seed of truth."

"Then maybe we should be keeping our eyes open instead of telling tales."

I didn't mean for it to come out harsh, but the Kinloch Forest had put me on edge. And the threat of a banshee or Grumus paled in comparison to that of a full-blooded fae lord. Especially one off his rocker.

"Sorry," Bree-yark said. "Just wanted to prepare you."

"No, it's me," I sighed. "I'm still coming down from the forest." I planned to leave it there, but I needed to get something off my chest. "I'm also feeling the pressure of Crusspatch being my last good shot. So if he's going to be crazy, I need it to be the pleasantly confused kind and not the eating-roasted-orc-toes kind."

"I hear ya," Bree-yark said. "It'll all work out. You'll see."

Though he was just saying it to pacify me, I found his words, spoken in his thick goblin voice, strangely comforting.

As we entered the trees, I began to think tactically. Was the better strategy to sneak up on Crusspatch's dwelling, or alert him to our presence way out here? Deciding the second hadn't done much for the orcs, I took the lead, wizard's senses on high alert.

I didn't pick up anything resembling defensive energies, but ornaments began to appear. They swung from branches on long threads: sparkling baubles and little figurines. The deeper into the trees we went, the more ornaments materialized until they were everywhere. They spoke to Crusspatch's oddness at the very least. Bree-yark squinted up at a wooden girl, Dropsy's light glinting from a single crystal eye.

"Don't touch it," I whispered.

"Don't worry. I like my feet attached to my ankles."

Soon, a small cottage appeared through the trees. With narrow walls and a sloping, moss-covered roof, it looked like something out of a fairy tale. Bree-yark and I crept to the edge of a small yard. A cobblestone path led to the front door. No lights shone from the windows, but it wasn't fully dark out yet. Thin curls of smoke issued from a stone chimney, suggesting someone was home—or had been very recently.

"What should we do?" Bree-yark whispered.

"I think it's time we announced ourselves."

He peered around nervously. "You really think that's a good idea?"

"If he's as powerful as everyone says, there's a good chance he already knows we're here." After all, not sensing any wards didn't mean there weren't any. They could have been beyond my abilities.

"Hope he's not preparing the skewers," Bree-yark murmured.

I tuned into my magic to be sure of my decision. It wasn't nodding, but it wasn't shaking its head either. Pulling Bree-yark up beside me, I uttered the Word for protection. The air around us hardened into a shield.

"Crusspatch?" I called. "I'm Everson Croft and this is Bree-yark. A friend of Seay Sherard's arranged for several of us to meet you. Unfortunately, not all were able to come. We would be honored and humbled if you would deign to grant the two of us an audience."

I shrugged at Bree-yark—a little flattery never hurt—and then we waited. Around us, night deepened and ornaments tinkled in the breeze. Dropsy's light shone toward the cottage with what seemed wariness. There was magic at work here, but it was strange and hard to nail down. It seemed to buffer us from the Fae Wilds while at the same time exposing us to something considerably more dangerous.

"Hello?" I called.

When no one responded, Bree-yark looked around. "Now what?"

"Keep watch out here."

"You're going to the door?"

I pictured Arnaud in his cell, waiting for me with his legs crossed and that little grin on his lips.

"I have to."

"I like you, Everson," Bree-yark said. "Be careful."

He retreated with Dropsy to a large tree on the verge of the yard. When he whispered something to her, the lantern's light dimmed, and they blended into the growing darkness. I scanned the cottage's front porch. No protections.

Swallowing, I drew my amulet and crept up the cobblestone path. The front door was slender, its frame canted to one side as if its designer was either whimsical or careless. But still no signs of wards or defenses, even up close.

"Hello?" I tried again. "Crusspatch?"

When no one answered, I winced and rapped the door with my cane. No defensive magic detonated, or even suggested itself. There was simply the plain sound of wood striking wood. With my final rap, the door opened a crack. A smell of smoke seeped out, and beneath it, something less pleasant.

I pushed the door open wider until I was looking into a one-room cottage. A kitchen crowded with hanging pots competed for space with an oversized bed and a chair-crammed wooden table. Pegged shelves stood from the walls, holding books and an assortment of odds and ends. From a stone hearth, a pile of embers illuminated a single chair on a round rug where a figure sat with his head slumped.

"Crusspatch?" I called.

The man wore a colorful robe. Long white hair fell from under a stocking cap, draping his knees and nearly touching his slippered feet. A thick book lay off to one side, presumably dropped when he'd dozed off.

"Crusspatch?" I tried, more loudly.

When he didn't respond, I eyed the threshold, then tested it with my cane. No protections, or at least none that I could feel. I wondered now if Crusspatch relied on his reputation to serve that function.

The other explanation, of course, was that someone had already breached his protections.

I moved the amulet across the cottage before stretching a leg over the threshold. Nothing blew up. Within a few cautious steps, I was close enough to prod Crusspatch's shoulder with my cane. His head lolled, showing his face.

I jumped back, a scream wedged in my throat. The fae exile's mouth was open, jaw canted to the side. But where his eyes should have been were blackened holes. The smoke corkscrewing from them carried the stench of sulfur.

A demon attack.

"You're too late," someone spoke in a low male's voice.

Shouting the Word to activate my blade's banishment rune, I dropped my amulet into a pocket and separated my cane into sword and staff. As I pivoted from the dead fae, my rune pulsed with holy power. But though the voice had spoken from mere feet away, I couldn't see anyone in the sudden play of light and shadow.

"Show yourself!" I called, heart pounding through the words.

A scuff sounded, and a hooded figure who hadn't been there a moment before stepped from behind the table. I pushed more power into the rune until the glow highlighted a blade-like nose and a chin of iron stubble.

"Who are you?" I demanded.

The hooded figure didn't flinch from the light of banishment. "An ally."

I opened my wizard's senses, but a powerful cloaking spell covered him. I was only seeing him because he'd allowed it. Whoever he was, his presence near Crusspatch's body couldn't have been a coincidence. We were either talking powerful demon or the fae who had fallen under shadow.

"I need a name," I said, pushing power into my wizard's voice, "or so help me God, I'll assume you're a demon and treat you like one."

"Yeah," Bree-yark barked.

He arrived in the doorway, goblin blade glinting in my light. When the figure's hands came up, I braced for an attack. But he drew his hood back by the sides. Dark hair spilled out, framing a rogue's face with cunning black eyes. Regardless, I didn't know him. Before I could say as much, he brought a finger to his lips.

"You once called me 'Sub.'"

As I repeated the name to myself, the fae's face began to smooth. His dark hair lightened and turned honey-blond. His lips filled out. I felt my sword arm sag as a pair of familiar, feminine eyes peered back at me.

Holy crap.

15

I'd given her the nickname "Sub" back when we had neighboring classrooms and I would show up late to find her teaching in my place. She had been Caroline Reid then, my friend, colleague, and crush. We'd made love once. Now she was a powerful princess who had bargained away her feelings for me.

She was also in the cottage of a dead fae.

"What are you doing here?" I asked carefully.

"Crusspatch was dangerous. He might have helped you, but not without harming you."

I glanced over at the slumped figure in the chair. My last hope to access the time catch. "So you killed him?"

"I planned to intervene, not harm him. The deed was done before I arrived."

Caroline held my gaze as if inviting me to weigh the truth of her words. Two years had passed since she'd helped me cast Arnaud into the Below. But having spent most of the intervening time in Faerie, she'd aged ten times that. While her face remained fae smooth, a certain hardness possessed her blue-green eyes.

Do not engage her, Angelus had warned. *She is not herself.*

I could feel the weight of the calling stone in my pocket. By holding it and speaking the word, I could summon him. As casually as I could, I moved the sword from my damaged right hand over to my staff hand.

"You're supposed to be missing," I said.

"My kingdom is compromised. I left of my own free will."

"Compromised how?"

"A demonic presence moves among us."

That jibed with what I'd gathered from Pip and Twerk's warning, but I needed an assurance that *she* wasn't the one doing the moving among. She remained strongly glamoured, either to hide from her kingdom or to conceal the truth from me, possibly both.

"Your husband's looking for you," I said.

Like I'd done with Angelus, I watched for her reaction, but she only nodded. "He doesn't see the danger."

"So you've been, what, hiding out in the Fae Wilds?"

"I've been waiting for you."

I slipped the hand into my pocket. "Me?"

"Osgood said you would come here."

My suspicions spiked. I hadn't even been considering this trip when I'd gone to the fae townhouse that morning. But as my fingers closed around the stone, I realized that Osgood would have overheard the Upholders and me discussing the Crusspatch option the day he'd intruded on our meeting. With my aid from the fae cut off, he might have divined that I would revisit that option.

"Why not just go to my apartment?"

"The portals between our worlds are being watched."

"Why are you helping me?" I asked pointedly.

"Because the demon threat is real, and the answer is in the time catch."

My magic had given me its first strong assertion when I'd said the same thing to Gretchen that morning.

"How do you know?"

She peered over at Crusspatch's body. "Because something is intent on preventing your return."

"There are no other fae who can send me? What about Osgood?"

Despite my suspicions of her, fresh hope crackled inside me. If she had been in contact with Osgood, maybe the powerful fae butler was back in play. But Caroline quickly smothered the notion.

"The entire kingdom is compromised. I can't discern friend from foe, and Osgood is no longer under my orders."

I turned the stone over in my fingers. Who to trust? Caroline or Angelus?

When I glanced over at Bree-yark, he appeared as baffled as I felt.

"I know our past is ... complicated," Caroline said, "but I need you to trust me. As your friend."

She was suddenly right in front of me. Her touch was gentle, even as she drew my hand from my pocket. An instant before the stone came into view, I let it tumble from my fingers, back into the well of fabric.

"Friend?" I said. "We haven't spoken in years."

Instead of replying, she gazed at my hand, turning it one way, then the other. The white knob of bone still showed where the rotten skin had fallen from my fifth knuckle. Concern lines creased her brow.

"Banshee?" she asked.

"Yeah, in the Kinloch Forest."

A warm force spread across my hand, thinning away the healing magic I'd applied. The damaged tissue suddenly felt raw and exposed. Caroline brought my hand to her stomach, folding her own hands over it.

"The purging will be harsh," she said, "but you must not pull away."

She was handling me with the familiarity of an intimate. And that was the problem. She looked and felt like the Caroline Reid I remembered. Almost human. But in the next moment, a dark throb of pain stole my breath. I felt the banshee curse spreading, eating through the rest of my hand, laying bare veins, muscles, bones. Sweat sprang from my brow, and I braced my teeth against a scream.

"Everson?" Bree-yark said from the doorway. "You all right?"

I was on the verge of tearing the hand away—the throbbing had deepened until I could hardly stand it. But Caroline pursed her lips and sent a soothing current of air into her cupped hands. The pain abated. When she separated her palms, my own hand was whole again. I raised it, flexing my fingers and then turned it over to inspect the knuckles. The skin was restored, smooth as a newborn's.

She had healed me.

"You're fortunate you caught it when you did," she said. "The banshee's curse nearly entered your bloodstream. Had the poison reached your heart, you would have joined the undead in the Fae Wilds."

"Not exactly how I was planning to spend retirement," I muttered. "Thanks."

Her soft smile lulled me once more into the illusion of our former friendship. We could have been at our favorite Midtown deli, but the fact was we were standing next to the body of a murdered fae. Smoke continued to wisp from his eye sockets.

"There is another way to get there," Caroline said.

I looked over to find her gazing at Crusspatch too.

"And what's that?"

"Arnaud Thorne."

The name landed like a shot in my gut.

"I know how that must sound," she said. "But he—"

I swung my cane toward her and shouted, *"Disfare!"*

Holy power blasted the length of the cane, swallowing Caroline in a cone of white light. I'd been fifty-fifty on the odds of her being demon possessed. But her "solution" to accessing the time catch had just tipped those odds to ninety-ten in favor. A banishment attack would settle the question.

Bree-yark stepped into the room, one hand shielding his eyes, the other clutching his blade. I listened past the blast for screams, but all I heard was the flapping of her cloak. After another moment, I recalled the power. Dimness returned to our space, and Caroline was standing where she'd been, golden hair fluttering back over her settling cloak. No sign the invocation had harmed her.

"Satisfied?" she asked.

Bree-yark looked from her to me as I lowered my cane.

"Why Arnaud?" I asked.

"He has a direct line to the time catch. Malphas made it so for all his demons."

"How do you know that?"

"Osgood. He left the information for me to find."

"And only two demons remain," I said, catching on. "Arnaud and the one who infiltrated the fae."

"Yes. Which is why I'm going with you this time."

I blinked at the unexpectedness of her announcement.

"You were correct in your letter," she said. "The plans of the demon Malphas threaten Faerie. Indeed, it's already begun. I have an interest in what happens. But once Malphas discovers you've re-entered the time catch, he'll send the final demon to stop you. One who wields fae powers. He'll be too formidable for you alone."

"He *won't* be alone," Bree-yark said, stepping up beside me.

The gesture warmed me as I turned back to Caroline. "So you know this fae?"

"Well enough," she said.

"Royalty?"

"Yes."

And someone pretty high up if he'd managed to turn Angelus against his own wife, but I didn't say that. I was thinking more about the nauseating prospect of having to bargain with Arnaud and what he would demand in exchange. A process that had the very real potential of turning Vega against me.

"Short of his freedom, Arnaud's not going to agree to help us," I said.

Caroline's irises darkened, and power stirred behind them. "He won't have a choice."

"You can do that? I mean, access his connection to the time catch?" I had known advanced fae possessed the ability to repurpose portals for their own use, but I hadn't guessed Caroline to be that far along. She must have cultivated some damned powerful contacts in Faerie, just as she had in our world.

"If he's subdued," she replied, "yes."

Though she didn't say it, I picked up a suggestion of *that's where you come in.*

"All right, *assuming* we go the Arnaud route," I said, a part of me wanting to vomit on the words, "there's the little problem of returning to our world. You said yourself that the portals between here and there are being watched, and I can vouch for the speediness of the reaction force."

I remembered how quickly Angelus and his fellow roc-riders had arrived. That had worked to our benefit the last time, but if Caroline was telling the truth—and after the failed banishment attack, I was leaning much more toward the idea she was—I doubted another run-in with Angelus would go so well.

"I know a way that's better hidden," she said.

"How far away are we talking?" I asked.

"Within the half hour."

Bree-yark's brow furrowed. "That close?"

Given the vastness of Faerie, I shared the goblin's skepticism.

"Not close," Caroline said. "Soon. The portal works off the moon's position."

Instead of allaying my skepticism, her answer only deepened it.

"A lunar door?" I all but cried. "You have a lunar door?"

I'd heard rumors of the gems, but they were said to have all been destroyed, if they ever existed in the first place. That was why the portals in Upper and Lower Manhattan were so valuable to the kingdoms that controlled them. Hell, the portals were the reason Caroline's mother had betrothed her to Angelus.

"Someone smuggled one to me, yes," Caroline said.

I deduced that someone to be Osgood, maybe another reason to trust Caroline.

"If he gave you a lunar door ," I said, "why can't he help you into the time catch?"

"Because the kingdom expressly forbade him. They issued the order after learning he'd helped you and the others. He is magically bound by such orders, whether they are influenced by demonic powers or not."

I had guessed rightly about that.

"And you were singled out for asking Osgood to help us?" I asked.

For the first time, her eyes glimmered with moisture. "Perhaps now you understand my situation."

I did. She might have left of her own free will, but she was also in danger. Her only hope for restoring her kingdom, and her place in it, was to end Malphas's menace. And that meant entering the time catch by the only means left. I could use her help, but I had to ensure we wouldn't be working at cross purposes.

"I have friends to recover," I said.

"I understand. What did you find when you went the last time?"

"Strangers. One each holding the half-fae and druids. Arnaud was there too, manipulating the ley lines around St. Martin's Cathedral. Or the plot, at least. The church burned down in the Great Fire of 1776 along with half of downtown. I think he was working on a portal for Malphas to enter the time catch."

"And from there, our world."

Finally, someone who understands the situation and the stakes.

"That's my guess too," I said. "But I'm not sure how Malphas plans to follow through without Arnaud at the controls. He must have found a replacement. Probably why he's being so protective of the time catch."

"I can attempt to access Arnaud's thoughts, understand what he was doing there."

"That would help." And it sure as hell beat attempting to finesse that info out of him.

"But I've little doubt the answer will be St. Martin's," she said.

"The power source."

"If we can cap the well, Malphas will have nothing to draw from."

"That should also restore stability to the domain."

"Making it safer to recover your friends."

For the first time, I smiled.

Bree-yark cleared his throat. "Hey, uh, mind if I have a word with you, Everson?"

"Oh, Caroline, this is Bree-yark," I said, remembering myself. "Bree-yark, Caroline."

The goblin hesitated before sheathing his blade and accepting her offered hand. "A pleasure," he grunted.

She nodded before shifting her eyes back to mine. "I know you have much to consider, but our window for action is small." She appeared to hesitate before adding, "You should know too that something hunts you."

A charge went off in my chest. "What?"

"It comes from the realm of the dead. It wants you or something of yours. That's all I can sense." When a comma appeared between her eyebrows, it took a moment for me to understand why her earlier show of concern had bothered me: she had sacrificed her feelings for me two years before.

"I'll prepare the portal," she said when I didn't respond.

As she strode from the cottage, her glamour returned, darkening her hair and restoring the roguish male features from before. Bree-yark waited until she was out of earshot before turning back to me.

"I don't trust her," he whispered.

"Well, I didn't either at first, but she stood up to my banishment attack without so much as a frown, so she can't be carrying anything demonic. Plus, everything she said makes sense."

"Of course it does. She's fae."

"Half-fae," I corrected him.

He seized my arm and walked me to the far side of the cottage. "One of the things I've come to respect about you is your judgment. I mean, that whole thing with me and Gretchen? You're no dummy. But fifteen minutes with this broad, and she's convinced you to do the one thing you've been dead-set against? Sorry, Everson, but that doesn't smell right."

Even though goblins held an inherent distrust for the fae, I considered what he was saying. *Was* she manipulating me?

"Did you pick up any magic?" I asked him.

"Just her glamour and some items she's carrying."

"No enchantments, though?"

"No," he admitted. "But there's more than one way to charm a person. Didn't you say you two had history?"

I pondered Caroline's show of concern, comparing it to the last time I'd seen her. It had been after the big press conference when the mayor had restored my good name in the city. Our gazes met across the stage, hers showing a vanilla recognition but nothing deeper, all of her feelings for me wiped clean.

Including concern.

"All right," I said, "maybe there's a little bit of manipulation happening, but I still believe our goals align. I want to recover my friends and head off a demon apocalypse. Caroline wants to restore her kingdom. And if Arnaud *is* the only way, she's going to need me to access him. She can't penetrate the wards."

"Is he the only way, or is she just telling you that?"

"Well, my magic's not giving me a hard no."

"Is it giving you a hard yes?"

The truth was, my magic was still in introspective mode.

"Maybe not, but she warned me about the death thing stalking me."

"Sure she's not behind that? Maybe as a way to rush your decision?"

Bree-yark was making a lot of good points, dammit. "All right, look. Before I agree to anything, I'll consult with someone else."

"Fine," he grunted. "But I'm keeping an eye on this."

I walked outside and found Caroline in the front yard. She had placed a crescent gem on a small mound of earth. The white gem with glinting flakes looked a little like mica, but if it was indeed a lunar door, it wielded the power of an ancient fae god. I looked from the gem to the tops of the trees, where an enormous Faerie moon glowed silver-white.

"The time is nearing," she said.

I stepped toward her. "I've come to a decision. I'll return with you to our world, but I need to consult with someone before we go any further with this."

"Whom?"

"Detective Vega. My fiancée."

I hadn't proposed to her yet, but that title resonated more strongly than *girlfriend*.

"Congratulations, and very well." Something flashed across Caroline's glamoured visage, but it was too fast for me to interpret. "I'll ask something in return, then."

"What's that?"

"That you leave behind the stone my husband gave you."

Damn, she sensed it. I reached into my pocket and palmed the calling stone, my insurance. If Caroline wasn't herself, I could be chucking my one solid line of aid. Bree-yark was clearly thinking the same, because when I glanced over, he shook his head. I turned the stone over in my fingers several times.

"The kingdom is using it to track you," Caroline said. "They'll know you've returned to your world and that you had help. They'll connect the dots back to me. I admit, it's for my safety as much as yours."

Was the stone acting like a GPS device, sending the kingdom my whereabouts? With my magic mute on the question, I went with my gut again. I pulled the translucent stone from my pocket and tossed it aside.

Bree-yark grumbled, but having made my decision, I felt better.

Caroline tilted her face back. I followed her gaze to the

moon. It orbited faster in Faerie than on Earth and had nearly cleared the trees. Off toward the lake, I picked up the gleeful singing of sprites, but Caroline must have cast a protection, because their song had no ill effect. As the shadows of treetops withdrew from the yard and more moonlight moved in, the crescent gem began to glimmer.

"The portal will open here," Caroline said, gesturing to the concave side of the gem.

Foot by foot, the moon's radiance overtook the yard. When it reached the mound, the gem seemed to absorb the glow until it was emitting the same light as the moon itself, only more brightly.

"There," Caroline said.

Indeed, a shadow was opening in the mound on the concave side of the gem.

"You may enter now," she said. "I'll need to go last to recover the lunar door."

"If you're playing some kind of game, lady..." Bree-yark grumbled.

"I assure you, I'll be right behind you."

The goblin gave me a doubtful look, but I nodded for him to go ahead. He stepped into the shadow with Dropsy and disappeared. Before following him, I peered back at Caroline. She'd restored her own visage just enough that her blue-green eyes glimmered back at me. Maybe it was an effect of the moonlight, but there was something in the look that recalled the late night she'd come to my apartment.

I dropped my gaze to the portal before my feet.

Hope you know what the hell you're doing, Croft.

Then I entered too.

16

A cold, splintering rain stung my hands and face as I staggered for balance across hard pavement. The enchanted moonlit yard was gone. In its place swirled brick walls and an odor of decomposing garbage.

"Whoa, there," Bree-yark said, grabbing my arm in one of his large hands.

I splashed through a puddle before coming to a stop, but it took another moment for the vertigo to wind down. I'd gone through four portals that day, five if I counted Gretchen dropping us behind the Met, and my brain and stomach were telling me that was at least four too many. This time we'd ended up in a narrow alleyway at night, a chain-link fence at one end and a dimly lit street at the other.

"Any idea where we are?" Bree-yark asked, water dripping from his jutting brow.

I swallowed my nausea and tuned into my wizard's senses. "Judging by the ley energy, somewhere in the upper half of the city."

"Yeah, and judging by the smell, not the ritzy part."

Dropsy rotated in Bree-yark's grip as though trying to get her own bearings. Fog plumed from her glass face. I peered up to see if I could spot any familiar landmarks, but the buildings on either side were too tall. The arrangements of their windows suggested apartments. A low cloud ceiling drifted past our wedge of sky, the moon glowing dimly beyond. Compared to Faerie's version, it looked sad and puny.

"Damn," I muttered.

"What?" Bree-yark asked.

"I told Vega not to worry about me until seven tonight, and it's probably past that."

The lunar door must have sent us through time as well as space to line up with the moon's position here. When I pushed back my sleeve and found a naked wrist, I remembered I'd left my watch in Bree-yark's vehicle, along with my cellphone.

"So where's Goldilocks?" Bree-yark asked.

"If she said she's coming, she's coming," I replied testily.

"Hey, I'm not trying to start anything. I've just had enough dealings with the fae in my hundred-odd years to be, you know, thoroughly distrustful of them. Then you throw in a demon's involvement—"

"Yeah, I get it."

I stepped away from him and tuned into my wizard's senses again. A pink orb swam into view. *Fae nexus*, I thought. Much like the wards my Order maintained throughout the city, the orb was one of several focal points of fae power. Glamoured, it was so transparent as to be nearly invisible. But it was clearly active.

I returned to Bree-yark bearing a steaming neutralizing potion. "There's a fae ward here," I said. "Caroline probably needed it as a focus for the portal, but it could be chatting with its neighbors."

"Told you I didn't like this," he grumbled as he tilted the tube to his pursed lips.

I was down to the dregs of my own potion when I caught

movement near the mouth of the alley. Four figures were separating from a pile of garbage. I wheeled toward them, a shield crackling to life around us. Spiking another of my empty tubes against the pavement, Bree-yark fixed Dropsy to his belt and readied his bow.

The figures' shambling approach had me thinking zombies, my mind quickly attaching them to Caroline's warning about my hunter being from the realm of the dead. But as the figures entered an amber cone of streetlight, I could see wool hats, newspaper-stuffed coats, and dragging pant cuffs.

"Bums?" I asked.

"Glamoured fae," Bree-yark answered.

Crap, he was right. A very thin, very faint sliver of magic glimmered around them. And the four were spreading out, blocking our escape. I glanced back. Beyond the chain-link fence two more glamoured fae were approaching. I peered up, weighing the odds of gaining a rooftop with a force invocation, but the buildings were too damned high. The group of four were about fifty yards from us and closing.

"Must've been staking out the nexus points," I muttered, palming the cold iron amulet in my pocket.

"Yeah, either that or your friend set us up."

"Listen, there are two behind us," I said, ignoring his remark. "Can you take leftie?"

We needed to move this fight from what felt like a claustrophobic shooting range to somewhere with better cover. And the alley beyond the fence opened out in a series of angles in the buildings' brick sides.

Bree-yark nocked an iron-tipped arrow. "Just give the word."

Bolts of silver light slammed into my shield as the four approaching fae unleashed an attack. Our protection wavered and shed sparks, but courtesy of the neutralizing magic, it held.

"Now!" I said.

Bree-yark and I spun toward the other end of the alley, the goblin's arrow already whistling from his bow. It threaded a diamond in the chain-link fence, and thudded into the shoulder of his target. The fae fell with a cry. Aiming my amulet to the right, I shouted, *"Attivare!"* A column of blue light shot from the charm and pummeled the second fae. He reeled backwards and went down with a hard splash.

I took off toward the fence, Bree-yark's bare feet slapping at my heels.

More blasts nailed my shield from behind. I incanted to reinforce it, but the potion fortifying me against fae enchantments was nearly exhausted. Shaping a force from my reserves, I aimed my cane at the approaching fence. The booming release flattened it in eruptions of metal links and concrete.

Bree-yark and I trampled over the fence and between the two fallen fae. The glamours that had made them appear common vagrants were dissolving now, revealing the elvish blue-skinned beings they were. Henchmen from Angelus's kingdom? The ease with which they'd gone down pegged them as lower-level, but there were still four at our backs, and my shield was starting to glimmer out.

With a muttered invocation, I took the hardened air and spanned it across the alley behind us. I then shoved Bree-yark toward a recess in the building to our right, while I stumbled toward the one opposite his.

"Use the light as a blind!" I shouted.

"What light?" Bree-yark barked back.

The fae's next assault took down the shield in a brilliant curtain of sparks.

"Gotcha," he said.

Nocking another arrow, he let it fly. The iron-tipped projectile punched through the light show and into the side of a disoriented fae, dropping him. Bree-yark let out a triumphant bark. "Want some more?" he called to the others.

I felled another fae with an amulet blast. But as my light blind glimmered out, the two remaining fae sighted on us. I ducked back an instant before a bolt nailed the corner of my building, blasting me with brick dust. Bree-yark poked his head out, then withdrew with a grunt as his own corner was hit.

We need another distraction.

I was wrist deep in a pocket of lightning grenades when the air warmed, and faint streams of gold and turquoise flowed past. When I noticed the fae had stopped firing, I peeked out cautiously. The lights were swimming around their heads. As the fae swooned and collapsed, the mesmerizing lights coalesced into the shape of a flowing hooded figure.

"It's safe," Caroline called to us, hardening into form.

Bree-yark looked over at me. Even across the alley, I could see the doubt in his eyes.

Raising a hand to tell him it was all right, I stepped from my cover. "Why the hold up?"

Glamoured in her male guise, Caroline strode toward us. "I was partway through the lunar door when I recognized the ambush. I backed out in time to escape detection and returned when their focus was elsewhere."

I gave a dry laugh. "A little warning would've been nice."

"Yeah, and you sure took your sweet time getting back here," Bree-yark added.

"A lunar door holds the consciousness of its creator god," she said. "Every passage requires a negotiation. I arrived as soon as I could."

Bree-yark gave a skeptical grunt, but her claim lined up with what I'd read about lunar doors. She peered at the downed fae, then over at the hovering nexus. "The kingdom is covering all transport points," she said. "Even potential ones. They'll soon discover they lost their sentry. We must go straight to Arnaud."

"We had a deal," I said. "Vega first."

Caroline trained her glamoured eyes on mine. "The kingdom suspects I'm in Faerie. Once they know I'm here, no amount of fae magic will hide me. If we're to enter the time catch, it must be now."

"Not before I talk to my fiancée."

"Everson, there isn't time." Her plea sounded more human now than fae. "Please."

I glanced over at Bree-yark, who had come up beside me, his face set in a scowl.

I was beginning to think we'd hit an impasse when something occurred to me. "What if I can keep you safe while I talk to her?" I asked.

The skin between Caroline's brows furrowed again. "How?"

———

WE CAUGHT A TAXI FROM WHAT TURNED OUT TO BE A neighborhood north of Harlem. Caroline enchanted the driver so he wouldn't see anything that would stand out in his mind, least of all a goblin holding a lantern that couldn't sit still. The enchantment also gave Caroline and me the opportunity to discuss our plans openly.

When we reached 1 Police Plaza, I arranged passes for Caroline and Bree-yark and had the guard alert the Basement we were on our way. As we stepped off the elevator, I greeted the members of the Sup Squad. Armed and armored with Centurion's monster-slaying tech, they looked formidable.

"How's he doing?" I asked, referring to Arnaud.

"Doing?" one answered brusquely. "He's just sitting there."

Another gave me a look that suggested having six of them on

the prisoner was a waste of personnel. The exchange reminded me how, underneath their impressive gear, the members of the Sup Squad were still very human. I thanked them anyway and led Caroline and Bree-yark into the holding area.

"Here it is," I said to Caroline, opening an arm toward the cell beside Arnaud's.

The day before it had held a newly minted vampire, released when the Sup Squad gunned down his master, restoring the young man's humanity. The cell featured some of my most powerful wards. But more important in Caroline's case were the dislocation sigils that would hide her from the rest of Faedom.

She looked them over now and nodded. "Yes, this will do."

"I'll power down the holding wards, but with the way everything is configured, other wards will have to stay up."

"I understand."

Caroline waited for me to perform the incantations before stepping inside. She took a seat on the bench against the back wall, the wards dissolving her glamour. Her hair and eyes lightened inside her hood, taking on the colors I knew.

I left the door open—there was no need to lock her inside. Still, she was putting a lot of trust in me. Maybe it was in the hopes I would reciprocate.

"She's not being held," I reminded the two officers at the desk. "This is just temporary."

One nodded her understanding, but the male officer became distracted by Bree-yark. After making a circuit of the holding area, the goblin had hopped onto a chair and was massaging his right foot. Dropsy, whom he'd set beside him, hopped around the chair, training her light this way and that.

"Oh, they're with me," I said.

"Apparently so," the male officer grunted.

"Hey, would you mind calling Detective Vega?" I asked.

I was not looking forward to our talk. Anything that involved keeping Arnaud alive was going to be thorny, but taking him with us into the time catch? I could already see the blowtorches in Vega's eyes. But before either officer could lift a phone, footsteps entered the holding area.

"You don't need to call her," she said. "I'm right here."

17

"I came this close to phoning your emergency contacts," Vega said.

"Yeah, sorry about that. The portal we took back from Faerie shuttled us forward in time. Sort of a long story."

"I'm just glad you're back. Saw you on the monitor coming in."

As I crossed the holding area to meet her, the skin across my girlfriend's brow looked as taut as a drum. I felt horrible for worrying her, and here I was, about to hit her with more worry. But any inclination I had to back off was met by Mae Johnson's stern admonition: *You need to figure it out together.*

I wrapped Vega in my arms and gave her a full-bodied hug. She reciprocated with a powerful embrace of her own. "I see you're with Bree-yark and not the Upholders," she said. "Was the time catch a bust?"

"Yes and no," I sighed as we separated.

"All right, I recognize those bad-news eyes." She circled her hand for me to spill it.

"The fae are compromised. Probably by Malphas. When we got to Crusspatch's place, he was dead. Murdered. No doubt to deny my passage back to the time catch. Malphas must need more time for whatever he's doing in there."

"So what does that leave? Anything?"

"Well..." I shifted my gaze over to the cells.

Her eyes followed before cutting sharply back to mine. "*Arnaud?*"

"He has a direct line to the time catch that we can access."

"So you'll be depending on that scumbag to get you there?"

"And back," I added.

"No. He's not leaving that cell unless it's in a dustpan."

"I've tried everything else," I said. "Claudius, Gretchen, the fae. It stinks to high hell, but this is what's left."

Gripping her arms across her body, Vega looked away and exhaled hard through her nose. "How long have you known?"

"I'm sorry?"

"How long have you known he offered a way back?"

She hadn't taken the Arnaud news well, and now she suspected I'd withheld info. Which, of course, I had.

When her eyes returned to mine, they were hard as obsidian. Would she consider my admission endangering Tony? Our unborn child? Once more Mae's frowning face appeared in my thoughts, nodding for me to go on and tell her. I opened my mouth. But before I could get the first word out, someone else spoke.

"I told him."

I turned to find Caroline walking toward us. The hood of her cloak was down, and though her golden hair and cyan eyes were less radiant than they'd been in Faerie, they still suggested the supernatural.

"And you are...?" Vega asked.

"Caroline Reid," she said, a hand appearing from her cloak as she arrived in front of us.

When Vega took it stiffly, I realized this was the first time the two most significant women in my adult life had met. And yet they couldn't have been more different—an academic turned fae royalty and a child of the projects turned NYPD detective. Surreal didn't come close to describing it.

I also noticed Caroline had used her maiden name.

"I think I remember you," Vega said. "Reported missing a couple years ago?"

I looked between them in confusion, even more so when Caroline replied, "Yes."

Holy crap, that's right. The night Caroline had gone to Faerie with Angelus, and subsequently married him, Vega and I had been following a trail of Arnaud leads to recover her son. Throughout the night, I'd taken intermittent stabs at locating Caroline. At one point I'd even had Vega check to see if anyone had filed a missing person's report on her. Though I'd never spelled out our relationship to her that night—which was at least a year before Vega and I got personal—she would have seen my anguish. She would have guessed that Caroline and I were close, if not involved.

Vega gave me a look now that was hard to read.

"We found her in Faerie," I hurried to explain. "Or rather, she found us."

"I have interests in the time catch too," Caroline said. "And Everson's right. Arnaud is our last recourse."

"What does Arnaud get in exchange?" Vega asked.

"This." I made a zero with my thumb and first two fingers. "The line to the time catch is embedded in his demonic makeup. We don't need his consent to access it. We just need him to be with us."

"To get there and back?" she said dryly. "And how do you plan to manage that?"

"Portable wards," I said. "They'll keep him cut off from the demonic realm."

"And if he escapes?"

"He won't," Caroline said. "He'll be under our power."

One of Vega's eyebrows went up. "Our?"

"The demon trap will be reinforced with fae enchantments," I said. "Caroline here is fae," I added awkwardly.

Vega's lips pursed into a tight smile. "Everson, honey. Can I talk to you?"

I nodded at Caroline to tell her she could return to the cell. I wondered now why she'd come out in the first place. To help? She may have sensed the tension between Vega and me, prompting the intervention. Though now that I thought about it, she'd more likely acted out of self-interest. She wanted to speed things along.

Vega moved off a couple steps, then turned to face me.

"I thought you said the fae had been compromised," she whispered.

"Yeah, someone high up in fae royalty. But when Caroline saw it happening, she left the kingdom, went into hiding."

"And you know this how? Because she told you?"

"Because what she told me lines up with what I've observed."

"And now she's telling you the only way to get into this time catch is to free Arnaud."

"He won't be free. He—"

"Yeah, I know. He'll be in portable wards with fae enchantments for 'reinforcement.'" She air-quoted the word. "*Her* fae enchantments. How do you know they won't be undermining your magic?"

She was sounding more and more like Bree-yark.

"You're going to hate this answer," I said, "but I just know."

"Everson, she's *fae*. You've never brought them up without using your next breath to list all the reasons why they can't be trusted."

When I caught Bree-yark nodding his head, I moved our conversation farther away.

"Look, you're right to be suspicious," I said. "Most fae are exactly how I've described them. But Caroline's human side tempers that. We're also ... old friends. She was the one working behind the scenes to get the Upholders and me into the time catch."

"Should I be worried you never mentioned that?"

"Oh c'mon, of course not. I just didn't think the name meant anything to you."

She studied my eyes for a moment. "Is there anything else you want to tell me?"

"About Caroline?"

"About anything."

Geez, where to begin? I was riffling through all that had happened that day—from my talk with Arnaud, to my vision of Malphas, to the pixies' warning, to my encounters with Angelus and then Caroline—when I blurted out, "I think there's another reason we're supposed to take Arnaud into the time catch."

"Another awful one?"

But her cynical remark barely registered. My words had arrived on the crest of an epiphany, and now the rest of it was crashing through me. I began pacing to compose my thoughts. "In that dream, Arianna told me the key to releasing her and the other members of the Order was to find Arnaud, right?"

"Mm-hmm," Vega said impatiently.

"While waiting for some kind of follow-up message, I've been trying to get back to the time catch to find the Upholders. When I went to Gretchen for that help this morning, I told her Faerie was threatened. But when that failed to move her, I claimed the key to defeating Malphas and freeing the Order was in the time catch. I was talking completely out of my backside..."

Vega gave me a deadpan look that said, *Really?*

"But," I thrust up a finger, "my magic agreed. It's been in this weird, almost meditative state all day. But when I said that, it suddenly snapped to and nodded. I think *that's* what Arianna meant when she told me to find Arnaud. Because she knew I'd need him to return to the time catch, where I can also help the Order."

Vega's brow furrowed. "But didn't the dream happen before you even went into the time catch the first time?"

"It did, but our collective magic isn't bound by limited constructs of time and space. None of us can access the extent of our magic's intelligence, but Arianna comes closest. She was relaying what it was telling her."

"I still have a lot to learn about your world," Vega muttered.

"So if my read on this is right, we have a shot at the Upholders, the Order, *and* stopping Malphas."

"You've got that manic light going in your eyes again."

"Which should tell you how strongly I feel about this." Because the more I considered it, the more sense it made. Increasingly, the thought of using Arnaud to access the time catch felt less like a problem and more like a grand and elegant solution. I just hoped Vega would see it the same way.

She sighed. "Fine."

I took her hands and squeezed. "Thank you."

"But I do have a condition," she said.

"What's that?"

"Regardless of whether or not you're right, the first thing you're going to do when you get back is destroy Arnaud. No discussion. No debate. I want his ass smoked. He can't be in our world anymore." For the first time, a kind of vulnerability crept into her eyes. She was asking for her son and our daughter.

I squeezed her hands again and nodded. "Done."

"So who's going with you besides Caroline?"

"That would be me," Bree-yark said, jumping up from his

chair and hustling over. Dropsy hopped to catch up. "Oh, and of course this little girl. She's good luck." When he stopped to lift her, she kicked excitedly.

"A pet lantern?" Vega asked.

"She's enchanted," I said. "We found her at Gretchen's."

Vega nodded as if that explained everything. "Have you considered support? I could arrange a unit to go with you." She cocked her head toward the members of the Sup Squad. "Help you keep an eye on Arnaud."

"Their weapons and tech can't make the journey. And without that stuff, they'd be more liability than asset." I thought again of how human they were beneath their cutting-edge equipment.

"I'll be all the support he needs," Bree-yark told Vega with a hint of insult.

"She's looking out for all of us," I said. "Anyway, you've helped enough. You don't—"

He thrust a palm at me, cutting me off. "Can it, Everson. You're not gonna shake this runt. I admit, I don't get everything that's happening here, but if it affects Faerie, it affects goblin-kind too. Besides, I started this thing with you, I'm gonna see it through to the flaming end. Debate over."

Vega smirked. "How can you argue with that?"

"I'm not even going to try," I said.

Bree-yark craned his thick neck around. "Is there a bath-room down here? I think the raisin bran just caught up with me."

"That way," Vega told him.

As Bree-yark hurried off, I said, "If nothing else, he'll be good company. And when we locate the Upholders, we'll have immediate reinforcements. Plus, there's the time catch version of my grandfather. If we need him, I know where to find him. We're going to have all the support we can handle."

"Still, it's Arnaud," Vega said. "He escaped Hell."

"Which means I'll be more careful with him than ever."

Vega squinted toward his cell. Though we could only see a sliver of window from our angle, the demon-vampire hadn't approached it. He remained in the back, waiting. Taking him into the time catch was the right call—I still believed that—but a part of me hadn't stopped recoiling at the idea.

"So, what now?" Vega asked.

"We build our portable trap," I said.

And make it damned strong.

18

I slick-gripped the door handle and pulled until only the oscillations in the charged air separated me from the demon-vampire.

"Mr. Croft," Arnaud said from the back of the cell. "How nice to see you."

The grin below his predatory stare caught slightly as I stepped through the wards. He hadn't expected me to enter. Up close, I could see the sunken skin around his eyes better. Less than twenty-four hours after being cut off from the infernal realm, and he was starting to waste away. The demon-vampire kept his composure, though, back erect, thin fingers laced around his folded knee.

"I trust your outing was fruitful?" he asked.

"After giving the matter careful consideration," I recited stiffly. "I've decided to enlist you in accessing the time catch."

His eyes snapped past me to the two members of the Sup Squad positioned outside the door, weapons aimed. They were wearing noise cancellers inside their helmets in the event he tried to talk to them. His grin steepening, he returned his attention to me.

"Of course you have," he purred. "Just as I foretold it."

"Good. Then I'm going to need you to stand and face that wall."

Arnaud chuckled. "You seem to be missing a key point, Mr. Croft. I am the sole proprietor of an asset you urgently need. More so now with the time you've squandered. Am I to surrender something so valuable without talk of recompense? Oh, no. That's not how this is to go at all. Indeed, I have some terms."

"Stand and face the wall," I repeated.

Anger flashed in his eyes, and he released his knee. "I will not be talked to like a—"

"*Balaur!*" I shouted.

The power I'd been withholding detonated from Grandpa's ring and drove Arnaud's flailing body into the rear wall. The cell's ward repulsed him, throwing him against the side wall, and then the wall opposite. Each collision wrung a scream from his scorched body. At last, he slumped at my feet, smoke drifting from his tangled robe.

I'd hoped the son of a bitch wouldn't cooperate.

Even so, I had held back. We needed him alive.

Dropping a knee onto his low back, I pulled a set of manacles from the rear of my pants. Arnaud moaned as I secured his wrists and then clamped a connecting manacle around his neck, covering the brand of his master. A warded muzzle went over his mouth, and I cinched it as tightly as I could.

I never wanted to hear that fucking voice again.

The restraint system was one of several implements I'd custom-made for the NYPD for use on supernaturals. With a few modifications it would be suitable for Arnaud.

From a pocket, I produced a pen with a tungsten carbide tip and began scratching out sigils in the restraint's alloy metal while uttering charged words in a long-dead language. The essential energies of the cell funneled through me and into Arnaud's new confinement. When I finished, I tested each sigil, then hauled Arnaud to his feet.

"You want recompense?" I whispered in his ear. "How about no one gives a shit?"

I dragged him from the cell and threw him onto the polyethylene sheet I'd pulled from my cubbyhole and spread over the floor. He collapsed into the casting circle and pulled himself into a tremulous ball. I retrieved my coat and cane and walked over to where Vega and Bree-yark were watching.

Caroline's turn.

As she knelt behind him, Arnaud's gaze rolled up to her. Recognition seemed to take hold. He looked over at me, eyes staring with a kind of bloodshot desperation. I returned a smirk and a shrug.

We had cleared the basement of extra officers, and the space was so quiet now that I could hear Caroline's fae energies whispering through his restraints. Some of them kept Arnaud subdued, while others bolstered the wards and sigils I'd installed, and still others wove in new enchantments. His eyelids quivered, then closed. After another moment, I sensed Caroline exploring his memory.

"What's she doing?" Vega whispered.

"Looking for what he was up to in the time catch," I answered. "Along with anything else that might be relevant to Malphas's plan."

As Vega slid an arm around my waist, I imagined the doubts running behind her brow. *How do you know she won't be undermining your magic?* The reasons I'd given her were sound, but in the end it was an odds game. Nothing was one hundred percent. I rubbed Vega's shoulder and pulled her against me.

Caroline turned toward us. "I'm afraid the memories are scrubbed out."

By Malphas, no doubt, I thought bitterly. *Probably before I transported Arnaud here to the cell.* "So, there's nothing?"

"Just fragments of him handling the energy you described, but not how or why."

Disappointment weighed on me like chainmail. It looked like we'd have to investigate the questions ourselves. When Caroline fell silent again, I sensed her exploring the line to the time catch. Hopefully *that* was still intact. As seconds stretched into minutes, my shirt clung damply to my back.

At last, Caroline opened her eyes. "The way is ready."

Surprised by the announcement, my voice snagged for a second. "To the time catch?"

She nodded and stood. Vega patted my hip before separating and helping me back into my coat.

"Are you sure you have everything you need?" she asked.

"I have everything that's going to make the journey."

With my coat on, I slung my pack over a shoulder. Everything was lighter. Like the last time I'd made this journey, there were restrictions on what I could take. No potions, combustibles, or electronics, and only two enchanted items. My cane was essential, and I wanted Grandpa's ring as a backup for Arnaud. But I'd also pocketed Gretchen's iron amulet, putting me one over the safe limit.

I turned to Bree-yark. "Hey, would you mind carrying this for me?"

I'd agreed that he could bring Dropsy—he kept insisting she was good luck, and she *had* bailed us out in Kinloch Forest. That left space on him for another enchanted item. He nodded and opened the mouth of his pouch.

"There's room in here, if it's not too big." He grimaced when he saw me tuck the amulet inside. "Cold iron?" Though not as susceptible to the metal as Faerie's magic-wielding beings, goblins still didn't care for it. Their own iron was forged in fire, making it less effective against fae creatures, but easier to wield.

"It's just for the trip. I'll take it back once we're there."

"You think we'll encounter fae?" He closed the pouch again.

I glanced over at Caroline, who was helping Arnaud to his feet. I remembered her warning about Malphas controlling a fae. But there was also Caroline herself.

"It's more a precaution," I said, returning my gaze to Bree-yark.

At my apartment, I'd stored some of his street clothes in my interplanar cubby hole. He'd gone ahead and changed into them and was back in his bomber jacket and a pair of steel-toed boots. He'd also traded his bow for a shepherd's sling that he could stuff inside a pocket. Less conspicuous.

Vega smoothed my coat lapels. "I'm not going to tell you to be careful."

"Then I won't tell you either. The thing that's hunting me is still out there, and the fae could come looking for Caroline." I touched Grandpa's coin pendant through Vega's blouse and topped off the energy. "Carry hybrid rounds, just in case."

"I'll have the Sup Squad escort me back to my apartment later."

"Given the time differentials, I should be back before your shift ends."

Vega managed to smile. "I'll look for you, then."

I pressed my lips to the top of her head. "I won't let Arnaud out of my sight."

"Come here, stupid." She gripped my lapels and pulled me into a real kiss.

When we separated, she blinked back some moisture and nodded. "You've gotta go."

"C'mon, Everson," Bree-yark said, jerking his head as he started toward the circle.

Reluctantly, I let my hands fall from Vega's. "I love you."

"I trust you."

Not the words I'd been expecting, which made them ring more powerfully.

Caroline's long cloak shifted as she stepped back to make room in the circle. Arnaud's entranced eyes stared above his muzzle. None of us were dressed for 1776 New York, but Caroline assured me she would take care of the needed glamours. Given her power demonstrations thus far, I believed she'd deliver.

"Is everyone ready?" she asked as I squeezed into the circle beside Bree-yark.

I looked over to find Vega standing in the same place, her face firming around the emotions clashing in her eyes. I'd given her every reassurance, but we both knew the danger was through the roof. I felt my gaze wanting to drop to her stomach, but if I started dwelling on our daughter, I was going to lose it.

Instead, we gave each other a final wave.

I turned back to Caroline. "Ready."

19

W ithout warning the bottom of the casting circle dropped out, and we fell into a steep, shuddering descent. Sulfur-yellow flames flickered, then roared past the sides of our column, some resolving into the visages of claimed souls.

Definitely a demonic line, I thought sickly.

"Holy thunder!" Bree-yark cried when one especially tortured face appeared inches from his. I gripped his arm, as much to calm him as to steady myself, because our plummet was turning increasingly turbulent.

Bree-yark shouted something else, but the rattling reduced his words to garbles. Dropsy became a chaos of jumping light. But Caroline remained the image of self-possession, eyes closed, hands on Arnaud's shoulders. Cool blue lines of fae energy rippled over our column, buffering our violent passage.

She got us through the lunar door, I thought. *She'll deliver us through a demon line.*

Unless of course she was the one who had fallen under shadow…

I was thinking of the cold iron amulet in Bree-yark's

bouncing pouch when the yellow flames dispersed, and we stopped moving. Bree-yark exhaled a few choice words, while Dropsy looked from side to side dizzily.

Above Arnaud's head, Caroline opened her eyes, her luminescent gaze meeting mine before peering around. Through the lingering dust of the infernal energy, the stone walls of a room were taking shape. Bookshelves and what appeared to be a large desk stood in the shadows just beyond Dropsy's glow.

"We're here," Caroline announced.

I peered down at my shoes, black leather boots now, alarmed to find them planted in a blood circle. Arnaud had rendered an identical circle in his Manhattan penthouse only days earlier, a portal to Malphas.

"*Everyone out,*" I whispered, shuffling from the demonic symbol.

"It's not active," Caroline said. "The connection's been broken, and no energy remains."

"Oh." I took another look. "You're right."

Though the circle served as a terminus for the demonic line, Arnaud was now cut off from his master. The reverse was also true. Without that connection, Malphas's energy couldn't access the symbol to trap us or hit us with any number of infernal spells. Bree-yark, whose furrowed brow suggested he had no idea what we were talking about, followed Caroline and Arnaud from the circle.

The heat of embarrassment sank back into my cheeks. Though rushing the journey here had been necessary, there were consequences. One being that beyond basic planning, I hadn't had time to think deeply. Ever since waking up that morning, it had been go, go, go just to find a way back here.

"We're alone," Caroline said.

She'd left off her male glamour, but she'd made adjustments to her attire—all of ours, in fact. Breeches and riding boots showed below the hem of her long cloak. Meanwhile, Arnaud's robe had become the disheveled attire of a rebel prisoner, his restraints featuring iron components and thick leather straps. Bree-yark looked like a dockworker, a ratty coat over a rough linen shirt and breeches.

I expected to find myself in a similar disguise as the last time, a common man. Instead, I was looking at a red coat over a brass-buttoned shirt and starch-white breeches. A British soldier? But when I took a second look at Arnaud, it made sense. The city was under English control, and he was my prisoner.

"Is it safe to be casting?" I asked Caroline, remembering Osgood's warning from the last time about magic drawing unwanted attention.

"Malphas already knows someone used an infernal line to arrive here," she replied. "How he responds is another question."

I walked toward a pair of arched windows. Stars twinkled beyond the paned glass. A full moon came into view and then its reflection, glistening from a broad river. When I caught the edge of a fort, I nodded.

"We're near the southern tip of Manhattan," I said, still not quite believing I was back. "In 1776, Arnaud was using this as a place of business slash fortress."

I remembered how he'd tried to lure me to this very building while a smiling Zarko—who had turned out to be the present-day Arnaud—grinned at his back. In our final confrontation, the real Arnaud had destroyed his 1776 counterpart, which meant one less worry now. The blood slaves he'd employed as henchmen would have regained their mortality or died. No doubt why the building was empty.

"Place has been ransacked," Bree-yark said, returning from across the room.

He'd lit several candle stubs, and in their guttering light, I saw what he meant. The drawers of the desk were sticking out like tongues. The bookshelves were barren. And a corner safe was pried open, a mess of papers spilling onto the floor.

I turned to Caroline. "How about we take a few minutes to search what's here?"

"It could give us some insights into his activities," she said, completing my thought. "I can start on the safe if you don't mind tackling the desk."

"What can I be doing?" Bree-yark asked.

I hesitated a beat before saying, "How about watching Arnaud?"

With an authoritative grunt, Bree-yark took the demon-vampire by an arm, sat him in a corner, and stood over him, blade drawn. Enchanted and bound, Arnaud's yellow-flecked eyes stared out at nothing. Even so, I couldn't stop thinking of my promise to Vega about not letting Arnaud from my sight.

"He can't go anywhere," Caroline assured me, already crouching before the safe.

My gaze lingered on Arnaud for another moment before I approached the mahogany desk. I spent the next several minutes leafing through papers on the desktop trying to make sense of them. Most were neatly penned financial statements or letters from loan-seekers. The sprouts of Arnaud Thorne's financial empire.

The drawers had been cleaned out, but a couple of ledgers remained. I removed the thicker of the two and started working backwards from the most recent entries. They listed deposits and withdrawals in various currencies. I swapped it for the other one, which appeared to catalogue commodities purchased. Before long, a block of entries caught my eye. They were for copper-plated panels. I mouthed the dimensions. *Six feet by nine. Twelve feet by sixteen.* Big copper-plated panels.

"I may have something," Caroline said.

The sound of her voice beside me made me jump. She spread a parchment over the desktop.

"There were several maps of Manhattan, most demarcating properties," she said, "but this one is interesting." I moved the ledger so she could shift the map more fully into the light of the candle. "It shows St. Martin's."

Indeed, the professionally drawn map was centered on the site of St. Martin's Cathedral. The Hudson, which I'd just viewed out the window, was depicted as a series of ripples. But someone had used dark ink to mark the area immediately around the cathedral with vertical and horizontal lines.

"Son of a bitch," I muttered.

"What is it?" Caroline asked.

"This is how Arnaud was channeling the energy coming from the St. Martin's site."

I showed her the ledger entries for the massive plates, copper being only second to silver as a container for energy, but considerably cheaper. I used copper in many of my casting circles and for the same reasons. Hell, I was carrying a tube of the shaved stuff in my coat pocket at that moment.

Caroline looked from the entries to the lines on the map. "He could have installed them in the sides of the buildings," she said, tracing one on the corner of Broadway and Stone Street with a finger, "then covered them over."

"He was also able to turn the plates on and off. Send the energy to very specific places."

I remembered our final encounter in the alleyway and how he'd deprived me of ley energy. When he'd done the same to the time catch version of my grandfather, Arnaud had inadvertently sent a current running back through me, allowing me to snag him and deliver him to the cell at 1 Police Plaza.

"He must have been tapped into the plates," she said. "Probably through demonic sigils."

"But what was the point?" I muttered in thought.

I was so absorbed in the map I didn't notice that Caroline's and my shoulders were touching until she moved her hand and tapped the St. Martin's site. "I believe the plan was to direct the energy back to the source."

A mental flashbulb went off. With a finger, I began drawing lines from every plate back to the center of the St. Martin's site. "Arnaud was only activating the plates selectively, but activate them en masse and, bam, magnified output. The ley coming up, *plus* the ley from fractions of a second earlier."

"Boosted energy," Caroline agreed.

"But that alone doesn't create a portal for Malphas," I said. "The energy would have to be converted somehow. I don't see anything on here about that, and the site was burnt to the ground the last time I was here."

"Nothing on the other maps, either," Caroline said.

"Arnaud was trying to buy the parcel, though. Probably with plans to construct something."

"Either way," she said, "I believe we've found our answer to how to stop Malphas."

"Destroy the plates and ward the site." It didn't seem like it should have been that easy, but that would definitely deny Malphas his power source.

"That should also normalize the energy here." Caroline began folding the map to take with us. "If you've noticed, it's a little irregular."

I had noticed, but it was far from the instability Arnaud had suggested. Probably a bluff to introduce urgency. It had gotten me moving, just not in the *Let's Make a Deal* way he'd planned. I glanced over at him now with a skintight grin.

Nice try, pal.

"It will also make it safer to find your friends," Caroline added.

While she tucked the map inside her cloak, I inspected the druidic symbol on my hand that once bonded me to the rest of the Upholders. Though I pushed power into it, I still couldn't pick them up. Was that because Jordan had released me from its obligation, or because the others were no longer in the time catch?

I lowered my hand again. "The church is only a few blocks from here."

"We can take Beaver Street over to Broadway." When I looked at Caroline in surprise, she returned a cagey smile. "Scholar of urban history, remember? I know the layout of the city back to its founding."

For a moment, she looked *exactly* like my classroom neighbor and friend. It was the light in her eyes, as if she were inviting me to come back with a quip, something I would have done those few years ago. The look also suggested that our shoulders touching a minute earlier hadn't been an accident.

I quickly turned to Bree-yark. "You ready?"

"Let's go," he said, hauling Arnaud to his feet.

We descended from the turret and arrived on a floor that looked as if it had been Arnaud's living quarters. But like the office, the space was ransacked. Dropsy's light glowed over a wooden floor where dark patterns showed the former locations of rugs and furniture. Arnaud's staring eyes gave no reaction.

The ground floor, where the day-to-day operations of Arnaud's enterprise had likely been conducted, were stripped too. Probably by British soldiers appropriating materials, but I wondered why they hadn't commandeered the building itself. The main door to the outside was ajar, and I pushed it open. As we filed out, the unpaved street felt warm underfoot, as if the sun had only set an hour or two earlier.

Bree-yark grunted what I was thinking: "Pretty quiet."

"Dark too," I said. "The last time I was here, the streets had oil lanterns."

"Something's off," Caroline said, squinting slightly, "though I can't say what."

"The best kind," I muttered. "All right, let's play our parts so we don't stand out. I'll take Arnaud. Bree-yark, hang back a few paces. And Caroline, can you watch the rear?"

It was only upon asking her that I realized I was assuming leadership like I had with the Upholders—the role coming more naturally to me now—but Caroline was fae royalty. If she minded, though, she didn't show it.

I seized Arnaud's manacled wrists and assumed the role of a British soldier delivering his rebel prisoner somewhere. To avoid the fort and governor's house, I marched up New Street before cutting toward Broadway. Under Caroline's subservience enchantment, Arnaud matched my clipped pace.

Behind me, Bree-yark scanned the houses to either side, one hand holding Dropsy aloft, the other touching the hilt of his sheathed blade. Caroline, meanwhile, moved like an apparition, her hood pulled low to hide her face.

Block by block, the silence of the city persisted. Every building we passed was either shut and shuttered or else thrown wide. But in all cases they were dark. Even the stench of raw sewage, so prevalent the last time, was minimal now. The cool breeze blowing against my face smelled of salt and marsh.

What in the hell could have happened for the city to clear out? As the question moved uneasily through me, I refocused on our immediate objective—destroying the copper panels and warding the site. Then we'd search for the Upholders.

We approached the wide dirt lane of Broadway to find it dark and empty. Blackened lots and the occasional husk of a burned building stood on the side opposite us. That much hadn't changed. When Bree-yark and Caroline arrived beside me, I pointed out the St. Martin's site a couple blocks to the north. Stone slabs from the original foundation showed through a layer of earth and cinder, but that was it.

"No new construction," I said.

Caroline consulted the folded map, then raised her face. "We're a block from the copper panels on the corner of Broadway and Stone." But she seemed to hesitate, a small fold forming between her eyes.

"What is it?" I asked.

"The ley energy is too diffuse."

I shifted to my wizard's senses. I could see the energy founting from where St. Martin's had once stood, but Caroline was right. The passing currents were way too weak. I wondered if it had something to do with the plates.

Bree-yark grumbled, "I'm picking up some strange smells."

Dropsy pulsed several times as if to announce something was bothering her too.

"We should go carefully," Caroline said.

With a Word, I hardened the air around us into a shield. But with the dearth of ley energy, the manifestation was feeble. It sputtered several times before stabilizing into something semi-protective. *Has to be the plates,* I thought. *Dismantle them and the energy flow will return to normal.*

I took the lead up Broadway, eyeballing the approaching corner.

Caroline started to speak when, in a blinding burst of sparks, something crashed through my shield and landed against my chest. The impact jolted Arnaud from my grip and drove me to the ground. Blinking rapidly to clear the bright afterimage from my eyes, I made out a reptilian head with large serrated teeth.

And it was lunging toward my face.

20

I met the oncoming head with a sword swing, the flat of the blade smacking off the snout. The creature reared back, giving me my first good look at it. Reptilian, yes—but its body was sheathed in gray feathers. It stalked around on a pair of legs that ended in lethal talons, head cocked to one side to peer down at me.

The hell is this thing?

From deep in its throat, a series of bass sounds emerged, like air pumping from a thick sac. And it did *not* sound friendly. Restoring my shield, I struggled into a backwards scoot. The creature pursued and was met by a wave of enchanted light. Caroline moved up beside me as the creature swooned, then thudded to the ground.

"Are you okay?" she asked.

I nodded, even though my sternum felt bruised and I was sucking wind. Taking her offered hand, I gained my feet and peered down at the feathered creature. It was at least eight feet from head to tail, with that reptilian jaw of carnivorous teeth. But its upper appendages appeared more wings than arms. Whatever it was, it didn't resemble any supernatural creature I'd ever seen or read about.

When Bree-yark joined us, I noticed with relief that he was holding onto Arnaud.

"Someone wanna tell me what a dinosaur is doing in 1776 New York?" he asked.

"Dinosaur?" I echoed.

Thoughtful ridges formed along Bree-yark's brow as he circled the creature. "Raptor, from the looks of it. Don't let the feathers fool you. Pretty common in the late Cretaceous period." When he caught Caroline's and my quizzical looks, he said, "Oh, yeah, learned all about dinosaurs on the Science Channel."

I trusted him, remembering how much cable TV he watched when he stayed at Gretchen's. But was this why the city had cleared out? An infestation of predatory dinosaurs? Though it didn't make a lick of sense, I peered around anyway to make sure no more of the feathered raptors were approaching.

"Native to North America," Bree-yark added.

"Yeah, but not two hundred fifty years ago," I countered, force returning to my voice.

"More like a hundred million. And that's what I smelled all right." Bree-yark's nostrils flared. "Prehistoric funk."

Before we could begin to dissect the meaning, Broadway disappeared. In the place of a building-lined street, a forest rose around us, bright moonlight filtering through a thick canopy. Sword and staff drawn, I jerked around. Caroline was beside me, fae energy glimmering from her hands.

A grunt sounded about ten feet in front of us. A large frond fell away, revealing Bree-yark, who'd hacked it down with his blade. He still had a hold of Arnaud. Dropsy rotated side to side from the goblin's belt, her light illuminating flying insects and an understory of ferns too giant to seem real.

Beyond the ferns, yellow eyes glinted.

"Heads-up!" I called as the rest of the raptor pack broke from their hiding and crashed through the brush. Thrusting my sword at the lead one, I shouted a force invocation. The whoosh through my mental prism was more air than ley energy, the emerging force barely enough to knock the raptor off balance and ruffle its feathers.

I need to scare them, I thought. *Give them something they've never seen before.*

Taking the shield I'd cast between us, I flattened it and rammed it toward them. The collision of raptors and wall created a predictable curtain of sparks. The raptors retreated from the light show in a chorus of bass sounds. But they didn't flee, the prospect of warm-blooded prey too enticing, apparently. Caroline followed up with a beautiful aurora borealis that swam around the raptors, dazing them.

"This way," she called.

I turned in time to see her cloak flutter behind a tree. But Bree-yark was stalking toward the enchanted raptors as if he meant to send them all back into extinction. Grabbing the scruff of his coat with one hand and Arnaud's arm with the other, I pulled them after me, high-stepping through the undergrowth.

We rounded the same tree as Caroline...

...and stumbled back onto Broadway. I didn't stop to look back. I broke into a full run, feet pounding the dirt lane for all they were worth. Bree-yark followed at my heels. We caught up to Caroline at the intersection with Garden, where she was waiting. I braced an arm against the cornice and peered back now, terrified of what I would see. But there were no trees or raptors, not even the one we'd put down. Just the empty thoroughfare, one side ruined by the Great Fire of 1776.

Bree-yark swung his stocky frame toward Caroline and bared his teeth.

"All right, you blasted fae," he growled. "What're you playing at?"

"It's not her," I said. "There's a time bleed."

"A time what?" he barked, his anger seeming to shift to me now.

"Another time catch is seeping into this one somehow," I said.

He jabbed his blade in the direction we'd just come from. "Then why can't I see it?" he demanded.

"Because this is the view from this time period," Caroline explained. "Just as our view from the prehistoric period was all forest. Though the two share a boundary, you can't see one from the other."

I moved my gaze along the blackened plots again until I arrived at St. Martin's. A shaky understanding sunk in. "So the church site isn't actually here," I said. "The time bleed displaced it."

"Which explains why the energy here is so weak," Caroline agreed.

I tuned into my wizard's senses again. With an intense focus that made my head throb, I could just make out a membrane about a half block up Broadway. I'd been standing on the boundary when the first raptor attacked.

"How does that even happen?" Bree-yark asked.

"The time catches move in something like orbits," Caroline said. "Arnaud distorting the energies and then abandoning them may have displaced the 1776 orbit, pushing it into another time catch."

"But instead of an apocalyptic collision," I said, "they became stuck together, creating the bleed." Though I had no experience with such things, I couldn't imagine that was a stable arrangement. I looked from Caroline to the demon-vampire. Maybe Arnaud hadn't been bluffing after all.

Bree-yark peered up and down the empty streets. "So everyone became dinosaur chow?"

"Or fled," Caroline offered. "As visitors, we don't feel the boundaries. For the inhabitants, though, a repulsive force keeps them in their respective periods. Even so, bleeds can occur along the boundaries."

I rubbed my bruised chest. "Yeah, no kidding."

"And the boundary is in flux," she continued. "After so many contacts with creatures of the prehistoric age, the surviving inhabitants of 1776 New York may have decided to relocate far from the boundary."

"Then it's just a matter of us avoiding the boundary, right?" Bree-yark said. "Following it around to wherever the real church site is?" He was shifting his weight like he was anxious to get going. Frankly, so was I. The sooner we got there and completed the tasks, the sooner we could recover the Upholders and go home.

"Caroline?" I prompted.

She was peering up Broadway at the church site—or where the church site *appeared* to be. She angled her face westward, as if following the boundary line through the burn zone and the former encampment of British soldiers, their field of white tents gone now. At the Hudson River, I lost sight of the line.

"I see no other way," she said.

Taking lead again, I headed east. The boundary ran at an angle to the northeast, which meant backtracking down Broadway and cutting over to Nassau.

After a few blocks, the line pushed us east again, this time to William Street. Still reeling from the knowledge I'd battled an actual dinosaur, and having no interest in a rematch, I kept a healthy distance between us and the line. At the next street, I paused to gauge whether we needed to detour another block, which would take us still further from St. Martin's.

"I don't quite get how this works," Bree-yark said, arriving beside me. "The boundary runs across the street up there, right? But we can still see past it?"

"Yes and no," I answered distractedly. "That's how the street would look if it *were* there."

"And someone on the other side looking this way? Same thing?"

"Same thing. The time catch plays on a loop, remember. It knows what it's supposed to look like at every point in its trapped time and from every perspective. Right now, it's filling in all that missing information."

As I set off east again, Bree-yark muttered behind me, "And I thought the Fae Wilds were screwy."

At the next block, I stopped and swore.

"What is it?" Caroline asked, coming up now.

I pointed north and drew my finger back and forth across the street. "The boundary line cuts straight across here, separating us from the rest of Manhattan." And that included my grandfather's farm, which was two miles north on Bowery Lane. Blowing out my breath, I looked toward the East River. Beyond Queen Street, I could make out its wharves, and beyond them, moonlight glinting off the water itself.

"What about going straight through the prehistoric period?" Bree-yark asked. "We'd come out the other side eventually, right?"

"*Eventually* being the kicker," I said. "It could be a hundred feet or a hundred miles."

"And we might emerge into another part of 1776 New York," Caroline added. "These realms aren't uniformly shaped. They twist and contort."

"Any boats around here?" Bree-yark asked.

"Probably at the harbor." His question got me thinking. "Hey, since we're already on this side of Manhattan, would you mind if we took a row out to Governor's Island? That's where I left the

Upholders. Could be a clue as to what happened, where they went." I was thinking reveal spell, but they could even have left a message. "If not, we can access Brooklyn and see how far the boundary extends over Long Island."

With both of their votes in favor, I led the way down King Street.

And found myself in the middle of a stampede.

21

Bodies rammed into me, sending me one way and then just as suddenly the other. Through a harsh whiteness—daylight, I realized—shouting faces jostled past my dazzled vision. The road had gone from packed dirt to mud-slick cobblestone, and I jerked my arms around like someone ice-skating for the first time.

The next hard collision sent me crashing into a pair of empty barrels along the roadside. A family of speckled pigs scattered as I landed ass-down in what I hoped was mud, my back slamming against a plank wall. My vision went gauzy, as much from the impact as the sudden displacement.

Pulling my cane against my chest, I stared at the human stampede.

They bore a crude look that matched the ungodly stench rising from the street. There were men in dirty hats and coats, women in patched skirts, and children with worn-through pant knees and shoddy shoes—when they had anything on their feet at all. But their common direction suggested purpose. Ahead of them, above a mad collection of leaning buildings, stood a dark column of smoke.

Usually people run away from a fire, I thought blearily.

The harsh clanging of bells made me turn. Men in red flannel coats and floppy hats were running a pump wagon up the street. They cleaved the crowd, which was beginning to tail off now, and disappeared around a corner.

Fire brigade?

"Are you all right?"

A pretty woman with blond hair approached. She wore a homely blue dress with large buttons down the front and a bow at the waist. Her arm was hooked inside a thin man's, a brown scarf wrapping the lower half of his face. A kid with a surly expression followed. I assumed the family had seen me go down before I realized I was looking at Caroline, Arnaud, and Bree-yark, all three glamoured to the gills.

"Fine," I said, coughing out a relieved laugh. Using a toppled barrel, I pulled myself upright. My British army uniform had become plain brown trousers and a patched homespun coat. "How about you guys?"

"When you vanished, we followed," Caroline said.

"Yeah, don't do that again," Bree-yark added in a scolding voice.

By the time I'd shaken the gunk off my pants, the stampede had dwindled to stragglers, the shouting and clanging rolling out like a spent wave. I looked around at a small dirt park bordered by cobblestone roads and a crowd of rickety wooden buildings. We'd clearly crossed into another time catch.

"I didn't even see the boundary," I said.

"That's because it was under you," Caroline said. "A seam in the road."

As I looked down at my mud-spattered boots, I remembered a brief, helpless sensation of falling.

"Someone wanna tell me where this is?" Bree-yark asked.

Before I could answer—because I had an idea—Caroline

said, "New York's Five Points neighborhood, around 1860. At the time it was a poor quarters of low-skilled laborers and immigrants, mostly Irish."

I was going to ballpark mid-1800s and the Bowery. It paid having an expert on the team.

Caroline peered toward the smoke now. "The crowd's in a race to reach the building before the fire brigade gets there or it burns to the ground."

"Why?" Bree-yark asked.

"To claim whatever's inside."

The goblin grunted as if that sounded fair enough.

"It appears we're sticking to another time catch," Caroline said to me.

I nodded, wondering just how many time catches ours had collided into. That couldn't be doing anything good for the stability factor, but at the moment I was more concerned with getting back to 1776.

Venturing from the spilled barrels, I shifted to my wizard's senses. I'd only gone a few steps upon arriving here, so the boundary had to be close. But where was the damned thing? I peered up and down the street, then tilted my head back, expecting to find the seam between me and the washed-out sky.

"I'm not seeing a boundary," I said, trying not to sound as panicked as I felt.

"No, I don't sense one here either," Caroline said. "But we're in a different part of the city than where we entered. This would have been country in 1776. In fact, there was a large pond right over there."

I remembered circling the pond on the way to my grandfather's farm.

"You're familiar with Columbus Park?" Caroline asked.

Two years earlier, I'd projected from my prison in Arnaud's vault to a clay golem I'd animated and that remained under my control. I arranged to meet Caroline at a pavilion at the north end of Columbus Park. There, she restored my magic and glamoured my thoughts for my final showdown with Arnaud, where I cast him to the Below. Shortly after, Caroline disappeared into Faerie, never even having said goodbye. Now her eyes looked as if they hoped to ignite some spark of nostalgia between us.

"Yeah," I said, feeling the same discomfort from earlier. "I know it."

"Well, this is the park's humble beginnings." She pointed to a plot in the center of the converging streets where the pigs I'd scattered were now rooting in the mud. Squalid kids played at the other end, while women pulled gray linen from a line near a public water pump. Thanks to Caroline's glamours, none of them paid us any attention. "This eventually becomes the park's southern end and the start of Chinatown, which puts us about a half-mile north of where we left 1776."

"But if we're near a boundary," Bree-yark grunted, "what's with all the people?"

That was a great point. I peered toward the smoke, where the distant clamoring continued to build. The sheer size of the crowd suggested people here weren't having the same boundary problems as the 1776 New Yorkers.

"They may not be dealing with boundaries," Caroline said. "The seam Everson disappeared inside was small. The periods could be sticking at discrete points, making it less likely there's a bleed." She turned to me. "Queen Street will take us back to the intersection where you dropped out."

"And you think we'll find a boundary—or point, rather?"

"It's where we should start."

"Hey!" Bree-yark cried. "Get back here!"

The goblin had taken a few strolling steps away from us, and now he broke into a run. A boy of nine or ten was fleeing ahead of him. The urchin had snatched something of Bree-yark's, but it wasn't until flashes began going off in his arms that I realized it was Dropsy. Caroline conjured a mist of fae light, but the boy broke through it and ducked around a corner.

"Bree-yark!" I called, right before he disappeared from sight too.

"Go," Caroline said. "I'll stay with Arnaud."

Drawing my cane into sword and staff, I started after the goblin. I soon arrived at the corner he'd rounded to find ramshackle buildings crowding a narrow lane. Several of the windows above featured propped elbows and grim faces. I spotted my teammate at the lane's far end, where it curved from view.

"Bree-yark!" I shouted again, this time trying to push power into my wizard's voice, but I was half-gagging from the stenches.

When he ignored me, I raised my sword—I'd knock him down if I had to. But the blade was jostling too much, and an errant shot could take down one of the teetering structures along with everyone inside. I upped my speed instead, adjusting my strides to avoid seeping channels of raw sewage.

Where the lane ended, a soot-covered church rose. Half a double door was rebounding from the urchin's headlong entrance. Bree-yark, who had gained on him, was almost to the door himself. Before I could shout or cast a barricade, the goblin lowered his shoulder and barged in after his quarry.

A disintegrated faith littered the church grounds like fallen ash. In its place, a malignant energy had crept up the walls, causing the spire with its broken cross to look like an infernal horn and the smashed windows to stare madly.

Dammit, Bree-yark.

At the church's threshold, I gathered what little ley energy there was, hardened the air into a defensive shield around me, and peered into the darkness. The goblin's panted breaths echoed ahead, each one jarring as if he were descending a staircase. Drifting in on cold, unseen currents came whispered voices and hushed giggles. The unnatural sounds sent goose pimples rushing the length of both arms.

"*Illuminare!*" I shouted.

A weak ball of light discharged from the opal end of my staff and illuminated the church's interior. The space was narrow but deep. Ragged black drapes hung from rafters and skirted a floor whose pews and wooden planks had been removed, exposing layers of excavated earth. The air inside wasn't as foul as it had been in the streets, but its staleness had a throat-gripping quality. The space was devoid of anyone, the whispers I'd heard seeming to have retreated into holes dug here and there.

With another Word, I activated the banishment enchantment on my blade and picked my way forward.

What kind of hellhole did you land us in, Bree-yark?

The goblin's grunts sounded from the far end of the church —only now they were returning. Moments later, he batted past the drapes. I noticed he wasn't carrying Dropsy. When his squash-colored eyes met mine, they were huge.

"There's a freaking vampire in here!" he gasped.

"Wonderful," I muttered.

That explained the big hole in the ground, not to mention the suffocating atmosphere: the church had been retrofitted into a giant tomb. Grandpa's ring came to life, pulsing with power, meaning the bloodsucker in question was related to a signatory of the Brasov Pact between wizards and vampires.

I aimed my fist with the ring around the room as I retreated toward the door. Bree-yark scrambled up the final level of excavation and was almost to me when the church door slammed shut. My ball of light shrank to a sputtering point. I pushed power into the invocation, but the air seemed to thicken around it. The best I could manage was a feeble glow that cast everything in brown shadows.

"Door's locked," Bree-yark grunted, tugging on the handle.

My wizard's senses showed brambles of vampiric magic growing along the frame.

"Fear not, travelers," a sultry voice called in a vaguely Irish accent. "No harm will befall ye here."

Rustling sounded, and I turned to find the long drapes drawing apart. Across the church, a female vampire sat on the altar. She was middle-aged and lean, dark-red hair spilling over the shoulders of a black dress. The dress's top was open to her pale sternum and girded bodice-tight above her waist before ending at her knees in a frilly hem. Laced up her shins were a pair of black boots. The thick heels kicked against the altar's side like cudgels.

"Indeed," she continued, "ye'll not find better sanctuary in the city."

"I seriously doubt that," I said.

The sealing magic over the door was weak. At my word, it fell apart.

"Yer looking for someone," the vampire called. "Perhaps Hellcat Maggie can help."

I'd pulled the door open, the pale sun like needles against my eyes, but what she said made me hesitate. When I looked back, a small army of children had emerged from the holes and taken up positions in the shadows around her. They were boys and girls, at least twenty of them, none older than ten. The youngest looked four. As I took in their small, pale faces, anger roared inside me.

"Like you helped them?" I growled.

"The orphans? Don't be so hasty to judge dear Maggie. Each one was sick, starved, and broken. Harry here was ravaged by consumption. And I found little Fiona in a trash bin at night, being nibbled on by rats." Bracelets jangled around Maggie's wrists as she stroked the hair from a girl's brow.

"So you made them your slaves?"

Maggie stopped kicking, her expression pinching around a pair of razor-thin lips. "I delivered them from death, traveler. And I made sure no one would hurt them again. Though a few fools have tried," she added darkly.

Unlike the urchins I'd seen in the street, these children were well dressed, their faces scrubbed and hair combed. The youngest girls wore ribbons. But the fact they were cared for didn't change that this creature had made them her undead slaves, and not out of charity. She was using them to enrich herself, our stolen lantern being just one example.

But even as I trained my ring on her, I reminded myself that I was witnessing an echo of a reality. Nothing I did here would change what had already happened. And the fact I'd never heard of Hellcat Maggie in the modern era suggested she'd met a violent end, whether by staking or burning. Her *orphans* would have all returned to mortality and ultimately passed too. I lowered my fist.

"Either way, we're leaving."

"Even if I can help shine a *light* on the one ye seek?" she called.

She placed teasing emphasis on the word *light*, no doubt referring to Dropsy. As for the rest, I knew vampires too well. Maggie had sensed the emotions coming off me. Now, having interpreted them, she was determined to manipulate me into doing her bidding, possibly even offering her my potent blood.

I snorted. "Thanks, but no thanks."

"So cynical. Maybe a show of good faith will change your stance. Liam?" she called sweetly. The boy Bree-yark had been chasing materialized at the front of the pack, the lantern dangling from his small hand.

"Dropsy!" Bree-yark shouted. "Are you all right?"

The lantern peered around before letting out two timid pulses.

"Go on," the vampire said to Liam. "Return what ye took."

I kept a close eye on the boy as he circled the excavation pit. When he arrived in front of Bree-yark, he extended Dropsy by her brass ring. Nostrils flaring, Bree-yark snatched her from his grip and backed away. The boy stared at him another moment before returning toward the altar.

"Does that help?" Maggie asked.

It suddenly occurred to me that she'd never meant to keep Dropsy. She'd had the boy steal the lantern to lead us here, to her domain. She smiled, lips breaking from teeth that had been filed to points to match her canines.

"Nothing gets past ye, eh, traveler?" she said. "I hope you'll forgive a smidge of trickery. I didn't know how else to bring ye into my company, short of force. And then you'd really be doubting dear Maggie."

"Let's go," Bree-yark muttered.

I waved for him to lead so I could cover our exit with the ring.

"Ye seek another traveler," Maggie called sharply. "One who walks through time."

I'd thought she was bluffing earlier, but that was too damned specific. I paused, my gaze ranging over the children. Twenty here, and who knew how many in the streets. That was a lot of eyes and ears, even in a city of eight hundred thousand. Had Maggie seen something? Heard something? One of the Upholders, maybe?

"Yes, I know of this person," she said. "I might even be convinced to arrange a meeting."

Negotiating with a vampire was never a good idea, especially when the vampire in question believed she had something you wanted. But what if one or all of the Upholders had stumbled into this period? For their sakes, I had to at least weigh the offer.

"In exchange for what?" I asked.

Maggie pushed herself from the altar so she was standing. "A favor."

"Everson…" Bree-yark said in his warning voice.

"I won't make any promises, but let's hear it."

A creak sounded as she limped forward. For the first time I realized the vampire's left leg was a wooden prosthesis, the knee flexing and extending on a metal joint. Maggie caressed her children's heads as she waded to the fore. "A man named Phineas T. Barnum has something that belongs to me."

"The circus guy?" Bree-yark asked.

"He runs a museum on Broadway and Ann Street," Maggie continued.

A very specific image fired in my memory. "Barnum's American Museum," I said.

"That's right. The artifact in question is a silver locket he keeps in his office. I would like it back."

"Then why not get it yourself?" I asked.

"Because the locket is warded. But methinks that won't be a problem for ye." When her eyes glinted, I understood the locking curse on the church door had been intended less to detain than to test me.

"So you want me to steal back something he stole from you?"

"He bought it from the one who stole it," she said, impatience creeping into her voice. "But all that matters is it belongs to me."

"And in exchange, you'll arrange for me to meet this traveler?"

"A straight up swap, no trouble or trickery. Maggie's word." She made the sign of the cross on her chest, but in reverse, I noticed.

"Can you give me a description of the traveler?"

"As I said, one like ye."

Typical vampire response, calculated to keep me interested. But though she affected a coy expression, something in her voice and stance told me she needed this artifact, hungered for it. Arranging the promised meeting in order to possess it was a cheap price as far as she was concerned.

I nodded. "Okay."

In a burst of electric energy, the vampiric deal took hold. The earnestness of the bonding suggested I'd been right.

"Do I bring the locket here?" I asked.

"When ye have it, one of the orphans will find ye."

With a tight-lipped smile, Hellcat Maggie retreated back into her blood slaves—another tell. With the destructive power I wielded on my fist, she knew she'd risked enough by bringing me here. Having gotten what she wanted, she was back to survival mode. She fluttered the talons of a hand in playful farewell, while her children stared at us from what was clearly a defensive formation.

Outside the church, Bree-yark hugged Dropsy tightly to his chest. "You're really planning on doing this?"

"It could lead to an Upholder," I said, "but I also want to check out the museum."

"What for?"

"I don't know where my grandfather lived in the 1860s—his old farm would be under the West Twenties by now. But I do happen to know he worked for one P.T. Barnum as a stage magician. I'd like to find him."

22

About a week following Grandpa's death, I'd found the poster in the back of his closet. It had been rolled up and bound with old string that fell apart when I pulled on it. Expecting another map, because it had been leaning among several, I was surprised to discover a vintage promotional poster.

ASMUS THE GREAT!
MASTER MAGICIAN!

The magician in question was a tuxedo-clad man with rosy cheeks, hand inside a top hat. Given the name, and the drawing's resemblance to a younger version of my grandfather, I assumed this was *his* grandfather. That was years before I would learn Grandpa had been a centuries-old magic-user.

Splashed across the poster's bottom:

BARNUM'S AMERICAN MUSEUM
NEW YORK CITY

"You recovered her," Caroline observed when we returned to Five Points.

"Not without a little negotiating," Bree-yark said, stowing Dropsy in his pouch and sliding me a dubious look.

I filled Caroline in on our meeting with Hellcat Maggie, finishing with our agreement. "My grandfather was a powerful magic-user. If he's at Barnum's, he could be an asset like he was the last time."

That said, I wasn't relishing the idea of having to prove who I was to him all over again. I'd succeeded with the 1776 version, but we were in a different period now. This Grandpa would have no knowledge of the other encounter.

"Worst case," I said, "he's not there, and we recover the locket. Then Maggie sets up a meeting with this 'traveler,' who could be an Upholder."

"*If* we can trust her," Bree-yark added.

Caroline's eyes diffused, and I felt her studying the vampiric agreement that obligated me. I took the opportunity to push power into the druidic symbol on my hand. Still no connection with the other Upholders, though.

"She'll keep her word," Caroline decided. "But we shouldn't spend too much time here. I've been examining the bonds holding this time catch together, and they aren't particularly strong. They could begin to unravel at any moment."

"The museum's nearby," I said. "Broadway and Ann."

We set out at a fast walk. Within a couple blocks, the buildings along the street sturdied and straightened, flower boxes appearing in windows. The Broadway that opened out ahead was a much different street than its 1776 counterpart. Paved now and enclosed by crowds of tall buildings, it also conducted multiple times the traffic. Horse-drawn carts and buses clattered up and down the thoroughfare while streams of people crossed back and forth and poured around shouting sidewalk vendors.

As we rounded the corner, Bree-yark flinched from several paperboys cawing the latest headlines.

"Kind of loud," he grumbled.

I slowed to check the date on one of the papers: October 13, 1861. Caroline had been really damned close. All around us, men wore vintage business suits and hats, many of them stovepipes like Abe Lincoln's, while the women's elaborate dresses spoke to a higher society than the neighborhood we'd left. I noticed Caroline had subtly altered our glamours to appear more middle class.

Walking south along the sidewalk, we passed the former sugar house where a Stranger had held Seay's friends captive and soon came upon the recently completed City Hall, an undeveloped park when I'd passed it in 1776. The ley energy was disorganized in this time catch too, but with each block south it seemed to be gathering strength. A plus if I needed to cast. At the southern end of City Hall Park, we stopped at a busy road.

"There it is," Caroline said.

Opposite us, on the corner of Ann Street, stood an enormous five-story building. Constructed at angles to conform to the wide corner, the white-washed edifice looked like the entrance to a baseball stadium. A line of world flags flapped from the building's top like pennants, a large American flag presiding over them. And painted above the windows on the third floor in giant circus font:

BARNUM'S AMERICAN MUSEUM

"C'mon," I said.

We hustled across the street, dodging carriages, and joined the back of a line. Placards shouted the admission fee—"Only 25 Cents!"—while posters glued to the wall announced the museum's various draws, from freakish acts to exotic animals to a brand new mystery attraction guaranteed to "Astonish and Horrify!"

I searched for *Asmus the Great* posters, but couldn't see any.

On an outdoor balcony right above us, a brass band struck up a lively tune, pulling in people from across the street to watch and listen. The clash of noises was clearly irritating Bree-yark's sensitive ears, but he gave a grudging nod.

"Man knows how to sell tickets," he muttered.

At the front of the line, I exchanged a glamoured one-dollar coin for four museum tickets, and we were ushered into a massive entrance hall full of people, their faces glowing with anticipation. Signs pointed to a grand staircase, the conveyance to the main attractions. We moved off to one side to get our bearings. From what I could gather, exhibits were on the second and third floors, while a performance hall occupied the fourth, shows on the half hour. An usher called out that the next would begin in ten minutes.

"Barnum's office is in back," Caroline said, nodding past the staircase. "To save time, I can take Arnaud and check it out if you and Bree-yark want to search the upper floors for your grandfather."

"Sounds good," I said. "Just be careful. The locket is warded."

Caroline flashed a smile. "I'll only be looking, not touching."

As Bree-yark and I took the stairs up, I watched her over the polished balustrade. She had glamoured the demon-vampire to look like a feeble man who needed escorting. Thanks to his restraints, that's about what he'd become. But he was still Arnaud Thorne, which meant dangerous. I'd promised Vega I wouldn't forget that.

"Something going on with you two?" Bree-yark asked.

I snapped my head around. "Huh?"

"The looks she keeps giving you."

"Who, Caroline? What looks?"

"You know, the sparkly-eyed kind."

"Not possible. She bargained away her feelings for me two years ago."

Bree-yark grunted skeptically. "Did someone bother telling her feelings that?"

I had noticed the looks, of course, but it disturbed me that Bree-yark had as well.

"Look, nothing's going on," I said testily. "She's married, and I'm with Vega."

"Yeah, well, in case you haven't noticed, things aren't going so well with Mr. Fae Prince. He's hunting her with giant birds."

"Which is exactly why she's here. To put everything right with her kingdom."

"I still don't trust her."

"Well, there's nothing I can do about that," I muttered, not wanting to rehash the debate.

We arrived on the second floor to find display cases stretched end to end. As we made our way to another staircase across the room, I glanced around. The displays ranged from the interesting—wooden tribal masks—to the absurd—a cat-powered weaving loom. I also kept a close eye on Bree-yark. There was no telling what he might find objectionable, and he had a bad habit of settling things with his fists.

We bypassed the third floor, where signs pointed the way to live animal enclosures, including an albino tiger and a monkey with two heads, and continued to the fourth.

Visitors were already lined up in front of "The Theater of the Otherworldly" for the four o'clock show. From inside came screams and rapturous applause. A door opened shortly to release the audience, all of them talking at once. I grabbed the arm of a young man in suspenders and a tweed flat cap who looked like he'd come from the Five Points neighborhood we'd just left.

"Is a magician a part of the show?"

"Aye! And a dead flash one at that!"

"Flash?" Bree-yark grunted.

By the man's animated eyes, I took that as slang for something good.

"Was his name Asmus the Great?" I asked.

"Didn't catch the name," he said, "but there weren't nothing hugger-mugger about 'im. No, siree. But wait till you catch the last act. Ooh-hoo! Best fist yer eyes so they don't pop from yer skull. Though yer lad there's liable to kak himself."

He was referring to Bree-yark, still glamoured to look like a boy who'd been in one too many playground brawls. If he was insulted, though, he didn't react. More likely he didn't understand what had been said.

With a nod, I let the young man go on his excited way.

"Think the magician is your gramps?" Bree-yark asked.

I considered asking another of the patrons streaming out, but our line was already moving. "We'll know soon enough."

The inside of the theater wasn't the gaudy venue I'd been expecting. With its Greek columns, decorative bunting, and two levels of balcony seating, it was almost elegant. Ushers directed Bree-yark and me to the main floor, where we ended up in the middle row facing a stage hidden by plush red curtains.

As the seats filled up, I opened my wizard's senses. No remnants of magic, but my grandfather had still been hiding his abilities from Lich while he worked with the Order in exile. Most likely he'd relied on stage tricks and sleight of hand during his stint here.

The crowd fell to a hush of eager whispers as the gaslighting in the theater dimmed. A circle of limelight swelled onto the stage until we were all looking at a rotund man in a three-piece flannel suit. Bright mustard hair glistened under an exaggerated stovepipe hat. His jowls were covered with trimmed side whiskers of the same color.

His sudden appearance drew murmurs of appreciation.

"Welcome to Barnum's American Museum!" he called in a barker-like voice. "The inimitable P.T. Barnum has searched far and wide, high and low, has navigated strange and perilous lands, risked treacherous seas, to bring you, esteemed audience, the *Theater of the Otherworldly*. For the next twenty minutes prepare to be educated and scintillated, mystified and stupefied, to feast your eyes on that which cannot be and yet absolutely is. Because seeing, ladies and gentlemen, is *believing!*"

As he backed to the side of the stage, the curtain opened onto what appeared a human pandemonium. Oohs and aahs went up, and a few children screamed. But the chaos was choreographed, resolving into a hypnotic rotation where sets of acts took their turn in the full glare of the limelight. There were unicyclists and stilt walkers, knife jugglers and fire breathers, contortionists and sword swallowers. The audience's reaction to each one was spirited, many jumping to their feet to applaud.

"They act like they've never seen this stuff before," Bree-yark grumbled.

"They haven't," I pointed out. "The modern circus hasn't been invented yet."

The performers all came to the forefront and bowed to more applause. The two knife jugglers, who had sent their dozen-odd blades spinning overhead, received an ovation as they caught each one, the final blades between their teeth. The curtain closed over the encore bow, and the barker bustled back into view.

"Did you enjoy that?" he asked.

Bree-yark palmed his ears against the enthusiastic response.

"Well, that's just the start," he said. "Next up, a conversation between two exceptional individuals: the world's largest man and Creation's most diminutive woman. I present to you, *Mimi and Biggs!*"

The curtain opened on a pair of chairs angled toward one another, one massive, the other of doll-sized proportions. A tuxedoed man lumbered in from stage right to murmurs and gasps. He must have been at least nine-feet tall and in excess of six hundred pounds. From stage left appeared a tiny woman in a white dress, no more than twelve inches from her heeled shoes to the little tiara atop her head.

A storm of wonderstruck approval met them.

"Th-they're from Faerie!" Bree-yark exclaimed.

I'd thought maybe their sizes were exaggerated through some trick of perspective, but Bree-yark was right. Biggs was an ogre, shaved and groomed to appear human. He bore a long cane for his clumsy gait, and was likely wearing a back brace under his jacket to correct the slumping posture characteristic of all ogres. Mimi was a pixie. Aside from her costume, which included a tiny parasol and hand fan, no enhancements would have been necessary. Pixies were already plenty theatrical.

"Look at them," Bree-yark grumbled. "Parading around like trained monkeys."

When the two beings arrived at center stage, Mimi thrust her little chin up at Biggs. "You're late!" she squealed.

Biggs dragged a massive hand through his slick hair. "Sor-rrry," he rumbled.

The crowd broke into a foot-stomping bout of laughter that rattled the walls.

"That's not even funny," Bree-yark complained.

I gave him a warning look that told him to cool it.

"Well, what's your excuse?" Mimi demanded of Biggs.

"A ... uh ... a cloud ... Got lost in a cloud."

He'd fumbled his line, but the crowd didn't care. The sight of Mimi giving the business to a man large enough to squash her underfoot—and him taking it—was the punchline. Men slapped knees and doubled over with laughter.

"Fine, then," Mimi said. "Shall we have a seat?"

"I ate … uh … I mean, I already had two for breakfast."

Bree-yark, who had seen enough, jumped to his feet. "This is an outrage!" he shouted.

Never mind his fear of ogres or that he couldn't stand pixies. They were all on team Faerie, and as far as Bree-yark was concerned, these two were making a fool of said team. Thankfully, his protest was buried under another tempest of stomping and laughter, and I managed to pull him back to his seat.

"This has already happened, remember?" I said between gritted teeth. "Causing a scene changes nothing."

He shifted like an unruly kid, hands balled into fists. "I still don't have to like it."

"Then close your eyes and plug your ears."

Following a few more rounds of give and take, Mimi climbed onto Biggs's lowered hand to show that they were, in fact, good friends, and they bowed. The crowd gave them a standing ovation as the curtains closed again.

"How about that Mimi?" the barker asked, hustling back to the fore. "I wouldn't want to try putting anything *over* on her."

Bree-yark gave me an exasperated look.

The barker's voice dropped an octave. "Now it's time for a journey to the mysterious, the esoteric, the arcane. And by that, of course, I mean *magic*. P.T. Barnum discovered him in a castle perched above the blackest forest in Prussia, perfecting his secret art. Ladies and gentlemen, please welcome…"

I leaned forward in my seat.

"…*Asmus the Great!*"

A bolt of exhilaration shot through me. This time the curtains didn't part. Instead, a door opened on the side of the stage and out walked a tall man in a top hat, shiny black shoes, and long swallowtail coat. The limelight followed him as he approached the barker, who stood waiting, right hand extended.

"Great to see you again, Asmus."

But instead of shaking hands, the magician pulled a wand from inside his coat. Thrusting it toward the barker, he boomed, *"Sparire!"*

A burst of smoke engulfed the rotund man to the shock of the spectators. Producing a handkerchief, seemingly from thin air, the magician waved it until the smoke dispersed. Predictably, the barker was gone. The collective gasps quickly morphed into an appreciative swell of applause.

"Your grandfather's pretty good," Bree-yark said.

"Yeah, but it's not him," I said, disappointment collapsing around the words.

"What d'ya mean? They introduced him as *Asmus*, right?"

"The eyes. My grandfather's were pale blue. Even in the full light, this guy's are way too dark. Plus, his proportions, his movements—they're all wrong." Grandpa had probably already come and gone by this time, but they were still using his name for continuity.

"What about the magic?" Bree-yark said. "He made that guy disappear."

"Stage magic."

I'd seen the smoke erupt from the floor and the curtain rustle prior to the barker vanishing. More applause sounded now as the magician passed the handkerchief through his other hand, changing the square of cloth from white to red—and then revealing that it was but the first in an endless stream of colorful cloths. A tired trick in the modern era, but no doubt still new in the 1860s.

"Sorry, man," Bree-yark said.

"Well, it's not necessarily a dead end. I'll catch the barker after the show, see if he knows where I can find the real Asmus."

We sat through the rest of the act, which included more sleights of hand and stage trickery. All well executed, but I was still bitter over him not being Grandpa. For the finale, the magician pulled a kicking white rabbit from his top hat, showed it to the audience, then transformed it into a small flock of doves that went flapping into the rafters. As he paced back toward the side door, the applause was thunderous.

Just before disappearing, he turned and tossed something. A plume of smoke went up in the middle of the stage, and the barker stumbled out in pretend confusion before gaining his footing and fixing his hat.

"I just had the strangest dream," he told us.

Bree-yark let out a chortle before catching himself and resetting his jaw.

"And finally," the barker said, "our most recent acquisition. Discovered in the Pacific Isles, this creature took more than thirty native sailors to capture, six of whom lost their lives, God rest their swarthy souls. But now, claimed, detained, and *mostly* tamed, I present to you the incredible, the horrifying ... *Fiji Mermaid!*"

The curtains parted on a water-filled tank that must have taken the entire last act to roll onto center stage. The audience fell silent and, starting with the front row, rose to their feet in a hypnotic wave. I followed, my breath catching at the sight of a muscled being with razor-sharp fins and turquoise skin suspended beyond the glass. From inside a floating mass of dark hair, a pair of orbs stared back at me.

It was Gorgantha.

23

I picked up snatches of the crowd's murmurs. They wanted to know whether the mermaid was alive or dead or even real. But Gorgantha was alive, and she was damned sure real. I could see the gills below her jaw—seamless lines when she was out of water—open now and cycling oxygen. And there was no mistaking that her eyes were fixed on mine. Waves of relief and sickness hammered me from all sides.

How in the hell had she ended up in here? Were the others around?

"What's going on?" Bree-yark demanded, straining on his tiptoes to see over the shoulder of the man in front of him. "What is it?"

"An Upholder," I said.

"One of yours?" He climbed onto his seat and turned to face the stage. "Holy thunder."

By now, the crowd's confusion was turning to impatience. The spectacle of the Fiji Mermaid was one thing, but they didn't want her just floating there. They wanted her *doing* something.

"Swim!" a man's vulgar voice shouted. Others in the audience took up the call.

As if in response, Gorgantha's body spasmed, and with a thrash of her legs and tail, propelled herself to the other side of the cylindrical tank. The crowd responded with a thunderclap of approval.

She stopped, webbed hands pressed to the glass—and there was the faint pattern of the druid bond below her right thumb. Her orblike eyes searched until they found me again. I raised a hand to let her know I recognized her. But my mind was reeling. I needed to get her out of here, but how? Tonight, when the museum would be mostly empty? I pushed my palm toward her to say, *Hang tight.*

"Do a trick!" a woman shrieked.

Gorgantha's mouth pulled to one side, and she thrashed wildly for the next several seconds.

That time, I caught the sparks. They had appeared in the back of the tank where a metallic box housed something. New York was still twenty years away from electrification, but not from the batteries that powered their telegraphs. Horror and rage stormed through me. They were shocking her.

The crowd began leaping now, faces shiny with elation, demanding more.

"C'mon!" I called to Bree-yark, and began shouldering my way down the row, making a special point of knocking patrons aside. A few protests went up, but most of the row was too transfixed on the stage to notice us.

I reached the aisle just as Gorgantha's tank was hit with another charge. This time, she shot straight up, colliding into the tank's sealed lid. Something dark and viscous spread from her brow—blood. I sprinted now, past the fist-pumping, throat-straining edges of a mob that wanted more, more, more. By now I could see the cable running from the tank's box to the side of the stage.

Whoever's at the controls, you just made the biggest mistake of your life.

I looked back to make sure Bree-yark was behind me. The stocky goblin, glamoured as a junior street tough, was shoving his way out into the aisle. A mustachioed man who took offense reached down and twisted one of his ears. Bree-yark responded by driving a fist into the man's kidney, dropping him.

Attaboy.

By the time I straightened, a pair of young ushers had stepped between me and the stage. I didn't slow. Inspired by Bree-yark, I thrust the blunt end of my cane into the first usher's belly, then reversed direction and smashed the other one in the jaw with the handle. Unfortunately, I didn't wield goblin strength, and the youth of nineteenth century New York were a hardier breed than your average Gen Z'er.

Grinning through bloodied teeth, the one I'd struck in the mouth answered with a roundhouse that caught me behind the ear. The theater swooned. The other usher stepped in and brought his fist up into my stomach.

As the air grunted out of me, Bree-yark arrived in my peripheral vision and tackled the gut-punching usher. But more were coming, eager for a fight. I hadn't wanted to resort to magic, not yet, but...

"*Protezione!*" I called, hardening the air around Bree-yark and me. Then, "*Respingere!*"

The pulse from the shield blasted the ushers in all directions, sending several into the seats. The crowd's attention was torn now between the spectacle on stage and the battle taking place in the aisle. Here and there, large men began wading toward us, laborers from the looks of them. Several pushed up their sleeves to reveal forearms as thick as cured hams. We were on the verge of a full-scale brawl.

In the tank, Gorgantha was thrashing from yet another shock.

All right, fuck this. Extending my cane, I shouted, *"Forza dura!"*

The emerging force didn't crack the tank. It demolished it. In a cascade of crashing glass, the front half of the tank was no longer there. Screams went up as thousands of gallons of salt water surged toward the audience.

"Grab hold!" I said, showing Bree-yark my back.

He climbed on and wrapped me tightly. Aiming my cane at the ground now, I summoned another force. The explosive counterforce sent us airborne, and we sailed over the hump of water dumping off the stage's lip and onto the first rows. Beyond the tank, I cushioned our landing with another invocation and came to a running stop. Bree-yark hopped from my back, and we both turned.

The water had already inundated the front of general seating. Entire families lay with their hair and clothes plastered to their bodies, children red-faced and shrieking. Beyond them, the audience was splashing and scrambling over seats—and one another—to reach the exits. The balcony levels were clearing out too.

My gaze dropped to the stage where the water had shoved Gorgantha's massive form to one side. I feared now my invocation had harmed her.

Rushing toward her, I nearly tripped over the battery line that ran from the tank. I peered over, tracing the cable to the side of the stage where, at the controls of a small booth, the barker sat in his top hat and flannel suit. The man responsible for shocking Gorgantha. My eyes narrowed as a growl rumbled from my chest.

The barker swallowed. "Did you, ah, enjoy the show?"

"Check on your teammate," Bree-yark said. "I'll handle this clown."

"Don't go easy on him."

"I wouldn't know how."

I continued to where Gorgantha was struggling to sit upright. At the sound of my approach, her fin-like ears cocked. She turned her head, dank hair spilling over one eye, until we were facing one another. I wasn't sure what to expect, but it wasn't the roar and swipe of a taloned hand that greeted me.

I skipped out of range and showed my palms. "Gorgantha, it's me! Everson Croft!"

She glared up from a three-point stance, her free hand drawn back for another strike. I tried to read her uncovered eye. Fluid from the gash she'd suffered ran around it. She'd been staring at me earlier—I hadn't mistaken that—but instead of recognition, her eye held a fog-searching quality.

It was as if my face *should* have meant something, but damned if she knew what.

I took a steadying breath. "I'm Everson Croft. We were on the same team. We called ourselves the Upholders. We were separated in a time catch in 1776 New York. Somehow you ended up here. Try to think back, Gorgantha."

Her lips drew from her sharp teeth, but I could see her mind working behind her eye. A constellation of burns marred her scaly skin, some fresh, others healing. Places she'd been electrocuted. From off stage, a string of yelps were punctuated by the satisfying sound of goblin fists pounding soft flesh.

That's right, you son of a bitch.

Turning my hand around, I showed Gorgantha the faint lines of the druid bond. "This was our symbol. You have one too. Below the webbing of your thumb." I nodded at the hand planted against the floor. But she kept her wary eye fixed on mine, as if ready to launch herself at the least provocation.

We remained like that for several moments. Then I had the idea to push power into my symbol. For the first time since returning to the time catch, faint white light pulsed along the lines. A moment later, the symbol on Gorgantha's hand glowed softly.

Holy crap, the bond still works.

With the disruption of ley energy, it must have required proximity.

Behind me, I heard Bree-yark returning. "That almost makes up for the satyr," he muttered.

He was dragging the unconscious barker from the wing of the stage, and he'd not gone easy on him. Dropping the bloodied man, he peered up and froze. On the balcony levels, uniformed men were spreading toward the railings. The ushers may have been willing sluggers, but the museum's hired security were armed with revolvers.

"Step away from the mermaid!" one of them ordered, aiming his weapon.

With an uttered Word, I shaped a defensive wall across the front of the stage. In the distance, alarm bells clanged throughout the museum. I thought about Caroline, reassuring myself that she could blend in with the crowds and escape. But Bree-yark and I were three floors up with more security en route.

"There's a back way."

Gorgantha was standing now, water dripping from her talons. She'd wiped the hair from her face so both eyes were visible again. Though they still lacked recognition, they appeared to hold more trust.

She cocked her head. "Over there."

"Lead the way," I said.

She took off toward the side of the stage, webbed feet slapping wood. Gunfire began popping behind us. I winced from the impacts against my shield, but it held until we were out of range. We raced past a line of stage props, including Mimi's and Biggs's chairs, and through a set of double doors, which I sealed behind us.

We were in a large gaslit room where the water tank must have been stored. There was a second, much smaller tank near the far wall, and I shuddered to think it had held Gorgantha when she wasn't performing. Just looking at it made me claustrophobic. A crane with a pile of netting stood near some long-handled brushes and shelves of bottled chemicals that leaked a stringent stench.

Gorgantha pointed out a door to our right. "Jokers who fed me came in and out through there. The fish were always spoiled," she added in a mutter.

"I'll check it out," I said, anticipating a stairway down to a back alley or loading area.

A *thunk* sounded, and a knife appeared above the door handle. I yanked my arm back and spun. The next blade punctured my billowing coat below the armpit and implanted itself beside the first knife. I darted for cover, but my pinned coat jerked me back against the door, and my cane clattered to the floor.

Oh, for fuck's sake.

When I stretched for my cane, a third knife punched through the other side of my coat, and my cane rolled out of reach.

"Pretty ballsy trying to steal off with the main attraction," the knife juggler said. He had entered from a back door partially blocked from view by the small tank. Another knife was flexed above his supple wrist while eight or nine more flickered in the light of the gas lamps from a belt around his waist.

"She's a friend," I growled.

"She fills seats," he countered.

His twin emerged from behind him, his knife cocked at Bree-yark. "Yeah, puts bacon on our tables."

"Then maybe you should make nice with the local butcher," Bree-yark snarled, "'cause she's coming with *us*." His goblin blade was drawn, but at his distance, he would absorb a dozen knives before he got within striking range. The jugglers apparently had the same read, because they smirked in response.

"Put that away, kid," one of them said, "before you hurt yourself."

"Oh, I'll put it somewhere all right," Bree-yark promised, but stayed put.

A lanky sword swallower with a shock of blond hair stepped between the jugglers, wielding a blade almost as long as he was tall. His grin was cold-blooded. With Bree-yark and me covered, he circled Gorgantha.

"All right, lovely," he said, slapping her thigh with the flat of his sword. "Fun and games are over. Back into the tank."

24

I looked over the preposterous scene—we were being schooled by the opening act, for crissakes—but the danger was real. The jugglers could release their blades in the time it took to blink, and with lethal accuracy. And I didn't like the sadistic grin on the sword swallower's face. But while they'd been talking, I'd been gathering energy, rehearsing the invocations I would need to cast in rapid succession.

When Bree-yark glanced over at me, I returned a nod.

In the next moment, my cane rattled over the floor and leapt into my outstretched hand. *"Protezione!"* I shouted.

The juggler's arriving knife broke through the still-forming shield, but the invocation was enough to alter the knife's spin and trajectory. The handle struck my shoulder and bounced to the floor.

Bree-yark used the distraction to put the small tank between himself and the other juggler. A knife spun past him. The twins rearmed, blades flashing from belts, but I'd already formed the next invocation in my mind. I allowed the barest moment for energy, breath, and intention to align before releasing the Word.

"Vigore!"

The force split from my cane and into each juggler's chest. I hadn't bothered calibrating—there wasn't time. The result was a pair of cannonballs. The forces plowed the jugglers into the wall with bone-fracturing force and dropped them among their spilled blades. One groaned weakly while the other kicked the floor in agony.

The sword swallower looked from his downed companions back to Gorgantha—just as her fist arrived. The blow collapsed his grin into his neck and sent his feet out from under him. He landed on his back, gurgling for air. Gorgantha wasn't done. She grabbed him under an arm and began dragging him.

"All right, *lovely*," she said, mimicking him from earlier. "Fun and games are over."

He was still clutching the long sword, but he couldn't even raise it. The blade rattled across the floor impotently. At the tank, Gorgantha hooked her other arm between his legs and dropped him into the water, sword and all. She slammed the lid closed and locked it with a lever. The swallower ended up in a hunch, lips pulling at the few inches of air beneath the lid, one hand clawing the glass.

"Bitch," Gorgantha muttered.

Clearly impressed with the mer's work, Bree-yark sheathed his blade and followed her from the tank at a trot. Meanwhile, I slipped out of my coat, pried the daggers free, and was pushing my arms back through the sleeves when fire burst from the back door.

"*Really?*" I complained.

Drawing his coat over his head, Bree-yark lunged in front of Gorgantha to absorb the brunt of the attack. As the flames petered out, four men with shaved heads and missing eyebrows emerged. *The frigging firebreathers.* And judging by Bree-yark's charred coat, they were breathing some heavy-duty shit. Gorgantha, with her sensitive skin, backed from their flickering torches and jugs of fuel.

"Not so tough now, eh?" one of them jeered.

Before I could force-blast the firebreathers into next month, Bree-yark charged. Legs churning, he went in low, coat still shielding his head. Eruptions of flames broke against him, but he didn't slow.

"You wanna see tough?" he roared.

Three of the firebreathers were smart enough to backpedal through the doorway, but the one who'd spoken tried to get off another blast. Bree-yark reached him first. Seizing his arm, the goblin rotated several times, his large feet pirouetting over the floor, and released the airborne man into the doorway.

The firebreather's jug smashed against the frame, and his torch landed in the spilled fuel. Flames burst over the sides of the door and up the plank wall. Bree-yark shuffled back and shed his smoking coat. Dragged by the legs, the downed firebreather disappeared beyond the spreading flames.

"You all right?" Bree-yark asked Gorgantha.

"Yeah, just a little dried out. Those were some dope moves."

Bree-yark blushed. "Well, I could say the same about yours."

The double doors we'd entered through began to shake.

"Don't worry," I said, looking over. "I locked it with magic."

No sooner had the words left my mouth than the frame separated from the wall, and the whole doorway collapsed into the room. Biggs the ogre ducked through the wave of dust and faced us. He'd shed his jacket, and his unshouldered suspenders were dangling from his beltline like a ship's rigging. He must have ditched his back brace too, because he was stooped, knuckles nearly scraping the floor.

Just keeps getting better.

His dull eyes roved from one of us to the other. He looked strong enough to, well, bust down a magically sealed door, but I wasn't going to expend power on him. Not when we could outrun the cumbersome brute.

"Let's go," I called to my teammates.

I opened the backdoor onto a staircase just as Mimi zipped in behind Biggs, her beating wings trailing purple-silver light. She smacked the ogre in the back of the head as she passed him. "Why are you just standing there? Stop them!"

"Ungh?" Biggs asked.

Sighing, Mimi fired off a bolt. Though the dusty burst of light above my hand looked tiny, the force jerked the door from my grasp and slammed it shut again. I yanked on the door, but fae magic sealed it now. I glanced over at the fingers of flames spreading across the wall. Were we *ever* going to get out of here?

"Well, if it isn't Miss Sell Out," Bree-yark said.

Oh, not now, I thought, digging furiously for my cold iron amulet.

"And what are you supposed to be?" Mimi squealed, dispersing his glamour with the wave of a hand.

Bree-yark drew himself up. "Someone with more self-respect in his pinky finger than you have in your whole body." That her whole body was only slightly larger than the finger in question stole some of the line's zing.

"Ha! *Self-respect* and *goblin* don't even belong in the same room."

"I'm not the one whoring myself out for laughs," Bree-yark shot back.

"Like you could whore yourself out for anything. Look at you!"

Bigg's deep-set eyes rolled from side to side, as if following a ping pong match. Behind me, Gorgantha had begun tugging on the rear door. If I could feel the fire's growing heat, she was suffering it fourfold. I needed to find the damned amulet, blast Mimi into Never Never Land, and unseal the door.

The amulet's still in Bree-yark's pouch, I realized.

I looked up as he swiped his blade at the pixie, her last remark apparently having struck a nerve. Mimi easily darted out of the way. I expected her to respond with a blast, but she only upped the taunting.

"What do a flower and a goblin have in common?" she asked. "A flower is pretty and a goblin is pretty ugly."

For the period, that wasn't bad.

"Bree-yark?" I called. "Mind tossing me your pouch?"

But he was swearing now and jumping up and down, blade whistling through the air.

"What do you call a wart on a goblin?" Mimi continued, zipping deftly around his futile strikes. "'Poor thing.'"

Absorbed in their petty contest, the two were behaving as if half the freaking room wasn't on fire. I was preparing to snag Bree-yark's pouch with a force invocation when Biggs lumbered forward, arm swinging. I stumbled over my words as I tried to redirect the invocation, but the ogre wasn't aiming for Bree-yark.

"You're mean," he rumbled.

"Hey!" Mimi cried, casting a protective sphere the instant before the ogre's hand closed around her. Bursts of fae light flashed between his clenched fingers, but he was apparently immune to her magic as well as her screaming threats. Beyond him, an army of footsteps stampeded across the theater stage.

"Go," he said. "I'll stop 'em."

I gave him a salute. "Thanks a lot, Biggs."

"Yeah, thanks, big guy," Bree-yark said. "And I'm sorry about, you know, what I said."

Though his insults had been directed at Mimi, they'd included Biggs by association. In the same waving gesture, the ogre told him it was all right and to get going. With Mimi's energies diverted to freeing herself, Gorgantha overcame the sealing enchantment. When the door broke open, I took the lead down the stairs.

Finally, I thought, blowing out my breath.

Gorgantha followed me, and Bree-yark moved in behind her. At each floor, I cast a locking spell on the door to the stairwell to avoid further encounters. Above us, bodies thumped and rolled. Several shots sounded, but unless the security were wielding iron rounds—which I doubted—Biggs would be fine. I was more worried about the upbraiding he was going to get from Mimi when he released her.

At least she'll be able to put out the fire.

I was thinking of the pixie's powerful enchantments, which would include frost, when a series of explosions sounded, rocking the stairwell. I'd forgotten all about the building's gas line. I imagined the pipe-fed lanterns throughout the museum erupting and spewing flames over wood and drapery.

"Keep going!" I shouted at Bree-yark, who had paused to peer up.

At the ground floor, I flung a door open onto a large loading area. The space was clear, workers apparently having heeded the alarm still clanging away inside. I led the way down a short flight of wooden steps to a cobbled lane.

Panting, I waited for Gorgantha and Bree-yark to catch up. Blown-out glass littered the narrow street, while smoke gushed from the top-floor windows.

The museum had already begun evacuating when I shattered Gorgantha's tank. If Caroline had exited with the crowds, she and Arnaud would be on Broadway by now. But the three of us couldn't very well circle the building to meet her: a marked man, a goblin, and a six-and-a-half-foot mermaid. There was also the matter of retrieving the locket for Hellcat Maggie, but not without getting Gorgantha somewhere safe first.

I was considering where that might be when a shout went

up. At the other end of the street, a group of men in navy blue caps and frock coats turned the corner and stampeded toward us.

"The po-po," Gorgantha muttered.

Sure enough, the copper stars pinned to their chests marked them as Vega's distant predecessors, early NYPD. But even in official attire, the crew looked rough-and-tumble, more likely to billy-club the peace into a crippled heap than preserve it. Lips snarled under broken noses and from jagged teeth.

"Here we go again," Gorgantha said, drawing her webbed hands into reluctant fists.

In the light of day, I could see the toll that captivity had taken on her. Her muscles lacked solidity, and her turquoise color had dulled to a depressed grayish blue. And then there were the nasty burns.

Another police unit appeared at the opposite end of the street, bringing their numbers to a healthy dozen. Bree-yark, still hot from his melee with Mimi, drew his blade and growled, "Their funeral."

"Be ready to run, guys," I said.

"Run?" Bree-yark echoed indignantly.

But the question remained, *run where?* We were at the beating heart of a mega city. We needed to find refuge, and I didn't know 1861 New York well enough. The immediate issue, though, was the cops. With a whispered Word, I hardened the air into shields on either side of us. Could I summon enough force to scatter the officers senseless? After my recent string of casting, the thought alone exhausted me. Hell, if Thelonious hadn't suspended our agreement, the depraved incubus would have been knocking about now.

A door across the street opened and a little girl's face appeared. "Come."

It took a moment for the dull eyes to register. One of Maggie's blood slaves.

I waved Gorgantha and Bree-yark toward the door. "Go!"

I had to give Bree-yark a shove to get him moving. By the time we arrived at the door, the first cops were colliding into the shields. The rest pulled up. While some pawed the invisible barrier, mouths gaping, others glowered as if the shield were a perversion and began beating it with their clubs.

That'll keep them busy.

Passing through the doorway behind my teammates, I slammed the door and locked it with magic. Bree-yark pulled Dropsy from his pouch, her eager glow illuminating a flight of steps that dropped us into a basement crowded with crates. Ahead of our sphere of light, the girl's dust-colored ponytail flipped back and forth.

We broke from the building, crossed a wide street—pedestrians and carriage drivers too transfixed on the smoke and clamoring of a major fire to notice us—and descended into the basement of a second building. The girl navigated the subterranean corridors like she'd done it a hundred times.

At the next building, she led us through a side door but upstairs this time. After several floors, the girl slowed and walked us into an empty room, the scent of stone dust suggesting recent construction.

I was startled to find Hellcat Maggie sitting in a large window opposite us, one leg perched on the sill, her prosthetic leg swinging below her skirt. Her eyes lingered for an extra beat on Gorgantha before moving to me. Maybe I'd overestimated her fear of Grandpa's ring. Extending an arm, she unfurled her long nails.

"The locket."

"We, um, didn't get that far," I said.

"It's still in there?" When she turned toward the arched

window, I inched forward. The window gave us a vantage over Barnum's Museum. Red flames lashed through the smoke that was pouring out from all sides now.

"Holy thunder," Bree-yark breathed, coming up beside me.

An enormous crowd had gathered around the museum, but now they were screaming and beating it the other way as animals from the live collection began spilling out. The albino tiger bolted down Broadway, a gaggle of men in pursuit, while the two-headed monkey scaled a building across the street in a shrill duet of chattering.

I glanced back to find Gorgantha peering past our heads, her lips set in a grim line. West of the museum, I spotted Biggs the ogre. He was holding the reins of an African elephant as if it were a pony, leading it to safety. Giraffes galloped past. My eyes cut back to the museum just as the rear section sagged.

"It's still in there?" Maggie repeated, heat rising in her throat.

"Where's Caroline?" I demanded. "The woman who was with us?"

Maggie would have had blood slaves watching the front door too.

"She never came out," the vampire replied in a scorched whisper.

I staggered back with a wheeze as the chill energy of the vampiric bond gathered around my neck and squeezed.

"And neither did my locket," she said.

25

"Everson, you all right?" Bree-yark asked.

I stumbled past him, reeling from the attack but also from the suggestion that we may have lost Caroline, not to mention our portal back to the present in Arnaud. With one hand, I clawed at the invisible bond cinching my neck. The other was already drawn into a fist, Grandpa's ring aimed at Maggie's face.

"*Balaur,*" I rasped.

But the expected boom didn't follow.

"Ye made the deal willingly," Maggie said, pushing herself to her feet.

I shook the ring and tried again, the Word emerging as a gasp this time, but she was right. Our agreement had effectively suspended the Brasov Pact, at least as it applied to the two of us. Now Maggie was using the energy of our broken agreement as a weapon to choke off my breath and voice.

"Not only did ye fail to produce my locket," she said, "you've destroyed it."

"Hey, what're you doing to him?" Bree-yark shouted above his drawn blade.

But as he rushed Maggie, her orphans appeared and were suddenly all over him. The goblin swore as he struggled to free himself. More of the diminutive blood slaves headed off Gorgantha, who had begun circling the vampire's blind side, her right fist cocked.

Hellcat Maggie's inflamed eyes never left mine.

"Do ye know what ye destroyed?" she demanded, limping toward me. "What it *meant?*"

I gagged as she upped the strangling force. But driven by the fire's intense heat, strong winds were gusting through the window now, tossing her hair. When a thick mass flipped across her eyes, I lunged forward and drove a heel into her prosthesis. Bolts snapped at the knee, and Maggie reeled.

I landed a forearm against her neck and pushed with my legs. Maggie's failing prosthesis buckled into a backward stumble until I had her pinned against the stone wall. Casting may have been out, but my blade didn't require words, and the tip was already buried in her sternum.

As smoke hissed from the penetration, Maggie's body locked up, suggesting the blade's silver edge had punctured a major vessel. Her head rocked back in a silent scream. Off to the side, Bree-yark and Gorgantha shook stunned blood slaves from them like they were rag dolls.

I adjusted my grip in preparation to cleave Maggie's vampiric heart. Destroying her would mean losing a possible lead to an Upholder, but we'd already lost that in the bonfire that had once been Barnum's Museum. And the broken agreement would continue to strangle me until either she called it off or I finished her.

"Don't do it."

Caroline stood in the doorway, her hood down from her golden hair. She stepped into the room, Arnaud behind her.

Though I'd sensed she had escaped the blaze, the sight of her sent relief rushing through me.

"Withdraw your sword," she said.

Can't breathe, I mouthed back. *Vampire bond.*

She nodded as if she understood but then repeated her command. Hesitantly, I pulled the blade free. Maggie came to immediately. Her thrashing arms knocked me aside. I stumbled to a stop beside Bree-yark and Gorgantha, hoping Caroline knew what the hell she was doing.

The vampire took quick stock of the room, her eyes wild from her near death. When she sighted her assemblage of blood slaves, her lips twitched up at the corners. But the smile quickly abandoned her mouth.

"Well, go on!" she snapped, meaning for the slaves to attack us.

Instead, they began turning and facing the wall like punished children. I sensed Caroline's subtle enchantment. Maggie must have too, because she trained her full glare on Caroline now, lips drawing from her filed teeth. Wresting a slave from a vampire's control was considered deeply insulting.

"How dare ye," she seethed.

But Caroline's demeanor remained unchallenging. "We've fulfilled the agreement."

"The fuck ye have."

Caroline reached into her cloak and withdrew something on a slender chain. The change that came over Maggie's face was immediate. One moment it was scrunched up and venomous; in the next, it was a child's on Christmas morning.

Maggie stared at the locket that swung pendulum-like from Caroline's fingers before heaving her damaged prosthesis into its first step. The vampire didn't seem to notice her buckling gait or care. Caroline met the lurching vampire halfway. But when she held out the locket, Maggie paused.

"It's no longer warded," Caroline said, lowering it into her hand.

With the agreement fulfilled, the pressure left my throat, and I took several heaving breaths. Maggie touched the locket in her palm, as if to make absolutely sure it was real. I expected her to fasten it around her neck, but she placed it carefully in one of her skirt pockets. When she looked up, moisture sheened her eyes.

"It's done, then." Maggie said it like a *thank you*, but her tone quickly turned vampiric. "Ye can find yer fellow traveler at the Old Bell Tavern at seven o'clock this evening." She reached into her skirt and tossed me something. I bobbled it before securing it against my chest: a pocket watch, so we could keep track of the time.

"Does the traveler have a name?" I asked.

"Yes, Lazar."

If the man in question was indeed an Upholder, that meant Malachi or Jordan. But I'd never heard either one referred to as "Lazar." We could be dealing with someone altogether different, possibly even demonic.

"How about a description?" I pressed.

"Ye can see for yourself tonight," Maggie snapped.

Following her elation at recovering the locket, the vampire seemed edgy now, anxious to return to her sanctuary. For no other reason, maybe, than to be alone with her prize. Her eyes flicked over each of us as she staggered toward the door. Released from Caroline's enchantment, the children filed behind her.

"Hey, what's so special about that locket, anyway?" Bree-yark called. The question clumped up his brow in a way that reflected my own curiosity. I'd sensed no magic or special properties in the locket.

Expecting the vampire to leave us guessing, I was surprised

when she stopped. "It belonged to my little girl," she said quietly, and left.

A vampire who turned children—even a time catch version of them—made my blood cook. But Maggie's parting words, and the tender way she'd spoken them, had me reconsidering her motives. I shook the notion from my head. Trying to moralize a vampire's behavior was a blood-slick slope best left alone.

Caroline joined us, Arnaud in tow.

"Nice going," I said to her. "But what happened to looking not touching?"

A smile brushed Caroline's lips. "P.T. Barnum's office was well defended. But then alarms began to sound, and the guards locked the office and headed upstairs. When cries of fire followed, I doubted we'd get another shot at the locket. The door was easily breached, and the locket easily found, thanks to the ward. Barnum had stored it behind a false wall in his closet, along with some other artifacts."

"Was the ward powerful?" I asked.

"The original would have challenged me, I'm sure, but being an echo, I was able to overcome it." She knew what I'd been asking, because she added, "And yes, the magic was similar to your own."

I suppressed my emotions with a measured nod. The 1861 version of my grandfather may have left Barnum's American Museum, possibly over the treatment of the other acts, but the active ward that resembled mine meant he was still around. Unfortunately, it didn't put us any closer to finding him.

Unless he's Lazar, I thought suddenly.

"I hate to interrupt," Gorgantha said. "But someone wanna tell me who you cats are and what the crunk is going on?"

"I'm Bree-yark," he said, stepping forward and extending a hand.

Gorgantha took it, even though he hadn't really told her anything.

"I'm Everson Croft and this is Caroline Reid," I said. "You and I belonged to a team called the Upholders." Once again, I showed her the symbol on my hand before indicating hers. "There were three others: Seay Sherard, Jordan Derrow, and Malachi Wickstrom. It was a mutual defense arrangement. Three of your groups were infiltrated by demons. We traveled to 1776 New York from the early twenty-first century to confront them, but we all got separated. You ended up here somehow."

The mermaid's scaly brow knitted as she studied the symbol below her webbing. "The Upholders," she echoed. "That does make a little jing-a-ling in my head. And those other names are kicking around like they should mean something too."

"What's your earliest memory?" Caroline asked.

"Honestly?" She ran a hand along the burn scars of one arm. "Pain."

The way she said it made me cheer the fire raging three blocks away.

"If it's all right with you, I'd like to try something," Caroline said. "An intervention to restore your memories."

Gorgantha looked over at me. As far as she was concerned, we'd just met, but she'd known me longer than Caroline, and I had the added cred of helping her escape the museum. "Let her," I said. "There's a lot missing from your memory, and restoring it could help us find the others."

She looked at Bree-yark, her other liberator, who also nodded his encouragement.

"All right," Gorgantha agreed.

SEVERAL MINUTES LATER, GORGANTHA WAS ON HER BACK, Caroline cradling her head from behind. To keep the mer from drying out, I'd soaked her with one of the water bottles I'd packed. The moisture also had a calming effect, allowing Caroline to induce a light trance.

"Think it was her treatment at the museum that affected her memory?" I whispered.

"More likely being in this period," Caroline replied. "The longer one spends in a time catch, the harder it becomes to connect with outside memories. Yet another feature of the phenomenon."

"Are we in any danger?" I asked.

"As long as we don't get stuck here, no."

From my post by the door, I glanced over at where Bree-yark was guarding Arnaud, our ride home. We couldn't leave before we'd found the others and the St. Martin's site. I hoped Gorgantha would be able to help with the first.

Magic stirred behind Caroline's closed eyes and around her hands. I paced as she began restoring the connections between the mermaid's mind and her far-off memories. A few times Gorgantha twitched and muttered, but Caroline's magic quieted her again. At last, Caroline opened her eyes and gave Gorgantha's head a gentle shake.

"Wake up."

Gorgantha stared at the ceiling a moment, then pushed herself into a sitting position. She blinked her eyes and looked at each of us in turn. When her gaze settled on mine, a huge smile broke across her face.

"You janky-ass player!"

"Wait, is that a good thing?" I asked.

But Gorgantha had already jumped up and seized me under the arms. She spun me like a child. As Caroline wheeled past my vision, I shot her with a little finger pistol. Whatever she'd done had evidently worked. Gorgantha pulled me into a spine-crunching hug and rocked me side to side before setting me back down.

She wiped at her tears. "Didn't think I'd ever see you again."

When I rubbed her thick arm, I noticed that her session with Caroline had also healed her burn wounds. "So you remember what happened?" I asked. "After I left you guys on Governor's Island?"

Gorgantha blew out her breath. "More than I care to."

"Just take your time," I told her, leaning against the windowsill.

She began slowly, as if revisiting the memories with a flashlight. "Took maybe two, three hours till everyone could walk that night. Seay and her friends kept us hid with glamours, but most of the soldiers were still busy on the river, trying to figure out what happened to the big ships." She was referring to the warships whose crews Pip and Twerk had enchanted. "We got to the pickup spot at the fort, or where we thought it was, and we waited. Nothing happened. We tried a few other places, but same story every time. No ride home."

"A demon compromised the fae," I said, glancing over at Caroline. "That's why they didn't bring you back."

I cursed myself again for not marking the place where we'd arrived. But something told me that if the fae hadn't used that loophole to deny the Upholders' return, they would have come up with something else.

"So Osgood left us hanging?" Gorgantha asked.

"He was bound by orders," Caroline explained. "Had it been up to him, he would have returned you."

"That's why Caroline's here," I said.

Gorgantha made a sound of semi-understanding and began walking the room in measured paces, her tail twitching. "It was gonna get light soon," she continued, "and Seay's gang was running low on glamour juice, so we returned to the boats, rowed over to Brooklyn. We found a wooded place to duck out. The druids used plant magic to make these wicked screens for us and the boats. By daylight, the warships had started moving again. Soldiers were rowing ashore, trying to find whoever had ganked the prison ship. The original plan was for us to stay put that day, try the fort again at night."

"But not everyone agreed," I said, reading her grim expression.

"No," she confirmed. "Jordan wanted to go somewhere safer. He talked about crossing back over to Manhattan that night and laying low at your grandpa's farm, waiting for things to settle down. He even mentioned joining his druid circle up in the forest. The two who'd helped us had flown back by then."

"Lorcan and Failend," I said, remembering their names. "Jordan was probably just worried for his wife." Delphine's abduction at the hands of the Stranger had driven him into an obsessive search, often involving recklessness. We'd had more than a few head-butting sessions. But after recovering her and the other druids, it sounded like Jordan had switched to an ultra-cautious mode to ensure their safe return.

"Maybe, but Seay wasn't having it," Gorgantha went on. "She wanted to stick to the original plan. They argued about it half the day. The rest of us stepped in, finally getting Jordan to agree to try the fort again that night. So that's what we did. But British backup had been arriving all day. That dirt fort looked like an anthill. The druids and half-fae had to push their magic to the max to keep all of us hid. We tried a few spots, like the night before, but nothing took."

I snuck a look at Caroline. She was listening with an elbow propped on her crossed arm, chin resting on curved fingers. Whatever guilt she may have felt was overshadowed by an expression of concern.

"Finally, we rowed back to our spot in Brooklyn. And if I thought the arguing was bad the day before..." Gorgantha shook her head. "We could all agree the fort was a bust, but Jordan was set now on going to his druid circle, seeing if they could muster the kind of magic needed to return us. But Seay wanted to keep closer to home base. In case you came back for us." She looked over at me. "The two went at it like a pair of bullheads, their groups lining up behind them. I tried to play referee, but without Malachi, we—"

"What happened to Malachi?" I interrupted.

"The day before, he was fine. Fact, he was the one who helped bring about the truce. But that day, he was acting all janky. Then he started saying things that didn't make sense. How we couldn't stay, but we couldn't go either."

"Kind of like the song," Bree-yark remarked.

I shook my head while wondering if Malachi had had another one of his premonitions.

"Thing is," Gorgantha continued, "everyone was so busy scrapping with each other to notice that Malachi was coming unglued. At one point, he just up and disappeared. I found him off by himself, sitting under a tree. When I tried to bring him back to the group he started in about worlds colliding."

Caroline's and my eyes met.

"What happened next?" I pressed.

"Well, we hadn't eaten in more than a day, so I offered to go into the city, fill up one of the boats. Figured some food might get everyone to chill. Also figured Jordan wouldn't run off till I got back. So wearing Seay's glamour, I set out. I stayed in the water for the trip, swimming behind the boat in case I needed to bail. I was maybe halfway across the river when a cannon went off. I didn't know who it was aimed at, so I dove under and waited a few minutes before coming back up."

She stopped pacing to give us all a look that said, *You're not gonna believe this next part.*

"When I *did* come up, it was nighttime. Not only that, the city was all trees, right to the shore. Not a building or boat anywhere. And Everson, there were things swimming in that river I'd never seen before. When this huge sucker came at me, it was haul butt time. Whatever the thing was, it had flippers and crazy big teeth."

It sounded like she'd crossed the barrier into the prehistoric period.

"I was too far from any shore," she continued, "so I dove down to find somewhere I could crouch. That's when I got snagged."

"In the weeds?" Bree-yark asked.

"In a damned net," she answered. "I was pulled out of the water and onto a boat. Daytime, now. And there was Manhattan again, all built up, even more than before. The warships were gone, but the river was full of boats."

She'd found one of the points into 1861.

"I was too stressed about the net to be worrying about any of that, though," she continued. "I was tangled from head to tail— and Seay's glamour had come off. Men were all around, swearing and shouting for others to come see. I heard one of them say something about fetching a good price at 'Barnum's.' Next thing I know, *crack.*" She drove a fist into her hand. "Clubbed in the head. When I woke up, I was in a tank at that damned museum." She hesitated. There was more, but I could see she wasn't ready to relive it. "Well, that's pretty much how you found me," she finished.

"Fiji mermaid," Bree-yark grumbled.

"How long were you there?" Caroline asked.

"I lost count of the days, to be honest. Stopped remembering where I'd come from too. Who I was, even. Just kept wishing that whatever day it was would be my last. I was legit funked out. Then one day, I saw *this* cat." Gorgantha's smile broke out again as she nodded toward me. "Just standing there in the audience. Could've sworn I knew him, but I couldn't say how or from where. When you busted the tank, I thought you were a rival of Barnum's, there to steal me away. That's how come I fought back. Better the devil you know, and all that. But then you started saying things that were just too damned familiar. And the way you took down those jokers? I figured you *had* to be a good guy."

"I helped," Bree-yark put in, still starstruck by her.

"I can't tell you how stoked I am we found you," I said.

Gorgantha gave me a sidelong look. "*You're* stoked?"

"And you haven't seen any of the others since you've been here?" I asked to be sure.

"Any of the Upholders? No, just you so far."

I sent out another signal through the bond, but once again, Gorgantha's was the only one to respond.

"So what's the plan?" she asked.

I turned toward the window. Scores of fire wagons had arrived around Barnum's, and water arced from hoses—Biggs the ogre was helping man one of them. But most of the museum had already succumbed to the blaze. I checked the watch Maggie had tossed me. Two hours until our meeting.

"How about we slip out under Caroline's glamour," I said, "get you some real food, and then find out who this Lazar is?"

26

W e rattled up Broadway in a hired carriage, the five of us freshly glamoured. For the whole ride, I stared out the window on my side. I couldn't help it.

Beyond the horse-drawn carts and omnibuses, people of every shade and stripe hurried past shops with goods ranging from pineapples to player pianos to giant bolts of fabric. It was like peeking under the modern district of glass and steel skyscrapers at this colorful, noisy ecosystem it had once been—a bridge between the 1776 version, population twenty-five thousand, and my city of more than eight million.

Scraps of passing conversation entered our carriage, some of it in the blunt, clipped voices that would become the New York accent. The big news was the fire at Barnum's. The bulk of traffic was headed in the opposite direction as us, New Yorkers wanting to see the spectacle for themselves.

The upshot is that when we arrived at a restaurant called Crawford House, we had it mostly to ourselves. We ordered platters of boiled cod with beets and potatoes, enough for Gorgantha and Bree-yark to have multiple helpings.

I ate slowly, partly from not being very hungry and partly to give myself time to think.

We'd recovered one Upholder, but there were three more to locate, not to mention the St. Martin's site. If the others had separated—which, knowing Jordan, seemed likely—they could have ended up in different time catches. Something told me there were more than the three periods we'd experienced thus far. That I couldn't link to my teammates' bonds in this one suggested they weren't close enough. Or hadn't survived. I had to be brutally honest. Either way, that put the identity of "Lazar" as an Upholder in doubt.

Grandpa? I wondered again. *Or demon?*

"When we get to the Old Bell Tavern," I said to Caroline, "I should go in first and check it out. See who we're dealing with."

"I can cover you," she said.

I nodded. That would leave Bree-yark and Gorgantha on outside watch. I peered past Caroline to where Arnaud sat, still glamoured in a thick coat and scarf to hide his restraints and muzzle. A quick check showed me that my wards remained at full strength. But his staring eyes looked more sunken.

"How's he doing?" I asked.

"Warded and entranced," Caroline said. "He's also weakening."

"How long before he's critical?"

"Hard to say with the time deformities. I'll keep a close eye on him."

A grim look of knowing passed between us. If Arnaud *did* become critical, we'd have to consider allowing some infernal energy back into him. It was either that or risk losing our line back to the present. And I remained convinced that he was somehow the answer to freeing the Order.

Leaning nearer, Caroline lowered her voice. "You should know that I've been cut off too."

I looked over in confusion. "From Faerie?"

She nodded. "My kingdom has denied my lineal rights. I can no longer access certain familial energies."

As I'd guessed, the demonic influence went high up the chain. Though Caroline maintained a stoic expression, the small crescent beneath her mouth deepened in either determination or sadness, maybe both.

"What does that mean for your casting?" I asked.

"I can draw from other sources, but they're not nearly as potent. I still have a reserve of familial energy. I just need to be judicious."

"Keep me posted on how you're doing."

"I will." She looked at me intently now. "I've missed you, Everson."

The quiet words arrived like a surprise blow to the chest. I glanced over at Bree-yark and Gorgantha, who were making garbled conversation between ravenous mouthfuls of their dinner. My neck warmed under the collar of my glamoured trench coat as I struggled for how to respond.

"I didn't think that was possible," I said at last.

But being cut off from her fae line probably explained why she'd seemed more human. Was it also weakening the bargain under which she'd sacrificed her feelings for me? As I considered the question, I shifted over, putting a little more space between us.

"I'm not telling you this to make things awkward," she said. "If anything, it's to clear the air." Her hands withdrew from the table to her lap. "I understand that you have your own life now, but in the small reservoir that's remained Caroline Reid, you've never stopped being special to me. I wanted you to know that."

A part of me let out a little. "I'll always consider you a close friend."

"The feeling's very mutual," she said. "Just don't ask me to cover your classes."

When she smirked, I chuckled. "How about running the occasional interference on Snodgrass?"

"God, I almost forgot about him. How's that going?"

"Better since he had me over for dinner a few weeks back."

Her eyes widened. "At his house?"

"Yeah, his wife insisted. Turns out she needed my magical *expertise*. She also wears the pants in the family. I never thought I'd feel bad for Snodgrass, but seeing him grovel was actually kind of painful. He's avoided me ever since."

She snorted a laugh. "I wish I could've been there."

I very nearly agreed, only because she had history with Snodgrass too. But though Caroline's admission *had* helped clear the air, I couldn't get too comfortable. Vega's parting words —*I trust you*—were layered. She was trusting me with Caroline, but she was also counting on me to be cautious.

"Speaking of the fae," I said, changing the subject. "Are you expecting them?"

Caroline's smile turned introspective. "Back when I was deciding between remaining human or claiming my fae blood, I would take long drives, always at night. Not to think, but to get out of my apartment, my head. One night I might end up in White Plains, another in Edison. Places I'd never been, no idea how I'd arrived there. But the same intelligence that steered me to these towns, often dangerous shells of places, would always bring me safely home. This experience feels a little like that."

Not sure whether she'd missed my question or was just being evasive, I said, "You're listening to your faeness."

She'd seemed to blur a little as she spoke, but now the lines of her face sharpened. "Yes, I suppose I am."

I poked a small potato around my plate with a fork. "I'm trying to do the same with my magic, but it's not saying much.

The only hard assertion I've gotten so far is to come to the time catch, that this place is the key to ... well, everything. The St. Martin's site feels like the epicenter, the answer to all the questions."

"That's where the fae will be waiting." It took me a beat to realize she was answering my question from a minute earlier. "One advantage of this mess with the time catches is that I'm much harder to find. But they know where I'm going to be."

"And this mess will give them time to get there," I murmured before gathering myself. "Listen, Seay and Jordan have half-fae and druids with them. By the time we arrive at the site, we're going to be a small army."

"A kickass one," Gorgantha agreed between bites, catching the last part.

I was trying not to think about how formidable Angelus had looked debarking from his giant roc and striding up to me, power radiating from his green eyes and tossing hair. He'd had others with him too.

"What does your magic say about me?" Caroline asked.

Her pointed question caught me off guard. "Well, it's yet to tell me to run," I joked, a part of me wincing at having shown my hand. "No, it's been in this contemplative state all day," I hurried to explain.

"Do you trust your magic?"

"Generally, yeah. It hasn't let me down so far."

"Maybe that's why it seems to be in an ambiguous place."

"I'm not following."

"It could be that it's talking, but you're not ready to hear what it has to say. But if it always leads you home..."

As Caroline returned to her meal, I considered her words.

Something about them resonated.

By the time we left the restaurant, dusk had fallen and gaslights flickered up and down the street.

I felt better as I stepped forward to hail a carriage. Better about Caroline, better about the uncertainty ahead, better about our chances. We also had a sound plan for Lazar. This wasn't going to be another headlong adventure where we could only react to whatever the time catch threw at us.

A spiky wave tore through me, and I pitched to the ground.

"Everson?" Bree-yark said, rushing up to me. "What the heck's going on?"

I tried to speak, but it felt like my guts were being twisted with a set of subzero skewers. I clawed at the sidewalk, panting protective Words through a fog-like scent of death. Hoofs clopped and axles groaned as a carriage pulled up in front of us. For a moment, I pictured a black hearse being driven by the Grim Reaper.

"Get him inside," Caroline said.

Gorgantha lifted me under the arms and Bree-yark got my legs. Together they lifted me into the carriage. I curled beside the far window and clutched the drapes, praying for the agony to end. Caroline gave the driver our destination, Old Bell Tavern, and the horses began clopping us toward Broadway.

Fae magic we couldn't spare stirred around me, and the gut-twisting sensation faded by degrees. Several more minutes passed before I was able to release the drapes and push myself upright, my hairline cold with sweat. The inside of the carriage rotated once before steadying.

"I'm all right," I said faintly.

Gorgantha leaned forward. "What the hell happened?" She was sitting opposite me, glamoured to look like a large man.

From beside her hunkered head, Caroline's knowing eyes met mine.

I stole another look out the window. "Something's hunting

me. Something from the present. I'm pretty sure it came to my apartment while I was out this morning, and I sensed it later in the Upper East Side."

"That thing followed you here?" Bree-yark asked.

"It looks that way." I wasn't sure whether to be freaked out or super annoyed.

Bree-yark squinted between me and Caroline. Earlier, he'd accused her of creating the threat. Now he appeared uncertain. If her intention *had* been to rush my decision to use Arnaud, there was no reason to keep up the ruse.

"But how?" he barked. "I thought coming here took serious magic or a connection to one of these guys." He hooked a thumb at Arnaud.

"It's from the realm of the dead, and it's locked onto Everson," Caroline said. "It will go where he goes. I've fashioned a glamour to hide him. Not a strong one," she added, anticipating my protest. "Just enough to muddle the connection, make it much harder for this entity to draw a bead on him."

"It's not a gatekeeper, I hope," I said.

Gatekeepers were powerful entities that guarded the realm between the living and the dead. I'd foolishly tried to trap one a couple years earlier while searching for info on my mother. Now I wondered whether the same gatekeeper had built up enough vacation time to come after me. It ticked a lot of the boxes.

"No, not a gatekeeper," Caroline said.

"That's a relief."

"A revenant."

I straightened. "A revenant?"

"The hell's a revenant?" Gorgantha asked.

"A spirit that returns to the world to track down and destroy its killer," I said. "Are you sure?"

Caroline returned a solemn nod. "The being was close enough that I could sense its undead fixation on you. It's powerful enough to ford planes, and it won't stop hunting until either you're dead or it's destroyed."

"Then we destroy it," Bree-yark said as if that settled that.

I dug a thumb and finger into the corners of my eyes. "Much easier said than done, buddy. Besides retaining whatever abilities they had in life, revenants are a special kind of nasty. Undead powers and immunities out the wazoo."

"How many suckas have you plugged?" Gorgantha asked.

I thought for a moment before replying, "A lot."

"Well, which ones would still have beef with you?"

"Since things tend not to like getting killed, all of them."

I flipped through the opponents I'd faced over the years. While most, if not all, had the motivation to come back for me, only a few would have possessed the means. Turning revenant required powerful magic.

"Old Bell Tavern," the driver called from outside.

"Listen, guys," I said. "I appreciate your concern, but our focus right now is Lazar. Let me worry about the revenant."

For starters, our time here was limited. I also didn't want to involve my teammates in something that freaking deadly. When our work was finished and we were back home, I'd deal with it myself. The one silver lining with a revenant was that it was only interested in its target. It wouldn't go after Vega or anyone close to me in the meantime.

But did it have to be hunting me now, dammit?

And here?

I declined Gorgantha's help down from the carriage, even though I was still queasy and my legs felt uncertain. Breeyark pulled Dropsy from his pouch, but told her to keep her glow on the down-low. As the carriage U-turned across the dirt lane, Caroline came to my side.

"How are you feeling?" she asked.

"Much better. Thanks for your help."

"You're hidden now," she assured me, referring to the revenant.

I nodded, even though I hated being a sink on her finite powers. "Just let me know how you're doing."

"We're in what will become New York's Upper West Side," she said, changing the subject.

As the horses clopped away, I looked around at the farmland that had been cleared and converted into building lots. For now, the result was a grid of dirt lanes, where ley energy trickled weakly. Plank homes were scattered here and there—squatter housing, most likely—but the city was clearly planning its thrust northward.

"Central Park is under construction to the east," Caroline continued. "Many of the laborers live around here, so that's who we can expect to find in the Old Bell." She nodded at the building catty-corner to us, a two-story tavern with a hanging sign out front. A mass of figures crowded beyond the windows, the rise and fall of their murmuring voices breaking into occasional bouts of shouting and laughter.

I checked the pocket watch. Seven o'clock on the nose. By the time I looked up, Caroline was back in her male guise. She had altered our glamours so that we looked like laborers now, dusty coats and sweat-stained shirts.

"Good work," I said. "Let's move."

I crossed the road, skirted some horses tethered to a post, and opened the tavern door. A rowdy wall of noise hit me first, followed by a yeasty wave of beer and body odor that made my eyes water. Every surface on which one could conceivably sit was taken, the bar in the tavern's back a solid five men deep.

I edged over to a plastered wall darkened by lantern smoke for a better vantage. My gaze went face to face in search of anyone I recognized. The place was mostly men, laborers as Caroline had guessed, the majority looking as if they'd come straight from their shift at Central Park. They were Germans, Irish, and Italians, all talking at once, their dialects as rough as their ruddy faces. No one stood out for me.

I peered back. Caroline had entered and was standing in an inconspicuous spot near a window. From there she could see Bree-yark, who'd taken over Arnaud duty and was watching the door from the outside. He had a line of sight on Gorgantha, who was keeping tabs on the side and back of the tavern.

Three men in aprons and drab shirts tended the bar, sleeves rolled to the elbows. While two of them busied themselves filling tumblers and steins, the oldest stood off to the side, a towel over one shoulder. He was tall with a lean, somber face and a widow's peak of iron-colored hair. I pegged him as the tavern keeper and the other two his sons. He seemed to be searching the tavern for someone.

An instant later, his eyes fixed on mine. I glanced away as if I hadn't been watching him. I waited several beats before walking my gaze back toward him. His eyes hadn't moved. He'd singled me out.

Lazar?

Before entering, I'd tightened my magical aura to avoid detection from supernatural types. Now I risked the use of my wizard's senses. Colorful arrays of astral energy overlaid the tavern. The man stood out for his subdued patterns, which was probably just sobriety. Nothing preternatural. But by moving to one side, arms folded, he was signaling to the thirsty bar crowd that he was no longer serving. They'd responded by pinching toward his sons, creating a narrow lane along the wall for me to traverse.

I edged along the opening until I was standing opposite him. The man regarded me for a moment, tongue searching a rear molar, before unfolding his arms.

"What'll you be having?" he asked in an English accent.

"Whiskey."

He prepared it quietly and set the small glass on the bar. Patrons shoved around me now, shouting out drink orders. The man raised a hand for their silence, his sober eyes remaining on mine. Though there was no magic in them, I saw an intelligence honed by decades of studying people.

"What else?" he asked, less a question than an observation.

"I'm looking for someone named Lazar."

"And what are you wanting with him?"

I sensed everything depended on how I answered.

"Someone believes we know each other."

"And who is this someone?"

"Hellcat Maggie."

His slow blink may have been a reaction—I couldn't tell. He walked over to his sons, leaned close to tell them something, then returned to me. He lifted a plank of bar and stepped aside for me to pass.

I sensed Caroline behind me, still watching.

As I joined the man, he lowered the plank again. Taking an oil lantern from the bar, he stepped out a back door and led the way across a small yard. I followed, reassured by having seen Gorgantha near the road. Given the dearth of ley energy, I was going to need backup if this were an ambush. The man stopped at an outbuilding, its door outlined in light.

"Lazar?" he called.

From inside came a moan and the sound of straw rustling.

The man turned to me. "He started early today, so I'm not sure how clearheaded he is."

It took me a moment to get that he meant drinking. When the man reached for the knob, I stopped him.

"Look, I'm not sure what I'm walking into here."

He lowered his hand. "Hm. Maggie's boy indicated as much."

That explained why the tavern keeper had been keeping an eye out for me. Maggie had sent one of her blood slaves to arrange the meeting, probably even including a description of what I looked like.

"I'm Everson, by the way."

I didn't bother with an alias since Maggie had already overheard my name.

"Jack," he replied, gripping my hand. "What're you wanting to know?"

"Well, who Lazar is, for starters."

"No one can say. Turned up when a tenement house caught fire. Lazar delivered several women and children from the blaze, but got burned awful bad himself. When he pulled through, he was given the name Lazar, short for Lazarus. We gave him work here, mostly out of charity. He's still not well." He tapped his temple. "Helps out during the day, cleaning and such. But he drinks sometimes. When he does, he ends up like this. Other times, he wanders off. Sometimes for months."

"Where does he go?"

Jack shrugged, which had me thinking about the time catches. "Makes his way back eventually," he said, "but each time looking considerably worse for the wear. When Maggie's boy said someone was coming to see about him, I'd hoped it was family. At this point, the old man needs caring after."

Old man?

"I'll leave you two," Jack said, and before I was ready, he opened the door.

Inside, a lit lantern hung from a peg. Against the opposite wall of a simple room, a man lay on a bed of straw-ticking. He was curled on his side, facing away from the door. A mass of gray hair burst from the top of his covers. I turned toward Jack, but he was already crossing the yard back to the tavern.

"Lazar?" I ventured.

The mattress rustled, and the man craned his neck around. A dirty hand emerged and cleared the hair from his face. The left half had been badly burned. A weeping gray eye peered from a bed of scar tissue.

I could see right away that I didn't know this person from Adam—if he was even a person. I gripped the handle of my cane sword. When the man's eye sharpened, he drew a sharp breath that triggered a coughing fit from deep in his chest.

I took a tentative step forward. "Are you all right?"

He nodded as he got control of his hacks, then rasped, "That you, Everson?"

I stopped and stared. *Did he just say my name?*

The old man pushed his covers aside and sat on the edge of the mattress. He was dressed in tattered clothes, dirty bare feet crossed at the ankles. "You remember me, right?" he pled. "You haven't forgotten?"

He gathered hair from his face with both hands now. The scarring on the left half extended from his hairline down to a threadbare chin. He tilted his head so the good half caught more lantern light. I examined the gaunt angles and leathery skin for some clue to his identity.

"I'm ... I'm afraid I don't recognize you," I said.

He released his hair from his sagging face. "No one does." Then very softly, "It's Malachi."

Malachi?

I dropped to my knees and seized his hands. Where the bond would have been was more fire-scarred skin. Pushing his hair from his face, I searched one gray eye, then the other. Age had paled the irises, but I could see the resemblance to the young man I'd known. I switched to my wizard's senses. Amid the chaotic pattern of his aura, I picked out familiar touch-stones, including currents of St. Martin's, where he'd spent so much time.

"Malachi Wickstrom?" I asked.

A light took hold in his eyes. "You remember?"

"Malachi Wickstrom of St. Martin's Cathedral?" I asked. "Of the Upholders?"

Clutching my hands, he sprang up and began shuffling his bare feet back and forth over the plank floor. "Yes, yes! You're the only one, but you remember!" He leaned his head back, his mouth opening to reveal a set of teeth ground down to pebbles. "He remembers!" he cried to the heavens.

Stunned by the revelation that this old man was somehow my teammate, I let myself be carried into his dance. But how in the hell was that possible? Malachi stopped suddenly and gripped my wrists.

"I chose you," he said in a conspiratorial whisper, the smell of gin breaking against my face. "Just as I chose the others. But time is short, is short." He looked wildly around. "The elements of the Night Rune gather."

"The Night Rune?"

"Come!" he cried.

He released me and dug under his mattress, eventually emerging with a Latin Bible that looked like it had survived hell. But even tattered and burned, I recognized it as the same one he'd carried into the time catch. He ignored the shoes at the foot of his bed and staggered past me, bare feet scuffing toward the door.

"Hold on a sec," I said, catching his arm. "You need to fill me in on what's going on."

Malachi thrashed his bony arm with surprising strength. "Time is short!" When I didn't release him, he started swatting my hand with the Bible. "Let go of me, dammit! *Time is short!*"

"Time for what?"

"To reach St. Martin's in, in, in 1776!"

I hesitated. "You know where the 1776 St. Martin's site is?"

He nodded fervently, sending his wild hair everywhere. "And the others!"

"The others—you mean the Upholders?" I stammered. "Seay and Jordan?"

"Yes, yes, but time is short, is short!"

"I understand, but let's sit down for a minute."

"No, the elements of the Night Rune gather!" he screeched. "The apocalypse is nigh! The demon apoc—"

Without warning, he swooned in my grasp. I caught him before he collapsed to the floor and lowered him down to the mattress. He was still breathing. The combination of elation, exertion, and inebriation had overwhelmed his aging body. When I examined his face again, I could see Malachi more clearly.

But what in the hell could have happened to him?

Heart thudding, I called for Caroline.

28

I stood back from the bed as Caroline worked on Malachi, fae energy already bathing his head. I'd called Gorgantha too, knowing she would want to see her teammate. When she arrived with Arnaud, I left the door open to keep a line of sight on Bree-yark. He remained on watch outside, Dropsy glowing sedately in his grasp.

"Damn!" Gorgantha exclaimed.

"I told you he'd aged," I said in a hushed voice.

She lowered her voice to my level. "Aged? He looks like a troll. How did this happen?"

"That's what Caroline's checking out. But he claims to know where Seay and Jordan are."

"Then why aren't they here?"

"Same thing probably happened to them as you—being in the time catches too long. I'm guessing Malachi tried to get through to them but couldn't. He said I was the only one who remembered him."

Gorgantha thrust her lower lip at Malachi. "How did *he* remember?"

Still in her male glamour, Caroline sat back from him.

"Because he never spent enough time in one time catch. Driven to stop the demon apocalypse, he's been jumping from one to another. The upshot is that he's retained his memories—or most of them. But the transitions also sped his aging."

"How many transitions we talking?" Gorgantha asked.

"Hundreds, possibly thousands," Caroline said.

Gorgantha's eyes popped wide. *"Thousands?"*

"It may sound implausible," Caroline said, "but the time structures are hopelessly distorted down here."

"And he's survived?" I wondered aloud.

"He's created a mental map of the time catches," Caroline said, eyes closing again. "Quite comprehensive. So, although his thoughts are fragmented, I believe he knows where to find the others and the St. Martin's site. I can't see details of the map, unfortunately. His mind is too ... chaotic. He'll have to lead us."

"Is he in any condition?" I asked.

"My enchantment will restore what it can. But he's made these journeys before."

I looked down at Malachi, who rested quietly now. The picture of what he'd become—a crazed mind inside a wasted body—kicked me in the heart. I remembered the timid acolyte he'd been at St. Martin's. He led me to the cathedral's catacombs, where I managed to channel the power of the church into the demon lord Sathanas.

When visions of an apocalypse began visiting Malachi's sleep, he became a de facto demonologist. He located Gorgantha, Seay, and Jordan, whose groups had been infiltrated by demonic Strangers, and he created the Upholders. Then, for reasons he'd yet to fully divine, he recruited me. By that time a zealotry to stop the demon apocalypse gripped him. But he retained an innocence that made me feel responsible for him, like an older brother for his younger sibling.

On the straw-tick mattress, the scarred corner of his mouth twitched.

"Did you find anything about a Night Rune?" I asked Caroline. "When talking about the apocalypse, he said 'the elements of the Night Rune gather.'"

She shook her head as she rose. "His thoughts are too tangled. Restoring them is beyond the magic I can invest, perhaps beyond any magic. I've smoothed as much as I could. He should be more coherent when he awakens."

"How long will that be?" With a host of fae on their way to head us off and a revenant tracking me, I was anxious to be moving again.

"As long as it requires." She smiled faintly. "How's that for a fae answer?"

"Not bad," I allowed, looking around the room. We'd left Arnaud in a shadowy corner, and as my gaze moved past him, the skin around his eyes seemed a little too tense for someone entranced. But by the time I took a second look, his eyes had assumed their prior slackness. A trick of the light?

"How do Arnaud's restraints seem to you?" I asked Caroline.

I kept a close watch on him as she walked up beside me. "Intact. Why?"

They felt intact to me too, humming with the warding energy that negated his powers and cut him off from the infernal realm. Arnaud's face continued to exhibit the sunken look that had begun to concern me in the restaurant. When I snapped my fingers in front of his eyes, they remained empty globes.

"Hey, guys?" Gorgantha called from the doorway. "Bree-yark's signaling."

I turned from Arnaud. Past the mermaid's body, Dropsy's light was pulsing an emergency sequence from the road.

Shit, I thought, pulling my cane into sword and staff.

"Mind staying here with these two?" I asked Caroline,

gesturing to Arnaud and Malachi. Now that she was drawing from a limited reservoir, we needed to preserve every ounce of fae energy for the essential work: glamours, Arnaud, and restoring the Upholders—not to mention getting us back to the present.

"Go carefully," Caroline said.

As I hurried from the building, Gorgantha fell into step behind me. I gathered the weak currents of ley energy and firmed the air into a shield, though I didn't know how much protection it would actually afford us.

We were halfway across the yard when Bree-yark backed into our view. He had hooked Dropsy to his belt and drawn his goblin blade. When he saw us approaching, he hustled into the yard to meet us.

"We've got a mob coming," he said. "And they don't look right."

I ventured past him to the road. Large crowds were coming down Bloomingdale Road from both directions, torches blazing above a sea of heads. But unlike the human stampede I'd encountered in Five Points, these crowds moved in utter silence. The only sounds were the march of boots and crackling of torch fire. Yeah, eerie as fuck. I opened my wizard's senses and swore some more.

"What is it?" Gorgantha asked when I returned.

"Remember the soulless soldiers from 1776?"

"That some kind of tongue twister?" Bree-yark grunted.

"Yeah, I remember," Gorgantha said, massaging a fist. "Cracked a knuckle on one of their noggins."

"Well, we've got two soulless mobs coming our way." I turned to include Caroline, whose glamoured figure split the light from the outbuilding. "It means there's a demon active in this time catch. One of Malphas's, judging from the interest in us. We've got about a minute to get Malachi out of here."

"I'll grab him," Gorgantha said.

Caroline emerged with Arnaud. "How many?" she asked.

"Fifty?" I guessed. "Too many to take on." Especially with ley energy scant and fae power at a premium.

"We could squeeze out through there." Bree-yark pointed to a space between the outbuilding and tavern where some old beer barrels had been stacked. "That'll take us east, away from the mobs."

I nodded quickly as Gorgantha emerged with Malachi cradled in one of her massive arms. She'd hung his shoes around his neck by the laces and tucked his Bible into the waist of his loose pants. I took lead, shoving the barrels aside. Behind the wall of the tavern, drunken laughter sounded. I was almost through when I spotted a third mob coming from the direction of Central Park.

How many frigging souls did he claim?

Signaling for everyone to stay low, I led the way around the back of the outbuilding and then cut northeast through a field of chicken coops. We were too exposed in this part of the city. Central Park would give us cover. But the southbound mob wasn't fooled. The glow of their torches veered from the road to head us off.

"I can glamour us," Caroline whispered from behind me.

"Let me try something first. You, Malachi, and Arnaud down here, against the coop." As Gorgantha set Malachi on the ground, I turned to Bree-yark and signaled for him to pass Dropsy to Caroline. He unclasped the lantern from his belt and handed her over. Caroline nodded, catching on to what I was planning.

"All right, everyone in close," I whispered.

Bree-yark, Gorgantha, and I arranged our bodies into a shield around the other three. Caroline's free hand was gripping Arnaud's far shoulder, holding him to her side. I searched the demon-vampire's eyes for any signs of cognizance, but they remained sunken and empty.

Caroline whispered to the lantern, and Dropsy's light pulled in, wrapping herself in a glamour of invisibility. The glamour swelled to encompass Caroline, Malachi, and Arnaud, but only caught the edges of the rest of us.

Knowing that might happen, I whispered, *"Oscurare."*

The shadow of the coop deepened around us until we were as concealed as we were going to be.

The southbound mob arrived moments later. They spread throughout the plot in a silent mass, torch light reflected in their hollow eyes. Judging by their appearances, the demon had selected them from the poor streets and shipyards—men and women who wouldn't be missed. As the mob neared, torches warped the shadows around the others coops, but the one concealing us remained an immovable block.

The westbound mob joined them, several members wandering within feet of us. I gripped my sword, ready to activate the banishment rune, but the lantern's glamour coupled with my low-level invocation were doing their jobs.

Soon, both mobs were beyond us. I waited to be sure no stragglers were coming up behind them before releasing the invocation with a shaky breath. As the coop's shadow lightened around us, the lantern's glamour contracted back inside the glass. Caroline, Malachi, and Arnaud returned to visibility.

I peered over the top of the coop at the diminishing torch lights. The mobs were moving east, which meant Central Park was out. While Gorgantha lifted Malachi, I helped Caroline to her feet.

"Know of anywhere nearby we might be able to lay low?" I asked.

I'd cycled through a few places before exhausting my knowledge of the period. My first thought, of course, had been a church—St. Martin's, even—but the threshold would strip my powers. Plus, through regular exposure, Malphas's demons had immunized themselves against the churches in the time catches. Our protection would be questionable.

Before Caroline could reply, Malachi murmured from Gorgantha's arm. "The bluffs..."

We all turned toward him. His eyes were closed, but his hooked hands were twitching as through trying to claw his way back from sleep.

"What bluffs?" I asked.

"On the Hudson," he slurred. "That's the way to ... to Seay's time."

"No jokin'?" Gorgantha said.

"What time period is that?" I asked.

Charges of anticipation were going up and down my body at the thought we could soon have eighty percent of the Upholders back together. But though Malachi's lips sputtered, no words emerged. I prompted him a few more times, but he'd lost his struggle and fallen back to sleep.

Caroline peered around. "The bluffs are northwest of us. And frankly, I don't think we're going to find much refuge here."

"Especially with an active demon," I agreed.

"I've had my fill of 1861 anyway," Bree-yark grunted.

"Damn sure know I have," Gorgantha said.

We crept from the coops and headed west under the light of a half moon. Beyond the squatter shacks, the landscape turned into cleared building lots and empty streets. Here and there lights burned from what looked like a boarding house or small estate. We avoided them, sticking to the most undeveloped parts of what would become the Upper West Side.

Soon, I made out the wooded heights over the Hudson River —the bluffs Malachi had mentioned. We could duck out there until Malachi recovered enough to show us the location of the portal.

"Riders coming," Bree-yark announced.

He had taken the rear, and I turned to find his glamoured ears perked up. Soon, I heard the distant rumble of hoofbeats. Torchlight glowed into view a moment later, flickers of orange over several streets.

"Dammit," I muttered.

Caroline pointed out a grove of trees. "We'll have better cover that way."

"Let's go," I said, pulling Arnaud by the manacles. "Gorgantha, see if you can wake Malachi."

We took off running toward the trees, Bree-yark stooping intermittently for stones to arm his sling. I attempted to speak a shield into being, but the ley energy was even more scant here than a few blocks back. After a few sputtering attempts, I gave up.

As we reached the grove, the cracks of gunfire sounded. The lead riders had come within about a block of us.

"Give me Arnaud!" Caroline shouted.

I passed the demon-vampire to her and waved for her and Gorgantha to continue to the wooded bluffs. Bree-yark and I followed them through the grove for several rows of trees before taking cover from the riders. There were about a dozen of them, their dead auras betraying their soulless states.

"Hit 'em hard," I called to Bree-yark. "There's no humanity left in them."

With a grunt, he slung his first stone. It smacked the forehead of the lead rider and sent him into a backward tumble from his mount. More shots cracked, splintering bark past my face. I had a handful of invocations that could have scattered them like bowling pins, but I lacked a decent energy source.

As Bree-yark loosed another stone, I eyed my blade's banishment rune and spoke a Word. Hallowed white light flickered around the etching—and just in time. A rider was charging up my row. I waited until he was almost even with me and swung. The contact of blade on rider was glancing, but it was enough to send holy flames ripping up his side. The horse bucked him to the ground and bolted. Meanwhile, Bree-yark had taken down another rider, but we had eight more coming.

"How you doing?" I called to him.

"A shot nicked me, but I'll live," he grunted. "You?"

"Fine, if I can get close enough to these guys."

More gunshots went off, pinning us behind our trees. I looked toward the bluff. Caroline, Gorgantha, and the others had disappeared from view, and I imagined them crouched inside another of Dropsy's glamours. I felt better knowing Gorgantha was with them in the event any riders got past us.

"Get yo' ass back here!"

I looked over to find the massive mermaid charging into the grove from the west. *What the...?* Ahead of her was what at first appeared to be a bag of rags blowing in the wind before I made out the shape of Malachi. His tattered clothes and long hair flew every which way as he raced toward us like a man possessed.

"Down!" I called to him. "Get down!"

But he kept coming. The remaining eight riders veered toward him. Bree-yark and I broke from our cover to try to head them off. I shouted to get their attention, but they were locked onto Malachi. If the riders took him out, we would not only lose our friend, but our guide to the time catches.

The demon Malphas clearly knew this.

I pumped my glowing sword like a relay baton, struggling for another speed. Bree-yark slung several stones, but they were off target. Malachi slowed, seemingly confused by the sudden attention, his Bible clutched to his chest.

As the first riders closed in on him, Bree-yark and I were still too far away. But Gorgantha wasn't. Reaching Malachi just ahead of the riders, she scooped up a thick branch and swung it. The branch split against a rider's head and knocked him to the ground. Two more riders aimed revolvers, but Gorgantha had the presence to duck behind a tree before shots exploded from barrels.

The remaining riders circled Malachi until he was blocked from our view. Shit.

I aimed my sword. Though there wasn't enough energy for a banishment blast, I had another option: drawing power from Arnaud's wards. It would mean weakening the demon-vampire's restraints, but to spare my teammate and friend, I'd have to chance it. A silent flash detonated among the riders.

But it hadn't come from me. A moment later, the riders thudded to the ground. Their horses remained a moment longer before bolting away. At their former center stood Malachi's hunched figure.

I completed my run toward him. "Hey, are you all right?"

White light lingered in Malachi's eyes as he looked around. Gorgantha stepped from her cover and peered from him to the fallen riders. "You were wondering how he's survived all this time?" she asked.

Yeah, no kidding, I thought.

Somewhere along the line, his banishment abilities had reached apostle level.

"Hey, uh, Everson," Bree-yark said, jogging up to us. "We've got more coming."

I turned and swore. In the middle distance, a second wave of riders was approaching.

Malachi snapped his fingers as if suddenly remembering why he'd run toward us. "You wanted to know where to find Seay?" he asked, the light that lingered in his eyes dwindling to points. "This way!"

He took off toward the bluff. The rest of us exchanged puzzled looks and followed. When we reached the trees, Caroline emerged from her hiding with Arnaud.

"He just got up and ran," she explained of Malachi.

"It's all right," I said. "He's taking us out of here."

Malachi led the way at a crooked run that was surprisingly fast. In fact, we had to call for him to slow down several times so we wouldn't lose him. Behind us, the fresh wave of riders had reached the grove. Ahead, the woodland fell steeply to the Hudson. We were running out of real estate.

"Watch out!" Gorgantha called.

Malachi's arms flew up and he dropped into a crevasse. The rest of us slowed to a stop and peered down. The fracture in the earth was rocky and littered with leaves, but there was no sign of our teammate.

"The opening is there," Caroline said.

A moment later, I picked up the small fold of multicolored energy.

"Let's go," I said, relieving Caroline of Arnaud and waving the others down.

Bree-yark wasted no time jumping into the crevasse. Gorgantha, who looked skeptical, chose to scale her way down. Both disappeared into the fold. Caroline gave me a small wave and stepped from the edge.

I took one final look at the approaching riders, then seized Arnaud around the waist and dropped in too.

29

I crunched into a foot of snow and nearly fell, but Gorgantha was there to steady me. I held her arm and squinted past the icy pellets stinging my face.

By all appearances, we were on the same bluff we'd left behind, only it was daytime, and we were in the clutches of a winter storm. A bracing wind flapped my trench coat while snow fell in a steep slant over the wide river below. The far shore —what would become New Jersey—was a pale presence thick with trees. We were somewhere else in New York's distant past.

"Can we go back?" Bree-yark asked.

The goblin stood in a shivering hunch, his back to the driving snow. Having shed his scorched coat at Barnum's, which had been his glamoured bomber jacket, he was wearing only a tight undershirt. Large goosebumps covered his tattooed arms.

I looked past him to Caroline, who'd raised the hood of her cloak. Beyond her, Malachi was pacing at the end of the ledge we'd ended up on, muttering and ticking items off his fingers. When I called his name, he hustled over, apparently unbothered by the weather despite his ragged clothing.

"Where are we?" I asked.

"Well, that's the Hudson River, and—"

"I mean when?" I interrupted. "What year?"

He squinted upward, then shook his head in apparent frustration. "That escapes me, but it's Dutch times."

"Dutch?" Gorgantha said.

"And this is where Seay is?" I asked to be sure.

"She's in the settlement, in the settlement with the others. In New Amsterdam."

New Amsterdam had been the predecessor to New York City, a 1600s settlement on the island's southern tip. "Then that puts her about six miles away, give or take."

"What's known as the Old Indian Trail runs east of here," Caroline said. "It follows the general course of what's now Broadway."

"All right, good to know," I said.

That would deliver us to the settlement, but we were looking at a three-hour hike in single-digit temperatures. I couldn't shield us for that long. If Caroline had been at full strength, she could have warmed us, but she wasn't, and my face was already going numb, my words turning mushy. Bad for casting.

"Is there somewhere we can shelter?" I asked Malachi.

He nodded readily. "There are some caves up this way, up this way."

Like a skipping record, he was repeating words and short phrases. Another effect of jumping between time catches, evidently. Without waiting, he scampered down the ledge to the ice-crusted shore. The rest of us followed, me guiding Arnaud while Bree-yark told the winter weather all the things it could do to itself.

"Not far, not far," Malachi kept calling back.

We soon arrived at a honeycombing in the bluff's stone base. Malachi led us inside the deepest one, out of the elements. As I shook the snow from my coat, I noted the blackened fire ring in the middle of the floor and the wood stacked against a back wall. I scanned the cave again to make sure we were alone.

"Oh, that's mine," Malachi explained, retrieving a small box and a handful of kindling from behind the wood pile. "I've stayed here a few times, a few times."

He opened the box to reveal steel, flint, and tinder. While he arranged the fire-starting implements, Bree-yark and I tee-peed the kindling inside the ring. Malachi got a spark to take, and we were soon blowing life into the budding flames. As Bree-yark began setting larger pieces in place, I saw the bloody gash on his neck where the bullet had nicked him. The ley energy was stronger in this period than the time catch we'd left, but when I offered to heal him, he waved me off.

"Save it for someone who needs it," he barked.

He snuck a peek at Gorgantha, clearly wanting to impress her. I hoped he wasn't forgetting Mae, but this felt more like hero worship than attraction. At least he hadn't mentioned Gretchen again.

Gorgantha remained near the mouth of the cave, water puddling around her feet following a plunge in the river to rehydrate.

"Aren't you freezing?" Bree-yark asked her.

"For a New England mer, this is beach weather. That fire would dry my scaly ass out. I'll keep watch on the river."

Appearing disappointed, Bree-yark pulled Dropsy from his pouch and set her in the spot he'd apparently been saving for his new idol. The lantern peered around, but soon abandoned the fire ring to explore the rest of the cave. Across the flames, Malachi was back to muttering and ticking his fingers.

"What are you doing?" I asked.

When he saw the rest of us watching, he chuckled nervously and stuffed his hands into his jacket pockets. I realized it was the same jacket—hell, the same everything—he'd entered the original time catch with. Nothing else would have made the transitions, much like the watch Maggie had given me. Gone now.

"I have a system for keeping track of the time catches," he explained. "Where to get in, where to get out."

"How did you find the interfaces?" Caroline asked.

"Some through wandering, others by divine inspiration."

Malachi used to have dreamtime visions, and I wondered now if the power that had boosted his banishment abilities had also done the same for his divine sight. It might also have helped preserve his clothing.

"How many time catches are we talking?" Bree-yark asked.

"Oh, hundreds probably," Malachi said offhandedly. "Most are from long ago, before there were people. I avoid those, but sometimes you have to go through one to arrive at another, to arrive at another."

Despite the repeats, he seemed more coherent than he'd been back at the tavern before Caroline's intervention. But I still wanted to test him. "Do you remember entering the first time catch with the rest of us?"

"That was a long time ago, but yes. I remember being worried about the British soldiers, the British soldiers."

"How long is long?" Caroline asked.

He searched the ceiling of the cave, lips pursed. "Fifty years?"

"Holy thunder," Bree-yark muttered.

I exchanged a glance with Caroline before saying, "You've been in the time catches for fifty years?"

"I'm estimating, but around that, yes."

"What have you been doing?" I pressed.

"At first, looking for you and the others, the others. I don't remember quite how, but we were separated. You went after a demon, I think..." He trailed off. "Is that him?"

I followed his gaze to Arnaud, whom I'd sat on the floor

beside me. Above his muzzle, hollow eyes stared at the flames. His infernal energy had dipped, likely from exposure to the extreme cold. I was hoping the heat would restore him.

"Long story, but yeah," I said. "And we need to protect him, keep him warm. He's our ride home." I cinched Arnaud's wrist restraints, which had begun to loosen around his emaciating limbs.

Turning to Gorgantha, Malachi continued his story. "You swam to the city for something. And, and Seay and Jordan had a fight. Went their own ways." He paused as though searching deeper inside his memories. "The Divine Voice was telling me that worlds were on a collision course, collision course. I only understood when I crossed into another time. It took me years to find the others."

Gorgantha made a confused face. "I was in that museum months, not years."

"It was different for you," Caroline explained. "You only passed through two time catches. Malachi here has transitioned through hundreds, each one with a different temporal structure. And all warped."

I was still trying to get my brain around the concept, but I was a professor of mythology, not theoretical physics.

Malachi continued as if we hadn't been talking. "The thing was, I couldn't make any of the Upholders recognize me. Tried everything I could think of, could think of. Went back more times than I can count. They thought I was drunk or, or crazy. But the Divine Voice kept saying I needed them, needed them." He wrung the dingy end of his jacket in frustration. The burned skin where his symbol had been gleamed in the firelight. "Then the Divine Voice told me to find the St. Martin's plot."

"The 1776 one?" I asked to be sure.

"Yes, the burned one. There are a few others, a few others, but a church occupies those sites in one form or another."

Making it too dangerous for the demon Malphas to attempt to manipulate that ley energy, I thought. *Hence the focus on the 1776 site, after faith had shaped the fount and the Great Fire had torn down the channeling structure.*

"That's where the demon apocalypse would commence, the Divine Voice told me," Malachi continued. "It took me twenty years, maybe more, but I finally found it, found it. A platform had been built."

I sat up a little straighter. "A platform? On the site?"

"Or what looked like a platform. I couldn't get close enough, close enough to tell. When I tried, I was met by a force. Felt like my skin was melting from my bones, my soul shaking loose. The energy was so raw, so *intense.*" He drew his burned hand into a fist, the passion of old returning to his eyes.

It sounded as though the copper plates were active, directing ley energy back at the massive fount, making it too strong to approach. I wondered now if the smarter course was to journey to the St. Martin's site first. We could shut down the plates, effectively thwarting Malphas's plans. That would also introduce some stability to the time catches. Who knew how much longer these realities would remain solvent?

"What if we went there now?" I asked Malachi.

A dreadful look came over his face. "Now?" He drew his fingers down his scraggly cheeks. "No, no, we must go together. That was why I chose you. Chose all of you." He looked over at Gorgantha to include her. "It's so clear to me, clear to me. The Upholders must face the forces of the demon apocalypse *together.*"

"But if we can disarm the site..." Caroline began.

Malachi shook his head, sending his hair in all directions. "No, no, no, no," he repeated.

When he didn't stop, I was afraid he was going to have a breakdown. *"Malachi,"* I said sharply, but he kept on. Bree-yark edged away from him, while Dropsy peered out cautiously from behind the woodpile.

But Caroline, who was on his other side, rested a hand on his back.

"Malachi, it's all right," she said in a soothing voice. "It was just a suggestion. We didn't know."

His words crumbled to sobs as he bowed his head to her shoulder. She stroked his head until it stopped shaking.

Eventually, he sat up. Tears wet the folds of his cheeks. In his eyes, I saw fifty years of fear, futility, and frustration. Even so, I checked him out again through my wizard's senses. His aura was all over the place, but it was Malachi.

"The ones who chased us," I said, "the soulless mobs. Have you encountered that before?"

Malachi sniffled. "From time to time, but not in those numbers. The Divine Power protects me, protects me and purges their evil."

"You can say that again," Gorgantha muttered, having just seen it in action and up close.

I wondered now if the demon Malphas had been using the soulless mobs to keep an eye on Malachi, only feeling threatened enough to deploy them en masse when we joined up with him. But what about the one who changed them?

"How about a demon?" I asked.

Malachi's face darkened. "I've not seen any here."

"Not even at the St. Martin's site?" Caroline asked.

Malachi shook his head. "The energy I felt there was raw but not infernal."

"Any visions?" I asked, hoping for some insights into this mystery demon's doings.

"Of demons?" He let out a high laugh that verged on crazed. "That's all I've been seeing. Nightmare visions of them flooding into the world. Wars, famine, pestilence, death. Billions of lives, of lives." That seemed to line up with Tabitha's premonitions that had her self-medicating with booze. Malachi swiped fiercely at the tears welling in his aged eyes. "We mustn't let it happen."

"We won't," I assured him.

"Not as long as I'm breathing," Bree-yark put in, glancing at Gorgantha again.

I felt like a bastard for being disappointed Malachi lacked info on the mystery demon. His knowledge of the time catches alone was a game changer for us, huge. It was just that demons of Malphas's caliber were incredibly hard to outmaneuver. And I couldn't help but feel he was setting us up somehow.

"You mentioned something about a Night Rune," I said. "What did you mean?"

The folds on the unburned half of Malachi's face deepened. "Night Rune?" he repeated.

"Yes, back at the tavern. You said, 'The elements of the Night Rune gather.'"

He gave me a pained look. "I'm sorry, I'm sorry." Tears stood in his eyes. "I don't remember."

"It's all right," I said before he could break down again. "Just let us know if it comes back to you. *Night Rune.*"

As he mouthed the words, I considered our next move. I was anxious to reach the St. Martin's site, especially with the knowledge Malphas was mobilizing to stop us. But Malachi was convinced we needed to recover Seay and Jordan first, and I felt obligated to trust his Divine Voice. Maybe because he'd come around to my magic's wisdom when it had led us to my grandfather in 1776. And Seay *was* only six miles away.

"What can you tell us about Seay and the other half-fae?" I asked him.

"They run a business in the settlement. Fashioning clothes from beaver pelts. Coats, capes, hats. Especially hats."

"They worked in fashion in the modern era," I explained to Bree-yark, who looked perplexed. "In the Garment District."

"And you've encountered them?" Caroline asked Malachi.

"Oh yes, several times, several times. But Seay thinks I'm crazy."

Before I could put the question to her, Caroline nodded at me. "I have enough power to restore her."

"Good deal."

And if all went well, we'd have twenty plus half-fae to help with glamours and enchantments, offloading the burden from Caroline. That made me feel better about recovering Seay before journeying to the St. Martin's site. The question now, though, was how to approach the settlement and get our teammate alone.

Gorgantha backed from the cave entrance and spun toward the fire.

"Two boats coming downriver," she whispered.

30

I spoke a Word, and the cave's shadows deepened, cloaking us and reducing the firelight to a faint dance in the darkness. Gorgantha led us back to the mouth of the cave, where snow continued to slice over the Hudson.

"There," she whispered.

Upriver, faint as ghosts, two boats were approaching. They were small, without sails, and as they drew nearer, I counted four paddlers in each.

"They're fur traders," Caroline said at my shoulder. "The front boat is Dutch made, the trailing one a canoe with native rowers, likely from one of the Algonquin-speaking tribes. Can you see the piles of pelts?"

"Yes, yes!" Malachi exclaimed.

One of the men stopped rowing and seemed to perk up. I clapped a hand over Malachi's mouth, and the rest of the team instinctively drew back into the cavern even though the shadow invocation still hid us.

"We need to keep it down," I whispered to Malachi.

His gray eyes flitted back and forth, still full of excitement. I waited for him to nod before removing my hand.

"Sorry," he said in a rushed whisper. "But they're going to New Amsterdam, to Seay!"

I watched the boats until the lead man resumed rowing. "How do you know?" I whispered back.

"When I was here before, I learned much about her operation, her operation. Most of the pelts are sold to merchants and shipped to Holland for tailoring into clothing for Europeans. But Seay and her friends created a local industry. She buys a portion of the pelts, the pelts and makes the clothing here, for the colonists."

"That's smart," Bree-yark said.

"It won't take much for me to enchant them," Caroline whispered behind me. "They could row us right to her." When I hesitated, she added, "It will save time. The other option is a twelve-mile roundtrip slog."

The boats were making their way swiftly downstream. They'd be even with us shortly, though a quarter-mile offshore.

I turned to Gorgantha. "Can you lure them in closer?"

A COUPLE MINUTES LATER, A THICK DUTCHMAN IN THE FRONT BOAT shouted and pointed ahead. The paddler opposite him was also Dutch, while two American Indians—Algonquins, Caroline had confirmed—rowed in the rear.

Gorgantha waved back at them from midriver. She then dove underwater, making sure to lash her tail. The crest of her fin created a V-shaped wake as she angled back toward shore. By now, all of the rowers were talking excitedly. Paddles dug in, and both boats began veering toward us.

Nicely done, G.

I waited until the boats were less than fifty yards out before hardening the air behind them and pulling them in. With fresh shouts, the men tried to back-paddle. One of the natives even rose as if to dive into the water. But Caroline's enchantment met them, and the men settled down and drew their oars in.

As the boats' hulls scraped onto the rocky shore, Caroline walked out to meet them. Gorgantha emerged from the water and stood beside me.

"How was that?" she asked.

"Perfect," I said, clapping her muscled back.

At the edge of the water, Caroline spoke with the men. As they climbed out and began transferring pelts from the canoe to the pile in the Dutch boat, I stared, wonderstruck, at another piece of living history. The tall Algonquins wore leather tunics and leggings, as well as thick capes that appeared to be bearskin. The two blond Dutchmen were in pantaloon boots and wide-brimmed hats.

When they'd moved about half the pile, the six Algonquins boarded the canoe, making use of the extra space. They shoved back into the water and were soon paddling upriver, ghosts once more.

"I'm sending them back to their village," Caroline said. "That leaves two spots with them." She indicated the Dutchmen, who had returned to their own boat.

"All right, huddle up," I said, waving in Gorgantha, Bree-yark, and Malachi. "Caroline and I will go to New Amsterdam for Seay, but your job here is going to be just as important, if not more so. You can't let anything happen to him." They followed my pointed finger to Arnaud, whom I'd sat against the cave wall. "No Arnaud, no getting home. Got it?"

I had strong reservations about leaving him, but with the extreme cold depleting his energy, I couldn't risk taking him along.

"You can count on us," Bree-yark said. "Right, Gorgantha?"

When she agreed, he smiled with all his teeth: extreme pleasure in goblin.

"Anything else we should know about New Amsterdam?" I asked Malachi.

"It's small, easy to get around—only fifteen hundred people or so, or so. Oh, but there is one person you should watch out for."

"Who's that?"

"The vampire Thorne."

"Of course," I muttered. *Fucking Arnaud.*

"He operates the biggest counting house on the waterfront."

I'd been hoping he hadn't arrived in the New World by this time. Avoiding him in the crowds of 1861 had been easy, but with only fifteen hundred in the settlement, our cover was going to be scant.

"What's he going by now?" I asked.

"Tristan," Malachi replied. "Tristan Thorne."

"Okay, thanks. We'll keep our heads down."

"The glamours I have in mind should help," Caroline said.

THE COLD WIND OFF THE RIVER MADE MY FACE AND HANDS HURT, but my fur coverings and the work of rowing warmed the rest of me. Caroline and I had taken the front positions, the Dutchmen the rear where they could steer as well as row.

Caroline's hair was glamoured into a long black ponytail that complemented her russet features. A bearskin, like the ones the men had been wearing, covered her body. She was saving on fae power by remaining female—wives occasionally accompanied their husbands on trading errands, she'd said. And I was the husband, glamoured into a strapping Algonquin. It was a smart glamour, even if it felt like I was being a little disloyal to Vega somehow. I retrained my gaze downriver.

"Remarkable, isn't it?" Caroline said, panting lightly.

"Rowing the Hudson in 1660? Can't say it was on my bucket list."

Caroline had estimated the year based on the population size. Now her laughter sent up a small plume of fog. "Mine neither, but as a former scholar of New York's urban history, it's surreal to be living it. I feel guilty for admitting that."

"Don't. I've caught myself gawking more than once."

"Glad I'm not the only one," she said. "These pelts, for example. Just think—they're the economic foundation of what will become one of the wealthiest, most vertical cities in the world."

I glanced back at the pungent heap of furs. "Beavers, huh?"

"'Soft gold,' the traders called them."

"Listen to you, Prof."

"It's Sooleawa," she corrected me.

My Algonquin name was Makkapitew, which knowing the Caroline of old, was very likely an inside joke.

"'Former scholar,'" I quoted her. "Does that mean you're not coming back from sabbatical?"

"I guess it depends on how everything turns out."

I'd steered the conversation there intentionally. "We're going to defeat Malphas."

"Even so, the faes' memories are long. Our kingdom could remain fractured. I may have no choice but to return to the city, go back to teaching."

"As a cast out?"

She nodded solemnly.

"You love him, don't you," I said after a moment. "Angelus."

"It took time, but yes. I do."

"But he's the one possessed."

I'd harbored the suspicion ever since encountering him in

Faerie. Not only had he tried to alienate me from Caroline, but he'd flown toward Crusspatch's refuge on the rocs following our encounter. And when I'd asked Caroline if she knew the fae who had fallen under shadow, she'd said, "Well enough."

She'd wanted to protect him. An instinct born from love.

Caroline glanced over with her dark, native eyes. "Yes. He's the one."

"But how did Malphas get to him?" I lowered my voice, even though the Dutchmen were enchanted to think we were speaking Algonquin. "He's one of the most powerful fae I've seen up close."

"My husband had been acting odd, pensive. When I pressed him, he mentioned a dream he'd had about an inbound darkness, a dream that had clearly disturbed him, but he wouldn't say more. He only grew more distant. Then one day he asked if I had been in contact with you. I hadn't seen you in years, but I *was* spending more time in the city. Partly to keep my father company after he retired from City Hall. Still, I couldn't understand why he would ask out of the blue like that. Until your letter arrived."

She was referring to my appeal for help to access the time catch.

"It was as if my husband had been expecting you to send it," she continued. "I noticed too that Osgood hadn't delivered the letter directly to me."

I took a break from paddling. "No?"

She shook her head. "But he left it where he knew I would find it. When I confronted Osgood, he admitted that Angelus had instructed him to intercept any correspondences intended for me. By this time, Osgood sensed something was off with Angelus too, and he began exploiting loopholes in his directives."

That must have been how the fae butler was able to continue collaborating with Caroline.

"My husband was barricading himself behind loyalists," she said, "holding meetings in secret. In your letter, you mentioned an infernal breach and demons infiltrating groups. That went a long way toward explaining Angelus's behavior, why he was so intent on blocking contact between you and me."

I snapped my icy fingers. "Back when Arnaud possessed me and locked me in his vault, he absorbed my thoughts—that was when you helped me at Columbus Park. Malphas would have had access to those same thoughts through his infernal bond to Arnaud. He would have known about our friendship. He clearly thought you were my one good chance to enter the time catch and disrupt his plans."

"And when you did," she said, "the repercussions came swiftly."

"Placing Osgood under even stricter orders. Forcing you into hiding. Severing your lineal claims."

"Murdering Crusspatch to keep you from returning," she added.

But something was still gnawing at the back of my mind. "Why didn't Angelus kill me in the Fae Wilds, then? I was helpless, trussed up, unable to cast. Malphas could have ended the threat of me going back right there."

"Because I would have gone in your place."

"And Angelus wanted me to lead him to you," I said in immediate understanding. "End two threats in one fell stroke."

Good thing I tossed the stone.

Plotting Malphas's moves like this was helpful, but too much remained shrouded. He'd infiltrated the fae and placed Angelus under his service, but he also had a mystery demon in the time catches, not to mention some sort of works going on at the St. Martin's site. Add to that the fact he knew we were here, but aside from a soulless mob that couldn't shoot straight, he'd offered no real resistance. I revisited what Caroline had said about attacking us, not where we were, but where we were going to be.

"How many fae can we expect at St. Martin's?" I asked.

"Angelus and his loyalists, certainly. So at least eight."

Damn. "How about help from the good fae?"

"I tried," she said wearily. "Believe me."

"Not even Osgood?"

"He did what he could, but he's dutybound to Angelus's family."

I was still curious how a fae as godlike as Osgood had become their servant, but now wasn't the time. "Do they have any weaknesses? Anything we can exploit?"

Caroline rowed silently for several strokes, snowflakes gathering across her lashes. At last she blinked them away. "When Angelus and I wed, he closed the ceremony with a heart vow. I wasn't expecting it—that wasn't part of the arrangement—but he was determined to prove his commitment to me."

"Wait, back up. What's a 'heart vow?'" Though I possessed a respectable understanding of the fae, many, if not most, of their customs remained veiled to outsiders.

"It's a bond that only I can access, and it endures for life."

"To his heart."

"To his life force."

Her troubled expression told me the rest. By pushing power through the bond, she could hit him where he was most vulnerable. Possibly to the point of destroying the possessing demon, but which could well destroy Angelus too.

"Does he have one to you?" I asked.

"I was given the choice, but I didn't grant it."

That gave her a big advantage, and a very grave decision to make.

We rowed in silence for several strokes, small waves slapping the side of the boat. Caroline had glamoured my cane into an ornamental stick, and I glanced down at it now. It held the means to banish demons, but my chances of getting the blade through a being as powerful as Angelus were next to nil.

"One more question," I said.

Caroline looked over guardedly.

"What does the name Makkapitew really mean?"

She let out a surprised laugh. "Man with large teeth."

"What? I don't have—" I broke off. "Oh, no you didn't."

"I couldn't think of any other names, and your glamour had to match."

"You gave me buck teeth."

Smirking, she dug her paddle into the water. I joined her, grateful to have drawn a smile. I couldn't imagine her pain. Her husband turned against her by a demon. A husband who could be awaiting us at the St. Martin's site. A husband she might have to kill. I exhaled an unsteady breath.

Right now, Seay.

31

R owing with the current, we covered the miles quickly. Before long, wooden palisades appeared on our left with a tower on its near corner. We were looking at New Amsterdam's northern defenses, which would become Wall Street. The impressive defense ran along the shore—a church spire and a couple of windmills rising beyond—and ended where a large fort began on Manhattan's southern tip. Further along, rows of gabled houses stood facing the harbor. I looked over at Caroline. Though her face remained serious, her eyes gleamed with interest.

As we circled the southern tip, considerably narrower than in the present thanks to the later addition of landfill, the people of New Amsterdam began to appear through the snowfall. I remarked that they looked like a cross between pilgrims and swashbucklers. "The majority are going to be Dutch and French," Caroline said. "Some Germans, some English. A couple hundred slaves and freemen. We may encounter natives, but they'll be here on business. No one will expect us to speak."

"Good thinking," I replied.

Buck teeth or not, she'd glamoured us well.

We made our way toward a large wharf, rowing past anchored ships, and pulled up to a pier. While one of our Dutchmen secured the boat, the other returned with a large handcart. I followed their lead and began unloading the beaver pelts. Caroline stood to the side, scanning our surroundings. Despite the weather, the waterfront was active with merchants and sailors porting cargo between boats and warehouses.

When we'd loaded the cart, the larger Dutchman took the handles and wheeled it down a muddied, snow-trampled road. Caroline and I followed. We hadn't gone far when a sharp whistle sounded.

"Oy! How much for the squaw?"

I glanced over to find a group of men huddled outside the door of a corner tavern. Their shirts were open despite the weather, and by their slouching, wavering stances, I could see they were already three sheets to the wind.

Brilliant.

"Oy! Chief!" the same one cried in a crude English accent. He was talking to me. "I'll give ya' a nice wampum for her."

The rat of a man dug into his pocket and pulled out a string of shells that looked like they'd been recovered from a pit toilet. When I realized he was proposing to swap them for Caroline, my hands balled into fists.

"Keep walking," Caroline said, her eyes fixed straight ahead.

The man staggered after us, holding out the dirty wampum. I returned a deadly stare.

"Aw, don' take offense, Chief. We're good mates, jus' off the ship. Cold and lonely is all. We'll go gentle on her." The other three men guffawed and stumbled after their spokesman in a slovenly trail.

Caroline had our Dutchmen speed their pace until we were turning the corner onto a street that ran along a deep canal. If I wasn't mistaken, this would one day become Broad. According to Malachi, Seay's place was only two blocks along the canal on the left. I was more anxious than ever now to get there.

"They'll lose interest," Caroline assured me.

She was right to ignore them, of course. A confrontation with the drunks would only draw attention. "Next time give yourself a set of buck teeth too," I told her, relaxing my hands. But Rat Face's boots crunched into a jog behind us.

"I'm tryin' to barter with you," he called irritably. "You know that word, don' cha, Chief? *Barter?*"

When we ignored him, his boots scuffed to a stop. Then, in a burst of resolve, he broke into an all-out run.

"Give us the squaw whore!" he cried.

I wheeled and met him, slamming the heel of my palm into his throat. He doubled over and seized the place in both hands where I'd felt cartilage crunch. When the others rushed up, I uttered a Word and swept my glamoured cane. A wall of hardened air broadsided them and sent them tumbling into the canal.

I leaned down until my lips were beside the gasping man's ear.

"Keep away from us," I said over the shouting and splashing below. "Or the next time, I'm gonna wear your scalp like a fucking cap." I pinched a greasy strand of hair atop his head and plucked it free. "Do you understand?"

He squealed and nodded desperately.

"That was subtle," Caroline said as we left him.

"I don't think anyone saw."

I glanced around the intersection to make sure. Fortunately, the steady snowfall seemed to be keeping the settlement's residents indoors. Most of the activity was off to the west, toward the fort. The people looked like little moving impressions, too busy and distant to have observed us.

But now I made out three stationary figures, one stout, the

other two lean. Whether they were facing toward us or away, I couldn't tell, but something about them made me itch. I lengthened my strides until we were beyond their view.

"Something wrong?" Caroline asked.

I shook my head, not even sure what I'd seen.

The Dutchmen turned a corner and parked the cart in front of a storehouse. A clothing shop stood immediately beside it, both buildings part of a larger estate with a sizeable garden and additional housing. The brightly-colored buildings with their neat trim suggested fae. The faint currents of magic sealed it.

"This is it," I whispered to Caroline, anticipation pumping inside me.

The door to the storehouse opened, and two men whom I immediately recognized as Seay's friends waved us in.

Pelts of various sizes and colors filled shelves and stood in neat stacks on pallets. Natural light glowed through high windows, while lanternlight entered through a doorway in back, where I could hear voices. Probably the workshop where the pelts were fashioned into clothing. I knew nothing of the trade, but this had the look and feel of a successful operation.

While the half-fae inspected the haul and talked with the Dutchmen, I pushed power into the bond on my hand. The lines of the symbol came to life, and a moment later, I had a connection. Seay was here.

I nodded at Caroline, then instructed the bond to summon our target. As the signal went out, I wondered if it could still compel her to respond. With the time distortions, there was no telling how long she and the others had been here. Judging from the operation, at least a year, maybe more.

Now I picked out a familiar voice among several coming from the workshop. A moment later, a woman appeared in the doorway. She said something over her shoulder and then faced the storeroom. Though the hair at the front of her bonnet was glamoured strawberry blond, the face that peered back at us was natural. She appeared a little older than I remembered and was sporting fewer freckles.

"Is this the shipment from the Hackensack?" Seay asked.

It took me a beat to realize she was referring to a tribe and not the city. When her associates answered in the affirmative, she came over to examine the pelts, running a hand over the fur. She kept her right hand behind her back.

"Six guilders per pelt," she declared.

The Dutchmen conferred and came back with seven. Seay agreed and signaled to the two half-fae. They disappeared through a side door, presumably to retrieve the payment. Under Caroline's enchantment, the Dutch traders moseyed to the far end of the storeroom, leaving us alone with Seay.

She glanced up at us, eyes glimmering green, then stepped around the cart. Her lips pursed as she searched my face. I'd rehearsed a pitch to explain who we were and why we'd come, but she spoke first.

"Nice teeth, Everson."

I stared back at her. "You remember me?"

Her right hand flashed into view. I stumbled backwards, the sting that spread across my cheek only adding to my confusion. Did she just slap me? She'd clearly seen through my glamour, clearly remembered me—so what was with the hostility? She advanced, but Caroline stepped over to meet her.

"Okay, calm down," Caroline said. "We're here to help."

"*Help?*" She thrust a finger past Caroline's shoulder. "Bucky here abandoned us in 1776. He left us in that hellhole to die."

"No," I said firmly. "Malphas blocked your return."

"One of his demons compromised the fae," Caroline explained. "Made it so you couldn't come back. Everson's been working his ass off to get back into the time catch so he could find you and the others."

"And who are you supposed to be?" Seay demanded.

Caroline relaxed her glamour, allowing her face to become her own. Recognition registered in Seay's eyes, but she maintained a surly expression as Caroline's fair-skinned features turned Algonquin once more.

"Wow, fae royalty," Seay deadpanned. "I'm floored."

"Look, we have Gorgantha and Malachi," I said. "And now we've found you. Only Jordan and his druid circle are left, and Malachi knows where—"

"Jordan," she cut in. "I'm almost as pissed at him as I am at you. He's the reason we ended up here."

"Yes, Gorgantha told us what happened," Caroline said gently. "And I'm sorry. But it's time to leave."

"Leave?" Seay snorted. "Not going to be that easy, your highness."

Assuming she was referring to her clothing business, I said, "We're in a time catch, Seay. This place has already happened. It's going to loop and loop until it comes apart—which could be any moment."

Seay was wearing a long coat over her gown. She unfastened it in front and raised her eyebrows at us as a round belly pushed into view. I swore to myself and exchanged a look of disbelief with Caroline.

Seay was pregnant.

Really pregnant.

"So, what happened?" I asked her.

"Do you really need the rod A, slot B explanation?"

"I mean everything," I said, flustered, "from the beginning."

We had moved the conversation to Seay's office, a small room off the workshop with an ornate wooden desk and velvet chairs. The Dutch traders remained in the storehouse helping count out the pelts.

Seay sighed. "After Jordan split for his druid circle, we stayed in the woods in Brooklyn, waiting for you." Though she narrowed her eyes at me, the look didn't hold the same venom as it had only a few minutes before. "Gorgantha was supposed to get us some food, but she never showed."

"She became trapped in another time catch," Caroline said.

"That explains it. A group of us went out looking for her but came back empty. Thought maybe she'd decided to throw her lot in with Jordan. Anyway, after a couple days, we were in sorry shape. There were some villages nearby, and we went out at night to see what we could find. Long story short, we got lost and ended up here. We enchanted our way into farm work on a huge estate up in Yonkers. It sucked, but we got food and shelter out of the deal and time to figure out how everything worked. The farmer's brother was in the fur trade. With a little more enchanting, we learned the ins and outs and started our own business. And then we'd forgotten we'd ever done anything else."

"But you recognized me," I said.

"Only because you activated this," she said, showing the symbol on her right hand. "Everything came back in an instant, all fresh. The fear and anger especially. Sorry about the hand-print on your face."

"No worries," I said, touching the still-prickling spot. As my gaze dropped to her belly, a nervous rush hit me. Partly at the thought of my own child, but mostly at what I had to ask next. "Is the father one of your friends, or...?"

"No, he's local," she said.

Dammit, that's what I'd been afraid of.

"We're not married or anything," she hurried to add. "He's this young merchant who works on the waterfront. I met him at a party at the governor's mansion. After a night of dancing, and yeah, drinking, I woke up under a pile of bedding between him and one of the scullery maids. Hey, it happens," she said defensively.

"No one's judging you," Caroline said.

"I hear a *but* in there," Seay said. "But what?"

I cleared my throat. "We're worried about the baby."

She placed a protective hand over her swell. "What about him?"

"With the way time catches work," Caroline said, "nothing can travel outside them, including people. They're locked in this particular place and time. Outsiders like us can come and go, obviously, but..." She gestured at Seay's belly. "We're just not sure how this is going to work, the baby having elements of both."

"Leaving the time catch could kill him?" Seay asked.

I nodded grimly. "We don't know, but potentially. Yes."

Seay stood and paced behind her desk, her green eyes sharp and pensive. I couldn't imagine what was going through her mind. Join us and risk losing her child, or stay here, where both would perish.

"I can't go, then," she decided.

I raised my hands as if trying to coax someone from jumping off the Brooklyn Bridge. "Seay, listen to me. I know this isn't an easy decision, but you have to understand how fragile the time catch is. If you stay here, it will come apart, taking out you and anyone who remains, by choice or circumstance."

"If I lose him, I'd die anyway." She cupped her swell in both hands now.

"But by leaving, you'd at least give him a chance at life," Caroline said.

Seay wedged a thumbnail between her upper teeth in anxious thought. At last, she turned to me.

"Is there anything you can do?"

She meant my magic, but how could I protect a child from something of this magnitude? I considered Seay's fearful, pleading eyes before swallowing hard and nodding. "I have a potion in mind," I said. "It's no guarantee, but it will buffer your child from the transition, improve his odds of survival."

It was a lie, but a necessary one to save my teammate.

Seay nodded. "Okay."

I PREPARED THE POTION ON A WOOD STOVE IN SEAY'S KITCHEN, which was in a nicely appointed house behind the store. Cats roamed the rooms.

While I worked, combining ingredients from her pantry with others I'd brought, Caroline filled Seay in on everything to do with the demon Malphas, the St. Martin's site, and the time catches. I caught bits and pieces of the conversation. Seay confirmed that a crazy man had approached her on a few occasions, but she'd had no idea it was Malachi.

By the time I finished, Seay was up to speed, and I had a potion that did nothing.

"Here it is," I said, handing her a warm tube. I'd made the liquid pink to appear as benign as possible.

Seay looked it over and placed it in a coat pocket. "As I told Caroline," she said, "I'm going to meet with my team. None have children, but several are in relationships with locals. Two are engaged to be married this spring."

Ouch, I thought.

"We'll meet you at the caves later," she finished.

"Wait, we're not going together?" I asked.

"Between restoring their memories, explaining everything, and preparing for the trip, it's going to take me the rest of the day," Seay said with a weary breath.

"And we have Arnaud to look after," Caroline reminded me.

I'd already left the demon-vampire longer than I was comfortable. "If for some reason we're not at the caves, use the bond to call me," I said. "And if on the very remote chance we're no longer in the time catch, go to Jordan's. Malachi said the portal is inside an unusual arrangement of boulders right above what's known as Hell Gate. That's a chokehold in the Harlem River before Randall's Island."

"I know Hell Gate," she said. "It's infamous among traders."

"Just be sure to drink the potion before you enter," I said.

"I ... I'm still not a hundred percent decided, Everson."

"Let us know either way," I said. "We'll wait."

Her eyes glimmered. "Thanks for coming back for me, you jerk."

"Thanks for being so understanding."

Smirking, she kissed the spot where her palm had landed, then hugged me, making me feel both better and worse about the fake potion.

"See you soon, Bucky," she said.

32

T he snow was still falling when we left. Seay arranged for the Dutch traders to boat us back upriver, which would save Caroline from having to enchant them again. I was worried that she had less in the tank than she was letting on. But as we walked toward the dock, I was more worried for Seay.

"Do you think she'll come?" I asked.

"I put a bit of suggestion into my pitch," Caroline said. "Between that, your potion, and her desire for her child to have a future, yes. I believe she will." Though Caroline didn't say it outright, she knew my potion was a fake.

"I feel crappy about lying to her."

"You did what needed to be done."

"I hope so," I said, but the thought of the child not surviving the transition sat like a massive brick in my stomach. The child wouldn't survive here, granted, and neither would Seay. But the look she'd given me... She was trusting me with the most precious thing in the world to her right now.

We took a different route to avoid the corner tavern, one that headed away from the canal before turning left to join the waterfront. As we followed the Dutch traders, I kept my guard up, but the people we passed paid us little heed. That didn't last. We were just emerging onto Pearl Street when a hoarse shout sounded.

"Oy! There they are!" The rat-faced man had been keeping lookout from behind a stack of crates near the warehouse. He emerged now, jabbing a dirty finger toward us. "There! Over there!"

His drunken cohorts weren't with him—probably still thawing out somewhere—but four men who had been milling around the wharf with muskets on their shoulders oriented to his pointing and hustled toward us, weapons aimed.

"The rattle watch," Caroline said under her breath. "They're patrolmen."

The crowds around the wharf paused in their bustling work to watch the developing scene.

"I can take them out," I whispered back, "but it's going to cause a huge stir."

"I only need to enchant one of them," she said.

Great, I thought, *more magic we can't afford to spend.*

The four patrolmen arrived around us and began shouting in Dutch. It wasn't one of my languages of fluency, but I picked out enough German to understand the threats. Imprisonment and death by hanging topped the list, and we just happened to be standing fifty yards from the gallows.

Rat Face arrived behind them, breathing hard. A too-big coat swam around his scrawny frame. "Struck me, he did," he rasped. "Threatened to scalp me. Used Indian magic on me mates. All 'cause I said his missus was pretty."

Caroline stood calmly, eyeing the members of the patrol. It took me a moment to understand she was looking for the dominant member, the leader. After a moment, the stockiest of them, a man with salt-and-pepper hair, turned toward his associates and spoke sternly. The others put up what sounded like token resistance, but when he gestured to our accuser and made a face, they broke into laughter.

Bingo. Caroline had found him.

Rat Face looked around wildly as the patrolmen dispersed.

"Oy, where ya goin'?" he demanded. "He attacked me! Did me bodily harm!" Realizing he'd lost them, he appealed to the gathering crowd. "Said he'd scalp the lot of us, he did! Then said he'd burn New Amsterdam to the ground!"

Oh, you little liar.

As the crowd pressed in, I whispered a Word. Power flowed from my glamoured cane, hardening the air around Caroline and me. Rat Face continued to talk, working the crowd into a murmuring mob. As I searched their faces, I saw more fear than anger—which I knew from experience could be twice as deadly.

"Be ready to make a run for the boat," I told Caroline.

But before I could invoke a repulsive force, heads began to turn and the crowd backed away. As they spread out, a man paced toward us, stout and sturdy with authority. A purple coat hung to knee-length trousers that revealed a right wooden leg, carved and knobbed like a dining room table's.

"It's the governor," Caroline whispered. "Peter Stuyvesant."

"*The* Peter Stuyvesant?" I'd learned about him in high school, the last Dutch governor before England claimed the city and renamed it New York. In the modern era there was a street and park in Stuyvesant's name, even a housing project. I was going to feel really bad if it came to blows.

With each limping step, curtains of gray hair shifted around the governor's somber face. When he'd come to within ten feet of us, he stopped and peered from the shadow of his wide-brimmed hat.

"Is it true you do magic?" he asked in broken English.

"He does, he does!" Rat Face cried, elated to finally have someone in authority interceding on his behalf. But Stuyvesant silenced him with a look. Rat Face stopped hopping and retreated into the crowd.

"Speak," he demanded.

"We're leaving now," I said. "Returning upriver."

I pushed power through my wizard's voice, but something was pushing back. Caroline must have felt it too, because I caught her subtle energy moving around the governor's head, warping his large nose and heavy cheeks.

Another enchantment we couldn't afford.

"Oh, but that's not what he asked," a slippery voice interjected.

He had been moving silently through the crowd, and now he arrived behind the governor with his head servant.

You have got to be kidding me.

"No, that's not what he asked at all," Arnaud Thorne said. "Was it, dear Zarko?"

"No," his servant confirmed.

Both vampire and slave were dressed for the period, though more extravagantly. Puffy sleeves bloomed from the cuffs of colorful coats. The gold buttons down their chests matched the shiny buckles on their shoes. Both wore wide-brimmed hats, similar to the governor's, but while Zarko's fit snugly over his monkish bangs, Arnaud's sat at a rakish angle. His predatory eyes gleamed above his spreading grin.

"Now, why not answer the governor truthfully, hm?" he said. "Then perhaps he'll release you *upriver*."

As I looked over the three of them—one stout, two lean—I realized they were the distant figures I'd seen right after my encounter with the drunkards. The itchy feeling I'd gotten had been from vampiric energy. With his preternatural vision, Arnaud would have seen everything. He would also have sensed my magic, and he'd evidently shared his findings with the good governor here.

"What do you care?" I shot back. *"Tristan."*

I was so frigging over these Arnauds from the past.

"My, my, what a temper," he said. "And a perfect command of the English language. Unusual for an Indian."

His teasing voice told me he knew we were anything but.

It was up to Caroline's enchantment now. If the governor dismissed us, what could Arnaud do? But the vampire's misty powers of suggestion were countering her efforts. With a look of exasperation, she withdrew, her enchantment dispersing. Stuyvesant, who had been watching us with dulling eyes, snapped to with a sharp intake of breath.

"We have an ordinance against magic," he said. "It is not allowed here."

"And I believe they've just attempted it again," Arnaud purred. "This time against *you*, dear Governor."

The flesh around Stuyvesant's eyes balled up. "Is this true?"

Without waiting for a response, he turned and limp-hopped away, crying out in Dutch. He was going after the patrolmen. I searched the crowd in the dim hope I might spot my grandfather. But he was still in Europe in the 1660s—I was sure of that. Instead, I picked out the cold gazes of blood slaves who stood from the crowd here and there. Two had headed off our Dutch traders to keep them from readying the boat.

I glared back at Arnaud, Grandpa's ring pulsing around my finger. "What do you want?"

"The ordinance is in place for a reason," he said. "Indeed, I advised the governor in the very matter."

I scoffed. "While he was under your influence, right?"

Arnaud's eyes glinted sharply as if appreciating the challenge. "Regardless, New Amsterdam only attained city status a few years ago. It's young, vulnerable. But ah, the potential. Growing trade, budding businesses, everyone working for and in opposition to one another. The spirit of enterprise and opportunity is everywhere." He closed his eyes and inhaled sharply as if he could smell it. "Now, my friend, imagine someone coming here with the advantage of magic. It would upset the balance. Nay, destroy it."

Yeah, just like you're planning to do.

As the apex predator, the vampire was poisoning the governor's mind, weeding out potential rivals, all to monopolize the crown jewels of the city: trade and finance. They would become his fortress, one he would command for more than three hundred years, ultimately heading a cabal of vampires downtown.

If he only knew he was looking at the two who would end his reign.

"Allow New Amsterdam to grow and flourish," he finished, "to become a city that rivals London or Constantinople. Then perhaps we can revisit the question of what's allowed within its walls and what is forbidden."

"We'll leave, then," Caroline said. "No harm done."

"But who's to say you won't be back?" He arched an eyebrow. "And under a different guise? No, no, that won't do at all. We must make *assurances* to our fledgling city. Isn't that right, Zarko?"

"Yes, master," he hissed through his grinning teeth.

"Did you know there's been a demon about?" Arnaud asked abruptly.

I'd been bracing my mind against his insinuative power, but now I faltered. "A demon?"

"Oh, yes. A nasty, nasty character. I've had to run the devil out several times myself."

This had to be Malphas's time jumper, setting the stage for his master's arrival. But what could he have been doing in 1660?

Trying not to sound overly interested, I asked, "What did he want?"

Arnaud chuckled. "What do all demons want? But that's no concern of yours."

"We're hunting a demon," Caroline said. "It could be the same one."

"Well, I'm afraid the hunt is over for you, my love. Magic is an egregious offense, on par with conjuring."

He spoke as if he were closing and bolting a door. He wasn't going to give us anything else on the question of the demon. When he reached for Caroline's arm, I thrust out my fist with Grandpa's ring.

"Back off, or I'll smoke your ass right here."

The vampire sprang behind his servant. But as he looked at the silver ingot with the rearing dragon, he relaxed and released a soft chuckle. "I thought your magic felt familiar. A fellow veteran of the war against the Inquisition. I believe we have an agreement not to meddle in the other's affairs. Your name, please?"

"Sure, it's We Go Our Way And You Go Yours."

"Cleverly spoken, but your affront is against New Amsterdam, not me. This is for the governor to settle."

"Keep talking," I said, holding the ring steady. "This baby is just itching to go boom."

"If I understand your unusual speech, you're threatening my life." He tsked twice. "Attempt it, and the city will become a savage dog pack. Especially with you being *hostile natives*. Even were you to escape its walls, all of New Amsterdam would be on the hunt, leaving you nowhere to hide. Even glamoured."

He'd called my bluff. Incinerating him would endanger our hideout as well as Seay's chances of reaching us.

And while we'd been talking, the town's patrolmen had returned. Stuyvesant was behind them, shouting and pointing. I remembered reading that he'd commanded an attack on a Caribbean island, and he looked the part now. Arnaud's blood slaves made their way to the front of a crowd that was fanning to the sides in a clamor. Amid the shouting, I kept hearing a single word: *"Executiepeloton."*

Firing squad.

"They're preparing our execution," I told Caroline. And with the fluctuating nature of the ley energy, I didn't know how many musket balls my shield could repel before we'd be able to get out of range.

"Or," Arnaud stressed above the commotion, "you can work for me."

As he turned to ply another affirmative from Zarko, I glanced at Caroline. Her eyes cut meaningfully to the left. The patrolmen, eight of them now, were standing and kneeling in two rows, muskets in firing position. Stuyvesant stood beside them, poised as though preparing to give the command. But that's not what Caroline was indicating. At the back of the crowd that had amassed behind the firing squad were several of Seay's friends. When Arnaud caught my nod at Caroline, he mistook it for acceptance.

"A wise choice," he purred. "Now, relinquish the ring, and I'll call them off."

I looked between Stuyvesant's firing squad and Arnaud and his blood slaves. The second group was the bigger threat. And the easier to eliminate.

"All right," I said.

I brought the fingers of my left hand to the ring, twisted the ingot, and held out my fist.

"Zarko?" Arnaud said through grinning lips. The blood slave stepped forward. But when I opened my hand, nothing fell into his waiting palm. I had an instant to relish the surprise on Arnaud's face as I aimed my right fist at his chest. Sleight of Hand 101. The ring had never left my finger.

"Balaur!" I shouted.

The power of the Brasov Pact gathered in the silver face and released with a ground-shaking *whoomp*. A storm of force and fire enveloped the vampire, flinging him through the air. He attempted to land nimbly, but I'd put everything into that Word, and the momentum carried him ass over ankles. He slammed against one of the counting houses and collapsed in a swirl of flames.

A moment of profound silence followed where you could hear the soft brush of landing snowfall, then all hell broke loose. Amid the screaming, shouting, and scrambling, a voice belonging to Stuyvesant rose into a single, sharp command.

"Schiet!"

Smoke billowed from the shooters' position in a collective crackle.

My shield was up, and I'd been pumping as much energy into it as I could, bracing for the inevitable volley, but not a single musket ball impacted. The patrolmen had aimed past us, toward the water, where I could see the likenesses of the Algonquin Caroline and me fleeing. As the patrolmen reloaded, Stuyvesant watched the glamours—courtesy of Seay's friends—with vindictive eyes.

Caroline pulled my arm. "This way."

She'd become a Dutchwoman in a pink petticoat and gown, a bonnet covering her pulled-back hair. I'd been glamoured into her male counterpart, minus the pink. We hurried from the wharf as part of the scattering crowd, making for a street that ran past the fort.

"This leads to Broadway," Caroline panted. "And Broadway will take us north, out of the city."

Another series of shots sounded. I looked back in time to see the likenesses of Caroline and me succumbing to a volley of musket balls. We fell from the pier's edge into the East River, the water carrying us under and away. Stuyvesant nodded at a job well done.

Spotting one of Seay's friends beyond the shooters, I gave her a thumbs-up. They'd executed the glamour beautifully. Arnaud was dead, but so too were the perpetrators. There would be no "savage dog pack" hunting us.

I looked at the vampire's burning body. Several bystanders were heaving snow over it, but the flames, born of enchantment, persisted. Though I'd only blasted a time catch version of Arnaud, it still felt good.

Something rammed into my shielded jaw, shaking my vision. I pulled up, holding Caroline's arm for balance. Zarko was in front of us, his preternatural senses seeing past our glamours. But what in the hell was he doing alive? He should have succumbed to mortality when Arnaud fell. A quick glance around showed a dozen more blood slaves, several I'd spotted in the crowd, converging toward us.

"You hurt master," Zarko said.

"That's a shame," I replied. "I wanted to kill him."

When he and the others rushed in, I shouted a Word. The shield protecting Caroline and me pulsed with white light, knocking the blood slaves back several yards. I drew my sword, already grimacing at the thought of so many decapitations. My gaze fell from the blade's banishment rune to the fire rune.

Incineration would be more efficient...

But the problem, as always, would be control.

Shouts sounded. I glanced around to find the group heaping snow on Arnaud rearing back from a blooming fireball. The charging blood slaves pulled up suddenly, hands to their chests and heads. Already, their faces were shriveling, bodies contorting. Some aged in years, others in decades or centuries.

But one by one, they dropped.

"About damned time," I sighed.

"Let's go," Caroline said, skirting Zarko's desiccating corpse.

We ran past the fort and around a large marketplace, where Broadway opened out. The wide thoroughfare extended past gardens and gabled homes to a gate in the same wall we'd seen from the river. I was dreading the idea of a six-mile hike back to the caves, when a pair of horses, fully saddled, trotted into our path.

"They're enchanted," Caroline said, smiling.

Once again, Seay's friends had come through.

"Remind me to treat the entire gang to ice cream when we get back to the present," I said.

Caroline and I mounted the horses and took off. Ahead, a pair of keepers opened the gate at Wall Street, and we were soon galloping from New Amsterdam and along a well-trodden road into the snowy beyond.

33

My enchanted horse followed Caroline's—a good thing, because my equine experience amounted to a two-minute pony ride at a Long Island fair when I was a kid. My sole job now, as then, was to hold onto the reins. The snow-covered road ran past small farming communities and large estates. As we galloped beyond rolling countryside and into woodland, Caroline relaxed our glamours.

"The caves are close," she called back, her hood fallen from her streaming hair.

The road angled through what would become the Upper West Side, and I could see the Hudson River through breaks in the trees. On the other side of a meadow, Caroline stopped and dismounted. I followed her example, landing on the snowy ground. We tethered the horses out of the weather and climbed down toward the river.

"We're back," I called to alert the others, but no one answered.

When I didn't spot Gorgantha near the cavern opening, my mind went into panic mode. I scanned the breadth of the river, but no mer head broke the surface. Had something happened?

Dropping the final few feet, I peered into our shelter. A small fire was still burning in the very back, but my teammates weren't around it.

"Hello?" I called.

Off to the right, a pair of squash-colored eyes glowed into view. "Over here, Everson."

My pent-up breath let out with a silent *thank God.* But I didn't like the worry in Bree-yark's voice. As my vision adjusted to the dimness, his squat form emerged. Gorgantha and Malachi were beside him, looking down at something. I cast a ball of light as I approached them, Caroline following.

"What's going on?" I asked.

"He just ... fell over," Bree-yark said.

Arnaud's restrained body lay at their feet, not moving.

Gorgantha looked back at us. "We tried sitting him up, but he won't stay."

"Might be dead," Bree-yark grunted.

They made room for me as I knelt down. Arnaud was on his side, facing the fire, but his dim eyes seemed to be absorbing the light instead of reflecting it. I looked over the rest of his face. The skin had gone a deep yellow and drawn taut against what passed for bones. *He can't be dead,* I thought desperately as I propped him against the wall. *He's our way home.* His head sagged over his chest.

"How long has he been like this?" Caroline asked.

"About a half hour," Malachi said, digging his hands into his long hair. He began pacing in nervous circles. "I didn't touch him, didn't touch him."

After what Malachi had done to the soulless mob, he possessed the capacity to kill the demon-vampire, but I believed him. This was Arnaud being cut off from the infernal realm coupled with the cold draining off his energy more than I'd realized. With nothing to replenish his lifeforce, he'd gone critical.

His body hadn't begun to sublimate yet, but that wouldn't be long in coming.

"I'm going to have to loosen the wards," I said. "Let enough infernal energy back in to restore him."

Dammit. I'd hoped it wouldn't come to this, because it *wasn't* just a simple case of loosening the wards. I was also going to have to ensure his line to Malphas wasn't reestablished, or the demon master would recall him. Then we'd be stuck in this clusterfuck of failing time catches without a ride home.

To this point I'd managed to keep my homesickness at bay, but now an image of Vega holding our infant girl in a blanket flashed through my head. I didn't want to miss that. Pulling myself together, I turned to Caroline.

"Will you need to remove the enchantments?" I asked.

She nodded. "Most of them, yes. I'll leave the subservience one in place."

"There's a smaller cave next door," I said. "Should make a better container for casting." I also wanted a buffer from the rest of my teammates in case anything went awry. "Can everyone else stay here and keep watch?"

They nodded and murmured their assents.

"Hey, what happened with Seay?" Gorgantha asked.

Without time to go into details, I said, "We found her, she's good. She'll be coming later."

Gorgantha pumped a fist and high-fived Malachi as he circled past in his pacing. I scooped Arnaud under the back and legs and lifted him. He weighed almost nothing, as if he were already starting to disintegrate from the inside. As I started out, I caught a sulfurous odor, possibly the first hint of sublimation.

"I'll tell you more when I get back," I said to Gorgantha.

The neighboring cave was small and scattered with leaves, reminding me of the grotto behind St. Mark's in 1776 New York. I shooed out Dropsy, who had wandered into the cave—and judging from her dim light, fallen asleep—and set Arnaud down. While Caroline went to work removing his enchant-ments, I cleared the rest of the floor and began fashioning casting circles from my copper filings.

"Do you want me to stay?" Caroline asked.

I looked from my completed circles to where she was rising from Arnaud's side. She'd removed the enchantments that had bolstered my wards and a few others. She looked fae-like again, her questioning eyes glowing blue-green beneath my hovering ball of light. It was the reclaimed energy. The only enchant-ments she was having to maintain were subservience and the one hiding me from the revenant.

"No, I can take it from here," I said.

She must have read something on my face. "Worried about Malphas?"

The truth was, yes. Because if I slipped up and allowed him to connect to Arnaud, he could decide to detonate him instead of recalling him. And if that happened, I'd rather it be just me in the blast zone.

"A little," I said. "I'll be careful."

As I stooped for Arnaud, she brushed my upper back with a hand. A warm current moved through me, sending up a sweet scent of spring. Before I could protest, she said, "It's not much. Just some extra protection."

"Thanks," I muttered.

I didn't like that she'd expended *any* energy on me, but as she left the cave, I felt less alone in my task. Maybe that had been the point. Setting Arnaud in the larger circle, I stepped into the one behind it and cracked my knuckles.

All right, Croft. It's go time.

With a Word, I recalled power from my light ball and pushed it into the casting circles. They glowed to life, drawing the cave back from darkness. Faint vapor trails drifted through the coppery light.

"Shit," I muttered. Arnaud was starting to sublimate.

Through my wizard's senses, I took quick stock of his bonds. Starting with the outer layer, I began switching wards off one at a time. An anchoring ward hummed in the shackle around his neck, its bands of energy feeding the dislocation sigil that concealed his whereabouts from Malphas. In fact, I'd etched the sigil right over the spot where Malphas's brand seared his neck. The trick would be tamping down the power of the ward while maintaining the dislocation sigil that hid him.

More vapor rose from Arnaud's body.

Gotta get this right, even if it takes extra time.

I sat down in my casting circle, legs crossed, eyes closed. Aligning my mind to the anchoring ward, I imagined it as a dial. Not wanting to take any chances, I'd cranked it to ten. Now I began turning it down. I was meticulous, pausing at intervals to check the ward even as the stench of sulfur strengthened.

Easy, man... easy...

At six, I felt the dislocation sigil fade. Heart bolting at the thought of Malphas rushing in, I bumped the dial back up to an imaginary seven and waited. After what felt like way too long, the ward strengthened again, returning power to the sigil while thinning the currents of infernal energy trickling back into Arnaud.

Would it be *enough* energy, though?

Or would Arnaud's deterioration outpace the meager flow?

Fighting the urge to open my eyes, I eased the dial down again, halfway between six and seven. The infernal flow increased, while just enough warding power remained to sustain the dislocation sigil. For the next several minutes, I made tiny adjustments. Satisfied I'd hit the ideal balance, I sat back, my shirt and brow soaked in sweat.

Now comes the moment of truth.

If I opened my eyes and he was still sublimating, I was going to have to shut off the ward entirely and attempt to power the sigil consciously. That would require a level of concentration and precision I wasn't sure I possessed in my overworked, underslept state. One slip and *Hello, Malphas!*

I peeked out. No vapor.

"Halle-friggin-lujah," I sighed.

Now I watched hopefully for signs of returning life, well aware of the irony of having just incinerated his 1660 version with gusto. But different Arnauds called for different measures. After several minutes, his drawn face began to fill in, pushing out the sickly yellow.

Looks like we've got our ride home again.

When a groan sounded from beneath his muzzle, my mouth broke into a weary smile. Yeah, he was coming back. But before I could feel too pleased with myself, the faintest voice whispered: *Listen to his words.*

The command came from a familiar place. Deep down, where the seat of my magic dwelled. It seemed my old friend had returned. But *whose* words? I squinted at the demon-vampire. Certainly not Arnaud's.

He groaned again, the muffled sound rising and falling. *Listen to his words.*

I reached for the straps holding the muzzle in place, then stopped. Where in the hell was this coming from? My magic, sure, but why would it tell me to listen to a creature whose voice was a living poison?

Caroline's suggestion about my magic came back to me now. *It could be that it's talking, but you're not ready to hear what it has to say.* She might really have been onto something, because I damned sure wasn't ready to hear this.

Arnaud's head tilted toward me, his eyes coming back into focus.

"Can't believe I'm doing this," I muttered as I unfastened the straps.

Very carefully, I peeled the muzzle away. A network of indentations crisscrossed Arnaud's skin where the restraint had been pressing. I moved back into my casting circle, unnerved at seeing his entire face again. It reminded me how deadly he was, even if he presently lacked the strength to lift his head. He gave up after a couple feeble attempts. A pale tongue emerged to wet his drawn lips.

"I know…" he rasped. "Know about … the Night Rune."

34

A part of me had been ready to dismiss whatever Arnaud told me, but now I straightened.

"What about the Night Rune?" I asked.

"It's to be Malphas's gateway."

"Into the time catch?"

His head nodded against the floor. I remembered the attentive look I'd caught earlier, in Malachi's lodgings. Even warded and enchanted, the demon-vampire had been listening. He'd heard me ask Caroline about the Night Rune. Though my magic was still nodding its own head, my rational mind was calling bullshit. This was Arnaud exploiting my need for information to his advantage.

"Fine, what is it?" I asked.

"Malphas didn't tell me everything. Only enough to perform the tasks assigned me."

"But he mentioned the Night Rune?"

"That he did, Mr. Croft."

"And you have no insights into what comprises it?"

Enough infernal energy had flowed back into Arnaud that he managed to elbow his torso upright. He slumped against the cylinder of hardened air rising from his circle so he was facing me.

"I'd hoped you would know, *Professor*. But I happen to have some theories. First, why do you suppose he went after half-fae, merfolk, and druids?"

I'd had the same question—human souls would have been more valuable in the Below—but I wasn't going to let Arnaud run this show.

"No. First, why are you even telling me this?" I said.

"What? You don't trust me?"

"Shocking, I know."

The corners of his lips twitched up. "Contrary to what you believe, I didn't work for Malphas willingly. I was enslaved. A status forced upon me by ... *circumstances*." The yellow shards in his irises flared. Through them I could feel his hatred for me, having cast him into the pits. He blinked and looked away. "The point is, I am too dangerous to him alive, and he knows this. If he succeeds, you and I both perish."

"The enemy of my enemy is my friend," I muttered.

"*Friend* may be putting too strong a point on it, Mr. Croft. But yes, we have a mutual interest in stopping him."

I glared at the creature opposite me, blood pounding in my temples. He'd killed the magic-user Pierce. He'd slaughtered Blade and the vampire hunters. He threatened to do the same to Vega. He'd even threatened our daughter. There was no way in hell I was going to collaborate with him. So why was my magic counseling me to listen?

"Even if you're telling the truth," I said, my voice raw in my throat. "You'll get nothing out of this."

"Nothing? I'll get to see Malphas defeated. He's bet every-thing on gaining access to your world and feasting on the souls of millions. He means to attain the exalted status of a demon lord. And when he fails, he'll have nothing. His competitors will tear him from his perch. He'll fall to the lowly ranks of the imps and pit devils and be torn to pieces." Arnaud's eyes brightened with the thought.

"Yeah, I'm not buying the 'and that will be reward enough' schtick."

The hinges of his jaw tightened. "You have no idea the depravations he's put me through."

"Be that as it may, you're too obsessed with your own survival."

"And you're planning to incinerate me when this is all over?"

"Not planning," I said, remembering my pledge to Vega. "It's happening."

"Perhaps you'll think differently."

"Absolutely not."

"You scoffed when I told you the way to re-enter the time catch was through me. And now?" Arnaud motioned around us. The gesture was weak, his voice still scraping from his emaciated body. So how could he be so damned confident?

"Malphas took what he could get," I said abruptly.

Arnaud blinked and pulled his hand back. "Come again?"

"Your question about why he went after half-fae, merfolk, and druids? Malphas needed soul fuel, and a demon already had the Strangers in place. The groups weren't pure humans, but he liked their numbers."

"A reasonable presumption. But what if I told you Malphas acquired the Strangers from three different demons?"

"Three?" I hesitated. "He shopped for them?"

"Yes, and why do you suppose he would do that?"

Why did anyone shop for anything? "For their particular properties," I replied.

"I believe so too. You were correct about the copper plates. I acquired and installed them to direct ley energy back at the source. And that, Mr. Croft, is where I believe the Night Rune comes in."

"To convert that energy into a portal."

"And what would that require, Mr. Croft?"

"An alchemizing process, for starters. A damned powerful one."

"Precisely why I believe the Night Rune is a container," he said.

I caught myself nodding. "To hold the essences he siphoned from those groups."

But what would be special about those particular essences? I wondered. Mer, half-fae, druid...

"Did I hear Malachi say he observed new construction at the church site?" Arnaud asked.

"Yeah, some sort of platform," I replied distractedly. "But if everything's in place, why isn't Malphas here already?"

"Because everything must *not* be in place."

I heard Malachi's distressed voice: *Time is short! The elements of the Night Rune gather!*

"What do you know about this other demon?" I asked.

"Hm, the revelation was as much a surprise to me as you."

"Malphas never mentioned this demon?" I asked suspiciously.

"Perhaps he was keeping him in reserve were anything to happen to me."

"But you knew about the fae being compromised."

"Only because Malphas is vain. Once he learned you'd entered our time catch, he gloated about having a demon doing his bidding in Faerie. He didn't want anyone believing you and the others had bested him."

"For someone who had his memories scrubbed, you seem to be recalling an awful lot."

"Ah, yes. I heard your fae friend's claim." Arnaud worked his lips into a tired smile. "Nothing was 'scrubbed,' Mr. Croft. There wasn't time. One moment we were in the alley, and in the next we were in your cell."

I gave a harsh laugh. "And there it is."

"I'm sorry?"

"Your ploy," I said. "Get Everson to doubt his teammates."

"Have I lied to you thus far, Mr. Croft? I said your friends were in the time catch, and they are. I said I was the only one who could return you here, and I did. I warned you that the time catch was unstable, and it is." He ticked each one off his fingers. "Now I'm telling you that my memories remain intact. Also true."

I still didn't believe him. There was no reason for Caroline to lie about that.

"Had *I* been the demon planted in Faerie," he went on, "I would have studied those in power for the weakest link. Caroline is only a *half*-fae, is she not?"

Instead of answering the question, he left it dangling. I'd pondered the question of how a lower demon had been able to subjugate a fae as powerful as Angelus. But what if he *hadn't* subjugated Angelus? What if Angelus's warning about Caroline not being herself was the truth?

The demon-vampire's eyes watched mine. "Allow me a little more freedom," he said, "and I can tell you definitively."

"Yeah, that's not gonna happen. In fact..." I retrieved the muzzle from where I'd set it.

"You'd be foolish to underestimate Malphas," he said.

"More foolish than underestimating you?"

"I'm much more valuable than you realize."

When my magic nodded, I paused. It was agreeing with *that*?

As much to shut up my magic as Arnaud, I placed the muzzle over his jaw and cinched it tightly.

"IS EVERYTHING ALL RIGHT?" CAROLINE ASKED AS I ENTERED THE larger cave, gripping Arnaud by his emaciated arm.

"Yeah, it was touch and go there for a minute, but he has enough energy coming in now to sustain him. Still far from full strength, though."

When Arnaud's legs buckled, I sat him against a wall. He closed his eyes heavily. As Caroline looked over the demon-vampire, I examined her aura again for any sign she'd been compromised. Nothing jumped out, but there were still enchantments swirling around her that could be hiding anything.

Yeah, like the revenant hunting you, I shot back.

I hated that I'd let Arnaud drive in that sliver of doubt, but it was there and nagging the hell out of me. Arnaud could well have had his memories of 1776 wiped and was lying about what he remembered, having pieced together the info from watching and listening to us. But his point about the demon in Faerie...

"Should I restore the remaining enchantments?" Caroline asked.

My gaze jumped back to hers. "Ah, not quite yet. I want to get a decent charge into him first. Avoid a repeat of what happened earlier."

"And when we can ill afford it," she agreed.

I turned toward the cave entrance. Outside, a wintry dusk was gathering over the river. I'd spent longer with Arnaud than I realized. When fae energy warmed my shoulder, I realized Caroline had come up beside me.

"Are you sure everything's all right?" she asked softly.

"Yeah, just thinking about Seay. Any word from the half-fae?"

"Not yet," she said.

Was this Caroline, or was the demon just this good?

"Hey, Everson," Bree-yark called. "C'mon over and try this fish Gorgantha caught."

He and Malachi were sitting on opposite sides of the fire, skewers hung with thick filets. Dropsy, done exploring for the time being, sat between them. Gorgantha emerged from the river a moment later, a striped bass hanging from one of her talons. "Plenty more where this came from," she said.

The cooking fish smelled amazing, but my stomach was an anxious fist. "I'll be over in a few," I said, then turned back to Caroline. "Hey, do you mind if I ask you something?"

I could either go back and forth in my mind about whether to trust her, or I could ask her outright if she'd lied about Arnaud's memories being wiped. In the corner of my eye, I saw the demon-vampire watching us.

"Sure," Caroline said, eyebrows raised.

A violent tremor shook the cavern, sending me into a stumble away from her. When I fell, cold water gushed around my hands and knees and surged toward the fire. With a shout, Bree-yark grabbed Dropsy and jumped up. Malachi went into a rambling fit and scurried back, hair flying every which way.

I peered toward the cave entrance at what was happening outside. But it made zero sense. The snow was falling horizontally, and the river seemed to be standing on end, the water along the shoreline crashing down. The cavern around us began to grind now. Stones cracked and plunged into the water.

"What in the *hell?*" I demanded.

I thrust my cane up, prepared to cast a shield invocation. And then, just like that, everything was back to normal. The water flowed back out, chased by smoke from the extinguished fire, and rejoined the Hudson. Caroline stepped from the wall where she'd braced herself and helped me to my feet.

"The time catch is failing," she said.

Malachi splashed up beside us. "Just here, just here it is. This one isn't very stable, never was, never was. We have to get to the next one."

"What about Seay and the others?" Gorgantha asked. She had grabbed Arnaud to keep him from being washed away, and now she dragged him by the arm as she joined us too. Bree-yark hustled up behind them.

"Seay will come, Seay will come," Malachi insisted.

He waved his hands to get us moving toward the entrance, but the others turned to me for direction. I flinched at what I thought was another quake, but it was just my body trembling from the wet and cold.

"Let's head back up to the road," I said, "see if the half-fae are coming."

If they weren't, I was going to have a really tough decision to make. We filed out and climbed the bluff along the route Caroline and I had come down. Several trees had fallen, which made me worry for the horses. But they were standing where we'd left them, skittish, but no worse for the wear.

"I'll check the road," I said, already hustling toward it.

I activated the bonding sigil, but it responded weakly. I sent a summoning signal to Seay anyway. At the road, I peered south into the dusky whiteness. There was no sight or sound of her or the others.

Dammit.

I was hurrying back to my teammates when a force threw me into a tree. I wrapped the trunk with one arm and aimed my cane around, but it was the time catch going through another spasm. This time, the tops of the trees seemed to bend toward one another. When they eased back down, the landscape remained cocked at an angle. Leaning to my right to compensate, I lurched toward the others.

"We can't stay, can't stay," Malachi was telling everyone.

Crazed or not, he was right. I'd never been in a failing time catch, but something told me ours could only tolerate so much twisting and bending before it split and succumbed to the vacuum that surrounded it.

"Start heading toward the departure point!" I shouted above the wind and driving snow. "I'm going back for Seay!"

Bree-yark faced me with bowed arms. "We don't know how much longer this is gonna hold together!"

"Exactly," I said, taking the horse's reins.

Malachi jerked them from my grip. "I'll go," he said, clambering onto the back of the horse. "I know the ways in and out. We'll meet you in Jordan's time, Jordan's time. It's more stable."

I lunged for the bridle, but Malachi swung the horse from my reach.

"You'll find him in Belvedere Castle," he cried over a shoulder. "The final jump is at the Morton Building."

Then he disappeared into a fierce swirl of snowfall.

35

S wearing, I looked from where Malachi had vanished to our one remaining horse.

"Bree-yark and I can hoof it," Gorgantha said.

The goblin stepped up beside her importantly. "That's right, you guys take the horse."

"It's going to be a three-mile journey through snow," I warned him.

"We're up to it," Bree-yark assured me.

I had no idea how his stubby legs were going to keep pace with Gorgantha's powerful strides, much less the horse's, but we were short of options. Caroline adjusted the saddle forward and mounted the horse. I set Arnaud, who still weighed next to nothing, behind her, then climbed on myself.

We headed east over the misshapen landscape, a shield invocation keeping the cold off Arnaud. Gorgantha followed in the horse's wake, while Bree-yark huffed and puffed behind her. I kept peering past them, hoping to see Malachi, Seay, and her friends charging up in our wake, but we were alone.

The horse plowed through woods and meadows, across what would become Central Park, then into the future Upper East

Side. When the East River appeared through the trees, Caroline veered north. We paralleled the thin stretch of Roosevelt Island, which sat mid-river, to where the shore bent out at the present-day mayor's mansion.

Caroline trotted the horse to a stop. Gorgantha and Bree-yark soon arrived beside us, the goblin panting like a bellows, steam rising from his soaked shirt. To his credit, he'd kept up. We were looking out over a narrow neck of the river, where the waters swirled and churned past a cluster of jutting rocks.

"Hell Gate," Caroline announced.

I peered around until I spotted a small snow-covered boulder field glowing in the moon light. "The interface must be in there."

I dismounted and lifted Arnaud down. He wavered but remained upright. When I gave Caroline a hand to the ground, the demon-vampire looked at me intensely. I ignored him. The priority right now was getting out of this time catch.

"Stay together," I called as I seized Arnaud's arm and led the way toward the boulders.

I'd felt low rumbles on the ride here, but now they began to grow. Tree-trunks fractured like popping knuckles, and boulders shifted. I scanned the field through the whipping snow, looking for any traces of the interface. Behind me, Caroline held her hood over her brow to screen her eyes.

"See anything?" I shouted.

She shook her head. "Not yet."

Reality suddenly flipped on an axis toward the river. We began to slide. Boulders dislodged from their deep embeddings, and trees toppled. Pivoting my cane toward my feet, I cried, *"Protezione!"*

The air hardened into a solid ledge, catching the five of us, along with a sheet of debris. I closed the shield around us as larger elements crashed and tumbled past. I looked back for our horse, but the poor thing was no longer there. I swore, even though she was part and parcel of the failing reality.

A massive tree split against the peaked roof of our shielding, prompting Bree-yark to wrap his head in his arms. "Holy thunder!" he shouted as the tree fell to either side of us.

Reality continued to rotate until we were perched on the equivalent of a cliff wall. Gorgantha stared between her webbed feet at the waters of Hell Gate raging below. The distorting forces were growing increasingly unruly. Molars clenching, I upped the effort to keep my shield from twisting apart.

"There!" Caroline called.

She was pointing at where the boulder field had been. With only a couple of the massive stones remaining, the interface was now in plain view. It pulsated in the ground like a large jellyfish, multi-colored and transparent. At over a hundred feet away, though, the challenge was going to be reaching it.

"Hold on," I said.

Gotta turn this baby into an express elevator.

Opening a hole in the floor of our protection, I aimed my sword down and shouted, *"Forza dura!"*

The force that blasted from the blade cratered the river's edge and produced a massive counterforce. Our conveyance rocketed upward, crashing through falling trees and debris— and overshot the target. With a second invocation, I hardened the air into a shelf below the interface. A plummeting boulder slammed into our ascent, and we landed hard on the shelf, ending up face to face with the swimming interface.

Praise be.

I quickly locked us in place. On the ride over, my plan had been to hunker near the interface and wait for Malachi to return with Seay and the others. I squinted toward what had once been south, but it was a pandemonium of warping terrain and falling wreckage. My shield twisted savagely, spouting sparks over us.

With a Word, I dissolved the wall of hardened air separating us from the interface.

"Go!" I shouted, waving my teammates in.

Bree-yark disappeared through the interface first, followed by Gorgantha, then Caroline.

I took a final look south. Still no one. With a pit in my stomach, I seized Arnaud and pulled him through as the shield failed behind us.

I FACE-PLANTED INTO THE GROUND, THE REST OF ME LANDING AT an odd angle that knocked the wind from my lungs. I rolled onto my back and gasped for air. The sun glared through leafy tree-tops, thawing my face and hands.

Wherever we are, it's not winter.

As my breath returned, I pushed myself upright. Arnaud, who had landed beside me, did the same. Caroline was already on her feet, checking on Gorgantha and Bree-yark. The two staggered from some bushes, Dropsy peering from the top of Bree-yark's pouch. An asphalt walkway wound past our weedy patch of lawn. Modern buildings rose beyond the trees, and I could hear car traffic. We were in one of the city's parks. More importantly, we were in a time catch that wasn't falling apart.

"Everyone all right?" I called hoarsely as I gained my feet.

"Better than a few seconds ago," Gorgantha said, giving her head a quick shake.

Bree-yark was rubbing his right hip, but he grunted his assent.

"How about you?" Caroline asked. She had the concerned look I'd grown accustomed to, but now it had me bristling with suspicion again.

"Fine," I said, spitting dirt and dead grass from my lips and brushing off my coat. "Any idea where we are?"

"Schurz Park," she said, "just below the mayor's mansion."

When I peered around, I found the East River sparkling through a span of trees. Geographically, this time catch lined up with the last one. I turned toward the street now. "That puts us at about East Eighty-seventh."

"And where did Malachi say Jordan was?" Gorgantha asked. "Some sort of palace?"

"Belvedere Castle," I said. "It's in Central Park."

"What would he be doing there?" Bree-yark grunted.

I had the same question, Belvedere Castle being a mostly decorative building that offered some nice views. "My guess is he tried to reach Harriman Park, but couldn't because of a time interface. The castle might have been the only refuge he could find. Of course, there's no telling how long he's been here."

"Must be after the recent Crash, then," Caroline said.

Half of Bree-yark's brow ridge went up. "How do you figure?"

"After the Crash, the city slashed the Parks and Rec budget, and that included security," she explained. "The only way he and the other druids are living there is if no one's visiting the park and no one's in authority to kick them out."

As she talked, I noticed the fresh graffiti covering a stone wall.

"Means the park's gonna be hella dangerous too," Gorgantha said. "Should we wait for Malachi and Seay?"

Bree-yark slid me a grim look. The chances of Malachi and Seay having escaped the failing time catch were toward the none side of slim, but I didn't want to have to tell Gorgantha that. I swallowed back an upwelling of grief and anger.

"Malachi will know to look for us at the park," Caroline replied.

I cleared my throat. "Yeah. We can walk there in thirty, but let's hail a cab."

"A'right," Gorgantha said. "Though you might wanna stick some clothes on me."

Before Caroline could cast a glamour, I took her hand. "That thing I wanted to ask you about in the cave? Do you have a sec?"

It was time we couldn't afford, but I didn't want to keep doubting her, either. That would only undermine what remained of our team. I signaled for the others to keep an eye on Arnaud as I walked off with her a short distance.

"What's wrong?" she asked.

I stopped and faced her. "Arnaud claims his memories of 1776 weren't wiped. He's saying you made that up."

"Is he also saying I'm the demon?"

"He suggested as much."

"Well, I'm not." A weariness weighed on her eyes that convinced me even more than her denial. Add to that the fact she'd been unphased by my banishment attack at Crusspatch's cottage—

"But yes," she said, "I lied about his memories being scrubbed."

I blinked twice. "What? Why?"

"Because I didn't want to worry your fiancée."

"Vega?"

I thought back to the holding area at 1 Police Plaza. When Vega asked how long I'd known Arnaud offered a way into the time catch, Caroline had covered for me. She may also have sensed my dilemma over the stability factor. Tell Vega? Remain silent? I'd gone with the second, obviously. And now Caroline was claiming she'd followed suit. Lying so she wouldn't have to announce that the time catch was as unstable as Arnaud had claimed.

"I also wanted to verify his memories," she said, "ensure they weren't lies. Which we were able to do in his office."

The copper plates and their placement. By Arnaud's own admission, that had been the extent of what he knew of Malphas's plans for the St. Martin's site. The rest was guesswork. His demon master had managed his scheme well.

"I'm sorry," Caroline said. "I should have told you."

"Was there anything else in his memories?"

"Nothing useful."

"Nothing about a Night Rune?"

She shook her head. "That didn't come up."

"He claims his master mentioned it," I said, "but he could also have heard us talking. He's been conscious most of this time."

Caroline's brow furrowed. "He has?"

"At least partially."

"Damn, something must have shifted with his draining energy. I'll need to monitor my enchantments better."

"It might have been for the best," I said. "My magic suggested Arnaud had something to say worth hearing."

"Did he?"

"Well, he claims he was enslaved to Malphas and that he wants to see him destroyed as much as we do."

"Should we believe him?"

"A dangerous proposition, but the brand on Arnaud's neck lends credibility to the enslavement part. I don't doubt he was mistreated, either. That's consistent with what I know about demons. So if a and b are true, I'm also inclined to believe c, him wanting Malphas destroyed. Arnaud's nothing if not vengeful."

"What's he offering?"

"At this point only theories," I said, not ready to go into them.

She peered past me at where he was standing with the others. "He must have an angle."

"Oh, Arnaud always does. We'll need to keep eagle eyes on him."

"So are we good?" she asked.

When I looked back, Caroline was watching me carefully. We were at a juncture where I had to decide whether I was going to trust her or not, and then stick with that decision. Waffling would only undermine our chances of success.

I pulled her into a hug. "We're good."

The strength of her return embrace told me just how much she'd needed that.

"Thanks for looking out for me and Vega," I said.

"Of course." When we separated, her nose was ruddy and she sniffled once. "Belvedere Castle?"

"Let's go."

"Oh, you're not going anywhere."

I turned to find a group of hoodlums climbing the steps from a lower tier of the park. The six of them barely looked teenaged, but that could have been an illusion created by their baggy pants and oversized jerseys. Judging by the brands and styles, Caroline had the period right.

"This is our turf," the lead one said. "And you're trespassing."

I searched his and the others' hands, but none were wielding weapons.

"C'mon," I whispered to Caroline, a shield already hardening the air around us.

I'd blast them if they came closer, but I doubted they would. This was a territorial display. A good thirty yards separated us, and running wasn't considered cool. We'd reach the street before they reached us.

"You owe a tribute," the leader called. "To the Raven Circle."

I'd been turning with Caroline, but I stopped now and squinted back at them.

The Raven Circle was the name of Jordan's druid group.

36

None of the hoodlums gave off druidic energy, but before I could ply them for info about this Raven Circle, Bree-yark shouted from behind me.

"You want a tribute?!"

A fist-sized rock shot past me and nailed the leader in the forehead. His sunglasses fell from his head in two pieces, revealing a pair of upturned eyes. He toppled straight back. Stunned by the sudden attack, the remaining hoodlums stood there instead of catching him. His body tumbled down the stone staircase.

"Anyone else?" Bree-yark barked, loading another rock into his sling.

A gunshot cracked in answer. Someone in the back of their pack had pulled a snub nose revolver from his pants. Before things could get out of hand, I swung my sword toward them and shouted, "*Vigore!*"

An arcing force discharged from the blade. Hoodlums went airborne, raining hats and shoes as they flipped over one another and disappeared down the hill they'd just climbed. Judging by the thudding bodies and wailing that followed, they were in no shape to pursue us. The Raven Circle name-drop was still bugging me, but if this was post-crash New York City, we'd already been in the park too long.

"Everyone all right?" I asked as I returned with Caroline toward the others.

Gorgantha relaxed her bowed arms. "Yeah, but I wasn't gonna feel right about smacking down a bunch of babies. Glad I didn't have to."

"Punks," Bree-yark muttered, letting the rock drop from his sling.

I took back ownership of Arnaud as fae magic stirred the air, glamouring Bree-yark, Gorgantha, and Arnaud into modern-day New Yorkers. Bree-yark was a neckless bruiser in a red track suit, his pouch now a gym bag. Gorgantha had become a large man, arms hulking from a sleeveless shirt while a Scottish kilt concealed her tail. And even though it had to be over ninety degrees out, Arnaud had reprised his role as a frail old timer bundled in winterwear, a scarf over his mouth.

Fanning my sweaty neck with my collar, I waved to the others and led the way toward the street. Still in my trench coat, I'd gone from hypothermic to borderline heat-stroking in the space of five minutes.

When a cab pulled over, Gorgantha hunched into the front seat, while Caroline, Bree-yark, and I sat three across in back. Arnaud went on my lap, eyes glaring at me above his scarf.

"Would you rather go in the trunk?" I whispered.

The cabbie looked us over with a sober face. "Usually I can guess where I'm taking someone," he said in a thick New York accent. "You five? No idea."

"Belvedere Castle," I told him.

"You some kinda wise guy?"

I caught my slip-up too late. Post-crash, the park had become a mecca for the city's nastiest creatures, both human and supernatural. Homicides through the roof. Which made me wonder how Jordan and the druids had ended up there.

"Sorry, bad joke," I said, releasing an awkward laugh. "The Metropolitan Museum of Art." That would put us close to where Seventy-ninth cut through the park, winding right past Belvedere Castle.

The cabbie muttered something about everyone being a comedian as he pulled from the curb. Caroline got my attention and drew out a newspaper someone had shoved into the slot in her door. I angled my head to read the date. Early September—no surprise there—but we were deeper into the Crash than I'd thought.

I glanced over the headlines. They all had to do with the city's budget problems and ballooning crime. There was even a column about the rapacious terms Arnaud's investment firm had set to manage the city's debt.

"Is this today's paper?" I asked the driver.

"Sure is," he responded without even looking.

He turned onto Eighty-third Street: a shallow canyon of apartment buildings and street-level businesses. Though we were still in a time catch, and in one of the most dismal periods in New York's recent history, a part of me embraced the familiarity. I squinted out my window, lining up the date with my personal timeline.

After Romania, meaning I've already been trained and inducted into the supposed Order. The true Order, headed by my father and Arianna, was still in hiding. *Vega will be an NYPD officer, pre-Homicide, whom I've yet to meet.*

I thought back to the night I'd failed to get to a conjurer in time and then exhausted my powers banishing the creature he'd called up. Before I could flee the scene, my incubus, Thelonious, came calling and raided the liquor cabinet. The police found me passed out on the apartment's couch with the victim's blood on my hands.

Vega handled the investigation. She knew I was withholding info—she'd always been good at spotting that—but without a weapon or apparent motive, she pushed obstruction. That got me a two-year probation. But it also led to us working our first case together, at St. Martin's Cathedral.

The rest, as the saying went, was history.

And let's see, I'm teaching at Midtown College. Caroline will be there too, still a few years away from marrying Angelus and becoming fae.

The day was Wednesday, meaning we would be on campus. The thought that a fifteen-minute ride could put us face-to-face with ourselves from five years earlier sent a wave of unreality through me. But there was no point and even less time. Our objective was to recover Jordan, hope to hell Malachi, Seay, and the half-fae showed up, and then get to the St. Martin's site and finish this.

The cabbie pulled up in front of the steps leading to the museum's columned main entrance. "The Met," he said wearily.

"Actually, would you mind taking us down a few blocks?" I asked.

Grumbling, he honked his way back into traffic. As the massive museum scrolled past the window, I thought about Gretchen transporting me to its back lawn earlier. *You want my help?* she'd asked. Beyond the museum, Central Park appeared. A line of cement barricades blocked street access at Seventy-ninth.

"Here's good," I said.

As I paid him, the driver looked from the park back to me. "You really are going to Belvedere, aren't you?" When I didn't answer, he muttered something about a group discount on coffins and drove away.

The paved pathway that entered the park was roped off and flanked by an AUTHORIZED PERSONNEL ONLY sign and another warning that the city wouldn't be responsible for anyone who trespassed.

We filed around the barrier and entered a dark tunnel of overgrowth that put me on immediate guard. Large gouges in the paved path looked claw-like. I pulled my cane into sword and staff and conjured a shield around us.

"Lots of baddies in here," I said. "Including a race of goblin that's especially warmongery. No relation to Bree-yark, though."

I looked over, surprised to find he'd fallen behind. He had been gimpy ever since landing in the time catch, but now his limp appeared more pronounced. With each step, his face drew into a sharp wince.

"You all right, dawg?" Gorgantha called back.

We slowed so he could catch up. "Need some healing magic?" I asked.

"Naw," he grunted. "Just need to walk it off." But when he waved the hand that had been clutching his hip, it was stained a dark red. And he was bracing the left hip, not the one he'd been favoring earlier.

"Whoa, hold it," I said. "You're bleeding."

"Yeah, that punk's bullet grazed me. No biggie."

"That's no graze," Gorgantha said. "I can smell the blood. Lots of it."

When Caroline dissolved his glamour, his left pant leg was soaked.

"C'mon," I said, supporting him under his left arm. "No more tough-guying this." I led him grumbling past a flattened section of iron fencing and into a small clearing beside the path. The others followed.

"Aw, this is ridiculous," he complained.

"Bree-yark, you've been shot," I said. "There's a frigging bullet in you."

"Yeah, and now I'm slowing everyone down."

"Just shut it and do what the man says," Gorgantha scolded.

I lowered him onto his good side and pulled his pants down past his bikini briefs. There was a sopping hole near his hip where the round had entered. "You're in luck," I said. "I've done this before. All you have to do is relax."

While Bree-yark protested, I removed Dropsy from his pouch so I could stuff it under the side of his head. The lantern hopped around to Bree-yark's front. When she saw his wound, she began flashing in distress. Caroline coaxed the lantern toward her and picked her up. Dropsy watched the procedure from Caroline's arms.

I began by touching my cane to Bree-yark's forehead to prompt an endorphin dump. As his eyelids turned heavy, I tented my fingers over the wound. I connected with the bullet energetically before snapping a Word off my tongue. The round dislodged from the bone where it had embedded and landed in my palm. I tossed it aside. Hovering my cane over the wound now, I spoke words of healing. The opal glowed, forcing a thick plug of blood from the hole before filling it with cottony light.

I sat back on my heels. "He's going to need some healing time before he can walk."

"How much?" Gorgantha asked.

"Considering that the round hit bone, at least a couple hours."

As I stood, Caroline knelt down in my former spot. "I can halve that, and without expending much magic."

I nodded for her to go ahead, time being at least as precious a commodity now as her magic.

"Maybe you and me could check out the castle," Gorgantha said. "Try and bring Jordan around like you did Seay?"

I peered west into the thick growth. Caroline had put up a light glamour to screen our clearing from outside view, obviating the need for Gorgantha's and the others' disguises. "Under different circumstances, I'd agree," I replied. "But we have no idea what we're walking into. I'd rather we go as a group."

"What are we supposed to do till then?" Gorgantha asked.

But I only half heard her. I was still puzzling over how Jordan had come to occupy the most dangerous piece of real estate in Manhattan. And what about the hoodlums demanding tribute for the Raven Circle? I didn't like it.

"I need to go somewhere," I said.

Caroline looked up. "Where?"

"My apartment in the Village."

"Do you think that's a good idea?"

"I want to cook up some potions. That will also give me time to check out a couple resources in my library. Alternate me will be at the college. I'll take Arnaud so you can focus on Bree-yark. Gorgantha, I'll ask you to stay here on security."

The mer nodded. "I can do that."

When Caroline's gaze lingered on mine, I had to remind myself that I'd chosen to trust her. No waffling.

"Go carefully," she said.

37

I peered up the four-story building that was my West Village apartment. A faint nebula of magic hung around the top floor, but it was ambient, left over from prior casting. I wasn't picking up anything fresh. And there was no sign of Tabitha on ledge patrol, either.

Big surprise there.

"C'mon," I said to Arnaud, taking his arm and heading up the steps.

I'd checked his infernal levels shortly upon arriving in the time catch. Satisfied they were ample, I restored the wards to full strength. It would deplete his energy, but I didn't want him tripping the citywide wards and alerting the time catch version of me that a demon was afoot. I'd open the wards out again before we left.

As we arrived at the building's doors, Arnaud moaned. I was preparing to ignore him, but like an echo from earlier, my magic suggested I listen. I unfastened his muzzle/scarf and removed it from his face.

"This better be good," I muttered.

"Have you forgotten about your wards?"

He was referring to the ones protecting my unit. "They're still under my control," I said.

Agitation edged the demon-vampire's eyes. "And if they're not?"

"Then you'll be incinerated."

"Which means you'll lose your ride home."

"Then what are you worried about?" Grinning, I pulled my keyring from my pants pocket and unlocked the building's front door. As we climbed the stairwell, I could feel the wards pulsing from the top floor.

So could Arnaud. Even under the power of the subservience enchantment, he managed to drag his feet. At the top floor, I had to pull him from the stairwell. Bound hands to his face, he shrank from the power emanating from my door. I incanted until the energy idled down. Arnaud watched warily as I unlocked the door's three bolts and pushed it open. The rack where I hung my coat and cane was barren, telling me I was truly out.

"After you," I said to Arnaud. "You're invited."

Creeping to the very edge of the threshold, he tested it with a toe, then jerked his foot back. Nothing happened.

"See?" I said.

As if to reclaim a modicum of dignity, Arnaud straightened and stepped through the curtain of weakened energy. I followed, bolting the door behind us. Hot sun illuminated the covered bay windows, while icy air-conditioned currents swirled around us. Except for some minor rearranging, my present-day apartment was much the same as this older version. Down to the orange mound on the divan.

As a pair of green eyes squinted out at us, a bolt of emotion shot through me. Not just at seeing Tabitha, but at seeing her so *young*. In this time catch, it had only been a couple years since I'd channeled the succubus into a stray kitten. Her hair was

brighter, her eyes a little more keen, and she was less volumi-
nous. Even knowing it would be a very bad idea, a part of me
wanted to rush over and smoosh my face against hers.

Her eyes closed again. "Oh. You."

On the ride over, I had considered how best to deal with her,
but now I remembered how little she spoke. She'd only just
progressed from her determined-to-kill-me phase to simple
hatred. The upshot was that pretending to be Everson from this
period would be easier to pull off than I'd thought.

"Nice to see you too," I said. "I'm going to be working up in
the lab."

The fewer words spoken, the better. I headed for the ladder,
waving for Arnaud to follow.

"Who's the old man?" she murmured, her body repositioned
away from us.

"Oh, just a … friend."

It took every ounce of willpower to force that word out.

"Are you sure he's not a ghoul?"

Indignation gathered on Arnaud's face. But before he could
respond, I held up the muzzle to tell him it could always go back
on. He compressed his lips, yellow eyes glaring at Tabitha
through his glamour.

From what I remembered of the two-year-old Tabby, he'd
gotten off easy.

We climbed the ladder to my library/lab. Spell implements
and ingredients littered the iron table, while a notepad and pile
of books occupied the desk beside my shelves. The hologram of
the city was dim, telling me the wards hadn't picked up Arnaud's
arrival into the time catch. One less worry.

"Have a seat," I told him, pointing to a stool in the corner.

As he complied, I went through the bins under my table to
see what I had to work with. This was before my pre-made-
potion phase, unfortunately, but I seemed to have stocked up

recently on spell ingredients. When I happened on a stash of lightning grenades, I pumped a fist and loaded them into a pocket.

I can definitely use these.

Thinking potions now, I cleared a space on the table for my portable range. I placed a cast-iron pot onto each of the two burners and split a bottle of absinthe between them. There wasn't time to prepare anything complex, but I had the ingredients on hand for basic stealth and encumbering potions and so prepared a pot of each. When they began to bubble, I snapped the burners to low so the potions could reduce.

Now research...

Turning toward my floor-to-ceiling bookcase, I whispered a Word. In a rippling wave, mundane titles became arcane tomes and grimoires. I'd reordered my collection as it had grown, but I quickly spotted what I wanted. Navigating the rolling ladder, I returned with two books considered authorities on rune magic. Arnaud remained silent on the stool, eyes fixed on a spot between his feet. He had to feel his energy depleting again and was likely trying to preserve his strength.

I made room on my desk for the books, settled into my chair, and flipped the notepad to a fresh page. Despite being an intruder in my own apartment, I felt right at home. The only thing missing was a pot of Colombian coffee.

"You won't find anything in there," Arnaud said after several minutes.

I finished scanning a section of the first book. "How do you even know what I'm looking for?"

"Information on the Night Rune."

"Why won't I find it?" I asked absently.

"I believe 'Night Rune' is just the name Malphas gave to whatever he's doing."

"I didn't know you were an expert," I said, flipping to another section.

"Don't be crass, Mr. Croft. Though I don't care for the connotation, I suppose I am a *survivor*, as you suggest. As such, I have cultivated an extensive understanding of the races, magics, energies, and artifacts that could potentially destroy me. While there are some powerful runes, as well as manipulators of said runes, none can break the demonic plane and permit the passage of one of Malphas's status."

"Hmm-mm," I murmured, turning now to a back section.

Though I was biasing hard against whatever Arnaud had to say, I found myself skimming more quickly. I finished book one —my notepad page still blank—and started on the other book I'd selected. The potions continued to simmer, filling the loft space with a bitter-smelling mist.

"Hellcat Maggie," Arnaud said.

I paused. The vampire we'd encountered in 1861? If Arnaud had intended to get my attention, it worked. I cut my eyes from the book until I could see his thin shadow on the very edge of my vision.

"What about her?"

"I couldn't help but notice that her revelation piqued your curiosity," he said. "The one about the locket belonging to her daughter? Would you like to know the full story?"

"It's irrelevant." I went back to the book.

"Oh, I disagree. I believe it's very apropos to the larger picture." When I didn't respond, his voice thinned. "For an accomplished magic-user—one who succeeded in expelling *me* —you disappoint me, Mr. Croft."

"I'm shattered."

After what seemed a brooding pause, Arnaud went on. "Maggie's daughter was murdered for the locket. It had historical value, but neither she nor her mother could have known this. Maggie was determined to find her daughter's killer. Being hopelessly impoverished and absent one leg didn't stop her. She crutched along the dodgiest New York streets day and night, questing for scraps of information. And yes, by her diligence, she was eventually given a lead to her daughter's killer. But he found her first."

I quit all pretense of reading and narrowed my eyes toward him.

"You can lose the sourpuss face, because it wasn't me, Mr. Croft, but a rogue collector. Only by happenstance did I find Maggie in the alley that night. The scoundrel had slit her throat. Most of her blood had pooled into the filthy cobbles and turned cold, so it had no appeal for me. I might have left the poor woman there to die, but I saw something in her dimming eyes that reminded me of my own mortal circumstances so many centuries before." A raw memory seemed to pass behind his visage.

"You turned her."

"I did, Mr. Croft," he said, straightening. "I granted her the *gift* of vampirism. And with it, she became Hellcat Maggie and destroyed her daughter's killer. She also began rescuing the orphaned and broken children she'd encountered on her nightly walks, but through the only way she knew how. By turning them into her slaves. An unfortunate turf war with another vampire led to her demise—by fire, if you were wondering—but that's neither here nor there. There are two things you must understand. First, very few of us *chose* vampirism. And second, upon becoming vampires, we can only act as such."

I scoffed. "And that forgives everything, right?"

"Absolution is a mortal concept, but it can *explain* many things. If you allow it to."

I didn't know where he was going with this, but his voice had turned teasing. I imagined slender, manipulative fingers trying to ply my will.

I steeled my mind. "Putting Hellcat Maggie in your league is a huge stretch," I said. "She didn't build a financial empire on mass murder and ruin. As vampiric as she may have been, her intentions were half decent."

"Oh, they often are in the beginning. In the early years, you convince yourself that you can hold on to your humanity, even as the bloodlust soaks your mind. Your kills are acts of *mercy*." He said it in a voice that seemed to taunt his own naivete. "I would feed on the very old, their bodies crippled from a lifetime of hard labor. It was the Dark Ages, you see, and my merchant duties took me through many small towns and villages. I witnessed much suffering. But then one day, your kills are simply kills, and you're forced to accept what you've become. It was the same with Maggie. Had you encountered her five years later, she would have struck you as a very different, very *brutal* creature. In the end, though, she was simply surviving."

"I'm still not seeing the connection to Malphas."

"Well, the study can be extended to demonkind. If vampires are survivalists, as you put it, what are demons?"

"Power mongers."

"Precisely. And how do they sate that hungered-for power?"

I wasn't keen on playing *Socratic method* with Arnaud, but with my magic still telling me to listen, I grudgingly went along.

"By amassing souls."

"And demon slaves," he added in a bitter voice. "But yes, souls are the prized currency. And what is the highest status a demon can attain?"

"Lord."

"And what are demon lords?"

I thought of the demon lord Sathanas, who represented Wrath. How in the catacombs beneath St. Martin's he'd tried to stoke my anger into a force he could command. How he'd almost succeeded.

"Elemental expressions of our darkest urges," I replied.

"Which makes all demonkind elemental beings," Arnaud said. "I've been thinking deeply on our conversation in the cave. We concluded that Malphas chose the mer, half-fae, and druid races for their 'particular properties' is how you put it, yes? Well what if those properties were elemental?"

"Elemental," I repeated.

A memory struck me. *The Met. The frigging Met.*

I was ten when Nana first took me to the Metropolitan Museum of Art. She'd known I was fascinated with ancient mythology, and the museum was featuring an exhibit on the Greeks and Romans. The pottery and sculptures all ran together in my memory, but in a section on philosophy, one drawing stood out: a depiction of Aristotle's five elements, also known as the Aristotelean Set. I'd become lost in it, the alchemy-like symbol speaking to some as-yet-awakened aspect of my bloodline.

Is that why Gretchen transported me there?

I pulled another book from my shelf and flipped it open until I was looking at the same depiction—a cross-like arrangement of the elements Earth, Air, Fire, and Water, with Aether in the center.

And with it came a vision I'd had twice now, of lying in a cross-like formation with four others, a dark energy building around us.

Arnaud stood and peered at the image too. "Yes, I was thinking of something similar."

I tapped the Water symbol and said, "Merfolk essence." From there I traced my finger to the Earth symbol. "The basis for druidic magic." I moved my finger to the symbol for Air. "The original fae were said to be Sylphs or air spirits."

Arnaud nodded. "I believe Malphas is using their essences in some form of elemental magic."

I looked at the remaining symbols. "That leaves Fire and Aether."

"Malphas can manifest Infernal Fire himself," Arnaud said. "He'll no doubt use his mystery demon as a focal point."

"Leaving Aether, which is synonymous with Spirit."

"And there, I believe, is your holy man," Arnaud said. "Malachi."

More understanding hit me. *That's why the soulless mobs appeared when they did. To claim Malachi before we could.* It also explained why the mystery demon was staying away. With the power Malachi wielded, my teammate could easily destroy the demon, and thus Malphas's plan to use them in his final elements.

"I'm now inclined to believe that my former master didn't mean 'Night Rune' at all," Arnaud said with a grim smile. "But rather 'Night *Ruin.*' A conflation of the terms 'eternal night' and 'mortal ruin.'"

The elements of the Night Ruin gather.

I looked over the Aristotelean Set again. The races-as-elements theory worked, but the pattern was meant to induce balance. It could amp up the energy at the St. Martin's site, sure, give it shape, but I wasn't seeing a demonic portal.

"We're making progress, I believe," Arnaud said. "But any further help I lend will require a formal agreement."

I turned toward him. "An agreement?"

"In exchange for my assistance, you'll release me from my bondage. In addition, you'll forego any and all acts of retribution —by you, your Order, or anyone you can think to contract. I, in turn, will pledge to leave you and your loved ones in peace. I'm proposing a permanent truce, Mr. Croft."

"You're proposing a lot more than that, and you can forget it."

"Not even for your family?" he asked, affecting surprise. "I'll fashion the agreement anyway. In case you have a *change of heart*."

"Don't bother." But I could already feel the demonic agreement taking shape in the psychic space between us.

"You have but to accept it," Arnaud purred.

I was telling him to get rid of it when the door opened downstairs.

I went silent and froze in place. *Oh, please don't let that be—*

"I'm home," someone called.

Shit. It was me.

38

I waved Arnaud toward a slot under the table, next to the bookcase. The demon-vampire gave me a withering look, but still under Caroline's enchantment, he obeyed, folding his slender form into the small space.

Downstairs, Tabitha murmured, "Again?"

I held my breath, but her remark didn't give the time-catch me pause. I could hear him cycling through my homecoming routines: hanging coat and cane, dropping a clutch of mail onto the table, rooting through the fridge. He'd be coming up here shortly to check the hologram. If only my damn stealth potion was ready.

"You hungry?" I heard the time-catch me call.

"Are you really asking me that?" Tabitha said.

"Let's see, I've got swordfish or flat iron steak."

"Can you stop pestering me with questions and just prepare both?"

"We have to save the other one for tomorrow."

"Like a concentration camp in here," she muttered.

"I can always start serving cat food, you know."

"Fish," she said.

As he began pulling out pans, I quietly slid the books I'd selected back into their slots, arranged the desk as it had been, and retrieved my cane from the table. I stood over the steaming pots. If he could give me about ten minutes, I could bottle the potions, get a stealth potion into Arnaud and me, and slip out.

Sure, it would have been fascinating to meet myself from five years earlier, but there wasn't time to convince him I was from the future. Also, I didn't want to have to tell him he was just an artifact and would cease to exist when the time catch collapsed, which could be in, oh, a few hours. I knew myself well enough to know he'd be skeptical of the first and super depressed about the second.

C'mon, c'mon, c'mon, I thought at the cooking potions.

"What happened to your friend?" Tabitha murmured.

Oh, crap.

"What friend?" he asked.

"The one with the hideous face and stench."

Arnaud glared at me from under the table. Downstairs, sizzling sounded as the fish landed in the pan.

"I don't know what you're talking about," time-catch me replied.

I peeked over the railing. Tabitha was still curled in a mound facing the window.

"Oh, stop being an ass," she continued in her languid voice. "You said you two were going up—"

I hardened the air around her into a soundproof dome.

"Going up where?" he asked.

But Tabitha couldn't hear him now, either. He returned to his cooking. I sustained the manifestation for another minute before removing it. Tabitha's body rose and fell in a steady rhythm, the lack of oxygen having dropped her back to sleep. And now the potions were reduced enough that I could start pouring.

I filled several tubes with each potion, the sizzling downstairs providing the perfect sound screen. Very carefully, I loaded all the tubes save one into my pockets, then placed the range, pots, and wooden spoon back inside a large bin under the table. Steam burst out as I opened the stealth potion I'd set aside.

A half dose each for me and Arnaud should do the trick.

The tube was to my lips when I sensed movement.

"Vigore!" a voice shouted.

The potion exploded from my fingers. I wheeled toward the ladder, mouth already moving to manifest a shield. A wall of air slammed into me first. I went into the bookcase hard, tomes spilling as I came off it.

The time-catch me leapt up the final rungs of the ladder.

Even as I staggered for balance, I experienced a flush of pride at the way he'd snuck up on me. He must have sensed the dome I'd cast around Tabitha. He thrust his sword—actually, the time catch version of Grandpa's sword, the Banebrand, that would one day destroy Lich. But my shield was in place now and stronger than his force invocation. He grunted and reeled from the blowback.

"Disfare!" he called.

My shield came apart beneath his dispel command. Made sense. We possessed the same mental prisms, which meant we were casting at identical frequencies. But talk about an inconvenience. I still held the edge in experience, though. Plus the advantage of knowing exactly what I'd have done in his situation.

"Disfare," I said at the same moment he spoke.

The orb of hardened air he'd attempted to manifest around my head came apart.

His aimed sword trembled slightly as he looked me up and down. He was wearing a rumpled shirt, sleeves bunched past the elbows. A dark blue tie I still owned hung loosely from his collar. Even though I might as well have been looking into a mirror, I could only think of him as someone else.

"Who are you?" Everson demanded.

"I'm, ah, basically you in a few years."

"Sure, courtesy of a mimicking spell. I want to know who you really are and what the hell you're doing in my apartment."

Wow, I actually looked a little menacing when I was angry.

I sighed. "Look, I could tell you about the scar on your first finger, inflicted by the same blade you're holding. Or how you acquired an incubus while in Romania searching for the *Book of Souls*. Or that you have a thing for Caroline Reid. Or about the ingrown nail on your right big toe that you pack with Q-tip cotton because regular cotton isn't thick enough. Or I could show you that we're wearing the same ring or holding the exact same staff. But what's it going to take to convince you?"

He maintained a skeptical expression, but his eyes gave him away. Only seven years into his gig as a magic-user—and largely self-taught—he had no idea what to make of me. He looked around the lab, probably to determine what I'd been doing up here. He had a little less gray at his temples, I noticed, and his face was slightly more filled out than mine. But considering all I'd been through in the years since his time, a side-by-side comparison would show I hadn't aged too badly.

"This stain," he said. "How did it get there?"

He touched his staff to a spot on the thigh of his khakis.

Oh, c'mon, I thought. *You were always spilling crap on yourself.*

Then it hit me. I'd left a ballpoint pen in my pocket before boarding a bus, and it snapped when I plopped down in the seat. Naturally, it had happened before class, probably that very morning, which was why he was—

"*Illuminare!*" he shouted.

Light detonated from the opal end of his staff, blinding me.

Son of a gun was only distracting me, I thought as I stumbled to one side. Once again, I couldn't help but be impressed with my younger self.

I threw up a defensive shield as I tried to blink away the twin glares. I expected him to follow with a series of invocations—it's what I would have done. Instead, he gargled on his next word. As my vision cleared, I saw why. Arnaud had sprung from his hiding spot and brought his manacles around my counterpart's throat from behind. He'd also managed to hook a leg over his sword arm, pinning it to his side.

I panicked. Was he going to bite him? Turn him?

"Disarm him, you fool," Arnaud seethed at me in a shaking voice.

I switched my sword's aim to Everson's flailing staff and dislodged it with a force invocation. I managed to do the same with his sword, even though Everson clung to it gamely. He drove his hands up under the manacles' chain to create breathing space, his eyes frantic with the effort to breathe, the will to live.

"Release him!" I shouted at Arnaud.

Below the ridge of his compressed brow, the demon-vampire's eyes burned with hatred, as if he intended to finish the job. But he relented. My counterpart responded by thrusting his weight back. He and Arnaud disappeared over the top of the ladder, falling into the main room below. The sounds of snarling and shuffling ensued.

When I rushed to the ladder, Everson was already on top of Arnaud, hands seizing his throat above his neck manacle. And he was speaking the Latin exorcism. Sulfurous smoke rose from his throttling contact.

Shit, he's going to destroy Arnaud.

"Stop!" I shouted, scrambling down the ladder. "Ballpoint pen, ballpoint pen!"

But Everson was determined to end him. With a running dive, I tackled him off Arnaud, and we went rolling across the floor.

"The stain," I tried again, this time in grunts. "Came from your ballpoint pen."

"If you doppelganged me," he grunted back, "then you'd have my thoughts too."

I may have been the more experienced magic-user, but he was filled with fresh book knowledge. And he was absolutely right, dammit. I had to think of something we could verify that hadn't happened yet, but I was coming up blank.

Meanwhile, our rolling tussle continued. Every time one of us uttered an invocation, the other shouted the dispersal Word, putting us at a casting stalemate. I was conscious of the vials clattering in my coat pockets, praying they wouldn't break—especially the encumbering potion, which would reduce me to slug speed.

Our momentum carried us into the leg of the dining room table. As the mail spilled around us, one parcel caught my eye. I could only make out "Midtown College" on the top line of the return address, but the envelope's slate gray color marked it as a Snodgrass letter. He believed, wrongly, that the color gave his missives added gravitas.

But now I had something.

Our arms had been locked, but Everson managed to glance a punch off my chin and seize my throat.

"Start talking," he said, "or I'll choke you out like I did your minion."

"Wait," I managed, gripping his throat back. "The Snodgrass letter."

His eyes cut over and back. "What about it?"

"He's moving the faculty bathrooms to the second floor. Reserving the ones on the first for department heads." I remem-

bered the letter at the start of that term vividly—and how much
it had pissed me off.

"What?" For an instant, Everson's fury shifted to Snodgrass.

"I know, it's ridiculous, but it's true. Open it and see for
yourself."

I released his throat and arm and scooted away, hands open
to show I had no intention of resuming the attack. He looked
from me to the envelope again before snatching it up. We stood
at the same time, lest the other have the higher ground, and
remained a safe distance apart. A glance back showed that
Arnaud was still down and in bad shape. I'd get to him, but I
had to sort this out first.

Tabitha, who was peering over a shoulder, smirked at Everson. "I told you that you were up in the lab," she said.

Scowling, he tore the side of the envelope with a finger, drew
out the letter, and shook it open. He glanced up several times to
make sure I was staying back. But as he read, he became increasingly absorbed—and vexed. By the time he reached the end, his
eyebrows were nearly touching in the center.

"That son of a bitch," he muttered.

"Yeah, there will be a faculty petition and everything, but
he'll still go through with it."

He let the arm holding the letter fall to his side as he looked
back at me. "The secretary handed this to me on my way out
today, so you couldn't have read it." He sighed. "Still, I need
more info about ... this." He gestured toward me.

"No problem, but first I need to tend to my minion."

Everson looked past me warily to where Arnaud was still
smoking on the floor. "What is he?"

"A demon-vampire." I didn't mention the Arnaud part.
While I was familiar with the name back then, I wouldn't
encounter him for another few years. "It's a long story, but he's
my ticket back to my plane."

"The future?"

I didn't want to get into the time catch stuff either. "Yeah."

"Go ahead," he decided. "But do you mind if I grab my sword and staff? As insurance?"

"As long as this is an honest-to-God ceasefire," I said. "I'm seriously pressed for time."

Everson nodded in a way that told me he'd honor the truce. As he climbed the ladder, I opened Arnaud's wards out again. A moment later, the foghorn alarm sounded upstairs, announcing that a demonic entity had just breached the city.

"Just us," I called.

"No worries," he said, shutting off the alarm.

I returned my attention to Arnaud. He lay there with his mouth open, eyelids at half-mast. A yellowish smoke still rose from where Everson had seized him. Just a day or two ago, I would have celebrated the beating my time-catch self had put on Arnaud, but now it placed our return in jeopardy.

I calibrated the wards until I found the happy medium again. Any weaker and the energy powering the dislocation sigil would be insufficient, and Malphas would find him. I lifted Arnaud's limp body and placed it on the couch. As I arranged his legs, Tabitha wrinkled her nose and shrank from the sulfurous stench.

"Smells like a corpse's turd," she said.

"Can't argue with you there," I muttered.

Everson descended the ladder and slotted his sword inside the cane. He took stock of the scene, his gaze lingering a moment on mine, then turned toward the kitchen. The fish continued to sizzle on the stove.

"Are you hungry?" he asked.

39

Ten minutes later, Everson, Tabitha, and I were sitting around a table set with plates of thick swordfish steaks, their seared tops buttered and dilled. Everson had also filled a large bowl with potato chips, which he set between us. My hunger had caught up to me, and I wasted no time digging in.

"I have a ton of questions, obviously," he said.

"The long and short of it is that I'm from the future, but not in a linear sense." As I paused to chew, I tried to remember if I'd been introduced to the concept of time catches five years ago. I didn't think so. "I'm here to recover a friend, another 'time traveler.'" I air-quoted the word. "And then we're leaving. Again, I'm sorry for breaking into your apartment and surprising you. That was a dick move. I just needed to stock up on potions and check something out in your library. I also helped myself to a few lightning grenades," I added sheepishly, even though I was confessing to myself.

He waved a hand. "I can always get more."

"Yeah, but let me reimburse you. I know money's tight."

"And the ... demon-vampire?" he asked, peering past me.

Back on the couch, Arnaud had stopped smoking, thank

God. Infernal energy was infusing into him again, and he'd stirred a few times.

"He's a conveyance more than anything," I said. "Once we're home, we plan to annihilate him."

"That sounds like bullshit," Tabitha remarked through a mouthful of fish.

"It's true," I said, more defensively than I'd intended. "I promised someone."

"Who? Everson's future wife?" she scoffed.

"You said you came back to recover a friend?" he asked.

"Are you familiar with a Jordan Derrow?"

He repeated the name and shook his head.

"How about the Raven Circle?"

Recognition sparked in his eyes. "Yeah, they're a druid group based out of Central Park." He seemed to grow cautious. "Why?"

Not wanting to say anything that could spook him, I turned cautious myself. "Well, we think our friend might've gotten mixed up with them somehow. What can you tell me about them?"

"The name started showing up sometime last year. The nasties that inhabited the parks after the Crash were freelancers, mostly. Then this druid group arrived on the scene. I heard rumors about a turf war in Central Park. Next thing I knew, this group was running the whole show. And not just in Central. If you want to do business in *any* of the parks, you have to go through the Raven Circle."

"We ran into some punks at Schurz Park earlier today who demanded tribute."

"Yeah, they operate like a supernatural racket. Thankfully, the parks aren't my beat."

This sounded like Jordan and his fellow druids, but what had made them go full mafioso? Jordan might have originally seen it as the price of survival—then, like Gorgantha and Seay, forgotten he'd ever done anything else. I dragged a hand through my hair. Something had told me recovering him was going to be a pain in the ass.

"We think our friend is at Belvedere Castle."

"Ooh, Raven Circle central," he said. "I feel you."

"I despise those filthy birds," Tabitha remarked.

"That was one incident," I shot back, knowing she was referring to the time a gang of ravens harassed her at Washington Square Park.

"And you did fuck all to protect me." She blinked, then looked over at Everson. "Or are you to blame?" Deciding it wasn't worth puzzling out, she exhaled and went back to work on her swordfish.

"Anyway," I said, "if they have shifters and gangbangers at their beck and call across the city, we're going to be dealing with a lot more than the Raven Circle. They're probably communicating through druid bonds."

"That you can scramble." With a raised finger, Everson excused himself from the table. When he returned, he'd retrieved a map of the city that he proceeded to spread beside me. "I'm visual," he explained.

"Yeah, me too." I stopped. "Well, clearly."

Everson smiled as he traced a finger around the section of park with Belvedere Castle.

Knowing where he was going, I said, "Bury copper at points along Seventy-second and Eighty-sixth and both avenues, push power into them until they link up, and presto, you've got a disturbance field."

"That would work, right?"

"Sure, if I had the time to set it up."

Everson cocked an eyebrow. "What about the help?"

"WE'RE BACK," I CALLED, STEPPING THROUGH THE THIN GLAMOUR.

As the clearing came into view, I was relieved to find my teammates there. At the same time, I was disappointed Malachi, Seay, and the others weren't with them. On the taxi ride to Central Park, I'd been hoping hard for their return. Gorgantha received me with one of her monster hugs. Bree-yark, who had been walking a lap around the tree with Dropsy, smiled at me with his goblin teeth.

"How's the hip?" I asked him.

"On the way to brand new. Thanks to you and Caroline."

Caroline stood from the grass and shook some leaves from her cloak.

"How did it go with you?" she asked, glancing at Arnaud as she walked up to us. He was frail and shaky but recovering.

"Interestingly," I said. "I was able to cook two batches of potions and do some research." I decided not to bring up what Arnaud and I had discussed about the races as elements in Malphas's "Night Ruin" scheme. I was still working it out in my mind, one. And two, I wanted our focus now to be on recovering Jordan and the druids.

"I also bumped into my time-catch self," I added.

Caroline's eyes widened, while Bree-yark and Gorgantha moved in to hear better.

"He caught me in his apartment, but it turned out to be a bonus. He had intel on the Raven Circle, a druid group running the parks in the city." When Gorgantha frowned, I said, "Yeah, it's Jordan's circle." I went on to share everything Everson had said and finished by telling them he'd offered to help.

"He's here?" Bree-yark craned his thick neck around. "Oh, this I gotta see."

"He's actually working the perimeter," I said. "Setting up a disturbance field so the Raven Circle can't call for outside backup. He'll signal me when he's ready, but that'll be the extent of his involvement."

"Sounds like you have a plan," Caroline said.

"A preliminary one." I sat and unfolded Everson's map.

Arnaud sank to the ground behind me, his muzzle back on. We had remained at the apartment until the demon-vampire was strong enough to walk under his own power. That gave Everson and me time to break down what we knew of Belvedere Castle and to talk strategy, all while ignoring Tabitha's many digs. Eventually, Everson ordered her out onto the ledge and sealed the cat door behind her.

"Having two of you doesn't just double the oppression," she'd remarked on her way out. "It increases it exponentially."

I lied and told Everson she would get kinder with age.

"All right," I said, angling the map so everyone could see. "First, what's the activity been like around here?"

"A group of punk asses walked by," Gorgantha said, "but then they walked right back out."

I nodded. "Everson thinks the mortals are working the smaller parks—like the group we met this morning—or hanging around the periphery of Central. We shouldn't have to worry about them. But deeper in, the druids are using weres."

"Wolves?" Caroline asked.

"Boars," I said. "They're easier to control, apparently."

"They're frigging bruisers," Bree-yark put in. "Saw one beat an ogre in a pit fight a few decades back. Dropped him with a charge, then started goring him. Ignored the ogre's tap out, too. Took eight refs to pull him off."

"Sounds about right," I said. "Which is why this won't be a frontal assault." On the map, I pointed out a body of water to the west of us. "Belvedere Castle abuts this lake. A drainage culvert was built to run out any water that got into the castle's sublevels, but it's underwater now. Gorgantha and I can enter the castle through the culvert. But we'll need a distraction to send the bulk of the wereboars south."

"A glamour should do it," Caroline said.

"How are you fixed for power?" I asked.

"I've been thrifty. That kind of glamour won't cost much."

"What can I be doing?" Bree-yark asked.

I unshouldered a duffle bag and unzipped it. From inside, I pulled out a pump-action shotgun and several boxes of shells. "Your job is to take down any ravens that try to fly out."

"Oh, hell yeah," Bree-yark said, inspecting the gun and raising it to his shoulder.

When Caroline slid me a questioning look, I said, "I made a quick stop in Chinatown. A guy I know owns an apothecary shop, but he also sells weapons and ammo on the side. The shells hold bird shot and silver dust. Enough to stun a druid, but do serious damage to any weres that show up." I still felt guilty about paying the time-catch version of Mr. Han in glamoured bills, but he'd been tickled to see me.

"Are we still holding out hope for Seay and Malachi?" Gorgantha asked quietly.

"They'll come," I assured her. "Malachi knows the time catches better than anyone." I dropped my gaze back to the map a little too quickly, though.

For the next hour, we went over our strategy, coloring in the details and making small adjustments. Finally, a distant shot from a revolver echoed over the park. Five beats later, a second shot sounded from the same gun.

"That's Everson's signal," I said. "The field is in place."

Bree-yark pumped the shotgun's action, chambering the first shell.

"Let's go find this Jordan," he said.

40

U nder the cover of stealth potions, Gorgantha and I picked our way through the trees. We soon emerged onto a stone shore where the eastern end of the lake began, the water green and edged with algae. Across the water, the high walls of Belvedere Castle rose above the treetops. Ravens circled the fort's conical tower.

"Should we get in?" Gorgantha whispered.

"Wait a sec."

Already grimacing at how bad it was going to taste, I pulled an encumbering potion from my pocket. Gorgantha had estimated that our time underwater could be anywhere from three to five minutes. On a good day, I could hold my breath for roughly one. Though designed for use on enemies, a sip of encumbering potion would slow my heart rate enough to make the trip on a single breath.

Tears sprang from my eyes as the sting of ammonia hit my throat, but I managed to gag it down. With a bitter face, I capped the vial and returned it to my pocket. The magic began to work immediately. It felt like someone packing my muscles with lead shot. Needing the effect to thin by the time we arrived in the castle, I'd gone with a small dose. I checked my pockets now to ensure they were all sealed, then gave Gorgantha a nod. Even that little gesture took effort.

The mermaid slipped into the lake first and helped me down off the rocks. On the tail end of a New York summer, the water that soaked me was bathtub warm. Clean too. Druids had an aversion to the unnatural, and that included pollution. Otherwise, the lake would have featured floating banks of garbage. Barely able to tread, I clung to Gorgantha's back, my heavy legs sinking to her sides.

To the south, a piggish cry went up. Others answered. A small stampede crashed through the foliage away from us.

The wereboars had taken Caroline's glamour bait.

I drew a deep breath and tapped Gorgantha's shoulder. She submerged and kicked off toward the castle. After several seconds I squinted my eyes open. Yellow light filtered through the pickle-colored water. Gorgantha cut left to avoid a group of turtles, then plunged deeper where we'd be less likely to disturb the surface. The water cooled and darkened. Plants along the bottom brushed us with slimy leaves. As we passed the two-minute mark, I still felt fine, like a creature of the underwater myself.

Ahead, the culvert's cylindrical opening grew into view. Gorgantha parked me beside it and held a finger in front of my face for me to wait. She then plunged inside. I leaned my head back. We were directly underneath the castle, but I couldn't see anything through the peaty water. Something squeezed my foot.

The hell?

I reacted in slow-mo, trying to draw my leg up, but it remained fixed. At first I thought the potion had deadened my leg, but something was holding me. It was the plants. They were writhing up my body.

Crap, an animation.

The druids must have placed a ward near the culvert. I'd marked several in the park, but this one I'd evidently missed. Swearing, I pulled my sword from my staff and inserted the blade into the leafy mass of tendrils now wrapping my waist. I twisted and sawed at them, but more were arriving all the time.

Going to need to cast.

Though I was in a watery medium, it wasn't briny enough to stifle my power. Gathering energy toward my prism, I glugged out a Word. The result was weak, but enough light and force discharged from my blade to scatter the bulk of the plant material. As I kicked my legs partway free, something grabbed my arm.

What now?

But it was Gorgantha. Dropping a torn-off grate, she pulled me into the cylinder after her. Her strength overwhelmed the remaining tendrils, which went snapping from my legs in putrid bursts of plant matter. More leafy arms searched after me, but they soon faded in our wake.

As darkness closed around us, my muscles tingled with returning blood. My lungs began to ache for oxygen. The small dose of encumbering potion was wearing off. Before I could panic, Gorgantha pulled me from the water and helped me to my feet. I sputtered and wiped my eyes as water cascaded off me. We must have been on the sublevel, but I couldn't see a thing in the pitch black.

I invoked a pair of shields around us and pushed power into them. The fields glowed, exposing a dank cinderblock room with a stairwell and a separate closet for a pump. I saw where Gorgantha had ripped off the grate that had once covered a large drain in the floor. The shields warmed us until we were damp rather than dripping, which had been the point. I didn't want a water trail giving us away.

I recalled power from our protection until the room fell black again. Gorgantha took my hand, the darkness not an issue for her mer vision, and led me toward the stairwell.

"We tripped a ward coming in," I whispered, "so expect company."

My invocations had burned through some of our stealth magic too, so I took another hit of potion and passed the rest to Gorgantha.

The ascending stairwell delivered us into a large basement. Light from a staircase opposite us limned the room. A neat arrangement of wooden crates and large sacks filled most of the space, their contents giving off plant and herbal smells.

I scanned the room for wards as we walked along a central aisle. Though the potential for magic hung thick, no dangers appeared in my wizard's vision.

"That company you mentioned?" Gorgantha whispered. "It's coming."

Faint snorts and snuffs sounded, and soon large shadows filled the stairwell ahead. *Damn, wereboars.*

My heart kicked into a flip-flopping rhythm as I motioned for Gorgantha to follow me down a side aisle. We concealed ourselves behind a stack of crates as two wereboars entered the basement. Beside me, Gorgantha swore under her breath. They were frigging huge.

The creatures wore hoodie shirts with the sleeves ripped off. From the ends of tusked snouts, porcine noses snorted this way and that. They stalked down the center aisle, clubs hanging from arms packed with muscles. As I shrank further back, Bree-yark's story about one of these things taking down an ogre didn't seem at all farfetched.

The lead wereboar stopped and stuck his snout down our side aisle and snorted several times. The stealth potion was designed to hide scent too, but these guys could pick up smells from five miles away. The wereboar straightened and pushed the hood from his head, revealing a thick mohawk of bristles above a pair of beady eyes. When he switched the club to his other hand, I braced for battle.

"Anything?" his companion asked in a gruff voice.

"Naw, this is bullshit," he said. "The action is down in the Ramble."

He was talking about the wooded area where Caroline's glamour had led the others. I relaxed my grip on my sword, even as my pulse continued to slug in my ears.

"Let's clear the lower level and head up," the lead wereboar decided.

I waited for them to lumber down the stairwell before invoking a shield over the entrance. It wouldn't hold the bruisers long, but I only needed it to keep them off us until we could find Jordan.

I led the way from our hiding place and up the stairs. The next level appeared to be the living quarters. Natural light entered through ports in the stone walls. Several potted trees rose and spread their leafy branches throughout a common area of wooden furniture. To one side, six cloaked figures conversed in low voices. Others went in and out of side rooms. We'd found the druids.

I recognized several from the prison ship rescue in 1776 New York, but none of them were Jordan. I peeked down at the symbol on my hand. Pushing power into it would mean compromising our stealth magic, but with time ticking down until the wereboars came back, I decided to go ahead.

The symbol began to glow at the same time the barrier over the lower stairwell shuddered. The wereboars had returned from the sublevel, and at least one was pummeling the barrier with his club. The next blows rattled the castle walls.

The druids turned toward the stairwell, all peering past

Gorgantha and me. Except for one. She squinted, then drew back, a quarterstaff seeming to manifest from the billowing flap of her cloak and into her hands.

"Intruders!" she cried.

The others moved into a defensive formation, quarterstaffs aimed outward. "Where?" one of them asked. The druid who'd spotted us lunged forward, magic gathering around the end of her staff.

A force met her chin and leveled her.

"Right here," Gorgantha said, rubbing her fist.

"Go easy," I reminded her. "They're friends, even if they don't know it yet."

I'd pulled a tube of encumbering potion from my pocket. Uncapping it, I shouted an invocation. The potion frothed and jetted from the tube. I canted it back and forth, hosing as many of the druids as I could. Their slowing motion made it appear as if the air had become a thick mud they were attempting to stir with their staffs.

The element of surprise was serving us well. Still cloaked in stealth magic, Gorgantha charged into the druids' midst, yanking staffs from grips and shoving druids to the stone floor. When my tube sputtered out, I grabbed and activated another. This time I aimed it at the druids rushing in from the side rooms. Several shifted to their raven forms and scattered, presumably in search of backup.

I managed to coat one with a jet of encumbering potion. Its slowing wingbeats failed to keep it aloft, and it tumbled to the floor. Gorgantha backhanded another into a wall. But two made it out, one disappearing up a stairwell and another out an observation port. A moment later, two shotgun blasts shouted.

Attaboy, Bree-yark, I thought, picturing the plummeting birds.

The symbol on my hand, which had been glowing softly this whole time, pulsed suddenly. It had established a connection with Jordan.

"He's upstairs!" I called to Gorgantha.

I just hoped the power of the bond would be enough to shake Jordan from his time catch-induced amnesia as it had done with Seay.

The mermaid tossed away a quarterstaff and stepped from the mass of druids writhing on the floor like slugs, too encumbered to push themselves upright. We were almost to the stairs leading up when I gasped from a hit of return energy. The barrier downstairs had failed. Hoofed feet pounded the length of the basement and climbed the next stairwell, accompanied by a storm of furious grunts.

I cast another barrier behind us. It shook as the first wereboar collided into it. I'd burned through enough stealth potion by now that he caught my spectral form fleeing up the stairs with Gorgantha.

"You're dead meat!" he boomed.

Gorgantha and I reached the next level as fresh pounding sounded below. This floor looked like an operations center, with tables spread out and maps affixed to walls. It was empty, though, and the bond was still pulling me upward. Taking the final stairwell three steps at a time, I dashed through an anteroom and out onto the castle's observation deck. I was familiar with this part of the castle—I'd brought a high school date here once—and quickly oriented myself to our surroundings. The lake Gorgantha and I had arrived by stood to the north while the thick treetops of the Ramble appeared south of us.

Pushing more power into the bond, I shouted, "Jordan!"

Gorgantha called his name too. "It's your old friends," she said, "the Upholders!"

A large raven burst from the trees, morphing into a human as he swooped down. He landed on the far side of the observation deck, cloak flapping, quarterstaff crackling with energy. The druid's head was shaven to a brown sheen, but I recognized the glowing sigils at his temples and the intensity in his dark eyes.

"I have no *old friends*," Jordan said.

41

B efore I could appeal to whatever memories he'd retained, Jordan's staff arced into motion. I threw up a shield, absorbing his blast, but the attack wasn't pure force. On impact, a faint cloud of druidic magic burst out. Some of it filtered past my protection. The observation deck fragmented, and I fought for balance.

"You all right?" Gorgantha asked.

"Yeah." I blinked. "Some sort of hallucinogenic attack."

She swung toward him. "It's us, dummy! Everson and Gorgantha!"

Jordan continued forward, another charge building on his staff. "All I see are invaders."

Shaking my head clear, I pulled an encumbering potion from my pocket. Jordan was too distant to attempt to hose him like I'd done the others. Instead, I shouted, *"Vigore!"* and let the entire vial fly from my hand. But with my vision still out of whack, I missed wide and the vial shattered against a stone wall.

Jordan thrust his staff, this time at Gorgantha. Once more, my shield stood up to the assault, but he'd smuggled in another follow-up attack. A dusty magic billowed past the barrier and stuck to Gorgantha's damp skin like chalk.

With a shouted Word, I sent a second encumbering potion at him. Jordan brought his staff around. *Shatter,* I thought urgently. *Shatter and soak him.* But instead of breaking the vial, the glancing contact sent it popping up like a foul ball. It smashed against a set of steps leading down to the park.

Dammit.

"I-I'm drying out," Gorgantha stammered.

When I glanced over, her scaly skin looked dull and brittle, and cracks were appearing along the lines of her muscles. Jordan must have used a desiccating spell. I jerked my head toward the parapet at our backs. "Go!"

Gorgantha hesitated, but when fluid began seeping from her eyes, she broke toward the wall and hurdled it. A moment later, a splash sounded from the lake below.

Hope to hell she's all right. From halfway across the observation deck, Jordan thrust his staff again. This time I met his blast with one of my own. The collision sent us each staggering backwards, dust exploding between us. From the Ramble, I could hear the snorting stampede of returning wereboars.

Yeah, just what I need.

I looked around for Caroline, who was supposed to be nearby.

"Don't know who you are," Jordan said. "But you're about to get a painful lesson in why no one challenges the Raven Circle."

"I'm not here to challenge your damn circle," I barked. "Think back, Jordan. You were part of a team called the Upholders. We went to 1776 New York to recover your druid circle, your wife. We found them on a prison ship in the East River. Time got screwed up, and you ended up here—in another time catch, about five years short of the present. Your real home is in Harriman State Park."

I was pushing power into our bond as I spoke. But though the symbol shone on his hand, it didn't restore his memories as it had done Seay's—or even give him pause. Jordan didn't so much as glance down.

"We came to get you out of here," I said.

"Oh, I believe that part." Jordan thrust his staff again.

Already seeing his aim was off to the left, I darted right while drawing out another encumbering potion. But I realized too late he'd been positioning me. When I bumped up against the stone parapet, a mass of vines swarmed around my shielded body like a carnivorous plant on anabolic steroids.

"Respingere!" I shouted.

The pulse ripped through them, but the vines regenerated before I could break away. Heavy footsteps sounded on the stairs leading from the park to the observation deck.

Aaand that will be the wereboars, I thought grimly.

But it was Bree-yark. The goblin swung the pump-action shotgun toward Jordan. "That him?"

Before I could answer, or Jordan could react, a raven appeared from behind the castle's conical tower. Still following my raven-shooting order, Bree-yark pivoted and fired. The raven shrieked as silver shot tore through its wings. By the time the plummeting bird hit the deck, we were looking at a human.

"Delphine!" Jordan yelled.

Shit. We'd just dropped his wife.

"Hold fire!" I shouted at Bree-yark. But he'd left his feet and was flying through the air, the recipient of Jordan's staff attack. The goblin landed in a tumble, body and shotgun rolling over one another.

Jordan backed toward his wife, staff held toward me. Deciding I was too busy with the animation spell to threaten them, he knelt and began working to revive her.

And I *was* busy. Even after another repulse invocation, the vines continued to pile over me. My shield buckled under the ever-mounting pounds per square inch. But I still had my encumbering potion in hand. I opened the vial, expelled it from my shielding, and watched the leafy mass consume it.

Within seconds, the writhing and squeezing slowed until it just felt like I was buried under a pile of dead weight. The next pulse from my shield shoved the plant animation off me, and I was free.

But now wereboars *were* stampeding up the steps, returning from their wild goose chase. Two more weres broke from the castle doors—the ones I'd trapped on the lower levels. As the hulking creatures arrived on the deck, they slowed to a menacing stalk. Eyes glared above tusked snouts. Truncheon-like clubs stood from fists. The wereboars' collective snorts sounded like a tractor convention.

"Bree-yark!" I shouted.

The goblin, who was sitting up groggily, saw the danger and scrambled over until he was beside me. He swung the shotgun from one advancing wereboar to another, but there had to be at least twenty of them. My shield would keep them at bay, but long enough to shoot and force-blast them into submission?

"Call them off!" I shouted at Jordan. "I'm just proposing we talk!"

I couldn't see him—the brutes had come between us—but I picked up his response: "Put them down."

Before the order could propagate through the ranks, I dug into a pocket and pulled out the lightning grenades from Everson's stash. Angling my mouth toward Bree-yark, I said, "Take the ones from the castle."

"Got it," he said.

He turned and fired into the left one, pumped the action, and emptied another shell into his partner. Clubs clattered to the concrete, and the shrieking wereboars threw their hands to their smoking, silver-blasted faces. Meanwhile, the large pack that had come up from the park broke into a charge.

Rolling the lightning grenades toward them, I shouted, *"Attivare!"*

A biting scent of ozone cut through the air an instant before jags of lightning crashed down. The lightning impacted at the front of the charge, blowing wereboars every which way. Those still arriving reared back with piercing squeals. Half deaf and with an electrical buzz lingering in my teeth, I pressed the attack.

Seizing an encumbering vial in each hand, I shouted, *"Vigore!"*

The potions erupted into jets, and I rained them over the mass of wereboars. Having incapacitated the pair from the castle, Bree-yark turned and began blowing silver shot into the main pack.

"Stop!" someone called. "Please, stop!"

The plea was coming from where Jordan had been tending to his wife, but the voice wasn't his. I signaled for Bree-yark to hold fire. The spreading wereboars turned—most in slow motion now—until I could see Jordan's wife. Rising to her feet, she looked from the observation deck to Jordan.

"Everson is our friend," she said.

"I still can't…" Jordan trailed off. "It's just so insane."

"Hey, I freaked pretty hard at first too," Gorgantha assured him. "At least you weren't in a damn fish tank."

We were gathered in a meeting room inside the castle. Following the ceasefire, events had de-escalated quickly. Jordan's wife ordered the wereboars off and convinced her husband to stand down. Caroline had apparently gotten to Jordan's wife in the park and restored her memories. Which was why Delphine had flown back—to tell Jordan who we were. Bree-yark muttered one apology after another for shotgun-blasting her, but it was my fault, and I let them know. He'd been following my orders.

Caroline had arrived shortly after with Arnaud, and Delphine convinced her husband to allow Caroline to work on him. Meanwhile, Gorgantha climbed up from the lake. Her plunge had washed most of the druid spell off her, and it only took a dose of my healing magic to finish restoring her body from its desiccated state.

"I'm really sorry, guys," Jordan said.

He had been holding his head in his hands, and now he looked up from the table. Delphine remained beside him stroking his back, while two more druids sat to his left. Everyone from my team, including a muzzled Arnaud, took up the table's remaining seats. We even gave Dropsy a place when she began fussing in Bree-yark's pouch. Now the top of her glass face poked above the table.

"I remember everything now," Jordan said. "But how in the hell did I forget it in the first place? How did I forget the Upholders?"

"It's just a feature of these time catches," Caroline said.

"Yeah, it would have happened to any of us," I said. "Go easy on yourself."

When his searching eyes met mine, he nodded back in what appeared gratitude. He and I had already exchanged bro hugs, which told me he was truly himself. His mind was just processing the aftershocks.

"You were telling us how you got here?" I prompted.

"Yeah, right." He inhaled sharply as though to anchor himself. "After leaving Brooklyn in 1776, we tried to get up to Harriman State Park, but we kept finding ourselves in different times. When we got to this one, we decided to set up base in the park and go about it more systematically—we were under the impression there was a portal back to the present, that it was just a matter of finding it. We didn't realize it was like you described, everything stuck together in the middle of nowhere."

"Problem was," Delphine said, "there was already a gang of wereboars here. Thinking they were smalltime, we drove half from the fort and charmed the other half for security. You know, to keep the freaks and nasties away. It was only going to be temporary, but it turned out they were part of a secret network."

A network Everson apparently hadn't known about, I thought.

Jordan gave an exasperated snort. "Yeah, and when word reached the rest of the network that the boars were in our service, they assumed there had been a power transfer. Before we knew it, we were the head of a citywide syndicate. We went along with it at first, mostly to avoid a major power struggle."

"Remember now, we weren't planning on staying here," Delphine put in.

"And then we just ... forgot." Jordan's expression turned incredulous again.

"Is that why you went with the tough boss look?" Gorgantha asked.

"Oh, this?" Jordan rubbed his glistening pate. "Naw, that had to do with something else that came up."

Delphine smirked. "He got gum stuck in his hair."

"Yeah, but then I decided I *liked* the look." He poked her side playfully.

When Delphine laughed, I caught myself grinning. Even though they'd landed in an impossible situation, they'd endured it together. By their distorted experience of time, that had been almost two years ago.

Jordan squared his shoulders back toward us. "So, do we know where Seay and Malachi ended up?"

I felt my smile shrink. "We found them, actually."

"No shit?"

With the others' help, I gave Jordan and the druids a summary account of everything that had happened. Jordan listened with his usual intensity. When we finished, he tapped his steepled fingers against his chin.

"So we have no idea if they made it out of 1660?" he asked.

"No," I said, glancing over at Gorgantha. "But they may have left by a different route. Malachi had already given us the portal location for 1776. The Morton Building downtown. They could be waiting for us there."

"And we don't know how much longer this period is going to be solvent," Caroline added. "The collapse of 1660 likely started a chain effect that will gain momentum as it rolls through the remaining catches."

"So obviously the sooner we can all get there," I said, "the better."

"And that's where you believe the demon boss is planning his big move?" Jordan asked.

"Arnaud confirmed that he placed the copper plates to boost the site's ley energy." When I looked over at the demon-vampire, he was staring back at me. "And I haven't discussed this with everyone yet, but I have reason to believe Malphas was interested in your races for their elemental properties."

"Explain," Jordan said.

The small furrow returned between Caroline's eyebrows. "Yes, please do."

"Malphas acquired rights to the Strangers through three different demon masters. The ones who infiltrated the mer, half-fae, and druids. Races that correspond with Water, Air, and Earth. That's why Malphas was holding them—holding you," I amended, gesturing to Delphine and the druids. "To draw out those essences. Malphas wields Infernal Fire through the final demon, who's probably already at the St. Martin's site. All he needs now is Spirit to complete his five elements, his Aristotelean Set."

"And what will that do?" Bree-yark asked.

"Presumably create a portal to Malphas, one that could trigger a larger demon apocalypse."

"That's it?" Gorgantha remarked dryly.

"You said *presumably*," Jordan pointed out.

"Well, an arrangement like that would alter the energy," I said, "but it still wouldn't be enough to blow open the kind of hole Malphas needs. That would require a super fuel."

"So there's the fount of ley energy, the copper plates, and this Aristotelean Set," Jordan said. "You think there's something else?"

"The energy from the failing time catches, maybe?" Bree-yark offered.

"That's a great thought," I said. "I'm not sure how he'd capture and channel it, though."

Plus, my magic was suggesting that Malphas already had what he needed, that those three components were the answer and it was just a question of how he planned to deploy them. Unfortunately, my magic wasn't spelling that part out.

"Where did all of this come from?" Caroline challenged more than asked me.

I pulled my lips in. Across the table, one of Arnaud's eyebrows rose slightly. If I told my teammates he and I had puzzled it out together, I was going to have to explain that my magic had advised me to listen to him. Otherwise, they'd think I was out of my mind. But at the same time, I didn't want Arnaud to hear the magic-advising-me part. He would use that to his advantage somehow.

"When I went back to the apartment, I did some research." I said. "I also talked with Arnaud."

I decided I didn't want to lie. Though surprised murmurs circled the table, being upfront with my teammates felt more important at this stage than ever. Soon, however, the murmurs turned angry.

"*Him?*" Jordan pointed at Arnaud. "I thought he was just a transport."

"He's also worked closely with Malphas," I said.

"Which makes him the skeeviest sort of bitch," Gorgantha snapped.

Their anger was understandable. Malphas's demons had murdered half of Gorgantha's pod and kidnapped Jordan's wife.

"You're right," I said, showing my palms. "Arnaud is who he is. But he's also our best potential source of intel."

"He could be telling you anything," Jordan said.

"Sounds like he already has," Gorgantha grumbled.

Heat broke over my face, and my voice thickened. "Well, it's either that, or us walking into a complete unknown."

Bree-yark shook his head. "You're better than this, Everson."

His remark stung the most, probably because to this point Bree-yark had been my most solid ally. From his corner seat, Arnaud watched us with pinched eyes. I imagined the grin behind his muzzle, a part of him delighting in the discord he'd sown. And all the time, his offer dangled between us, awaiting my assent to snap firmly into place. I would never agree to the terms of his proposed truce, of course, but I wondered now if my teammates were right. Should I have been listening to him at all?

"I think we need to trust Everson's judgment," Caroline said over the others.

She met my gaze in a way that told me she remembered our talk in the restaurant in 1861. She knew I'd finally listened to my magic, to what I hadn't wanted to hear. I also sensed she appreciated my honesty.

"We wouldn't have even reached this point if it hadn't been for him," she added.

Delphine turned to Jordan. "I've been having those dreams about our sacred tree falling over, part of the root structure missing. And the Raven Circle *has* felt weaker. It's like part of the Circle's power is somewhere else."

Gorgantha cleared her throat. "I've felt off too. Hard to explain, but it's like me and water aren't quite on the same page anymore."

"Both could be explained by Malphas holding your racial essences," Caroline said.

When Jordan raised his eyes to mine, I saw an extended olive branch. "Was there anything else?" he asked.

"If Malachi is the final element," I said, "and he got there ahead of us, then Malphas's plan could already be in motion."

Jordan pushed himself up by the knuckles. "We should get moving, then."

"There may be fae who will try to stop us," Caroline said. "Royal fae."

"Damn, do we have a plan for them?" Jordan asked.

Remembering what Caroline had told me about the heart vow, I watched for her response. Moisture stood in her eyes as she nodded. "Yes."

"The portal is downtown," I said. "On the other side of Arnaud's wall, unfortunately."

"One of the boars drives a city bus," Jordan said. "I'll have him grab one from the fleet. That'll take care of getting everyone down there, anyway. We can worry about the Wall when we reach it."

42

The druids packed light—the clothes and cloaks they'd arrived in, plus herbal kits and quarterstaffs that would disappear the moment we transited to 1776. Jordan's was the only staff that would endure, having originated outside the time catches. As we filed down the steps from Belvedere Castle, I saw him look back, his dark eyes roving the fortress before he shook his head and continued walking.

I stepped up beside him. "Hey, good seeing you again."

He draped an arm across my shoulders. "If I'd known that was you earlier, I might have put on a better show."

He was referring to our sparring session on the observation deck. "I don't know. If you'd put on a better show, I might not be standing here. Packaging magic inside your blasts? What the hell, man?"

"Some cantrips I've been working on. You liked them?"

"Pointed at someone other than me or Gorgantha, maybe."

He chuckled and withdrew his arm. "When we get back, the ales are on me." He clapped my shoulder and showed his hand. "I know, I know, we have to get back first. Believe me, I've learned that lesson. Two freaking years."

He took a final look at the fortress before it disappeared beyond the trees.

The city bus was idling curbside when we reached the western border of Central Park. The large being hunched behind the wheel was in human form, but he still had the spiky hair and surly eyes of his boar half. A lit cigarette protruded from a hairy fist. As we boarded, Bree-yark sidled up to him.

"Hey, think I could bum one of those?" he asked.

I winced when the wereboar grunted, but he pulled a cigarette from a pack in the pocket of his shirt. He even lit it. Bree-yark clapped his shoulder in thanks and took a long drag. "Man," he said, exhaling as we walked down the aisle. "Ever since watching Barnum's go up in flames, this is all I've been thinking about."

"Well, you've earned it," I said.

Still, I took a seat with Caroline and placed Arnaud in the growing plume of smoke beside Bree-yark. Gorgantha sat ahead of us, while Jordan and the rest of the druids spread out here and there. When the driver got the confirmation we were all on, he closed the door and pulled from the curb.

"We look like the express bus to Narnia," I said.

That drew a faint smile from Caroline, who had spoken little since our meeting in Belvedere Castle. She was thinking about Angelus and our impending encounter.

"Hey, thanks for getting my back with the Arnaud thing."

"Is your magic talking now?" she asked.

"More like I'm listening to what I didn't want to hear. You were right about that."

"Then I have no choice but to trust you," she joked.

"Your advice actually echoed something my grandfather said. I've been looking for him in these time catches, thinking he could help. But he already gave me all the help I needed when I found him the last time."

"How so?"

"Well, when we were at his farm, he said he'd felt a change in the ley energy. He sketched it out for us, showing energy lines being directed back at the St. Martin's site. We now know that was from the copper plates. The sketch also reminded me of a vision I'd had of being in a cross-like arrangement with four others and rotating, the motion generating an intense, malevolent energy."

"The Aristotelean Set?" Caroline said.

I nodded. "Malachi had the same vision, which makes me think I was tapping into him through our bond. If he represents Spirit, the other four were the rest of the Upholders, plus a demon. Earth, Air, Water, and Fire. My grandfather said it sounded like someone meant to perform powerful spell work."

"So far, spot on."

"But his real help came at the end. He said we only needed to worry if it came to pass. And that my team was in the presence of 'one who heeds his magic'—though I think he was challenging me more than making an observation. That's all a long way of saying thank you, because I believe that's what it's going to take."

"You're welcome, and I *do* trust you," she said, echoing her vote of confidence from the meeting. "But the biggest challenge will be seeing it through." I sensed she was telling that to herself as much as me.

"Sounds like you've come to a decision as well," I said.

I left it out there in case she wanted to talk about it. I wasn't sure she did. Blocks shot past as the wereboar weaved in and out of traffic. At a corner bus stop, a group waved their arms, believing we were their ride. We blew through a briefcase that a man thrust into the street. Papers burst everywhere.

"With the heart vow, I'm the only one who has a realistic

chance against him," Caroline said at last. "If he's waiting at the St. Martin's site, I'll do what needs to be done."

"Malachi could be there too," I reminded her. "He has potent powers of banishment."

"If he's not, I'll need you and the others to buy me time."

"Of course, whatever you—"

The driver swore and slammed the brakes. We pitched forward while the rear of the bus fishtailed in a shrieking peal. Trailing cars braked and crunched into us.

We rocked to a stop across Broadway. More thuds sounded from a growing pileup. I'd thrown an arm across Caroline to brace her, and now we peered out our south-facing window.

A fog of burned rubber scudded past our view. Beyond, a formation of tall figures stood in the road, their skin a familiar cobalt blue. The one in front had the chiseled face of a deity and a mane of copper hair.

"Caroline," Angelus boomed.

Shit, they're early. I squeezed her hand and rose. "Stay here."

"Where are you going?"

"To buy you that time."

The rest of the bus was beginning to stir as I made my way down the aisle. "What the hell's going on?" Jordan asked.

"It's the fae," I said. "The *demon-possessed* fae."

"Come out, Caroline," Angelus called. "I'm taking you home."

When I passed the wereboar, I whispered, "Keep the bus running."

He grunted at my back as I descended the steps. We were far enough south that Broadway had become one way. Behind me, I could hear the shouting and commotion that was the aftermath of the pileup. Ahead, the street was eerily quiet. Pedestrians along both sidewalks stood and stared. Several began filming on their phones. Angelus and the seven fae with him had made no attempts to blend into the period—or to even appear human. Like in Faerie, they could have been a race of gods.

"I've come for Caroline," Angelus said.

"Oh, is that why you were calling her name?"

"We don't want to harm anyone, Everson."

"Then maybe dropping into the middle of Broadway wasn't the brightest move."

His intense green eyes cut from me to the fishtailed bus and back. Though Angelus carried no weapons, the same light-skinned male and female who had flanked him in Faerie wielded a sickle-shaped blade apiece.

"You were to have summoned me," he said.

"Yeah, about that..." I pretended to pat my coat pockets. "I must have tossed your stone somewhere."

"I just want Caroline."

"Unfortunately, the feeling isn't mutual."

For all my bravado, my knees were quaking. I was standing in front of a demon housed in a formidable fae's body. There was the banishment rune on my blade, sure. But I'd need to pierce him first, and with the kind of powers Angelus wielded, he could reduce me to cellular powder the moment I flexed.

Right now, the game was to keep his attention on me.

"So why don't you run along back to Faerie?"

"I've always tolerated you, Everson. Don't make this personal."

I snorted even though being tolerated by a royal fae was rather high praise.

"You want to talk about personal?" Bree-yark barked. "How about you making it so my friends here couldn't go home?"

When I looked back, I was surprised to see that he had come off the bus, along with Jordan, Delphine, and a host of druids. They were all arrayed behind me, weapons in hand. Through the window I could see Gorgantha standing over where Caroline was presumably crouched, out of sight.

"We have no fight with you," Angelus replied.

Bree-yark pumped the shotgun's action. "Then let's keep it that way."

I showed the goblin a hand for him to cool it. But something about this whole thing felt off. If Malphas was controlling Angelus, why the fixation on Caroline? Why not engage the rest of us? He had to know we were gunning for his portal now. It was almost as if Angelus was just being ... himself.

"Stand aside, Everson," he said. "She's not the woman you knew."

When he stepped forward, a rustle of cloaks sounded behind me, and the collective hum of druidic magic took up in staffs. Angelus's eyes glowed, while the flanking light-skinned fae readied their blades. The energy issuing from the fae prince sent ominous waves through the time catch: a promise of mass destruction. In the distance, approaching sirens rose and fell, but they felt a world away.

"Then who am I?" Caroline asked.

I looked over to find her moving through the druids. Gorgantha was with her, still acting as her protector, but there was no fear in Caroline's eyes. Angelus watched sternly, but I felt his power draw down.

"It's time to come home," he said.

Gorgantha dropped off as Caroline stopped beside me, keeping Angelus a good fifteen feet out in front of us.

"Why?" she asked. "You've already severed my lineal claim."

"You're under the influence of a malevolent being. You don't know what you're saying, what you're doing."

Caroline shook her head sadly. "No, Angelus. It's you who's been corrupted."

In the next moment he was towering over her, hands gripping her arms. Before I could react, he and Caroline were fading from the time catch. *He's taking her!* But Caroline's mouth wrenched down, and Angelus cried out. They returned to solidity, only now Angelus was on his knees, one hand gripping his chest.

She'd done it. She'd attacked him through the heart vow.

The remaining fae faltered as if the attack had stunned them too. It suggested they were joined in a fae bond, possibly to move in and out of the time catch.

The short silence was broken by hooves pounding asphalt and the cries of pedestrians. Our driver had gone full wereboar and was charging the fae. I shouted as his monstrous form bounded past me, trying to call him off. The last thing we needed was a full-blown battle before Caroline could overwhelm the demon.

But the wereboar ignored me. Snorting, he drove his thick head into the chest of the male twin and gave a savage twist. The fae cried out as tusks tore through flesh and threw him through the air. Pedestrians screamed and backed away. The wereboar wheeled on the female, but she was ready for him.

I cast a barrier between them, but the fae's enchanted blade smashed through it. The wereboar absorbed three rapid slashes and his bulky form disintegrated to the street. Behind me, the druids reacted with blasts from their staffs. The fae blocked them, but like Jordan's attacks on me earlier, these carried sneaky cantrips. With each seismic collision, yellow dust burst out and wisped around the fae.

"Time displacements!" Jordan shouted.

Indeed, like videos being rewound, the fae underwent a rapid dance until they were standing at attention as they had been shortly after arriving.

"How long?" I asked him.

"Fifteen seconds, give or take."

I glanced at where Caroline stood over her husband. Fae

light radiated from her eyes. Angelus remained down, a hand clawing at the asphalt, clearly weakening. I could just make out the tight cord of power she was driving into his heart. She had to be pushing her limits, both energetically and emotionally. And if Angelus recovered, we were going to be looking at a major fight against him and his loyalists.

"Hit the fae," I called to my teammates. "Hard."

Bree-yark didn't need to be told twice. His gun went off in a rapid series of pumps and shots, silver ammo blasting into the seven standing fae, knocking them around. Under the cantrip, the fae didn't resist. They were viewing everything as it had happened seconds before the magic possessed them.

Pushing power through my cold iron amulet, I dropped the reeling fae with a cone of blue light. Transparent white flames burst over their protective magic. I withdrew my attack as the druids moved in with quarterstaffs, pummeling the downed fae with charged blows and then pummeling them some more.

We were cheap-shotting the hell out of them, but we needed to bring their power down to a level we could manage before they recovered. With time winding down on the cantrip, I turned to Caroline.

"How's it go—?" I started to ask, then broke off.

She had drawn a fae dagger from under her cloak and raised it overhead. The tip was aimed at the center of Angelus's back. He remained on the street. One of his hands crawled to her ankle and gripped it weakly. Beneath the faltering light in her eyes, tears streamed down the sides of her face.

Unable to purge the demon through the bond, she was left with an enchanted blade.

A moan-scream sounded, and I looked over to find Arnaud staggering from the bus. With Caroline's energies spent, her enchantments had fallen from him. The vampire-demon thrust his bound hands toward Caroline and Angelus, while his jaundiced eyes implored me with the urgency of whatever he was trying to say.

Listen to his words.

I flicked an invocation off my sword, and Arnaud's muzzle released and fell to the street. He was already shouting in a strained voice, but with the surrounding commotion, I couldn't hear the message.

I labored to read the shape of his lips.

Not him! he was saying. *The demon isn't him!*

I looked from Caroline to Angelus. Was Arnaud trying to spare Malphas's demon, or was Caroline about to make the biggest mistake of her life? Off to my right, the fae were recovering from the cantrips. They leapt to their feet and began repelling the druids with bolts of fae light. The twins recovered their blades from the street, and the air whistled as they sliced at the retreating druids.

Aiming my sword, I shouted, *"Vigore!"*

The force invocation slammed into Caroline's hand and knocked the dagger from her grip. As it went clattering away, I hoped *I* hadn't just made the biggest mistake of my life. Pulling her hand to her chest, Caroline's shocked face snapped toward me. Though I felt my mind tugging at the question, I refused to revisit it.

It's not her.

But if the demon wasn't Caroline or Angelus, who did that leave? I looked at Arnaud, but he was scanning the action from the steps of the bus. To be safe, I cast an invocation that bound him to the door.

The druids were holding their own against the weakened fae. But the stalemate wasn't going to last, not with the fae's magic returning. And the twins were no longer engaging the druids. They'd disappeared. As I searched for their pale-blue faces, I reflected on their likenesses to Angelus.

Half-siblings, I thought suddenly.

If their other halves were human, they would have been vulnerable to the demon that Malphas planted in Faerie—and I'd heard of a single demon possessing twins. *A shadow demon.* In the pixies' song, Pip and Twerk referred to the one claimed as "they"—not gender neutral, but truly plural. The fae twins would have been capable of influencing Angelus through their common bloodline.

As I looked around anxiously for the twins, I imagined their early meetings with Angelus. Malphas's goal would have been to undermine Angelus's trust in Caroline, to convince him that she had been compromised. Everything the twins advised him to do would have been with the purported goal of restoring his wife. And Angelus would have responded out of his love and devotion to her, when, in fact, the goal was to prevent anyone from disturbing the 1776 St. Martin's site.

The twins had been too late to stop Osgood from sending us the first time, so they took measures to ensure I couldn't go back. They murdered Crusspatch in the Fae Wilds, but failed to find Caroline or Arnaud.

I threw myself flat an instant before a blade broke through my shield. I'd been around fae glamours enough now to have sensed the subtle distortion at my back. When the male twin materialized, he was grinning wickedly. I scooted back and leveled my sword at him, banishment light already bathing the length of my blade. But in a blur of his sickle, my sword went clanging from my grip.

I still had ahold of my iron amulet and shouted until power haloed the metal and then my body in a field of blue light. The twin drew back, his free arm across his face. He might have been a demon, but he was still packaged in a fae's body.

"Turn that *off*," he hissed.

"Yeah, or what?" I said, upping the power.

Behind me, Caroline cried out. I looked over to find a sheet of her hair wrapped in the female twin's fist. The demon's lips pinched upward as she raised her blade and said, "Or your friend loses her head."

43

I looked around desperately. Angelus, who was still recovering from the attack through his heart vow, remained down, his skin a sickly shade of blue. The battle out in the street had turned against the druids, who were in retreat. Bree-yark had dropped his shotgun to drag Gorgantha to temporary safety behind a bus shelter—she was moving at least, but it didn't look good for the allies. Not good at all.

My eyes cut to where I'd contained Arnaud, but he was no longer there. The manifestation I'd used to bind him to the door must have fallen when the twin sliced through my shield. The little bastard had fled.

But at that moment we had bigger problems.

"Turn it *off*," the demon-fae backing away from me repeated.

His sister yanked Caroline's hair, drawing a small cry from her. The demon's blade was still raised, the edge glimmering with the same magic that had disintegrated the wereboar. A dusty cloud of his remains happened to blow past us at that moment.

"Yeah, yeah, all right," I said.

I withdrew the power from my amulet as slowly as I thought

I could get away with. I still had one last recourse—my magic's wisdom. Focusing past the adrenaline-fueled pounding in my head, I listened.

My magic nodded.

That's it? That's all you have to say?

When my magic nodded some more, I lost it.

Well, what the fuck's that supposed to mean?

The last of the blue halo glimmered back inside the amulet.

"Toss it aside," the demon above me ordered.

I complied weakly, watching it roll and then rattle to a rest. *At the first opening, I'll reclaim it with an invocation.* The demon-fae swept his blade toward the amulet like a golf pro teeing off, and an invisible force launched it into the sky. *Or not,* I thought as the amulet disappeared from view.

The wail of approaching sirens grew through the silence.

"Everson Croft," the demon said in a taunting voice. "The wizard who doesn't quit."

Though his twin had relaxed her grip on Caroline's hair, her blade remained poised above her neck like a guillotine.

"What do you want?" I growled.

The male demon signaled to the fae, and in the next moment, Jordan and the druids were bound up in enchantments. Bree-yark and Gorgantha too. Caroline, Angelus, and I remained unfettered, but Angelus was in critical shape, and the twins had Caroline and me under the threat of their sickles.

"We're going to play a game," my demon said, tossing his blade from hand to hand. "It's called the Will of Croft. Your tenacity, while admirable, can't go unpunished. The game is simple. You choose the order in which your comrades die, and their deaths will be swift. No tortures, no cruelties, no pain. The only catch is that the tortures they would have undergone will be conferred to you."

"How original," I said dryly.

There had to be a reason my magic was acting so damned nonchalant. I scanned the empty sidewalks down both sides of Broadway. Here and there, faces peered from windows, but they were no one I recognized.

"Pay attention!" the demon shouted.

He extended a hand toward a street-level drugstore. The plate glass window shattered as a man in a blue business suit came flying out. The demon-fae caught him around the neck and drove his blade into the man's gut. With a severed cry, the man crumbled to powder. Even though we were in a time catch, I reacted, reaching an impotent arm toward the victim. The demon grinned as he wiped off his hand on his hip.

"A little demonstration of the kind of swiftness I'm talking about," he said. "So go ahead, choose your first one."

"Release her..." Angelus said.

He had struggled to his hands and knees and was pawing toward the female demon, fae energy warping the air around his outstretched fingers. The demon brought her blade down. Angelus's severed hand fell to the street. Caroline cried out as her husband pulled his arm to his body and collapsed again.

"Choose," the demon above me repeated impatiently.

Past him, down Broadway, someone peered around the cornice of a building and quickly withdrew. It was me, Everson.

Is he the answer, somehow?

"You're not paying attention!" the demon roared.

He thrust his arm back. Stonework crumbled from the cornice, and then my time catch counterpart was sailing through the air, coat flapping. Like the businessman moments before, Everson landed in the demon's grip.

The demon paused, looking between us. "Well, isn't this interesting."

"No!" I cried.

He drew back his blade—and the whole block went bright white.

I crouched against the street, arms over my head, but the light vanished as suddenly as it had appeared. In the place of the demon was a smoking pile of sulfurous debris. A figure stood beside the remains, but it was no longer Everson. A glance back showed me that the female demon had been smoked too.

Freed, Caroline wrapped an arm around Angelus and spoke into his ear. The remaining fae were down as well, no longer a threat.

The figure approached me. "I believe this belongs to you, to you."

I stood, accepted my sword, and embraced Malachi. "You son of a gun."

"I told you I'd meet you." He hugged me back in the awkward way of someone without much experience in human contact. "And look who I brought, I brought," he said, turning and waving down the street.

A block away, Seay and the half-fae appeared. Everson was with them.

I shook my head, still dazed at our sudden reversal in fortune. "They glamoured you to look like me."

"I felt that a holy blast would be more effective, more effective at close range," he said. "We arrived at the castle after you'd left, but you—I mean, Everson—told us about the bus." Spying on my future self sounded like something I would have done. "We took the most direct route until we reached the pileup, the pileup."

"But how in the hell did you make it out of 1660?"

"There was a portal down in New Amsterdam, but from there it took a lot of detouring to arrive here." He shook his head wearily. "A lot of detouring."

I kissed his forehead and ruffled his hair. "Let me check on everyone."

Freed from their confinement, the druids had begun helping the injured. Jordan and his wife looked to be all right. In fact, Delphine and another druid were assisting Gorgantha, while Bree-yark looked on in concern.

The five fae, dropped following Malachi's holy blast, gained their feet. No longer under the influence of the demon twins, they made their way toward Caroline and Angelus. Upon arriving, they knelt around their prince, each placing a hand on his back. I was worried he had perished until Caroline spoke.

"He needs your strength," she told Angelus's loyalists.

Currents of energy flowed from their touch, encasing her husband in a corona of healing light.

"Is there anything the druids or I can do?" I asked.

Caroline's eyes were puffy when she stood. "Anything done here can only sustain him. He needs elder fae magic and quickly. I'm so sorry, Everson, but we have to take him to Faerie. I'll send Osgood back to help you."

"Do you have a way of getting there?" I asked, still brooding on Arnaud's disappearing act.

"The line they arrived by is still active. With our collective power, we'll be able to traverse it, but it must be soon."

Had we not been through so much together, I would have been deeply suspicious of what she was telling me. Now, I nodded without hesitation.

"I understand."

She glanced past me. "The Upholders are reunited."

"Thanks to you. With Malachi back, we can destroy the final demon and take down whatever Malphas has built at the St. Martin's site. I'm thinking this was his last-ditch attempt to stop us before we got there."

The fold between her brows deepened. "Where's Arnaud?"

"He took off, but he's still warded. He'll be easy to track."

Indeed, finding him was going to be a minor pain in the ass more than anything.

"Thank you for everything," Caroline whispered, and pressed her lips firmly against my cheek.

I nodded and watched her kneel beside her husband and the other fae.

"I'll send Osgood," she repeated.

In an implosion of fae light, they disappeared.

44

"That wasn't dramatic or anything," a voice said at my shoulder.

Turning from the lingering point of light where the fae had just been, I found Seay and immediately pulled her into a hug. "You came."

"The collapsing reality didn't leave me much choice." When we separated, she turned serious. "I took your potion."

Crap, I'd all but forgotten about that. "And?" I asked carefully.

A shadow crossed her face as she cradled her belly. "He's been quiet. Probably sleeping."

I felt the brick in my stomach again, but before I could follow up, Gorgantha limped toward us. "Is that the prego?"

"Gigi!" Seay exclaimed, running over and throwing her arms around the mer.

Gorgantha was banged up from her encounter with the fae, but powerful druidic magic moved through her.

"They told me you were big, girl," she said. "But *dayam!*"

Malachi looked as if he were trying to keep up with the rapid exchange that followed, but he was fidgeting with his Bible, anxious to get going, it seemed. I shared the sentiment. I was about to say something when Seay's laughter cut out suddenly. I followed her pinched gaze to where Jordan was approaching.

He stopped several feet away, quarterstaff planted at his feet.

"Before you say anything about what happened in 1776," he said, "I'm sorry."

Seay stared at him another moment, then eased from her bowed-up stance and nodded. "In that case, get your stubborn ass over here."

Jordan chuckled as he walked up and hugged her. "I am sorry."

"It's history," she said. "Literally. It's lovely to see you."

"You too, and congratulations."

The remaining druids and half-fae, who had all been encamped in 1776 Brooklyn together, took their cues from Jordan and Seay and began greeting one another. Hugs and a few kisses went around.

"Holy thunder," Bree-yark said.

He was standing off to one side, staring between me and my time catch counterpart, who had stopped on the verge of the reunion. Everson looked as if he'd been debating whether to intrude or slip away.

"It's all right," I said, waving him over.

"I'm sorry," he said. "I know the original plan was that I wouldn't be involved beyond the park, but well…"

"Believe me, I understand. At least this way, I get a chance to thank you." I gripped his hand and pulled him into a bro hug, clapping his back with my sword hand twice. "The disruption field worked to perfection."

"Good," he said.

Embracing ourselves seemed to make us both a little self-conscious, and we didn't linger. When we moved apart, Everson's eyes dipped to the street before looking up again. "Listen, I had some time to think while I was setting up the copper stations. And you can, you know, give it to me straight." He squinted as if someone were about to throw a baseball past his head. "Is this a time catch?"

"You know about time catches?"

"I did some extra reading over the summer. In a tome on alternate planes, there's a small section on them."

Shit, that *had* been this summer. I looked at my younger self for a moment, considering how—and even *if*—I would have wanted to be told I wasn't really me, but actually a spliced-off echo in space and time.

"Yes," I said at last. "This is a time catch."

He inhaled solemnly and nodded to himself. "I feel better hearing it from you."

I'd figured he would. The fact a future version of me was still living suggested things were going to be all right, somehow.

"But I have to ask," he said. "That woman who just disappeared...?"

"Caroline Reid," I confirmed. "Your colleague. And it's a long story."

"No doubt," he muttered.

"Are you going to be all right?"

The revelation about the time catch had turned his face a shade of bone and given him a thousand-yard stare, but he snuffed out a laugh. "Maybe this will get me to take more risks in my personal life," he said.

With Vega, Tony, and a little girl on the way, not to mention all the people I could now call my friends, it was easy to forget how lonely I'd once been. But the man in front of me was testament to that solitary period.

I nodded. "That's a good plan."

"In the meantime, what else can I do to help?"

I was about to thank him for the offer and tell him he'd

already helped enough, but I still had to move everyone out of there. I gestured toward the bus. "We're going to need to get this big guy downtown."

"Past the Wall?" When I nodded, he checked his trench coat pockets before looking up in sudden realization. "Do you happen to have any more of the stealth potion you cooked at my place?"

I pulled out a vial. "Last one."

As he palmed it, he said, "All right, take Broadway south. By the time you get to the Wall, I'll have that checkpoint open."

I punched his shoulder. "Thanks, kid."

He punched mine back. "Don't mention it, old timer."

I smiled sadly as he ran off to hail a cab.

"I didn't want to interrupt," Bree-yark said, walking over, "but that might be the wildest thing I've ever seen."

When I peered around, I noticed that just about everyone had been watching my reunion with myself as well. Meanwhile, the approaching sirens had stopped somewhere beyond the far side of the bus.

"Is everyone here?" I called.

When Jordan and Seay answered that all of theirs were accounted for, I waved them toward the bus. As they boarded, I filled them in on where Caroline had gone and that we could expect Osgood shortly.

"We'll start making our way downtown," I said, "but we're going to have to take a side trip to track Arnaud."

"No, we won't," Bree-yark said.

Before I could tap into the wards that bound Arnaud, the goblin stuck his hand under a seat and hauled up the demon-vampire by the back of his neck manacle. I stared for a moment, not believing he hadn't fled. Had his fear of Malphas's demons overwhelmed all other instincts? Is that why he'd stayed? Or did he believe his best chance at freedom was the infernal deal he'd proposed to me?

"Unhand me, you brute," Arnaud hissed, swiping his manacled hands around.

With a growl, Bree-yark shoved the demon-vampire up the aisle. "Do we even need him anymore?"

I caught Arnaud as he stumbled against me. "What do you mean?"

"If Caroline is sending us Osgood," Bree-yark said, "having a demonic line is pointless now, right?"

That got some mutters of agreement from the rest of the bus. Though Jordan and Gorgantha remained quiet this time, I could see by their eyes that they were ready to dispose of Arnaud too. Even Seay was giving him a black look. And Caroline was no longer here to defend me. My gaze returned to Bree-yark. I might have considered what he was suggesting if it hadn't been for Arianna's dream visit.

Find Arnaud, she'd said.

There was a connection between him and freeing the Order from the Harkless Rift, one I still hadn't found.

"He's our backup plan," I said firmly. "He's coming."

Though Bree-yark grumbled, the others fell silent. They'd already experienced firsthand the consequences of *not* having a backup plan for returning to the present, and it had sucked big time.

With no wereboar to drive us, I inherited the responsibility by virtue of being the last one to board. I settled into the air-cushioned seat, then pulled down a narrow seat beside me that was probably used for training.

"Sit down," I told Arnaud.

Though no longer under Caroline's enchantments, he complied. As I leaned over to strap him in, he hissed in my ear.

"The alert was a freebie," he said, referring to his warning that Caroline's husband hadn't been the demon. "The next time, it will mean invoking our little agreement. In exchange for my help, you'll release me," he reminded me. "Not only from these wards, but from any and all acts of retribution—by you, your Order, or anyone you can think to contract. For my part, I'll promise to stay away."

I ignored him, telling myself it would never come to that.

But had I ever thought he would end up sparing Angelus's life?

I looked out the driver window. The pileup against the side of the bus ran three and four cars deep. The backup extended for several blocks now, even overflowing onto the sidewalks. Several ambulance and police vehicles were trying to nose their way through, while a small army of first responders had already disembarked and were hustling through the backup to reach the accident scene.

I do not want to deal with these guys.

As instructed, the wereboar had left the bus running, and it only took a moment for me to orient myself to the transmission and pedals. By going into forward and reverse several times, I was able to separate from the wreckage by degrees. Soon, I had enough room to turn the bus south toward the empty road. As I accelerated, the frame squealed against the left front tire, drowning out the shouts of the arriving officers.

"They're going to be looking for a city bus," I called.

"We're on it," Seay answered. "Want anything special?"

"Yeah, not a city bus."

Fae magic stirred, and when I checked the side mirror, I saw that I was now driving one of those pink party buses. I couldn't complain though. The half-fae were also glamouring the traffic lights, giving me green clearance for as far as the eye could see. I only had to slow to round Union Square before picking up

Broadway right before it angled south toward the spires of the Financial District.

Beside me, Arnaud had fallen silent. Something in his small, pensive frown suggested the mortal he'd once been.

I blew through the Village and Soho, and before long we were passing City Hall and the intersection where Barnum's Museum had once stood. The formidable Wall loomed ahead along Liberty Street. Only there were four armed guards at the checkpoint, all signaling for me to slow down.

C'mon, kid, I thought. *Tell me you got there ahead of us.*

I kept my foot on the gas, but cast a shield over the front of the bus to be safe.

When I got to within two blocks of the Wall, the guards raised their rifles. At one block, a force scattered them. A row of bollards that had begun to rise from the pavement behind them sank again, clearing our way.

"Hell, yeah!" I shouted, pumping a fist and pressing the accelerator.

As our pink bus sped through the checkpoint, I gave a thumbs-up to the phantom in the control booth, a young man who looked remarkably like me. I then narrowed my eyes toward Wall Street, needing to reach our target before the time catch version of Arnaud reacted to the egregious breach of his domain.

At the next block, the bedrock under Manhattan shuddered.

Forget the damned vampire. The time catch is starting to fail.

Pedestrians fell to the sidewalks and red brake lights glared ahead of us. I swerved around a line of cars pulling over, then slowed to push between a pair of cabs stopped in the middle of the street. Metal keened as the bus shoved them apart. I accelerated again, our destination just blocks away now.

Hold it together a little longer, I told the time catch.

A violent rumble shook the bus, tottering it onto one set of wheels and then the other. Ahead, the asphalt undulated like waves. Water shot from a sudden fracture in the street, soon joined by fire from a ruptured gas line.

"Shit," I muttered, veering onto Cedar Street.

"The buildings are really swaying," Bree-yark said in a worried voice.

In the rearview mirror, I caught him angling his neck to peer upward. I straightened my gaze as chunks of masonry began landing around us. One flattened a sleek Mercedes Benz I was passing, its glass spraying the side of the bus. As I extended my shield to cover our rooftop, Malachi shoved his wild head of hair between me and Arnaud.

"How's it going?"

"Oh, could be better," I said, jerking our ride south to avoid a yawning crevasse.

"At the next intersection, turn right," Malachi said.

"I was going to try to hook back up with Broadway."

He shook his head. "No, no, that way's blocked." He jabbed a finger at the upcoming turn. "Right, right!"

I followed his direction. "Divine Voice?"

"Divine Voice," he said, his own voice wild with conviction. "It's going to get us there."

After what I'd seen him do to the twin demons, I believed him. Still, the world was coming apart fast, and we were getting farther from our target.

"Left!" he cried.

"There's no turn."

"Left!"

I swerved onto the sidewalk, blowing through a line of vendor wagons. Hotdog and falafel carts exploded to either side of the bus, while their umbrellas tumbled past my view. The ground shuddered as two massive pieces of falling building burst against the road where I'd just been.

"Good call," I said in a shaky voice.

From there, I followed every command Malachi gave, avoiding more falling building parts, while swerving around ruptures, geysers, and sudden gouts of fire. As smoke closed around us, his directions became even more essential. I found the switch for the headlights, but I could barely make out the street signs now.

"The portal is at the bottom of an excavation site," he said during a rare lull.

"I thought it was at the Morton Building."

"*Behind* the Morton Building. It was a planned addition, planned addition."

"Financed by Chillington Capital," Arnaud put in, referencing his old firm.

"Construction was put on hold during the Crash," Malachi said, prompting Arnaud to mutter something about a spineless builder.

"How deep a pit are we talking?" I asked.

"The project had only begun," Arnaud said. "So, not very."

"Turn!" Malachi called.

I followed his jabbing finger to the right. Suddenly, we were rushing up on a block ringed in tall construction fencing and yellow signs. The street shook violently, and the rumbling around us turned into a roar. I didn't have to look to know that buildings were coming down. Before I could ask Malachi what to do, the time catch itself bent. Our street fractured and canted down, sending us straight toward the fence.

"The entrance!" Malachi shouted.

I angled the bus toward a short ramp that ended at a closed gate in the fencing.

"Hold on, everyone!" I shouted, peering up at the mirror. They were already hunkered down.

Beyond them, a pale cloud of smoke and debris was

charging toward us. We smashed through the gate at the same moment the cloud swallowed us. Darkness filled the bus. I stomped the brakes and incanted another layer of protection around us. The bus banged and rattled and then the nose veered down.

Holy shit, we're plunging.

As I gripped the wheel helplessly, Malachi remained at my shoulder.

"It's okay, the portal is below!" he shouted. "The final reckoning is at hand, is at hand!"

A dizzying show of lights rippled around us, and then blackness.

45

The cool breeze that brushed my face smelled of salt and marsh.

Seized by a feeling of plunging, I shoved myself upright. The world rocked violently for a moment, but only in my head. I was sitting in the middle of a wide dirt road under a full moon. Stately buildings rose in a procession along one side of the thoroughfare, while the other side was a blackened ruins.

This looked for all the world like 1776 New York. But where was everyone else?

"Hello?" I called, grasping my cane from the ground beside me. "Seay? Gorgantha?" I wobbled to my feet. "Jordan? Malachi?"

There was no bus, no druids or half-fae, no Upholders. A block away, my gaze stopped on a familiar foundation of stone slabs scattered with earth and cinder. The St. Martin's site. Only I was viewing it from the north side now. It had taken one hell of a journey, but I was finally around the barrier.

And alone.

"Bree-yark?" I shouted, panic growing inside me.

Wiping dirt from the bonding sigil on my hand, I pushed power into it. A moment later, I felt the faintest tug.

Okay, I thought, exhaling, *the Upholders are here somewhere.*

I pivoted in a circle, shouting their names again. "It's Everson!"

Still no answer, and the bonding sigil wasn't giving me a direction. My trench coat rustled as I strode toward the St. Martin's site and pulled my cane into sword and staff.

Through my wizard's senses, I watched ley energy gushing from the foundation. In four surrounding locations, dispersed energy was being collected, concentrated, and channeled back at the fount. Two of the locations were buildings on the far side of Broadway. The other two were structures that stood in the blackened field beyond the site, cleverly disguised to look like casualties of the fire. All four held the copper paneling Arnaud had installed, and all were active, creating the cross-like pattern my grandfather had observed.

There were secondary and tertiary locations for energy amplification set farther back, but these four were the main ones. And presumably being operated by Arnaud's replacement, Malphas's final demon.

Was he waiting for us? I thought with stinging dread. *Did he get to the others?*

As I neared the St. Martin's site, I felt the growing intensity Malachi had described. Raw, concentrated ley. But where was the platform he'd seen? Where were the containers for the essences Malphas had siphoned? Where was the rest of his Night Ruin?

"Everson!" someone cried.

I wheeled to find a lone figure running down Broadway, all ragged hair and tattered clothes. I breathed a silent prayer as Malachi covered the final block, but I checked his aura to be sure. The chaotic pattern was a match to my teammate's.

"Have you seen the others?" I asked.

"No," he panted as he arrived in front of me, his Bible clutched to his chest. "I was going to ask you the same, the same."

"This is it, right? The 1776 site?"

"It looks different than the last time I was here, but yes. It has to be."

"What about the final demon? Can you sense anything?"

He peered around, then shook his head.

"Where did you end up?"

"Couple blocks over, by New Dutch Church." He pointed toward the northeast.

"There's a good chance we're all scattered, then." When I noticed Malachi shying from the intensity of the St. Martin's site, I said, "How about you go look for the others, and I'll start dismantling the copper panels, cripple the power source. It doesn't look like Malphas has his Night Ruin up and running." Until we found the others I was going to be on edge, but the fact we'd arrived here in time was a huge relief.

But Malachi was peering back at me with a meditative face, the burned half shining in the moon's glow.

"Did you have another idea?" I asked.

"When I was returning with Seay and the others, I had some time to think. And now I'm wondering, I'm wondering..." He rubbed his forehead agitatedly. "Did we just do Malphas's work for him?"

"What do you mean?"

"The Aristotelean Set, the five elements. He needed a container for the essences, right? What if the containers, the containers were us? Jordan, Seay, Gorgantha, Arnaud, and ... and me, I guess?"

As I looked from Malachi to the St. Martin's site, icy fingers crawled down my back.

"What if that was his plan?" he pressed. "What if that was the reason for manipulating you into coming back the way you did?"

"Manipulating...?" A flash of irritation hit me. "The hell are you talking about? He was trying to block me."

"Or did he just narrow your choices?" He raised a finger. "To one?"

Though still peeved, I considered the steps the demon Malphas had taken. Removing Osgood as an option for my return, alienating Caroline, and then murdering Crusspatch.

That had left Arnaud—a demon he couldn't reach, because of my wards and sigils, but that perhaps he still needed? And when I asked Caroline how she knew about the demon lines, she said Osgood had left the information for her to find. But what if one of the demon twins had in fact left it?

"The rest of us were already here," Malachi went on, "in 1776 New York, but then you captured Arnaud, and the time catches collided. I don't believe Malphas was expecting that, expecting that. But like a powerful demon, he adapted. When we became separated, he needed someone to find us and bring us here. Someone we trusted."

I was caring less and less for his suggestion that I'd been an unwitting pawn in Malphas's plans. But I thought back to how we'd found Gorgantha and Malachi in 1861. Hellcat Maggie had intercepted us, sending us on a mission that led to both team-mates. That had seemed a lucky stroke, but what if Malphas's final demon had pointed the vampire at us?

And upon finding Malachi, we'd effectively acquired a guide. Locating Seay and Jordan would have been impossible, otherwise.

But there was a problem with the theory.

"Then why send his soulless mobs after us?" I asked. "Why try to stop us?"

"No, no, I think he wanted to speed us along," he said, pumping his elbows in a running motion. "Keep us moving."

"Because of the instability of the time catches?" I mused aloud.

"Though maybe he sped their demises too," Malachi said. "He did get us to jump from 1660 to the present to 1776, bam, bam, bam."

"Still, it seems too risky. The whole thing."

"Maybe another reason for placing it in your hands. You seem to succeed where so many others would have failed."

"That doesn't explain the fae intercepting us, though."

"Yes, I've been puzzling over that." Malachi paced in a circle, rubbing his ear. "The demon twins corrupted Angelus through their common bloodline. Still, he's a powerful fae, and then there's his love for his wife. Those factors may have overwhelmed the demonic influence, but what did Malphas care if Angelus reclaimed his wife at that point? She'd already served her purpose, and it would mean one less wild card at the end. That was the plan, I believe. Take Caroline and let the rest of us go on our way. The attack, the battle—unexpected, but you wouldn't have held your own against them otherwise."

"We didn't," I said, feeling vindicated to have something solid to push back with. "They overwhelmed us and would have slaughtered us if you hadn't shown up and holy-blasted..." I trailed off, seeing my teammate with fresh eyes.

"What?" he asked.

Malachi had freaked out when I suggested we skip to here before recovering all of our teammates. *The Upholders must face the forces of the demon apocalypse together,* he'd insisted. He was also the one who had rescued Seay from the collapsing time catch and then steered us unerringly through a failing downtown Manhattan. And he seemed to have deduced an awful lot about Malphas's plans.

I noticed something else too.

"You're not repeating yourself anymore."

His mess of hair spilled to one side as he cocked his head. "Huh?"

"Ever since we found you, you've been skipping like a record. But start pontificating on Malphas's *brilliant* deceit, and presto—you smooth out. Not only that, you actually sound lucid."

Though the lion's share of ley energy was being redirected at the St. Martin's site, an energetic field had taken hold around it, one I could draw from and draw powerfully. I summoned a form-fitting shield and activated the sword's banishment rune until the entire blade sang with resonant white light.

I was also remembering how the 1660 version of Arnaud claimed to have had several encounters with a demon in the small settlement of New Amsterdam, but Seay reported none. Just a few run-ins with a crazy man, who had turned out to be Malachi.

His burned skin glistened as he continued to squint at me in apparent confusion.

"I don't think you *holy-blasted* anyone," I said, stepping back. "Not the soulless mobs, not the fae demons. The light you manifested was a cover to conceal the fact you were absorbing their infernal essences. And it got the rest of us to deepen our trust in you, to follow you without question."

I shifted to my wizard's senses. It *was* Malachi, but through what must have been untold tortures, the demon had fragmented my friend's mind and faith, giving himself gray regions to hide out in.

"The only *Divine Voice* you heard was Malphas's," I said. "You're his final demon."

By the time I refocused, a shrewd, almost gleeful look had come over my teammate's face.

"Admit it, Everson." He tore the Bible in half and flung the pieces aside. "We played your ass like a fiddle."

In his grip, a fiery sword and shield roared to life.

46

By the demon's smugness, I could tell he had wanted me to find out who Malachi really was. Just as he'd wanted me to understand how thoroughly his master, Malphas, had deceived me. Arnaud was right about demons. Incurable gloaters.

"Do you have a name?" I snarled.

"Yes, but you can call me Forneus."

Good, because thinking of the demon as Malachi sickened me. Distorted fragments of my old teammate remained—enough to have fooled me, to have fooled all of us—but the question now was whether he would survive a banishment. Or was this infernal parasite the only thing holding him together?

"Malachi," I shouted, "can you hear me?"

Forneus laughed. "You might as well be talking to a vegetable. He hasn't had an original thought in the equivalent of fifty years. I wouldn't count on him starting now."

But I didn't believe him. Malachi had leaked about the "Night Ruin," and from there we'd pieced together what the demon Malphas was building.

"You should also know the fae won't be riding to the rescue," Forneus said. "Now that they've served their purpose, we've sealed the time catch against them. It's just us and your poor friends. Malphas's *elements*."

"Vigore!" I shouted.

Force and divine light stormed from my extended sword. But Forneus brought his shield up. The collision of holy and infernal energies threw off a crackling fount of sparks.

I uttered another invocation, hardening the air around him. He cleaved it with a savage twist of his sword. Energy from the collapsing manifestation rushed back into me, stealing my breath. The field around St. Martin's was enabling me to cast at a high level, but Forneus was matching it somehow.

"You must be wondering how we got to Malachi."

I turned as he circled me, each of us looking for an opening.

"Let me guess," I said. "More of your master's sparkling brilliance?"

"We were lucky, actually. Following the mess with the time catches, Malachi came back to the city and wandered into Arnaud's fortress. Upon entering his sanctum, he found the demon circle."

The same circle we'd arrived in when Caroline hacked Arnaud's infernal line.

Perhaps seeing my recognition, Forneus said, "Yes, the residual energy in the circle was intended for you, but Malphas saw how he could use Malachi instead, to prepare the way for your arrival. He was a servant of the Church, yes. But once inside the demon circle, the sorry mortal had no chance." In Forneus's eyes, I saw him reliving the evils he had visited on Malachi. My teammate's burns, which had conveniently destroyed his bonding sigil, hadn't come from any tenement fire. That whole story had been a fiction, fed to the tavern keeper, then fed to us. The flames had been infernal.

"Once we'd broken your friend," Forneus continued, "my master infused me into what remained. And together we embarked on a journey to map the time catches and locate your teammates."

Sounded like we were dealing with another shadow demon.

"And you couldn't bring my teammates here yourself?" I challenged.

I wanted to fluster him. Demons didn't like being called out for their weaknesses.

His eyes narrowed. "I could have, but why use force when persuasion is far more efficient? And with you on the way, well..." He gestured around with his flaming sword. "Here we all are."

Something about his answer rang false, but I didn't have time to dissect it. Because in the next instant, his face contorted in pain. His pants were growing out in the back, as if he were giving birth to a giant watermelon.

What in the...?

When his pants split open, a massive arachnid-like abdomen emerged and flopped to the street, still expanding. The legs that had once been Malachi's burst apart, replaced by four segmented spindles on each side. Pieces of bloodied fabric and flesh fell as the spindles separated and lengthened into spider's legs. They then pushed against the street, hoisting Malachi's still-human torso into the air. I craned my neck back as I stepped away.

Forneus looked like a grafting experiment gone horribly wrong, but I was seeing something closer to his true demonic form.

"Now that you've delivered my master his elements," Forneus said, "all that's left for you to do is die."

He covered the distance between us in a fast skitter. Holding my ground, I pushed energy into my shield. His blade came off it in a plume of fire. But before I could get my sword into his abdomen and shout the banishment Word, Forneus continued past. We were talking a mid-level demon, tops. And with the amount of raw energy thrumming around my casting prism, it wouldn't take much to expunge him.

Then I can begin to heal what's left of Malachi and search for the others.

I just needed a damned opening. I considered launching my sword, but I'd used that move on another of Malphas's demons, the one overseeing the half-fae. And Forneus's flaming shield appeared poised to block whatever came at him.

He chuckled now as he circled me. "You should have seen your stupid face when the Upholders were reunited. So confident, so full of yourself." His swollen abdomen shook above the ground. "That was one of the greatest joys of my demonic life. You doing just as master intended and having no earthly idea."

I grunted into my next sword swing. He raised his shield, but not before an edge of holy light glanced off his shoulder. White flames erupted along his sword arm, and he skittered back with a scream.

"Where does that rank on your joy meter?" I asked.

His lips curled, and he yanked his abdomen back. It wasn't until I was tugged from my feet that I realized that all the time he'd been circling me, he'd also been wrapping my body with infernal strands of energy. My body rotated now as his many legs went to work, turning me over in an attempt to cocoon me.

"Respingere!" I shouted.

The force that detonated from my shield ripped the strands apart and slammed me to the ground. Forneus went airborne and landed on his side several yards away. His spider legs righted him quickly.

Seeing me down—and dazed—he rushed me, sword roaring with infernal fire. I gained my feet and parried his blow. I couldn't see Forneus's face, but I could feel his fury in the contact of our blades. Sparks from the collision fizzled over my shielded body.

When he backed away, so did I, moving to the left to keep him out in front of me. I wasn't going to let him circle me again. And with every backward step, I could feel the growing power of the St. Martin's site behind me. Power I could use.

With my next step, I left the dirt lane of Broadway and crunched onto uneven ground. When he'd first appeared, Forneus-as-Malachi had shied from the power of the St. Martin's site, and he was hesitating now.

Just need to lure him in.

Alternately thrusting staff and sword, I released a series of invocations in succession.

The first one bound Forneus's left set of legs in hardened air. He staggered and swung his sword down to break up the manifestation. But a force blast was already slamming into his shield. With his legs still constricted, the violent collision of opposing energies knocked him onto his back.

He leapt up quickly, unfettered legs spreading apart again, but now walls of hardened air were arriving from both sides. Grimacing with effort, he got his shield against one and his sword through the other. But the shock of the dispersing manifestations shook him, setting him up for the *coup de grace*.

"*Vigore!*" I shouted, and opened my sword hand.

White flames rippled as the blade shot toward him.

And then past him.

Forneus laughed. "What a pity."

I stumbled backwards into the roar of ley energy and fell, landing hard on one of St. Martin's foundation slabs. Seeing his opportunity, Forneus skittered forward and leapt. His ponderous spider abdomen landed on my shielded legs, pinning me. Beyond him, my blade clanged against a copper panel. As he raised his fiery sword, I threw a hand toward his abdomen and shouted the Word for retrieve.

Forneus hesitated and turned.

My returning sword skewered his gut, the end of the blade punching out his low back. Bullseye. With a shriek, he twisted back toward me. My sword handle protruded from his navel, a thick black liquid oozing around it.

Seizing the handle, I shouted, *"Disfare!"*

Banishment energy flashed from the blade's topmost rune, but something was pushing back. With the volume of ley energy storming around me, I'd only opened my casting prism a crack. I braced myself now as I willed it wider. The light of banishment swelled from the blade, engulfing the demon to his fraught eyes.

Forneus held his form, though.

He shouldn't be this strong, dammit.

Malphas, I thought suddenly. *He's forcing energy through the demonic line, matching me.*

I searched until I found the opening in Forneus where infernal energy was pouring in. It might have been helping his demon, but it made Malphas vulnerable. By forcing enough banishment energy back through the opening, I could cripple the demon master, if not destroy him. Then I could recover my friends, dismantle the site, and return home.

The thought of Vega's embrace filled me with renewed conviction.

With a prayer to Saint Michael, I adjusted my grip on my sword handle and threw my prism wide.

Only once before had I attempted to channel a raw fount of ley energy. I'd been facing the demon lord Sathanas. I was green then, my abilities limited. If it hadn't been for divine help in the form of Father Vick, I would have failed. My casting capacity had since grown, and I was facing a demon master, not a demon lord.

But it was just me this time.

The deluge of raw energy drowned out all else. Amid the thrashing and smashing, I struggled to maintain my casting prism, to funnel power through the blade's banishment rune and down the demon line, but the prism was already starting to shake apart. The effort to hold it together was agony.

At the other end of the connection, I felt Malphas recoil.

Confidence surged through me, and with it strength. *That's right, you son of a bitch.*

Malphas recovered, pushing back with his considerable infernal might. Though every cell in my body was screaming for me to close my mental prism, to shut it down and let go, I refused, even as the pain became excruciating.

This was for my teammates. For Vega and Tony. For our daughter.

Forneus's hands seized the sides of my head, his murderous eyes inches from mine.

I drew a giant breath and boomed, *"Disfare!"*

Forneus withdrew and came apart. The banishment invocation continued down the demonic line, bowling through Malphas's resistance. At the other end, something massive screamed, and an implosion, deep and violent, followed. The time catch shuddered for several seconds before falling still.

I sat up in the center of the St. Martin's site, still clutching my sword.

"Malachi?" I called weakly. But whatever had remained of my friend was gone.

Swallowing a thick knot of grief, I stood on shaky legs. That had taken everything I had, but I'd felt the result. The demon Malphas was either destroyed or I'd dealt him a critical enough blow that he was being torn from his perch and cast down the ranks. Either way, he was no longer our problem.

I peered around 1776 New York, the setting lonely and

unpeopled under a full moon. My bonding sigil continued to glow faintly, telling me my teammates were near. I may have delivered them to Malphas unwittingly, but I'd denied the demon the chance to use them as containers for his infernal portal.

"So suck it," I muttered at his memory.

But now I remembered something. When I'd asked Forneus why he hadn't brought my teammates to this site himself, he'd claimed my persuasion would be more efficient than his force. I understood now why that had bothered me. All of the elements Malphas had needed were already there for the taking: Gorgantha for Water, Seay for Air, Jordan for Earth, Malachi for Spirit, and Forneus as a medium for Fire.

He hadn't needed me.

I hesitated. *Unless he did.*

I thought about my prayer to Saint Michael and the power I'd just channeled. What if *I* was meant to be the container for Spirit? What if the demon master's manipulation hadn't ended with us arriving here. What if, once more, I'd given Malphas exactly what he wanted? He was a demon master after all.

And what had he mockingly called me in my vision? The *great savior*?

As the horrifying questions corkscrewed through me, something red strobed against my face. I jerked back with a grunt and peered around, but I couldn't see where it was coming from. As the strobing continued, something bumped the side of my head.

Open your eyes, a child's voice whispered.

Open my eyes?

47

Open your eyes, the voice repeated.

Already, the St. Martin's site was beginning to blur and come apart, but not in the way of a time catch collapsing. More like in the way of a dream dissolving. I put my will now into coming out of it.

The result was like awakening to a nightmare.

I was on my back, staring up at a rotating black sky. Harsh energies burned through the atmosphere, the stench of ozone so thick I could barely breathe. I'd been here before, in two separate visions.

This time, though, it was real.

This was the true 1776 St. Martin's site, not the mirage Caroline, Bree-yark, and I had seen from the other side of the boundary upon first arriving, and not the hallucination I'd just left. Forneus's hybrid form lay off to one side, his spider's legs drawn in, infernal smoke drifting from his body. Others lay around me, oblong forms in the dark.

I tried to sit up, but I was bound. Something flashed several times and nudged my head again. I looked over to find an antique lantern peering up at me.

Dropsy?

She hopped back a step and expanded her light, revealing a raised platform, round and built from stone. Her light passed over the other figures: Seay, Arnaud, then Jordan. I had to crane my neck back to see Gorgantha, who was behind me, the four of them forming a cross-like pattern around me. Fluid-filled cocoons encased us to our necks. Cocoons made from sticky strands of infernal energy.

Containers, I understood. *Spun by Forneus.*

Thick cords joined us and ran to levels below I couldn't see.

I shouted my teammates' names until my vocal cords went raw, but I could barely hear myself above the roar of ley energy and the sizzling and crackling overhead. *If can shout, I can cast.* Inside my cocoon, my hands were gripping my sword. I could even see the faint glow of the banishment rune.

"Vigore!"

Raw energy poured through my casting prism, but instead of blowing my container open, the power from my blade shot along the cord to Arnaud. Infernal power pushed back. At the same time, I felt currents of elemental energy running from Jordan's, Seay's, and Gorgantha's containers toward us.

I pulled back in horror, understanding now what Malphas had created.

We were the five elements of the Aristotelean Set, alright. Only this living alchemical symbol hadn't been designed to create balance, but opposition. Between light and dark, Heaven and Hell, Spirit and Infernal Fire.

Through my blood line, I was connected to Michael, a First Saint. Arnaud was bound to Malphas, a demon master. The other three—Jordan, Seay, and Gorgantha—were acting as earthbound grounding elements, their containers bolstered by the druids and half-fae, who must have been on a lower level, as well as the claimed souls of the merfolk. Their job was to hold the Aristotelean Set together while I channeled high-octane Spirit energy and Malphas pushed back through his line to Arnaud with Infernal Fire.

That opposition, pushed to its limits, had created the implosion I felt. The energy of the implosion had overwhelmed Forneus, whose toxins had induced my hallucination, and who had likely been speaking right above me the whole time, goading me into attacking, but it hadn't touched Malphas.

It had freed him.

Above, a deep tear sounded.

From the center of the rotating sky, winged figures began to appear. Shriekers, by their piercing cries. The first of Malphas's arriving legion. I strained against my confinement, but I couldn't move.

The visions *had* been telling me something, dammit. In the one behind the Met, Malphas had pierced my forehead with a talon, rendering me powerless. I assumed he'd smashed my casting prism—but he'd thrown it wide. An aim he just achieved by getting me to believe I could destroy him through Forneus.

I turned to Dropsy and shouted, "Can you get me out?"

I didn't know what the enchanted lantern could do, but she'd surprised me before. She hopped around my confined body as though assessing the situation. High above, the ripping continued. More shriekers and winged devils circled like arriving carrion birds. And now I could see a pinpoint of sulfurous yellow light.

Shit. The opening of the portal.

Dropsy turned suddenly, her light illuminating the demon Forneus. His spider legs had twitched under his torso, and he was pushing himself upright.

Okay, this isn't good either.

Dropsy drew back in a contraction of light. Forneus lurched for a few steps, then fell, catching himself against my cocoon, his head poised above me. I recoiled, but the eyes that peered into mine weren't demonic. They were watery gray and benevolent.

"Malachi?" I said.

He gave a pained smile. Using the razor-sharp edges of his front legs, he began sawing the length of the cocoon. When he reached my midsection, I pushed with my hands, creating an opening large enough to wriggle from. Thick liquid dripped from my body as I gained my feet and retrieved my sword and staff from the goo.

"You all right, all right, are, are, are?" Malachi shouted above the hellish racket.

I turned to find four of his legs braced against the cocoon for balance, while his hands steadied me. Forneus had been blown from his demonic form, but some patchwork of what had been Malachi remained.

"Yes." I gripped his forearm. "Thank you."

With a network of cords running between everything, the Night Ruin looked like a cross between a spider's web and a mad alchemist's lab. The druids and half-fae were arrayed on lower levels, along with a multitude of pods holding sickly colored liquids. Mediums for Malphas's claimed souls, most likely.

Ley energy gushed up from the foundation, supplemented by the reclaimed energy beaming in from the four locations I'd seen in the hallucination. Supercharged by all that raw energy, the elements of the Aristotelean Set had performed their parts well. Too well. Ultimately, the opposition of Spirit and Infernal Fire had collapsed the space that separated Malphas from the time catch.

Which put him a stone's throw from the present.

Above, the portal continued to open. A pair of eyes peered in now, enormous and demonic.

"He's coming through!" I shouted to Malachi.

"Balance!" he yelled back. "Sustained, through, through, the portal is, is, is, balance!"

He fell to the platform, pulling me down into a kneeling position beside him. His hands were cold, and his eyes had gone glassy.

"Hold on," I pled. "We'll help you."

Dropsy, who had been peering out from behind my cocoon, hopped forward. Malachi's gaze drifted toward her light. He tried to smile as he mouthed, *Balance.*

As the glow fell from his eyes, I slipped my hands from his dead grip and peered skyward. Malphas's appearance was kraken-like—enormous and incomprehensible. Harsh bursts of energy highlighted the contours of a craggy face as more of him pushed through. The rupture created by his violent passage wouldn't end with him. Many, many more would enter. A demon apocalypse would ensue.

My instinct was to thrust my sword skyward and unleash the full force of the banishment rune. But that was what had created the portal in the first place. When deep laughter rumbled like thunder, I heard Malphas's voice from my vision:

This was inevitable, Croft. You were inevitable. The great savior.

I had acted predictably, according to my nature. Just as he'd known I would. Anything I cast in the name of Spirit would be met with a counterforce of Infernal Fire. A force Malphas commanded.

The portal is sustained through balance, Malachi had been trying to tell me.

What if I were to cast a force that went against my nature? I thought suddenly. That upset that balance? I eyed the runes of my blade, then dropped my gaze to Arnaud.

When my magic nodded, I swore.

That was going to mean accepting his demonic deal, shredding my promise to Vega. I imagined her face when I told her I had not only released Arnaud, but sworn to never seek retribution against him again. That he would be free to roam the world with only a vague promise to stay away from us.

I'll lose her.

The time catch was shuddering now with Malphas's arrival, the shrieks of his legion growing stronger and more soul thirsty. I looked around at my other teammates, then back at the demon-vampire Arnaud.

My magic nodded again.

"Shit," I spat, and struggled toward him through the hot, swirling winds.

Dropsy followed. When she peered over the edge of the platform, her light picked up a squat body on Broadway. It belonged to Bree-yark. He was lying face down in a haze of infernal smoke, his goblin blade beyond his outstretched hand. Ever the bulldog, he'd tried to fight Forneus when they'd arrived.

You better fucking be all right, buddy.

The open pouch beside him told of Dropsy's journey all the way up here. I didn't know how she'd managed it, but I was glad she did. She backed from the edge now in a mournful hunker.

"We'll check on him in a sec," I told her.

Arriving at Arnaud's cocoon, I began cutting it open from the neck down. As I pried the shell from his throat, I saw that the manacle had been removed, probably by Forneus. The same was true of his wrist shackles.

"Wake up!" I yelled, slapping him.

Arnaud's head rocked, but he didn't stir. I dragged him from the thick suspension and onto the platform. Thinking of Vega and our daughter and everything I stood to lose, I paused before opening my mouth again.

"I accept," I whispered.

The energy of the demonic agreement reacted, seizing me hard enough to shock the breath from my lungs. Arnaud's eyes opened and he sat bolt upright. He peered around, seeming to comprehend everything at a glance. Overhead, Malphas's form was growing, along with his demon horde. A look of fear and loathing gripped Arnaud's face. Finally, his eyes locked on mine.

"You've accepted the agreement," he said, an angle of surprise in his voice.

I nodded, but my heart was pounding sickly. "If you're serious about stopping him, I need your help."

Arnaud peered skyward again, then felt around his naked neck. Though his body was brimming with infernal energy, much of it courtesy of Malphas, there was nothing now to hide him from his master's wrath.

"What do I do?" he demanded.

I pulled him to the center of the platform, where the fount of ley energy was thickest, and aimed my sword upward.

"Grasp the handle!" I shouted. Arnaud's slippery grip came up under mine. "When I give the word, push your infernal energy through the blade. As much as demonically possible. Do you understand?"

He nodded, eyes glowing yellow.

With a Word, I activated the banishment rune. Powered by raw ley, the white light shot like a jet's contrail toward the portal. The winged demons shrieked and darted from it, but I felt infernal energy pushing back with equal force, reestablishing the balance of opposing energies, wrenching the portal still wider.

All right, here it goes...

I shifted power from the banishment rune to the one beneath it, fire.

"Now!" I called to Arnaud as a spire of flames roared up, consuming the light of banishment.

His face hardened with malice and effort. Dark tendrils of energy burst up the blade and joined the elemental fire. Arnaud and I labored to hold the shuddering sword, to keep our aim true. Arnaud then shrieked something that made it sound as though he were vomiting a lung. But it was Malphas's true name.

The spire of Infernal Fire steadied and collided into his former master's face. The entire portal shook. And then Malphas made his first mistake. Believing I'd upped my power, he responded with an even greater output of infernal energy. This time, the portal buckled. Panic seized Malphas's eyes.

Yes, yes, it's working!

I could feel Malphas trying to pull back, to correct the balance, but it was too late. The portal was contracting, collapsing around him. Beside me, Arnaud let out a savage cry of glee. When I looked over, he was giving his former master the finger.

"Hold on!" I shouted as the sword started to waver. "Keep pushing!"

Arnaud brought his free hand back to the hilt and willed more energy into the blade, further tipping the balance that had held the nascent portal open, upsetting it further and further toward the infernal.

Malphas's monstrous face contorted into impossible shapes. With a roar, he thrust a clawed hand down as if intending to seize and crush us. Even though he was far away, I instinctively ducked lower. His winged legion took up the cry and began circling down his arm, spiraling toward us.

Those guys can reach us.

"Push!' I shouted at Arnaud.

The word was barely out of my mouth when, in a deep, thunderous crack, Malphas broke apart. His winged legion dispersed in shrieks. Some dove back into the collapsing portal, joining their master in ruin. Others remained, flying aimlessly. But with the portal's demise, our time catch was failing.

When I recalled the power from my sword, the rune obeyed, the fire returning to its symbol. I pulled the sword from Arnaud's grip and waved it toward my bound teammates. "We've got to get them out!"

Fallen pieces of Malphas were impacting around us now. One burst to my left, sending me into a stagger. A shrieker swooped in. With a grunt, I swung my sword around. The blade tore through the creature's wing, sending it off with a shrill cry. I plunged my blade through the chest of another and blew it apart with a Word. The damned things were everywhere. I summoned a shield around the platform, but it was weak, and it wasn't going to be worth a damn when the time catch decided to break down.

I looked around for Arnaud—our ride home—but I could no longer see him.

I was shouting his name when my shield failed in an eruption of sparks. Energy roared in my ears while plummeting pieces of Malphas crashed around me. The time catch was entering its final throes.

I tried to shape another shield, to hold our world together a little longer. Stones rushed up from the collapsing platform, and I fell. Images of my teammates and Vega sped through my mind. But my final thought was of our little girl.

Safe now.

48

"It was foolish of me to carry that plate of gingersnaps inside," someone said, "because it told her I was, in fact, home. Just one of those things I didn't stop to consider. Like so many other things I do, I suppose."

A slightly hunched man wearing a silk robe that matched his dangling curtains of black hair came into focus.

"So there she was," he continued, "going door to door, window to window, shouting that she knew I was home. And I'm crouched behind the refrigerator like a spooked cat. You'd think after all these—"

"Claudius?" I interrupted.

He stopped pacing beside the full-sized bed I was tucked into and trained his tinted glasses on me. "Yes?"

"Where in the hell am I?"

My surroundings had the vanilla look of a guest bedroom.

"Oh, my place in Peoria. Or is it, ah—"

"Yes," I said, "but what am I doing here?"

"I thought I explained all of that to you." He blinked several times. "Didn't I?"

"Maybe, but I'm not sure I've been conscious."

"Hm, your eyes were open. Though that might have accounted for the vacant stare."

"What happened to the time catch? To everyone else?"

I shoved the covers off and sat on the edge of the bed. I was wearing wool socks and a black silk gown, one of Claudius's no doubt. Underneath, my body felt roughed up and hollowed out. But I could also feel warm currents of healing magic running through me. Powerful elder-level magic.

I hesitated. "The s-senior members?"

Claudius chuckled. "Yes, yes, they're out now. In fact, they're the ones who placed you in my care."

"How? The last thing I remember is the time catch collapsing."

"When you destroyed Malphas, a powerful trap he'd set around the Harkless Rift came apart. You were correct about him being responsible for their confinement. Freed, the senior members went straight to the time catch. They were able to preserve it long enough to extract you and the others. They would have waited for you to awaken, but there are points along the rupture site that needed shoring up." Claudius smiled broadly. "The Order is very much in your debt. You prevented a demon apocalypse."

"I had help," I said distractedly. "Where are the others?"

"They're..." He glanced away. "They're being cared for."

"But not all of them made it," I said faintly. "Did they?"

"Most will be fine. But no, some were beyond the Order's help."

I saw the light fading from Malachi's eyes and Bree-yark lying face down on Broadway and the entire platform disintegrating...

"I don't know the names of the fallen," Claudius said, "or I would tell you."

The room blurred, and I wiped my eyes. Claudius came over and patted my shoulder uncertainly.

"'Find Arnaud,'" I whispered.

"What's that?" He leaned nearer.

"When I asked Arianna how I could help her and the others, that's what she told me: 'Find Arnaud.' It was by his hand we were able to collapse the portal and destroy Malphas. And that's what freed the Order."

I knew I'd done the right thing, but I was still thinking of the cost. With Claudius's report that some hadn't made it, the one faint glimmer of a silver lining was that maybe Arnaud had been among them. But I could still feel the demonic energy of the agreement that bound us, cold and jeering.

"Well, Arianna's a sharp bird," Claudius said. "She knows what she's talking about. Oh, that reminds me!" He straightened suddenly. "She said there was something you needed to take care of when you awakened."

"She did?"

He pulled me by the arms until I was standing, then signed in the air behind me. By the time he turned me around, a portal was yawning open.

"Wait," I said, "what about my clothes?"

"They're still in the dryer. Oh, but here's your cane." He inserted it into my hand.

Before I could ask where I was going, he gave me a shove.

"Good luck!" he called.

49

F ollowing a series of somersaults through a cloudy vacuum, I landed in a familiar casting circle on a sheet of poly-ethylene in a large basement space. I was back in 1 Police Plaza, performing a half-split on the same spot we'd departed from.

Holy hell, I thought, wincing upright and straightening my gown.

The holding space was empty. The clock above the desk read 3:10 in the morning. So why had he sent me here?

"Welcome home."

Vega uncrossed her legs and stood from a chair in the corner of the room dressed in her detective blacks. A rumpled blanket over the armrest suggested she'd been dozing. The sight of her sent a dozen raw emotions pouring through me. The net effect was an all-consuming numbness, and I drifted toward her like a man in a dream.

She pressed her cheek aggressively to my chest, fists balling up the back of my gown. My arms swallowed her. This was the moment I'd kept returning to over the course of the journey—through 1776, 1861, 1660, the recent past—this idea that she would be at the end of it. We remained like that for a long time.

"How did it go?" she asked at last.

"Malphas is gone, and the Order's back. The demon apocalypse has been postponed indefinitely. So, about as well as it could have."

She breathed a quiet *thank God*.

"How long was I away?" I asked.

She checked her watch. "Almost six hours."

I snorted a laugh of disbelief and leaned down to kiss her.

"Is that Mr. Croft I hear?" someone called in a singsong voice.

I stopped and closed my eyes. It had come through the speaker to the cells.

"What's he doing here?" Vega asked in a dangerous whisper.

I'd been hoping to savor a few more moments with Ricki before having to tell her what I'd done. But this is what Arianna had meant when she'd said that I had something to take care of. She must have noticed the infernal bond between the demon-vampire and me, and she'd returned him to the freshly warded cell. Now I had to fulfill my end of the agreement if I didn't want to forfeit my soul.

I shut off the speaker and returned to Vega.

"Look, I have something to tell you." I rubbed her arms, then held them. "My magic was right. The key to recovering the Upholders, stopping Malphas, and freeing the Order was in the time catch. Well, time catches, plural." Her head tilted in question. "That's another story. The thing is, Arnaud's role turned out to be much bigger than just getting us there. He helped us to destroy Malphas."

"And that's why he's still alive," she said, her gaze cutting to the cell.

"I made a deal with him for that help."

"A demonic deal?"

I sighed and nodded. "In exchange, I can't destroy him. And

neither can the Order or anyone I hire. So basically, once I let him out of that cell, I can't touch him. It wasn't something I negotiated. He formed the agreement and left it out there. I never, in a million years, thought I'd take it."

"What did your magic say?"

Her voice was tired but neutral, like her eyes.

"It told me to listen to his words. I think my magic knew the opportunity would come for Arnaud to destroy Malphas."

That must have been why it hadn't issued a warning during the entire journey, despite that I'd largely been playing into Malphas's hands. It was just a matter of me listening when it told me to listen.

Vega sighed. "Then we have to trust it."

I was starting to tell her I didn't like it either, but I stopped.

"Call it a detective's intuition, but when you left here, I sensed that Arnaud remaining alive was a possibility. And while I've been waiting, I've had time to think. I gave you shit over your magic, but it's only because I don't always understand it. All right, it scares me. But it's a part of you, and I don't get to pick and choose which parts I love and which parts I don't. That's not how it works." Her mouth leaned into an almost-smile. "Plus, you always seem to pull through, so it's obviously doing something right."

"Yeah, but what about my promise?" I said dismally. "About destroying Arnaud?"

"I want him gone more than anything." Her thumb tapped a button on the stomach of her blouse. "But I can't imagine the kinds of choices you had to face in there. I'm not going to second-guess what you did."

I pulled her in close and pressed my lips to the crown of her head. "Before I do anything else, I'll talk with the Order," I said. "See what our options are for—"

I grunted and doubled over as a savage force twisted my guts.

"What is it?" Vega asked in alarm, kneeling beside me. "What's wrong?"

"It's the agreement," I managed. "Arnaud did his part, and now I have to do mine."

She helped me to my feet and drew my arm over her shoulder. "Then we'll do it together."

With Vega supporting me, we made our way to Arnaud's cell. When we arrived, I nodded and whispered that I could stand under my own power. Though the pain lingered, the brunt of the soul attack had passed.

She drew her service pistol, the magazine loaded with hybrid rounds. I unlocked the door and pulled it open. Beyond the oscillations of warding energy, Arnaud rose to his feet in his prison scrubs and neat robe.

"For a moment, I thought you were going to stand me up." He strolled forward, hands behind his back. "And after saving humanity together," he tutted. When he spied Vega behind me, he leaned over and smiled. "Hello, lovely."

"I just want one assurance," I said.

His eyes snapped back to mine. "Oh, I'm sorry, Mr. Croft. You accepted the agreement as is. There was no talk of amendments or assurances. And what did you say when I attempted to establish the terms for delivering you into the time catch? 'No one gives a shit'?" He opened a hand. "Well, then."

"That you'll really stay away from my family," I pressed on.

"My history as a vampire is one of persevering. And as a demon, I'll increasingly crave power. We had this conversation, Mr. Croft. I can't help what I am. And neither can you. As my ambitions grow, so will my enterprises. I'll do things that will offend who you are and what you stand for. You may not be able to challenge me directly, per the terms of the agreement, but you'll make every effort to frustrate my plans. That's a cart of bothers I won't tolerate." He leaned over to look at Vega again, this time making a point of fixing his demonic gaze on her stomach. "And family, I've found, make excellent pressure points. If you *could* promise to leave me to my work—work you deem reprehensible—then I might honor your request. But you can't, so I won't. Now, kindly release me."

Arnaud's smug voice and subtle threats needled my rage centers. I accessed the pulsating wards. Did I test the strength of the agreement and throw them wide? Reduce the demon-vampire to smoke before he knew what hit him? The gut-twisting pain seized me again, and I dropped to my knees.

"Stop it!" Vega shouted, placing a hand on my shoulder.

Arnaud laughed heartily. "Oh, I'm not doing a thing, Miss Vega. Your shillyshallier is doing this all to himself."

I could feel the pleasure he took in my pain, in Vega's fear. But beyond that, I could feel his raging hunger. Free of Malphas, immune from the Order, and with no demonic rivals on this plane, the world was truly his oyster. The minute he walked, he would start seeding his hellish empire in Manhattan. One that would exceed his reign as a vampire in misery and butchery many, many times over as he pursued the rank of demon lord.

Yellow flames flickered in his eyes as he grinned down at me. "Come now, Croft," he purred. "You're only delaying the *inevitable*."

Vega was right. An evil like his couldn't be allowed in our world.

When a third attack hit me, this one carrying a stench of putrescence and death, I realized something. The pain wasn't coming from the demonic agreement. Shuffling footsteps echoed down the corridor.

"Um, Everson?" Vega whispered when I'd caught my breath.

I followed her gaze to where a figure stood across the holding area, a long blade extending from one hand. Vega pivoted her service pistol, but I placed a hand on her forearm and brought it down.

"It's all right," I said, standing again.

Vega's nose wrinkled sharply. "What in the hell is it?"

I turned back to Arnaud. "Since visiting your cell yesterday morning, everything you've told me has been true. You didn't deceive me once. Though I suppose that was a play in itself— accumulate trust points so that when it really mattered, I'd be more prone to give you what you wanted."

Arnaud had been trying to see who Vega and I were talking about. Now his eyes slashed back to mine. "Free me," he said, insistence scoring the words. He might not have been able to see the presence, but he could feel it.

"I believe, from our talk in my library, that you were a decent person in life," I continued. "From the sounds of it, you were attacked and left for dead, probably for your cargo. And that's how a vampire found you, much how you would later find Maggie. I believe your claim that you resisted the bloodlust for as long as possible before it became all-consuming, and you accepted the creature you had become."

Arnaud winced as the footsteps shuffled across the holding space. I could see the figure in my peripheral vision, the swinging blade glinting under the fluorescence. Vega seized my arm, but I kept my gaze fixed on Arnaud.

"The same with your demonism," I said. "I don't question the power lust that grows inside you like an infernal blaze, the bloody ambitions it feeds. It's who you've become. It's your nature now. The thing is, I can't allow it. Not in our world."

"We have a *deal*," he seethed.

"We do," I agreed. "But she doesn't."

I stepped back as the revenant arrived. Arnaud's eyes shot wide, and he recoiled with his whole body. I couldn't blame him.

Blade looked even more gruesome than the night I'd discovered her slaughtered body in her apartment. Dried blood spattered her disheveled scythe of pink hair. A hoodie jacket hung around a tank top that was blood-brown and in tatters. Arnaud had driven the vampire hunter through multiple times with her own katana swords, then left her pinned to the wall. From a pale green face, Blade's vengeance-hardened eyes swung toward him.

"No, no," Arnaud babbled. "You can't hire anyone to come after me. It goes against the agreement."

"My contract with Blade ended with her murder," I replied. "This is between you two now."

In desperation, Arnaud flung himself at the doorway. The ward met him in a burst of force and flames and threw him to the floor. He kicked himself backwards, smoke scattering from his trembling body.

"Per our agreement," I said to him, "I release you."

As the oscillating wards disappeared, my pain vanished along with the energy of the demon bargain.

I gestured Blade toward the open doorway. "He's all yours."

She stepped inside with her enchanted sword. There was a brief scuffle followed by Arnaud's shrill scream and the crunch of metal spearing demon flesh. Mercifully, Blade closed the door behind her, muting what followed.

"Do you want to tell me what the hell is going on?" Vega asked in a shaky voice.

"At some point in her life, Blade underwent a ceremony with a powerful necromancer," I said, walking her a few paces from the cell. "Maybe as payment for a job, I don't know. But it ensured that were she ever murdered, she would return as a powerful spirit, a revenant, to avenge her death." That seemed like Blade. "The thing is, because of the dislocation sigil I'd placed on Arnaud, she couldn't find him."

"So she locked onto you."

"Exactly. She knew I'd been hunting him, so she calculated I could lead her to him. She came to my apartment yesterday morning, then tracked me to the Upper East Side. She also managed to find me in the time catch. Because her revenant powers were set on me, I reacted in the same way her intended target would have. It's awful, like exploratory bowel surgery but without the anesthesia."

Vega held up a hand. "I get the picture."

"But I was never in danger. Blade's objective was always Arnaud. Caroline used an enchantment to hide me, but when she had to leave, so did the enchantment's effect. Blade tracked me here."

"Damned good timing," Vega remarked.

The door to the cell swung out. For a moment, I was afraid Arnaud was going to step around the door, a victorious grin on his bloody lips. But it was Blade who came into view, wiping her sword on the leg of her cargo pants. Though she was still covered in dried blood, a healthy flush had replaced her green tone from earlier. As she looked at us, her eyes softened, becoming more human, more living.

"Paybacks are a bitch," she muttered.

"Blade," I stammered. "Are you ... all right?"

I felt like an idiot for asking, but I'd never talked to a revenant before.

"Am now," she said, sliding her sword into the sheath on her back. "Sorry for going psycho stalker on you."

"No worries," I said. "I'm just sorry for what happened to you and the others."

She waved a hand dismissively. "Don't be. We knew the risks when we got into the business. It's why I took out this little insurance policy." She gestured down her vengeful spirit body and winked.

Vega whispered to me, "What happens now?"

Assuming she really has destroyed Arnaud, she passes on, I thought. The fact she was still here made me nervous. Maybe she had only cast him back to the Below, where he could reform and return someday.

"I'll be damned," Blade said.

A rosy light warmed her tilted-back face as though she were watching the sun come up over the Sierra Nevada. The light grew and brightened, suffusing her form until it was simply too beautiful to watch. Vega and I turned away.

"So long, party crasher," she called as the light receded again.

A parting jab at the night I'd met her, when I was under the influence of Thelonious.

"She's gone," Vega said.

I turned back, blinking, to find the holding area empty. I walked over to the cell and peered inside. A faint thread of Arnaud's vapor lingered where Blade had slain him, its residual malice dwindling and breaking apart.

"So is Arnaud Thorne," I said, exhaling heavily. "For good."

With a weary smile, I walked back toward Vega. I was intending to hold her again, to revel in the end of a chapter in our lives. But as I arrived in front of her, I knew I was ready to start the next one.

"I admit, this isn't how I pictured the moment. In the wake of a grudge match between a revenant and a demon-vampire, and me wearing a silk gown, but..." I dropped to one knee and beamed up at her. "Ricki Serrano Vega, would you do me the incredible honor of becoming my wife?"

Somewhere, I imagined Mae nodding her approval.

6 months later

On the first Saturday in May, we were married in St. Martin's Cathedral in downtown Manhattan.

Ricki wore an elegant ivory satin gown with thin straps and a v-neckline. I chose a conservative wool suit, Irish brown. We made a nice portrait. Much of the ceremony seemed to speed past, but exchanging vows with her under the stained-glass image of St. Michael was one of the most profound moments of my life. And our kiss following the pronouncement of holy matrimony one of the happiest.

It was made sweeter by the applause of our friends and family who had come, and a touch more sentimental by the absence of those who couldn't.

We reserved a nice courtyard in Brooklyn for the reception, which was catered by one of Ricki's cousins. All of her family attended, and as a perfect spring day deepened into blue evening, and hanging lanterns glowed over Mediterranean cypresses, nieces and nephews scattered into a rowdy game of chase.

Tony, our ring bearer, turned to his mother. "Can I?"

"Go ahead," Vega said. "Just take it into the yard over there."

He looked at me with expectant eyes.

"What your mother said."

"Thanks, Dad!"

As he jumped up from the head table, I took Vega's hand. Her far hand rested over her very pregnant stomach.

"Pretty kicking wedding, huh?" I said.

She smirked. "We'll have to do it again sometime."

The rest of our long table was taken up by members of the wedding party. Tony's sitter, Camilla, had acted as maid of honor, while Ricki's oldest brother, Diego, had walked her down the aisle in her late father's stead. Now, two of her other brothers, Alejandro and Gabe, were laughing about something with their wives, while the youngest of them, Carlos, picked sternly at his plate of flan at the table's end.

Carlos had been dead set against the wedding and let the family know. Deciding she'd had enough of his shit, Ricki threw down an ultimatum: either shut up and come to the wedding or stay out of our lives for good. He'd come.

"Ugh," Tabitha grunted. "Is it *over* yet?"

I'd leashed her to the chair beside me, where she lay slumped on her side affecting a miserable face. Consuming her weight in roasted pork probably had a little to do with it. The rest was just Tabitha.

I grinned. "Still having fun?"

"Wake me up when it's time to go," she moaned.

"The dancing starts in twenty and *could* go all night," I teased.

Muttering several choice words, she flopped to her other side. I'd placed my father's sword and mother's emo ball on the table between us. It may have been my imagination, but the blade seemed to hum with new energy, while the emo ball glowed a little more brightly.

"We did good, Croft," Vega said.

I looked from her to the small sea of tables, where our guests were chatting over dessert and coffee. We'd accumulated our share of friends and associates over the years. When I thought of the time catch version of me from the recent past and how lonely he'd seemed, I lifted Vega's hand and kissed it firmly.

"Yes, we did," I agreed.

The NYPD took up two tables. Vega's partner, Detective Hoffman, had given us his best at the beginning of the reception. He remarked that we'd chosen well. Though said grudgingly, he sounded like he actually meant it.

Behind them was a table of my fellow professors and their significant others. With the Order back in action and the demon threat stalled, I'd resumed full teaching duties in the spring and freshened up old contacts at the college. I'd even sent an invite to Professor Snodgrass. He would have trashed it, no doubt, but his wife, Miriam, was a fan of mine and the first guest to RSVP.

She was presently holding court at their table. When Snodgrass reached for a carafe of water, she slapped his hand, telling him he was going to spill it, then snapped her fingers for one of the servers. Snodgrass gave me a disconsolate look that said he hoped I'd have better luck with my partner.

One table over sat Caroline and her husband, as well as several members of their fae court. Angelus, who had received emergency healing, looked as handsome and formidable as ever. He was even sporting a freshly grown hand.

Caroline had attempted to send Osgood back to us that day, but the 1776 time catch was locked. In the weeks following my return, gifts had arrived from Faerie, much of it foods that couldn't be found in our world. The lion's share ended up in Tabitha's belly, of course. And when the gifts tapered off, she fell into a mild depression from which she was still recovering. Caroline had included a personal letter in the first package, thanking me for my trust in her and for helping to restore her husband and their marriage.

She smiled warmly at me now across the courtyard, her sentiments of friendship no longer being blocked.

The fae butler had come too. Sporting a silver tuxedo, Osgood was drawing a healthy amount of attention from the fifty-and-older female crowd. Above their table I could just make out the circling contrails of Pip and Twerk. The demon twins had recalled them that day, it turned out, not destroyed them, and I'd told the pixies they were invited as long as they remained out of sight and didn't prank the guests.

Carlos was fair game, though.

"Great wedding," a barking voice said.

I turned to find Bree-yark limping up on a cane, Mae beside him. They had been seated on my side of the head table, but they'd gathered up Dropsy the lantern as well as the pet carrier holding Buster.

"Not thinking of bailing on me, are you?" I said to Bree-yark. "Best man?"

Though I winked, he gave an embarrassed chuckle. "Aw, we'd love to stay, but..."

"*But,*" Mae took up, "this old lady is pushing her bedtime, and Bree-yark is being a gentleman and making sure I get home safe." Their courtship was still going slow and strong, and they seemed happier than ever.

"I'm so glad you two could come," I said, standing. "Truly." When Buster chirped and wriggled his tendrils through the mesh door and Dropsy set off a pair of flashes, I chuckled. "You guys, too."

"It was beautiful," Mae whispered as I hugged her over the

table. "And I'm not ashamed to tell you I cried like a proud momma."

"Thanks for all your advice."

"Anytime, sweetie."

As she turned to gush over how amazing Vega looked one last time, I regarded Bree-yark. He'd been in bad shape when the Order recovered him from the time catch. Heavily scored by infernal fire, his chances of survival were doubtful. But true to his warrior spirit, he clawed his way back from the brink. And now here he was, having my back once again, and on my most important day.

"Thanks for everything," I said, the words barely making it around the knot in my throat.

"Aw, c'mon. I keep tellin' you I'm fine." He held up his cane. "Another few weeks, and I can ditch this thing."

I pulled him into a hug. "Anything you need, man, just let me know."

"Same for you, Everson. Anytime."

They left, passing a mostly empty table I'd reserved for the Order. Following Malphas's expulsion, the senior members had repaired a chain of ruptures before returning to finish work in the Harkless Rift. Though the major tears were sealed, it was the constellations of minor ones that were taking forever to find and fix. Knowing the importance of the work, I noted their absence with silent thanks.

Claudius was the only high-level member who could come. He'd brought a date, an older woman with a coif of frosted pink hair. The gingersnap lady. He smiled like a baby now as she spoon-fed him her coconut pudding.

Across from them sat a young man wearing a cowboy hat and a smart linen vest. James Wesson was the magic-user who had covered the city's outer burroughs before the Order sent him to western Colorado. I'd gone out there when he was still getting his feet wet, and we'd had a few adventures. He looked from Claudius and his date to me with a *wtf?* expression. I laughed and shrugged.

James had also attended the Order's ceremony that winter, which commended my efforts in repelling the demon Malphas and freeing them. Arianna hung a charmed medallion around my neck. Having insisted the honor be shared, I returned home with additional medallions for Bree-yark and the Upholders.

I turned my attention to the latter's table now. Glamoured as a tall, striking woman, Gorgantha had come down from the Maine coast, where she'd returned with her fellow mers to rebuild their pod. She was giving Jordan and Delphine her skeptical face, then said something that made them all laugh.

The druids had survived the collapse, save one I hadn't known. They journeyed back to their sacred woodland and tree in Harriman State Park. I'd gone up to visit once they'd gotten settled, and Jordan had delivered on the promised ale. It turned out he was a really cool guy when not stressed out of his head.

Beside them was an empty setting with a medallion and a Latin Bible to honor our fallen friend Malachi. The one who had foreseen the demon apocalypse in his visions. The one who had founded the Upholders. He succumbed to Malphas, but not before assembling those who would ensure the demon master's final ruin.

Divine Voice, indeed, I thought.

But with devastating loss had also come surprising life. Everyone at the table now turned toward Seay, who was coming back from the restroom cradling a freshly changed baby boy.

Seay never mentioned the potion, and I never brought it up. Maybe she already knew I'd lied about what it could do. But against all odds, little Tyler had survived the transition, and that likely forgave everything. Seay had already sworn Vega and me to regular playdates when our daughter was old enough. She didn't want to get stuck with the "yoga pants mafia," as she called the mortal mothers her age.

Tyler gurgled now as the others shook his little grasping hands and wiggling feet. I was smiling at them when I glimpsed a large figure lurking behind one of the plants in back.

"Mind if I step away for a sec?" I asked Vega with a sigh. "There's someone here I want to talk to, and I may not get another chance."

"Only if you leave some collateral to prove you're not running."

I kissed her. "I expect that back with interest."

"Be careful what you wish for on your wedding night."

"Ooh, wanna take Tabitha's lead and ditch this joint?"

"I'll tell you when you get back."

With a laugh, I got up and circled the venue until I was standing on the other side of the plant. When I cleared my throat, the figure jumped.

"They left," I said.

"Who?"

"Bree-yark and his girlfriend. The ones you were hoping to spy on."

My teacher, Gretchen, stepped from behind her cover. She was wearing a plain green housedress, probably chosen for its camouflaging properties, and a hat with a white plastic flower. She scanned the guests.

"Well?" she asked.

"Well, what?"

"Is she better looking than me?"

"She makes him happy. That's all that matters."

"So you're saying she's a cow."

"I'm saying you need to get over it."

Gretchen responded with a disconsolate grunt.

"Where have you been, anyway?" I asked. I hadn't seen her

since our showdown in her kitchen. I sent her a wedding invitation, never expecting her to show, but I'd underestimated the pull of jealousy.

"Around," she said in a moping voice.

"Well, I'm glad you're here. I never got a chance to thank you."

"For what?" she snapped.

"For the massive assist. Yeah, don't give me that face. You may not have known what you were doing, but coming from your magic, you knew it would help. The morning you transported me to the Met, you gave me a companion in Bree-yark, an enchanted item in Dropsy, and a major clue to Malphas's plans —the Met was where I first learned about the Aristotelian Set. I wouldn't have succeeded without them."

"I don't know what you're talking about."

"Sure, you don't. How about joining us for some dessert?"

"Good gods, no. Crowds and I do *not* get along." She burped loudly and drew an arm across her mouth.

"I would never have guessed," I said.

"I hope you're not planning a long honeymoon."

"A couple of weeks on the Spanish coast. Why?"

"Because we have training to get back to, and you've missed too much already."

It wasn't worth pointing out that I'd only missed because she'd up and disappeared.

"Just tell me when," I said. "I'm anxious to jump back in."

"That makes one of us."

Oddly, I took the casual insult to mean I was forgiven.

"Well, I have things to do," she said abruptly, and disappeared.

I turned from the empty space beside the plant and looked over the courtyard. My gaze lingered once more on all of our friends, colleagues, and teammates, some mortal, many magical, before returning to my wife. She was standing now and waving at me. It took me a moment to realize the music had started.

I hurried through the crowd, absorbing their cheerful congratulations and shoulder claps, and met Vega in time for our first dance.

"I'm back," I said.

THE END

But the Prof Croft series continues. Keep reading to learn more...

SHADOW DUEL

PROF CROFT BOOK 9

Beware the shadow of many faces, but fear the master of many places...

It's Monday morning, and I've recovered a strange glyph-covered chest from a landfill. By Monday afternoon, someone's stolen it from my warded loft.

Before I can suss out who, why, and most importantly, how, I'm neck-deep with the NYPD on a murder case. A bigshot CEO is dead in his penthouse, his kidneys harvested in a way that screams black magic. Only there's no magic in evidence.

The two crimes connect somehow, and the key may be an old explorers club in the heart of Manhattan. But this mage needs to get moving. More victims are turning up sans organs, and twice now I've found myself in a shadow realm—a darker, more dangerous version of the city, where a mysterious entity wants me dead.

And here I thought the summer's biggest chore would be persuading my talking cat to play nice with my wife.

Spoiler alert: she's still Tabitha.

AVAILABLE NOW!

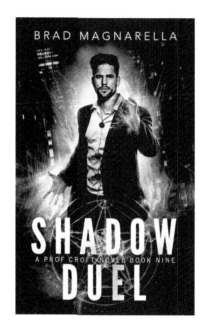

Shadow Duel
(Prof Croft, Book 9)

AUTHOR'S NOTES

At some point while writing *Night Rune*, I stopped and cried out, *"What in the actual hell?"*

I was trying to fit Everson's story into a four-act structure, which is more or less how I plot all my books, but it wasn't working. At all. Appropriately enough, it took a long walk on New Year's Day for me to realize I was writing a hero's journey. And that meant a different ball of yarn.

The hero's journey begins with a call to adventure, which the hero initially refuses. Interestingly, the call in *Night Rune* is initiated by Arnaud. He tells Everson that he and only he can get him into the time catch. Everson tells him no frigging way.

By refusing the call, and searching out alternatives, Everson picks up some key allies and supernatural aid. Caroline, Bree-yark, and Dropsy the lantern not the least of them. Only after a perilous trip through the Fae Wilds, and compelled by circumstances, does Everson accept the call, but he's better prepared.

We also see the beginning of a central conflict: Vega wanting Arnaud dead versus Everson needing to keep him alive.

So having accepted the call, Everson enters the time catch with Arnaud and his new allies. If you noticed, his goal—the St.

Martin's site—at first appears very close. But it's an illusion, thanks to the time-catch mashup. And arriving there is going to require Everson undertaking a lengthy journey full of trials and adventures.

Everson's immediate objective is to recover the Upholders, but the threat of Malphas and the apocalypse looms ever larger. There's also the question of whether Everson will be able to listen to his magic when the time comes. Especially if it tells him to do something really messed up. Such as jeopardizing his future with Ricki.

By the time Everson arrives at the St. Martin's site, all the elements are in place for Malphas's grand scheme, but also for Everson's final victory.

If he can only listen...

In that critical moment when he tells Arnaud, "I accept," Everson is not only agreeing to the demonic deal, but to what his magic is counseling. Acceding to Arnaud would seem to go against his good-guy nature, but he's made the mental transition to magic-user. He's accepted that in order to attain the highest levels, he must listen to his magic, no matter what it tells him.

But it took a journey, the hero's journey I didn't realize I was writing, for Everson to face that final trial and pass. A trial he would have been unprepared for had the St. Martin's site been as close as it first appeared.

Though Everson completed *his* journey, it felt important that Ricki do the same.

When Everson leaves for the time catch, she says, "I trust you." The test of that trust, though, is when she learns about his deal with Arnaud. What will she do? After accepting she can't separate the man from the magic, she helps him to the cell so he can fulfill his end of the deal by performing the one act she's been most set against—releasing Arnaud.

If that's not marriage material, I don't know what is.

I'm guessing some of you did the champagne shake and spray over Arnaud's sublimating body at the end. Though I enjoyed writing his character, I was just as ready for him to exit stage right. I'm glad we got a glimpse of his origins, because I always wondered who he'd been in mortal life. A merchant in the Dark Ages makes sense. And a decent person, no less.

But aiding Everson for his own benefit was the closest Arnaud was ever going to come to redemption as a demon-vampire, and so ends his story.

As for the manner of his demise, I actually hinted at Blade's return in the last book. Some of you may have caught it. During Everson's lengthy dream vision, the just-murdered Blade tells him, "I'm coming to help." Not understanding what she means, Everson tells her to stay put. Luckily for our gallant hero, she ignores him.

Some of my advanced readers have asked whether this is the end of the Prof Croft series.

It's the end of a chapter in the Croftverse for sure, one that spanned eight books and two prequels and saw Everson go from a lost and lonely truth-seeker to a leader and capable magic-user. But he's clearly on the cusp of another chapter, one that will have him balancing marriage and fatherhood with his wizarding duties.

I'd like to see what that looks like. I'm also curious to see how Tabitha adjusts, heheh.

As always, I have several people to thank for helping bring *Night Rune* into full realization.

A big thanks to the team at Damonza.com for designing another stellar cover. Kudos to my beta and advanced readers, including Beverly Collie, Mark Denman, Lin Ash, and Susie Johnson who provided valuable feedback during the writing process. And thanks to Sharlene Magnarella and Donna Rich for taking on the painstaking task of final proofing. Naturally, any errors that remain are this author's alone.

I also want to give a shout out to James Patrick Cronin, who brings all the books in the Croftverse to life through his gifted narration on the audio editions. Those books, including samples, can be found at Audible.com.

And none of this would be possible without the Strange Brigade, my dedicated fan group whose enthusiasm serves as motivation jet fuel, book after book.

Last but not least, thank you, fearless reader, for taking another ride with the Prof.

Till next time...

Best Wishes,
Brad Magnarella

P.S. Be sure to check out my website to learn more about the Croftverse, download a pair of free prequels, and find out what's coming! That's all at bradmagnarella.com

CROFTVERSE CATALOGUE

PROF CROFT PREQUELS

Book of Souls

Siren Call

MAIN SERIES

Demon Moon

Blood Deal

Purge City

Death Mage

Black Luck

Power Game

Druid Bond

Night Rune

Shadow Duel

Shadow Deep

Godly Wars

Angel Doom

SPIN-OFFS

Croft & Tabby

Croft & Wesson

BLUE WOLF

Blue Curse

———————

For the entire chronology go to bradmagnarella.com

ABOUT THE AUTHOR

Brad Magnarella writes urban fantasy for the same reason most read it...

To explore worlds where magic crackles from fingertips, vampires and shifters walk city streets, cats talk (some excessively), and good prevails against all odds. It's shamelessly fun.

His two main series, Prof Croft and Blue Wolf, make up the growing Croftverse, with over a quarter-million books sold to date and an Independent Audiobook Award nomination.

Hopelessly nomadic, Brad can be found in a rented room overseas or hiking America's backcountry.

Or just go to www.bradmagnarella.com

Printed in Great Britain
by Amazon

44308637R00249